HIS COVER WAS BLOWN.

His failure at a routine ignition of the Soviet Su-9 Sukoi jet sent the duty sergeant running back to the command post to double-check the pilot's orders. Garrett knew it was now or never.

Going over the start-up checklist in his mind, he found his mistake and fired up the Lyulka turbojet engines. Garrett jerked his helmet left, then right, saw no incoming aircraft, and released the brakes. Easing the plane to the center of the runway, he gave himself a twenty-degree flap angle and ran the throttle forward. His speed was up to forty-five miles per hour before he saw the flashing red light in the control tower.

It was the signal to stop. Garrett ignored it and increased speed.

Two miles ahead on the dark runway, a flurry of activity and blinking red vehicle lights caught his attention. They were blocking his departure with emergency equipment and fire trucks.

"Damnit!" Garrett grunted into his oxygen mask, and engaged the afterburner.

Slapped back into his seat as the massive engines punched out their full 19,000 pounds of thrust, he was airborn in seconds, on his way to Ivan's secret weather base in the Kamchatka Peninsula.

Phase One was complete.

COLD
FRONT

WILLIAM H.
LOVEJOY

ZEBRA BOOKS
KENSINGTON PUBLISHING CORP.

ZEBRA BOOKS

are published by

Kensington Publishing Corp.
475 Park Avenue South
New York, NY 10016

First printing: June 1990

Printed in the United States of America

For Jane, who waited patiently, and for Joe, who could not.

Cold Front

One

The flight leader had a great deal of experience in the MiG-25 high-altitude aircraft, but he hated these missions. Though dawn had long since arrived at his altitude, the view outside the canopy was of dark streaky clouds, and he could not even see his wingman fifty meters off his right wing.

Every flight in the last three months, plus the test flights of last winter, had taken place in the same highly turbulent conditions. It was a requirement of the project. The 37,000-kilogram airplane was a toy, a yo-yo snapped up and down by the unseen hands of a novice operator. The aircraft leaped in gusts, sank abruptly in downdrafts, and yawed unexpectedly, skidding across the dark sky at Mach .9. And again tonight he would see the red and blue bruises on his skin, the effects of tight straps on his chest, shoulders, and waist.

Far too frequently, the decision of the project commander was to have them wait out deployment for twenty minutes, dangerously close to the point of no return, but the flight leader was heartened this morning when the message came through so quickly: "Falcon One, Code Ruby. Say again, Falcon One, Code Ruby."

"Ruby" meant salvation. He could deploy the canisters, advance the throttles to afterburner ignition, and climb at Mach 2.2 into the serenity of calm air at 24,000 meters. Shortly thereafter, he would begin looking for his refueling tanker. Until he was refueled, he was always nervous about reaching his base.

By order, he was not to acknowledge any radio call, and he had to assume that his wingman, Falcon Two, had also heard the order. The pilot simply retarded his throttles and then activated the release by pressing the stud under his thumb on the control stick.

On the underside of the jet's nose, a curved panel pushed hydraulically downward as the aircraft slowed to under 1,120 kilometers per hour. One by one, six globes were ejected from the storage cavity, a tethered metal plug pulling free from each. Loss of the plug activated a timer which opened the valve on a compressed carbon dioxide cartridge. When the aircraft were fifty kilometers away, on their homeward journey, the gas forced two pistons upward, ejecting a triangular piece of fiberglass from the top of the shell. The skeletal, hinged struts rose out of the module and unfolded, spreading above the sphere into a wide framework with an attached nylon fabric.

The paravane gliding mechanism made the module look like an obese angel.

Of the twelve spheres ejected from the two aircraft that morning, eleven spread their wings successfully. The carbon-impregnated fiberglass struts of one sphere cracked, then snapped in the maelstrom. The structure collapsed, the nylon shredded, and it began a torturous journey downward. It was tossed about by gale-force winds, tumbling and spinning, until it crashed into the heavy swells of the sea. Its heavy cargo dragged it quickly under the surface.

The launch survivors, whose spread paravanes activated a UHF transmitter, bleeped eleven separate coded messages in one-fiftieth-of-a-second bursts. The signals were gathered by the Molniya I satellite in

10

orbit above the Sea of Okhotsk at the time. The Molniya I was a communications satellite with an elliptical orbit rate of twelve hours, and three satellites in sequential duty were required for the project. The Molniyas had store-and-dump capability; they could retain information for later transmission. On that morning, the satellite relayed the eleven data-impregnated messages to a microwave relay station on the tip of the peninsula, and forced them northward on confidential frequencies to the secret compound where the computers decoded them. Finally, the telemetric data were fed back to the operations room.

Since the predominant makeup of the spheres was of fiberglass, to avoid radar detection, the sophisticated electronics were necessary to provide a homing signal to the satellite, so that not only the satellite's computer, but the personnel on the ground would know exactly the altitude and geographical coordinates of each module. Since the beginning of the operation, the telemetry readings had never failed to be accurate, perhaps because the telemetry circuits were almost exact copies of similar devices employed by NASA.

In the jet stream itself, the modules with the hang-glider wings tossed and bounced, burbling through the dark skies, not losing a great deal of altitude, and following the only guide they had: the wind.

The specially modified MiG-25's were on the final approach leg to their home base when the computer aboard the Molniya I received instructions from the ground, verified the classification, and then examined the directions carefully in microseconds, aligned the sequence, and transmitted the triggering codes.

When the coded transmission was interpreted by the receiver in each module, a relay was closed. Twelve volts of electricity shot through the circuit, detonating a small TNT charge which disintegrated

11

the thin fiberglass shell of the sphere at the same time that the key component initiated a chain reaction in the passive crystals. The miniature fission took place in nano-seconds, and the crystals scattered into the darkly clouded skies in a wide pattern.

It was a pattern that would affect a continent.

TWO

By November, the *Farmer's Almanac* prediction of a winter milder than normal appeared to be slightly out of whack. Judd Petersen stood in his warm kitchen, finishing his second cup of coffee, and stared out the window. A blustery wind piled tumbleweeds against the north side of the barn. The sky was leaden in the direction of Thedford, Nebraska, and a new coating of snow had covered the tracks in the yard. The long fortress of baled hay back of the corrals looked smaller than ever. He turned back to his wife sitting at the kitchen table. "Dee, you remember the name of the fellow we shipped hay to during the drought a couple years ago? Down in Arkansas?"

"We've got it in a file somewhere."

Judd Peterson shrugged into his blanket coat. "You want to look it up and give him a call? See if he can spare a few tons?"

Dee rubbed her tired eyes with her forefingers. "You think we're going to need more?"

"Just a feelin' I got."

Judd Petersen's forebodings were shared by others across the plains of Nebraska, Montana, Minnesota, and the Dakotas. For people whose ancestors had pioneered the high plains, weather forecasting was part of the psyche—a careful interpretation of the

13

clouds and the vane over the barn, a sniffing of the wind, and an experience that arose from within.

Something was twitchy. It did not feel right.

The trees had shed their leaves a few days early this year. The first snowfall in September was not unusual, but had been heavier than expected. A sudden snow flurry in Bellingham, Washington, combined with salty sleet off the sound, had caught traffic on Interstate 5 unaware and resulted in a forty-two-car pileup. Denver's airport had already been closed down twice in late October because of snow and low visibility. That happened in Denver, but not usually so early in the winter. A light snowfall in northern Michigan had transformed itself into a raging blizzard when eighty-mile-per-hour winds descended from Canada. Utilities crews were still repairing telephone and electric lines, and the snapshots of ten-foot drifts were still a staple on the evening news.

To people old enough, like Judd Petersen, it felt like 1949.

About twenty miles out of Denver's Stapleton Airport, still in a steep climb, Brandon Garrett began to regret his decision to bring the Cherokee. He should have rented a twin or flown commercial.

Ahead of him to the west, the snow-capped peaks of the Rockies were brilliant, almost dazzling, in the morning sun. Beyond them, however, the sky was a dead gray. At the top of the stratocumulus, the edges were silver, but at the bottom, and spread from his left horizon to his right, the color was considerably darker. They offered a gloomy omen for the afternoon.

"Cherokee seven-one, you are cleared for fifteen thousand feet," the air controller told him.

"Cherokee seven one. Confirm clearance fifteen thousand feet. Thank you, Denver. Seven-one out."

Denver Air Control was actually located in Longmont, Colorado, to the north of the city. Garrett did not worry about it.

He worried about his airplane. It was a 1978 Dakota model with the Avco Lycoming 235-horsepower engine. The plane was perfectly suited to his weekend flying out of College Park Airport in Maryland, where he kept it. With a 17,500-foot ceiling and a maximum speed of 170 miles per hour, it was also adequate for mountain flying. That meant he could clear the peaks in the rarified air of Colorado.

Garrett was a competent pilot, and a cautious one outside of combat flight, and he approached winter mountain flying with an eye to the dangers involved.

The rough air he was currently bouncing around in was typical of the foothills of the Rocky Mountains, a result of updrafts, and did not concern him. But the storm clouds in the west did, and intuition told him the storm would move in faster than the meteorologists had calculated. He was following Visual Flight Rules, currently using Interstate 70 as his guide, so he dialed his Nav/Coms into a weather channel. He turned the volume down until the broadcast was a murmur in the overhead speaker.

By ten-thirty, Garrett had achieved his altitude, trimmed out the controls, and poured himself a cup of hot coffee from his thermos. Idaho Springs was passing by on his right. The town looked to be about knee-deep in snow. Snow was piled high along the streets and the exits from the interstate highway, and cars were moving, but it was a hell of a lot of snow. Garrett thought that he had read somewhere that the snowfall for October and November was far above normal. It would be a record season, if it kept up.

The syndicates and the few individuals who had a proprietary interest in things snow-worthy were probably doing handsprings once a day. Skiers bound for the multitude of Colorado resorts had snapped up

15

most of the available motel and condominium accommodations. Garrett had had to make a number of calls before landing reservations at the Aspen Lodge for himself and for Harv and Connie Landers.

This was going to be an impromptu get-together, sparked on Garrett's part by a desire to get out of his Pentagon office and to use up some of his accumulated leave time before the paper-pushers started X-ing it off his records. Though he was a full colonel, the U.S. Air Force still insisted upon a ceiling of ninety days of accumulated leave. He had to use it, or lose it.

Then too, after the operation in West Germany, working out of Rhein-Main, he decided he could use the rest. Seven days of that mission had been conducted on what had been the eastern side of the Wall, pursuing rumors of an intelligence pipeline out of the Air Force's electronic security section at Tempelhof Air Base in Berlin. It had been a little dicey at times.

As a special assistant to the Deputy Director for the Operational Intelligence Directorate of Air Force Intelligence, Garrett was a troubleshooter who was often assigned to run such rumors to ground. In this case, the rumors proved to have foundation, and Garrett had traced them back to a personnel staff sergeant and a headquarters clerk at Tempelhof. Their motivations in delivering personnel assignment and squadron battle plans to the military liaison division of the German Democratic Republic's *Volkspolizei* had been 10,000 *Deutsche marks* a month. For the equivalent of a couple thousand American bucks a month, the two had been willing to risk not only their personal freedom, but also NATO's position in Europe.

Garrett thought that the upcoming Air Force court-martials for the two NCOs would effectively restrict their freedom to the immediate vicinity of Fort Leavenworth, Kansas, for about twenty-five years. It was about fifty or sixty years short, in his opinion, but a lot better than current civilian courts would mete out.

The mountain coming up on his right felt a little close, so he banked away from it to the left and passed directly over Georgetown. It too was inundated in snow, but the highway climbing up to the Eisenhower Tunnel was clear, twin black ribbons snaking through a white wilderness. It looked cold as hell.

It had been cold and gray, a German winter constant, when he had left Munich for New York City on the last weekend in October. The Big Apple had been dismal too. Garrett remembered slush when he remembered New York in winter, not snowpack. He remembered face-tingling cold, not numbing, bitter impact.

His Trans World Airlines flight had arrived at Kennedy three hours behind schedule, at eleven in the evening, and he had elected to taxi into the city for the rest of the night, rather than hang around for a shuttle flight to Washington. The shuttles were backed up.

He stayed at the Marriott Marquis on Broadway. Garrett had a fondness for first-class hotels, if not for the pornographic sights and amusements of Times Square and 42nd Street.

After checking in and carting his single suitcase up to his room, he hit the lounge at twelve-fifteen. At twelve-eighteen, Harvey Landers hit him squarely in the middle of the shoulders.

"Garrett, you son of a bitch!"

He wheeled around on the stool to face his attacker. "I'll be damned. Harv. What in the hell . . ."

"Come on. I've got a booth over here, and I'll do the buying."

Settled in a banquette booth with Johnny Walker Black Label on ice, Garrett and Landers eyed one another with fondness. The two of them had gone through the University of Southern California on ROTC scholarships, then the fixed-wing school at Lackland Air Force Base together. Landers had stayed in fixed-wing craft, while Garrett had also picked up training in rotary-winged craft.

In his more than two decades in the Air Force, Garrett had met a lot of people. If he sat down and compiled a list—which he would not do because he hated paperwork—he could probably come up with over a thousand names of people he knew fairly well. He guessed there would be less than ten on the list that he would call a true friend.

Landers was on the shorter listing.

"You give up L.A. for New York?" Garrett asked.

"Hell, no! Who wants this snow-and-cold shit? I'm here on business."

"Same business?"

"What do you think?"

"I'd say no."

"And you'd be right," Landers grinned.

Harv Landers had left the Air Force after two tours of Vietnam, four years of service, a captaincy, a Distinguished Service Medal, two Silver Stars, and three Purple Hearts. One of the Silver Stars and one of the wounds came during his second tour, when he was flying a Cessna 0-1 Bird Dog as a forward artillery observer for an artillery brigade. Like many FAOs, he had rigged two rocket launchers to the struts of the high-winged aircraft, in addition to the marking flares. Firing the rockets in flight nearly brought the plane to a standstill.

At that time, Garrett had transferred to Nathan Petrie's Special Operations Group, working out of the Saigon Embassy. Garrett and three ARVN officers, en route to a rendezvous in Laos, lost the turbine of their UH-1H Huey to ground fire and went down west of An Khe. They were under heavy machine-gun fire by a platoon of NVA regulars and calling for extraction by rescue choppers, when Landers heard the radio transmissions. Garrett would forever remember Landers's call on the radio emergency net: "Sounds like that fuckin' Brandy Garrett to me. Hey, Tiger Base, I'm going to go check it out."

Landers came in low and unleashed his two rockets on the NVA position, but did not do much damage. On the second pass, he came in behind them, cut power, and crashed the Cessna into the middle of their emplacement. He killed seven of them, disabled three, and walked away from it with only a gash in his forehead.

Since his release from active duty, Landers had sold insurance, become an insurance broker, sold cars, bought three automobile dealerships, sold real estate, become a realty broker, built houses, become a general contractor, sold airplanes, and become an airplane dealer. He still owned pieces of the action on all of it.

"So what is it now?" Garrett asked him.

"Couple of things. We're doing a hostile takeover of a Southern California restaurant chain, and while that's going on, I've set up a holding corporation for all of it. I've been here for two weeks screwing around with the underwriters who think I'm going to make a few bucks by taking the holding company public. Most of them are assholes."

Garrett sipped his drink and grinned. "You don't put up with the establishment very well, Harv."

"Look who's talking. I remember seeing your name in the paper a few months ago. As I recall, you were testifying at a Senate hearing on intelligence leaks, and you told a prominent Senator on the panel that he was the biggest hole in the dike."

"His staff is, in reality."

"I don't see why you're still with Air Force Intelligence," Landers said. "If I were the boss, I'd have canned your ass the next day."

"Because it was the truth. It's hard to bitch about the truth."

"The truth is," Landers said, "you should take your exalted pension and get out of it, Brandy. Hell, you know you're not going to make brigadier general, not with the brass you've pissed off."

"Problem is I like what I'm doing."

"Yeah, I know. Somebody's got to do it. Shit, you could be making triple the money if you took over my aviation outfit."

"You offer me that every time we see each other," Garrett said.

"It's always open. And we'd see each other more often than—what? Three years?"

"I guess it's been that," Garrett admitted. "You're on the wrong side of the continent."

"The hell with that. It's warm on my side."

"How's Connie?" Garrett asked in order to change the course of the conversation.

"Great. Better looking every day. Just last month, she was saying she missed my twin, though."

Garrett and Landers were constructed from similar molds. Both were six feet tall, but Garrett was the heavier at 180 pounds. He had lost six or seven pounds in Germany. Both had a few scars on their frames. Garrett's most notable souvenir was a burn scar on his left bicep. Landers and Garrett both had blue eyes, though Garrett's were a shade darker—a gunmetal blue that lightened to gray when his temper was on the rise. Where Garrett's hair was a sun-bleached blond, Landers's was brown. Landers's face did not yet show any of the pressures of his multiple businesses. Garrett had a few lines at the eyes and at the corners of his mouth.

At one-thirty in the morning, the two of them went up to Landers's room, broke the seal on a fresh bottle of Black Label, and talked until four A.M. The upshot of the accidental meeting was the planned three-day holiday in Aspen.

By the time the Cherokee passed high over Dillon Lake, the sun had disappeared into the gray concrete of the overcast skies. The low clouds in the west appeared closer, their lofty peaks roiling in fast-moving air currents. Overhead, large bluish clouds had formed.

Garrett spread the chart on his lap and looked up the frequency for Salt Lake City Air Control. He spun the thumbwheels on the radios to the indicated numbers and turned up the volume a little.

Checking the chart since he was going to abandon Interstate 70 after passing Frisco, he chose the 14,000-foot peak of Mount of the Holy Cross for his landmark. He peered ahead through the growing gloom until he found it, and then banked left to put it on his right oblique.

It started snowing. Tiny, brittle flakes flashed past the side windows.

From the speaker above his right ear, Garrett heard Salt Lake start to issue advisories. He could not hear the aircraft end of the dialogue, but Salt Lake Control told a few of the smaller airplanes within its range of control to start looking for a place to land, or to divert their flight plans into Arizona and New Mexico.

Aspen was just a hop over the mountain, fifty-five miles away as the crow flies.

As long as the crow did not ice up.

Connie Landers dozed very peacefully in the right seat of the Beechcraft King Air. She was fitted snugly into the juncture of the seat back and the side of the cockpit. From time to time, she snored. She would never admit she snored, but she did, when she was sitting up like that.

Sometimes, when they were flying into a warm sun on a trip to Tahoe or Vegas or Phoenix, Connie stripped to the skin and sunbathed in the copilot's seat. She was very fit after bearing two children, both boys. The younger, Tad, was now twenty years old.

Harvey Landers did not tire of looking at his wife. He remembered some of those long business and vacation trips where, at 25,000 feet, they had left the controls to the autopilot and slipped back into the six-passenger cabin to test the softness of the carpeting.

Landers was happy that she was asleep.

He did not want her to become alarmed.

Not that she would see anything. The windscreen was white. He had the de-icers going, but the ice formation was beating them out. Out the side windows, he could see each of the 550-horsepower Pratt and Whitneys, but he could not see the wingtips. The rubber-booted wing de-icers were also working, but there was a half-inch-thick coating of ice clinging to the upper panels.

Through the yoke, the airplane felt heavier.

A few minutes before, Landers had seen a dim glow on his left that may have been lights in Hotchkiss or Paonia. He had resisted the impulse to circle back, looking for them. He would only have gotten lost.

The Nav/Coms were set to Aspen, and he kept the Omni Bearing Indicator lined up on it. It was only forty-eight miles away. It was only twelve minutes at the cruise speed of 256 miles per hour.

But he had lost speed with the ice buildup. Call it eighteen minutes.

Below was the Gunnison National Forest. There would not be a friendly clearing to put down in, if he needed it. The forest was also closer than he liked. He was flying at 16,000 feet, and had to pass between the 14,000-foot summits of Snowmass and

22

Castle Peak.

He was slowly losing altitude.

He tried the throttles once again. They were against the forward detents.

Harvey Landers considered the odds, said to hell with Aspen, and put the King Air into a right bank.

An updraft bounced the plane a couple feet.

Connie awakened, stretching her shoulders, coming upright in the seat.

She looked out her window. "Jesus, Harv. It caught up with us."

Landers dialed in a new frequency on the radios. "Yeah, babe, it did."

"You're turning. What are you doing?"

"We've got some ice," he told her, "and I'm not going to risk the mountains. You suppose there's a good restaurant in Montrose? It's about twenty miles away."

"I'll bet they have a warm motel too."

The right engine coughed.

"Shit."

"What?" she asked.

It was slowing. The tachometer jerked and stuttered its way down the numbers as the RPMs came off. The manifold pressure dropped radically.

"Ice in the fuel line, probably."

He played gently with the mixtures, prop pitch, and throttles, but he could not get it back.

Landers feathered the prop.

"We're at 11,000, Harv. Rate of descent 300 feet per minute."

They had maybe 3500 feet of ground clearance.

"I know, hon. You want to try the radio?"

In his routine of checking instruments and indicator lights, Garrett had introduced a sequence of checking his wings for ice every two minutes.

It did not look good. Thin sheets were forming, breaking loose, and disappearing into windstream.

Visibility was down to maybe a mile. The snow flashed past his side windows in streaks that blotted out the landscape. It was an eerie wonderland.

He switched the radio to the Aspen Control Tower.

And caught the end of a transmission. ". . . Air five-three, say again."

There was ten seconds of blank carrier wave.

"Aspen Tower to King Air five-three. Come back to me."

Garrett only heard the control tower's side of the transmissions, but the King Air was obviously not responding to the tower's queries.

Harvey Landers's company plane was a King Air.

"This is Aspen Tower. Do I have an aircraft in my southwest sector?"

Silence.

"Aspen Tower. Thank you, United one-one. We have lost radar and voice contact with a Beech King Air en route to Aspen, but turning back to Montrose. He may be down."

Garrett squelched out some background static coming over the air and turned up the volume. He did not realize that he was holding his breath.

"Aspen Tower to all aircraft. United one-one confirms Emergency Locator Beacon operating west-northwest of Montrose. We are alerting sheriff's department, Montrose. Advise all aircraft weather conditions deteriorating rapidly . . . advise Aspen closed to departing aircraft . . . advise Aspen will close to arrivals shortly . . . go ahead, Lear nine-six . . . Lear nine-six, you are cleared for landing, runway two-seven. Wind two-five-eight at one-two knots, gusting, visibility quarter-mile, runways icy. Give yourself plenty of room, nine-six."

Garrett picked his microphone from its clip on the instrument panel and pressed the button. "Cherokee seven-one to Aspen Tower."

"Go ahead, seven-one."

He glanced out at his wings. "Aspen, Cherokee seven-one is approximately fifteen miles out and icing rapidly. Request straight-in on runway two-seven."

"Seven-one, you are tentatively cleared for straight-in landing, runway two-seven. Final clearance dependent upon Lear nine-six. Wind two-five-eight at one-two knots. Visibility down to quarter-mile, runways slick. Give me an IFF, seven-one."

Garrett reached out and flipped on the Identify Friend or Foe transmitter to identify his blip on Aspen's radar screens. "Seven-one to Aspen. IFF operational. Thank you. Advise that King Air may be out of Burbank. Pilot Harvey Landers, passenger Constance Landers."

"Thank you, seven-one. We'll check it out."

Garrett dropped the mike in his lap and concentrated on lining his Omni Bearing Indicator on the compass heading for the airport. He eased the throttle back a notch and began losing altitude at twenty-five feet per minute.

He could no longer see anything on the ground. His whole world was whited out.

He wanted to be able to see the mountains that surrounded the ski resort. The airport was nestled into a valley, and incoming aircraft had to clear the peaks, then drop quickly for their landing approaches.

"Aspen to Cherokee seven-one."

"Seven-one. Go ahead, Aspen."

"Hold that altitude for awhile, seven-one. Repeat, hold at eleven thousand."

"Seven-one holding at eleven thousand," Garrett said, watching the rate-of-climb gauge while easing in throttle. The needle came back to zero.

It took more power to hold it there, though.

He saw the ragged edge of mountain peaks snake

out of the snow ahead of him.

"Aspen Control to Cherokee seven-one. Lear nine-six has landed . . . nine-six has cleared the runway. You are cleared for direct approach and landing. Wind is still two-five-eight, but gusting to two-five knots."

"Seven-one. Thank you, Aspen."

As soon as he passed over the last of the mountain range overlooking the Aspen valley, he lost sight of the earth. Garrett retarded throttle and eased in ten degrees of flaps. He lost 1,500 feet before he saw the ground again. A snowy road was off to his right, but he would not have known it if it had not been for four cars with their lights on.

The Cherokee sank lower. It felt as if it were wallowing in the thickening snow. He saw a line of telephone poles.

Pushing the throttle in, Garrett extended the flaps fully for maximum lift.

The plane continued descending, and he gave it more power.

A quick glance showed him ice rinks on both wings.

There were the runway lights. A quarter mile to his right.

Sideslipping gently to the right, Garrett got the Piper lined up. The gusting wind attempted to roll the plane, and he fought it with gentle movements of the yoke. He dropped the landing gear, heard the clunks, and checked the panel lights. All green.

"You're a little low, seven-one."

He would not give up his grip on the control column for the microphone.

The throttle handle was as far forward as it was going to go.

The airplane cleared the outer fences by at least ten feet, he thought. It wallowed, sluggish, striving to reach the end of the runway.

The runway lights ran on ahead into infinity.

He hit short of the runway, but the snow and ground were frozen, and the plane bounced high. Ice broke from the wings and cascaded backward. On the next touchdown, he reached hard black surface.

Black ice.

The Cherokee slewed sideways, her tail going to his left. Garrett countered the yaw with the rudder.

A gust of wind off the left quarter caught the tail and straightened his landing path.

The plane was on a shallow angle, running off the left side of the runway. He glanced at the air-speed indicator. It told him eighty-five, but with the wind scream and gusting, it felt like a hundred.

He gave it a touch of right rudder pedal.

The Cherokee straightened out.

Speed sixty.

The gust of wind must have been at least fifty miles per hour.

The Piper's tail jumped hard to the right as the left wing tried to come up. The tricycle landing gear went sideways to the line of travel.

Garrett toed in rudder.

The plane whipped around the other way, the left wing went down, and the wind kept it down.

He was down to forty miles per hour when the left wing hit the ground.

It scraped along the runway, snagged a runway light post, and the plane ground-looped.

Garrett was thrown towards the right seat.

He killed the engine before the Piper came to a rest, off the left side of the runway. When he sat up, he found he was staring at the runway. He figured it had rotated about 450 degrees.

It was damned quiet, except for the moan of the wind and the snow. The snow was slanting in, brittle flakes clicking against the glass.

Looking out the left window, Garrett saw that he

had lost his left wing. The outer ten feet of it was sheared off. The aileron was gone, and the left flap hung loose, one end of it dragging the ground.

He sighed, and reached into the back seat for his parka and squirmed into it. He found his gloves and put them on. Pushing the door open against the wind, he pulled himself and his suitcase out, slammed the door, and slid off the wing.

It was damned cold too.

Five minutes later, a Jeep Wagoneer slid to a stop next to the plane, the driver rolling down his window.

"You all right?" he called above the wind.

"Yeah, I'm fine."

Garrett walked around the front of the Jeep and got into the passenger seat.

"What about the airplane?" the driver asked.

"Fuck the airplane. How do I get to Montrose?"

He got to Montrose by renting a Chevy Blazer and fighting snowpacked mountain roads for 165 miles in four-wheel-drive.

The trip took him more than six hours, as he listened to the radio for news reports. He had turned south at the small town of Hotchkiss, taking Colorado 92 down to its intersection with Highway 50 above Blue Mesa Reservoir. It was beautiful country, deserted and clean in its white blanket, but Garrett did not pay much attention to it.

The radio reports said the Beechcraft had gone down in the Black Canyon of the Gunnison National Monument, ten miles short of reaching the Montrose Airport.

Search parties had already reached the crash site by the time he turned off Highway 50 and headed north toward the Monument Headquarters. The road into the park was closed off by a Colorado State patrolman, but he let Garrett by after hearing the explanation.

Six miles later, he reached the Monument office. It was surrounded by four-wheel-drive pickups and utility vehicles. Many of them had empty flatbed trailers used to transport snowmobiles.

Garrett parked to the side of the lot, got out, and pulled on his gloves. They were ski gloves. He had come to Colorado prepared to ski.

He went inside the office, which was heated to sauna levels, and found a dozen men clustered around a radio.

A wizened old man in a ranger's uniform looked up at him. "Help you?"

"The pilot of the plane may have been a friend of mine."

"Oh. Well, have a seat. They've reached the crash site."

"Any survivors?" Garrett asked.

"No. Man and a woman. The plane went into the side of a cliff."

Garrett shook himself out of his parka and gloves and sat down and waited.

At two in the morning, the snowmobiles came in, pulling two sleds. Garrett went out and identified the remains of Harvey and Constance Landers.

What was left of them.

Three

Kijuro Yakama descended the steps of the American Consulate briskly, with a hint of a new concern for balance. He inhaled the fresh November air and surveyed the city he loved. Up the hill behind him, a noisy crowd of American and Japanese tourists were impatiently waiting for the tram to Victoria Peak. On his left was the east wing of the Government Offices, and he reminded himself that he must call Sir Kenneth. A year had passed since he had shared tea with Kenneth Foster-Camden, and he did love to converse with the man, enjoying immensely the dated British accent. He would call.

Behind him, the imposing facade of the Governor's residence faced the vista of the Victoria Central District, shining in the sun. The scene was a dear one to Yakama, somnolent and disguising the teeming and sometimes tawdry intrigue that supported his life-style.

Three-quarters of a mile across the harbor from Hong Kong—meaning "Fragrant Harbor"—was Kowloon. The boy Emperor Ping had named it the "nine dragons" 800 years before because the ancients believed that a dragon resided in each of its eight mountains, as well as in the emperor himself.

Many years before Yakama had been code-named Yellow Dragon.

30

He was five feet, five inches tall, immaculately tailored in a custom beige suit with the merest of pinstripes peeking from it. He shot his cuff, peering intently for a stray thread or a frayed edge. There were none, but the suit was a year old, worn several times, and he was due at his tailor, James Lee, in Kowloon for replacements for it and several other suits closeted aboard the *Eastern Orchid*. Reassured that his appearance would not offend discriminating eyes, Yakama strode toward his taxi waiting on Garden Road.

At sixty-eight years of age, his energy was still frenetic, though he was somewhat restrained in his posture and his pace. There was not a wrinkle on his smooth, admittedly broadening forehead, nor a worry clouding his brown eyes. Yakama had smiling eyes.

Yakama had just completed a satisfying visit with Howard Carson, American Vice Consul and, incidentally, an agent of the Central Intelligence Agency. He knew Carson from their postings to Saigon, he as protector of Japanese national concerns and Carson as a liaison in the American Embassy. Later, they had met in Bangkok in the same capacities. Carson had been assisted then — or "dogged," as he liked to say — by the American Air Force Intelligence people Garrett and Eaglefeather. They were good days, those.

As with any other foreign intelligence service acquaintance, Yakama prolonged his friendship with Carson past the year of Yakama's retirement five years before. He accomplished that with occasional visits or with a carefully structured correspondence directed by the yacht's computer. It could be considered a pre-crisis intervention. If he ever needed assistance, he wanted to know that it was there. By the same token, he always offered his competent aid to his friends, and was generally able to bestow a favor now and then.

31

The practice arose not only out of his ancestral tradition, but also out of his training in postwar Japan. He was thirty-three years old when he first became associated with the Office of Strategic Services, which later evolved into the CIA. A captain in the Japanese Imperial Army at the end of the war, with no civilian future before him in a devastated Japan, he had offered his humble services to the intelligence office serving MacArthur's occupation headquarters in the Dai Ichi. His service had been accepted tentatively at first, with nominal cash rewards, until the Americans discovered the compelling need for Oriental physiognomy and the Japanese and Chinese languages in undercover operations in occupied Japan.

Since his approach to the Americans was founded solely in the desire for sustenance, Yakama was surprised by his eventual embracing of MacArthur's goals for the country. With the natural exceptance of women's suffrage. There were, after all, some traditions that should have been maintained. Yet the development of a democratic government, after he came to understand it, encouraged him and he found himself generally supportive of those objectives — and consequently, increasingly trusted and utilized by his foreign employer.

When governmental functions were returned to Japanese control, Yakama also returned to Japanese employment, as a section head in charge of international intelligence. Twice before he retired, he had been offered the post of head of the Japanese intelligence service. He had declined both offers, preferring the relative anonymity of his field position. He saw the elevated stature as one that would restrict his other, and most satisfying, activities. Yakama, extremely loyal to his country, had one higher loyalty, and that was to himself.

In the years of his postings in southeastern Pacific Ocean countries, he had learned that favors, the transport of millions in the cash of foreign currencies and art objects and the support of foreign clandestine operations, offered the promise of enhanced retirement. Over those years, Yakama had provided for himself modest commissions from yen and piaster and peso and dollar, from jade and sapphire, diamond and silver. In addition to his self-imposed commissions, there were always the little gifts, such as the pride of his collections, the delicately carved jade elephant with the inlaid diamonds and sapphires.

The repositories of his pension could be found in Malaya, Bangkok, Tahiti, Manila, Singapore, and Hong Kong. There was, of course, also the pittance provided him by a grateful Japanese government.

Two years before his retirement, Kijuro Yakama had purchased the *Eastern Orchid* from an aging ex-Nazi industrialist with embarrassing ties to American oil companies, the details of which could have been cataclysmic and very likely indictable. At five hundred dollars a foot, the purchase price was agreeable to Yakama, though perhaps less so to the German. In any event, the beleagured German did not have a choice in the matter.

The yacht was seventy-two feet long and powered by a pair of gigantic and powerful Mercedes diesels. She was luxurious and fast, and her sumptuous staterooms and salon were furnished in brocade and Persian rug, in the Picasso and Monet of taste and investment. She was home to him in the South Pacific, in the Indian Ocean, off the Japanese Out Islands, often in the harbor of Hong Kong, and wherever else the climate was congenial.

Aboard her, Yakama indulged his insatiable desire for travel and for well-deserved rest from a life of occasional danger. Aboard her, with his computers and his global communications equipment, he kept his mind alert to international intrigue, maintained clandestine friendships, and provided an occasional expensive or free—depending on the circumstance—service. The recipients of his services were American, Chinese, Cambodian, Thai, Indian, and South Korean friends. He never worked for the Soviets. And he never dealt in narcotics, except perhaps when the outcome influenced a desirable political end.

Kijuro Yakama—Kij to his closest friends—enjoyed his retirement immensely.

The taxi driver got out to open his door for him. Yakama smiled at the driver and nodded his thanks. The driver was a selected man provided him by shadowy friends in Hong Kong's chief triad.

"Dor jeh."

"Aw hui Kowloon?" the driver asked.

"Hai." Yakama directed him to the Star Ferry for the waterborne journey to Kowloon and his tailor. Afterward, he would return to the yacht.

Outside of Washington, D.C., deep inside the complex at Langley, where there were no windows to let him contemplate the frozen rural setting, Major Clarence Swallow sat in his small office staring at the high-resolution color monitor of his computer terminal. The thermostats had been set at sixty-six degrees as a result of the President's Executive Order, and Swallow was cold.

He hit the return key, and yet another of the endless photographs replaced the last on the screen.

Clare Swallow was a studious man, thirty-six years old, with eleven of those years spent in the Army. He wore heavy, black-rimmed glasses that contributed to his professorial image, even in the Army green winter uniform. He wore the jacket of the uniform as a defense against the frigid environment.

He tapped the return key again, tasted his coffee, and found it cold. At the side of the room was a small automatic-drip coffee pot, from which he refilled the ornate ceramic mug his wife had given him. Then he returned to his desk and hit the key again. It was boring as hell, scanning the photos, but Swallow was good at it. He had an eye for irregularities, incongruities in the brown and gray, white and black satellite photos.

In this sequence, each of the multi-spectral photographs covered about 100 square miles, the detail excellent where cloud cover had not obliterated the earth. Small white print in the upper right corner of each scene indicated the coordinates of the shot and the time it was taken.

The photos had been obtained by a KH-11 satellite in near-Polar orbit. The KH-11 was slowly replacing the earlier Big Bird, KH-8, and KH-9 satellites, which dropped their film in canisters for recovery on the earth's surface. The KH-11 used a digital imaging system that provided resolutions nearly as good as Big Bird's. The digital data was flashed through one of the NATO communications satellites in code, then to the computers of the National Photographic Interpretation Center. The NPIC was a function utilized by all of the intelligence services in the U.S., and some friendly services outside CONUS, but which was administered by the Central Intelligence Agency.

Clare Swallow was Army and on loan to the NPIC. He sipped his coffee, called up the next photo, stared, then recalled the photo before it to the screen. Okay, the submarine tender *Dovar* was departing Vladivostok. He raced ahead for a few frames, to get a directional heading for the ship, then punched in a command and brought up the current file on the vessel. She had been in port for over seven weeks, probably a retrofit. He updated the file with the new information, and went back to the photos.

In twenty minutes, he completed the sequence, finding nothing more of importance.

Checking the next memo on his desk, Swallow entered the code, and a new series was extracted from the mainframe computer and entered into the smaller memory of his terminal. This sequence was of forty-two larger photos, larger in that they covered about ten times more area. Mostly, he saw cloud coverage in northern Pacific areas, and he began to wonder why one of the analysts in his section, Asian Continent and Pacific, had given him the computer codes for these photos. The memo said, "Please review."

He looked again at the memo providing the computer code. It was signed by Plessy, a GS-7 civilian in his section, but had no notation telling Swallow what strange activity the man had seen. Still, Plessy must have been bothered by something that appeared unusual, and Swallow quickly sped through the photos again.

In Photo 5, he saw a flight of two MiG-25s, emerging from the cloud cover. By Photo 6, they had once again disappeared from view. In 41, there was another dim, wispy view of two aircraft, probably the same MiGs. Then he looked at the upper right corners for the photo IDs. The aircraft were estimated to be at an altitude of 76,000 feet in both shots. So, okay. The 25s were an interceptor aircraft, primarily used for high-level reconnaissance. They were the only aircraft in the Soviet fleet that even approached the service ceiling of the American SR-71 Blackbirds.

Again perusing the ID information, he spotted the anomaly. This photo series was from the passes of two different satellites, and the elapsed time between the first sighting in Photo 6 and the sighting in Photo 41 was slightly over two hours.

Strange.

The coordinates. Photo 6 was way in the hell out over the Pacific. It was not a normal area for Foxbats—the NATO designation for the MiG-25. Photo 41 was southeast of the Kamchatka Peninsula. Quick estimate, close to 3,000 miles apart.

Plessy's concern: The Foxbat cannot do it.

The damned thing flew faster than shit through a goose, but only had a combat radius of 700 miles, or 1,400 in a straight line. Stretch the range with externally mounted fuel tanks, and an economy cruise of less than the pedal-to-the-metal, scorching 2,100 miles per hour max, and it still could not make it.

In-flight refueling.

Risky as hell in that weather, in heavy clouds, but still possible if the MiGs dropped to around 30,000 feet to meet the tankers. Then climbed back to 76,000?

Why?

And what the hell was there for them to photograph in the middle of the northern Pacific anyway? U.S. reconnaissance ships would be much closer to land masses.

There was something else. This was not a first.

Last year sometime.

Swallow sat up in his chair and unwrapped a cigar, clipped it with his chrome-plated tool, and lit it. Then he leaned forward, tapped in his access code on the terminal, and entered a global search command with the key words "MiG-25" and "Pacific."

It took three passes through the file before he found the report, again identified by Plessy in January. It was a similar situation, with the suggestion of Foxbats on an extended flight, but nothing to show they had not been refueled while airborne.

Nothing conclusive.

Nothing to show that they ought to be worried by a Foxbat that could fly 3,000 miles. If it could, it was damned well something to be worried about.

A rumor. A vague concern. A wisp of something seen, but not really there.

Okay, what to do about it?

Swallow would enter the information in the file,

and any one in any of the intelligence agencies who had computer access to the file could call in on their computer links and read it anytime they wanted to do so.

If they ever did.

He should call it to someone's attention, he decided, rather than just let it hang, even if it were only a suspicion. But whose attention?

The NPIC worked for everyone, but Swallow, who had come up through the commissioned ranks in Army Intelligence, did not know anyone he trusted very well here at the CIA.

He had spent a number of years at Army Intelligence, and he recalled his supervisor there with good feelings. The man was now at the Defense Intelligence Agency. With a long drag on his cigar, he called through the open doorway to his secretary, "Susan, get me Colonel Eaglefeather on the phone, will you? At DIA."

In the forty-square-foot space which contained his desk, chair, and computer terminal, Peter Forsyte tapped away at the keyboard over his lunch hour. He worked his normal free time in order to leave early for the meeting in New York City.

If the trains were running. The damn weather had made train schedules idealistic ramblings of some optimistic planning department.

Peter was a data-control officer, and he was entering into computer files the pertinent data from the monthly reports of Nuclear Regulatory Commission monitoring officers across the nation. Once entered, the data could be fed through an evaluation program on its way to data storage, or it could be flagged, then queued up to await its turn at the printer. The paper report would then be scanned by some analyst and sent down to the bulging archives or forwarded to a supervisor. Forsyte could also bypass the analysis program and send the data directly to storage.

With this batch, he bypassed analysis and stored the data, then picked up the stack of original reports and carried them into the copy room. As he slowly fed each sheet into the copier, he thought again about how strange the recent reports were. All across the northern United States, the roving monitors were discovering minute traces of atmospheric radiation, and some of the findings were located hundreds of miles away from reactors.

Forsyte knew that if he had brought the reports to the attention of his supervisor, either he or the supervisor on the level above him would bury them. For such minimal showings, they were not about to act on potential dangers that could shut down nuclear plants in a terrible winter, with energy sources already stretched tightly. Coal utilized for heating could not very well be diverted to electrical generation plants if the nuclear sites were taken off-line.

Better, he would take the reports to the meeting tonight and let Joseph decide how to use them. Usually, the leader of their unit of No-Nukes Incorporated would leak the information to the New York newspapers.

Peter Forsyte's job with the NRC did not dictate how he thought, and he often felt that the special tasks he performed would eventually be recognized as a tremendous service to mankind.

A few blocks away, in the Environmental Protection Agency, in a similar warren of desks, Conrad Shafer was keying data into his own terminal, but his mind was not on the information. He was thinking about how Bobbi Lester's tits jounced when she ran and about the long weekend they were taking at a hopefully winterized motel on the shores of the

Chesapeake.

He was running twenty minutes late, but he had only three more documents to enter before he was to meet Bobbi for a late lunch. He might come back late. Fuck 'em all.

Conrad Shafer was a data-entry clerk making $43,200 a year, plus benefits. A month before, he had been a Management Information Officer, but that position had been eradicated in the stupid desire to reduce the cost of government. In line with Civil Service rules which guaranteed his old salary for two years, he had been demoted, and the girl whose job he had taken had been fired for a total savings of $19,500 a year. It was utterly stupid. The goddamned taxpayer did not care.

What really irked Shafer, though, was the fact that he must now punch a clock, place his own phone calls, and give up his two- and three-hour lunches. Not observing that clock could get him fired before the two years ran out.

Cursing the administration in general and the EPA in particular, Shafer tapped away at his terminal:

Location	Air Quality	Comment
Portland	Good	New: Trace Radiation
San Francisco	Acceptable	
Los Angeles	Poor	
Seattle	Good	New: Trace Radiation
Minneapolis	Acceptable	New: Trace Radiation
Denver	Poor	
Omaha	Acceptable	New: Trace Radiation
Detroit	Poor	New: Trace Radiation

He threw the last report into the basket for filing, punched the send key, and consigned the information to data storage. Then he retrieved his hat and topcoat before punching the damned clock. He would not give them one damned minute more than they had coming.

Nathan Petrie received what he considered to be a well-earned promotion.

For years he had been a special assistant to the Director for Consular Operations. In that position, he was allowed to rove about the world, chasing assignments fed to him by the Director. But it was a dead-end job, a staff position with no real authority.

Now, he was head honcho in the operations directorate.

With its embassies and consulates spread all over the world, the State Department was naturally a prime tool for the collection of economic, political, and military intelligence. And just as naturally, the Central Intelligence Agency used diplomatic positions as cover for their chiefs of station and for their agent-control officers. The State Department, however, had its own intelligence and security needs, separate from those of the CIA, and it took care of those needs through Consular Operations.

And Petrie was the new Director. He was in a line of authority, for a change, with all of the operations divisions reporting to him. The line-authority was more important to him than the nine-thousand-dollar annual increase in his salary. Money had never influenced Petrie. His father had left him several millions.

Also important was yesterday's move up one floor, to a spacious office suite located on the same floor as the Secretary. Status-wise within the Department, that counted for a great deal.

Petrie had also brought Mimi Paake, his secretary for many years, along with him. She was elated, of course, but more for her one-thousand-dollar increase in annual salary than for any change in his influence or her office site. Mimi had spent all of the day before supervising the moving of files, the installation of new office furniture, and the setting up of the telephone system. The furniture bill had run to twenty-six thousand dollars, but the State Department did not pay for it. Petrie had bought his own.

Petrie spent much of moving day selecting artwork for his newly papered walls. He walked around his office a lot, testing his new view of the Navy Bureau of Medicine and Surgery across 23rd Street. Beyond the scattered buildings, he could see the Kennedy Center and Theodore Roosevelt Island in the middle of the Potomac River. History. He loved it.

It was about time, he thought. He had joined the CIA in the mid-fifties, when Allen Welsh Dulles headed the agency. It was a time when the emphasis was on recruiting Ivy League talent, and his Boston address, his Harvard degree, and his inherited money had made him an instant candidate. He had spent twenty years in the Agency before allowing himself to be enticed over to State by his predecessor, the just-retired Dean Morrison.

Petrie was a formidable man at six-four and 240 pounds. His hair had silvered nicely, and he wore it at medium length, combed back over his ears. He thought of his eyes as boring tools. He spent a lot of money on his wardrobe, and his self-confidence in appearance, condition, and intelligence was enough to cow most political or professional adversaries.

On the second day in his new job, Nathan Petrie and Mimi Paake sat at the new big conference table in his office with stacks of personnel files spread over its polished teak surface.

They had spent all morning and most of the afternoon reviewing the file on each of the key positions reporting to him. Petrie was looking for reasons to make personnel changes. There was nothing like a quick firing, an unexpected demotion, or a snappy re-assignment to let subordinates know who was in charge.

He tossed the file for Haverford to the "okay" pile. "Next, Mimi."

"Soviet Bloc, Mr. Petrie. Barbara Morris."

He knew her. She was a competent analyst, but had no field experience.

"Is she around?"

"On vacation time. In Indianapolis, I believe."

Petrie took some time going through her file. She looked impressive on paper: thirty-six years old, B.A. from Bryn Mawr, law degree from the Harvard Law School, divorced from a State Department analyst over in the South American section. She had nine years in Asian analysis, spoke Russian, and had risen rapidly in her section. There were a number of letters of commendation.

"She's going to be unhappy with me, isn't she?" Petrie asked.

"Sir?"

"I mean, Morris may well have expected to get this—my—job."

"Oh, I wouldn't know about that, Mr. Petrie."

He decided to leave her where she was for the time being. She might scream a little, but tough shit. Or maybe he could find something else for her to do. Petrie did not like screaming women.

He went through the last few files, occasionally adding to his yellow legal pad of notes. When he was through, he stacked the folders, slid them across to Mimi, and pursed his thin lips.

"Okay, let's set up a schedule. I want to see all of the division heads, beginning first thing in the morning."

"Yes, sir." Mimi wrote quickly on her steno pad.

He ripped the top sheet from his legal pad and sailed it across to her. "Then make appointments for each of those people."

"Yes, sir. Should I tell them a reason for the appointment?"

"No. When they get here, I'll be the one to tell them they're fired. It's my job."

Four

General Nikolai Zhukov was head of the Department of Disinformation in the Committee for State Security, and he cheerfully read the coded message just routed through Moscow Center from one of his agents in New York City. The man was successfully entrenched as a cell leader in an organization called No-Nukes Incorporated, and one of his well-meaning members, usefully employed in the American Nuclear Regulatory Commission, had brought to him a number of reports concerning radiation leakage around nuclear power plants.

Zhukov smiled, extremely pleased with the information that had become available to him. Anything that further inculcated fear in the American masses was a tool to be used.

He nodded to his secretary, a KGB lieutenant. "By all means, send a coded message and instruct 'Jozev' to release the information to the American press. They have always served us well."

The cab driver cursed pleasantly as he threaded through the needle holes in the traffic. The trip was not without excitement, with unexpected icy patches appearing in unlikely spots on the D.C. streets, and with traffic jammed closely together. There were warning signs on the bridges over the Potomac River.

Garrett paid attention to neither the driver nor the *Post*'s headline:

RADIATION LEAKAGE WIDESPREAD

He had scanned the article on the second power failure in upstate Maine, the third failure in Montana and North Dakota, the stranded hamlets along the northern border of Minnesota, and the final slide of half-million-dollar homes into the Pacific Ocean north of Malibu, but none of it registered clearly.

Brandon Garrett felt a little numbed, though his condition did not result from the three-degree temperature of Washington, D.C.

He had personally escorted the bodies of Harv and Connie Landers back to Los Angeles. He had stayed on to help the boys, Jay and Tad Landers, through the rituals of American death and memorial. The boys had been devastated, but both of them were at an age where they were determined to remain fiercely independent.

Jay was a junior majoring in business at USC, and Tad was a computer science freshman at UCLA. Garrett had known both young men from the time they were toddlers. He was the dashing, swashbuckling uncle. In a display of his maturity, Jay had offered Garrett the presidency of Landers Holding Corporation. While it was a minor temptation, he had declined. It would not be the same without Harvey around to heckle him.

Getting back to the East Coast had been something of a trial too. The snowstorm had achieved blizzard proportions in parts of the Midwest, and most of the commercial flights had been fully booked, or diverted, or cancelled.

Garrett had hitched an Air Force ride from March Air Base to Chanute Air Base in Illinois, then to

McGuire Air Base, and finally to Andrews outside Washington, D.C. Wherever he was forced to sit and wait, in an airplane seat, in a motel, in an operations room, the years had come back to him. Most of them were pleasant memories, but they weighed heavily now.

The cab deposited him at the curb outside the Pentagon, and Garrett carried his suitcase inside, stepping hurriedly through the inch of snow on the walks. It was brittle and made cracking noises under his feet.

Garrett was a little rumpled. He had taken one suit with him to Colorado, and it was badly in need of pressing after five days in Southern California and three days of erratic travel.

The building was not that much warmer than the outdoors, he thought. He passed through the concourse with its shops and restaurants and salons and barbershops, identified himself at the checkpoint, and took the elevator up to the third floor of the C-ring. He walked the familiar hallway down to his office. It was a typical government hallway. Stacks of cardboard boxes were spaced along it, leaning against the beige walls like paper Towers of Pisa, waiting to be carted somewhere for storage. Paper. The damned city generated millions of tons of paper, all of it waiting to be stored somewhere for someone's posterity.

He was surprised to find the door to the outer office locked. Fishing his keys out, he opened up and turned on the lights.

The place was deserted.

Jessica's desk was immaculate, as usual, but barren. The blotter, calendar, and telephone console were neatly aligned, but the little silver picture frames and her personal coffee mug were gone. He looked around. The watercolor landscapes she had hung on the walls were also gone.

"Oh, shit!"

47

Garrett went through the anteroom to his office and found it in typical disarray. Stacks of paper were strewn over the credenza and the small round conference table. When Garrett was not on one of the assignments provided by his boss, Lieutenant General Merlin Danton, the deputy director of operations tried to keep him busy with analysis. That meant paper, and Garrett scanned it for what he needed and tossed the rest aside.

There was a plain white envelope in the middle of his desktop. He opened it, read the short goodbye note, then settled into his chair and searched through the directory for her home phone number.

She answered after the first ring.

"Jessica, this is Brandy." Garrett did not care much for his natural nickname, but it came easily to people. He allowed his close friends to use it.

"It's nice to hear from you, Colonel." There was more than a little frost in her voice.

"Jess, I'm damned sorry I missed your retirement party. It wasn't on purpose, believe me."

"I'm sure it wasn't. With you, Colonel, I know something always comes up."

He told her about Harv and Connie.

"Oh, my. I'm very sorry about that, Colonel. I understand."

"Anyway, I just got back, and I wanted to wish you happy days."

"Thank you."

After some chitchat about unfinished files and office gossip, Garrett tapped the telephone plunger and dialed the duty office. He requested a messenger. While waiting for him, Garrett unlocked his credenza and got out the small gift-wrapped box. He had not forgotten Jessica's retirement. The timing was screwed up. He had wrapped the present himself, and it was not very neatly done, but he thought Jessica would appreciate the personal attention.

Garrett had a small collection of precious stones in a Washington, D.C., safety deposit box. They were an odd assortment of trinkets he had picked up along his particular roads through Southeast Asia, Europe, and the Caribbean, and none of them were set. Many had never been cut. He had selected three diamonds that were relatively close in color and brilliance and had them cut and mounted as matching earrings and a pendant. The design of the settings was simple and executed in platinum. The final total weight in high-quality brilliant diamonds was a little over five karats, and the jeweler had offered him twenty thousand dollars for the set.

The messenger arrived slightly breathless. He was an Army corporal.

"You bonded?" Garrett asked.

"Sir?"

"You're not going to lose this?" Garrett gave him the package.

"No, sir, I'm not."

"Okay." He wrote Jessica's address on a memo sheet, and then peeled a couple of hundred dollars in twenties from the roll in his pocket. "Stop along the way somewhere and buy a bottle of Mumm's champagne. Get an arrangement of white roses too."

After the corporal took off, Garrett locked the office and went up one flight to Danton's office. The general's secretary, Donna, grimaced when she saw him. "You're six days overdue, Colonel. He's been looking for you."

Garrett smiled his best smile for her. "That's because he loves me."

"He uses funny terms of endearment. None that I've heard around home."

"He's just not as sophisticated as I am, Donna."

"Pooh. I'll bet Jessica's happy she retired."

Garrett pushed open the door and went into Danton's office without knocking. It was one of the little

49

irritants he enjoyed forcing on Danton.

The general sat at his oversized walnut desk, his large head tilted over a file folder. An oil painting of his Virginia home hung on the wall behind him to remind him that he had a family as well as a country. Merlin Danton had close-cropped gray hair and even white teeth that were revealed in an occasional grin. He was one of the practical generals around town, and Garrett admired him greatly, but would never say so, of course.

He looked up at Garrett, and his grin was not one of the happy ones. "Garrett, do the regulations of the United States Air Force ever get in your way?"

"Frequently, Merle. I try not to let it worry me."

"I'd hate to have you worried about a little thing like AWOL."

"I'll call Personnel and straighten it out. They can take it off my leave time. They've been raising hell anyway about my not using it."

"I suppose you have some kind of a rationale?" the general asked.

Garrett told him about the Beechcraft going down in Colorado.

"Ah, shit! I'm sorry about that, Brandy."

Garrett shrugged. "Harv was a damned good pilot, Merle, but it's difficult to predict mechanical failures. He was turning back from the mountains at the time. The NTSB investigator said the right prop was feathered and the engine was fuel-starved. It was probably ice."

"What about your own plane?"

"It can be repaired, but I sold it to a dealership. The next plane I get is going to be a twin."

"It doesn't always help."

"Yeah."

"You want a few more days?" Danton asked.

"No. I'm going go home early today, if I can get there, and catch up on my naps. Then I'll be bushy-

50

tailed in the morning."

"See me first thing, then. I'd like to have you look into some rumors out at Suitland."

"Naval Intelligence?"

"I'm afraid so. There's a suspicion that some of their data is appearing in the wrong places. Admiral Clanton wants an outsider to have a look, and he asked me. I owe him the favor."

"Damn. This is getting to be a damn dismal profession."

"Yeah. You want your day perked up? The Secretary of State has confirmed Nathan Petrie's appointment as Director of Consular Operations."

"Jesus! What kind of hole did he have his head stuck in?"

"Don't say that in front of a reporter, please."

"Can you imagine a Nathan Petrie with power?" Garrett asked. "Scares hell out of me."

"He believes in the same things you do. You can't fault him on his loyalty, ethics, or morality."

"Sure. But his methodology and his personality are wacky as hell. He still lives as if Dulles and McCone are looking over his shoulder."

"Maybe they are. Go home, Brandy."

Garrett went back to his office for his suitcase and his topcoat, then out to the parking lot to retrieve his black Corvette. It was a '65 roadster model, with the 396-cubic-inch engine, and he frequently turned down nice offers for it. The car had been sitting for awhile, nosed into the northerly winds, and it took a few tries of the starter to get it turned over. He let it warm up for five minutes before leaving the lot.

When Garrett had rotated to Washington ten years before, his first assignment had been as a liaison officer on the Hill, so he had purchased an elderly townhouse in Georgetown. Shortly after that, the Air Force brass had decided he was not tactful enough for Capitol duty and put him back in intelligence where he belonged. He suspected he was one of a very few who commuted *into* the District at night.

The house was not large. Besides a half-bath and kitchen, a dining room and living room, there was only a single garage on the first floor. On the second floor was one bedroom and a room he had converted into a den. Garrett had had the oak flooring refinished and the walls papered in a rough-textured burlap before he moved in. The furnishings were simple, the emphasis on oak tables to match the woodwork and earth tones in the fabrics. It was masculine and comfortable for him, though it seemed as if he did not spend much time there.

Parking the roadster in the garage, he shut the door with the remote control, then got out of the car and unlocked the door to the foyer.

Before he even removed his topcoat, Garrett crossed the living room and started a fire in the big rock fireplace. He moved to the open shelving next to the fireplace and powered up the 100-watt Pioneer amplifier. It was a Peggy Lee kind of afternoon, he thought, so he shoved one of her cassettes into the tape deck.

Unusual for him, he hung his topcoat in the front closet. He jerked his tie loose as he headed for the kitchen.

Checking the refrigerator, he found that his twice-a-week housekeeper, Daffy Quinn, had stocked it for him. He would not starve. He built himself a Johnny Walker Black Label with ice and skipped the water.

Climbing the stairs to his bedroom, he took off his suit coat and tie. He threw them on the king-sized bed and kicked his shoes after them. He looked at the bed, but suddenly did not feel like sleeping.

Back down in the living room, he settled into one of the big chairs in front of the fireplace and absorbed the growing warmth of the blazing logs. A few cars slushed along the street, and he studied them through the window.

He thought that he would not mind getting snowed in. He was getting a little tired of the things that were going on out in the world.

Barbara Morris hated flying in the first place, and this was the worst she had ever experienced. The Boeing 737 dipped and swayed, swerved and jumped for the entire flight. Around her in the packed cabin, several people made extensive use of airsickness bags, and the putrid smell did nothing for her own stomach.

She was sitting in one of the unpopular window seats, and she watched the blankness on the other side of it, intent for any sign of an Earth that should not be there. At any minute, she expected to see a strange mountain, other airplanes, or high radio towers. Finally, she felt a change in the airplane's attitude, followed by the blank view transformed into a rushing of flakes past the window. Soon, rows of streetlights were visible far below. She envisioned runways coated with ice and snow. Tightening an already taut seat belt, Morris knew there would be black and blue marks across her hips if she survived.

An horrendous banging in the fuselage startled her, and Barbara forced herself to remember that it was only the normal lowering of the landing gear. The wing that she could barely see parted, and hunting for the logical explanation, she said aloud, "Flaps."

The pilot was very good. He set the main wheels on the ground within three feet of the end of the runway, which was shiny and slick under the runway lights. The funny clamshell behind the engine spread open, forcing reverse thrust, and she felt the brakes being applied, the tail rising. There was a light slewing from side to side. Again the brakes were forced, the plane skidded, and she could see the other end of the runway coming up too rapidly.

They came to a bouncy stop, the engine whine dying as the airliner turned and followed a taxiway where the snow was piled six feet high on either side, the wing tips appearing to barely clear it. She did not loosen her belt until they were parked at the gate. Then she clutched her overnight case and headed for the lounge in the main terminal.

Morris sat at a small table and ordered a brandy. Now she was in no hurry and had time to get her nerves untangled. In fact, she had nothing at all that was pressing, and had returned to Washington two days earlier than planned in order to beat the weather. She was afraid of being stranded in Indianapolis.

She certainly did not want to be sitting in Indiana while Petrie was ripping up the office. The announcement of his appointment had caught her by surprise. She had been harboring a tiny thought that the Secretary might call her in Indianapolis and ask her to take on the new job.

Her record was impeccable. Her abilities had been recognized time and again. But Barbara also should have known that the bastards in the White House would seek every excuse to avoid putting a woman in a position of responsibility. She had let her hopes carry too high.

Damned politics. They always got in the way of facts and expertise. Barbara had planned her career carefully once she had a position in the Department. She had worked diligently at every task, specializing in one area, then another—language, culture, politics, industry, agriculture. All for one purpose, so she would have the knowledge to assume a leadership position. Well, she had the goddamned knowledge, but a good old boy, for Christ's sake, had the position.

The brandy relaxed her, and she had to admit to some reality; the papers had provided more of Petrie's background than she had known through her previous casual contacts with him. Maybe he did have expertise in the area, but it was just not fair. She had been working carefully toward the spot into which he'd so blithely stepped.

She considered resignation as a sign of protest, then rejected it because the message would go unheeded and because she needed the money to keep her independent of people like Phillip.

Maybe a transfer to another section or division within State?

God. What if she ended up like Phillip, stuck in a back corner of some minor analysis section?

She put four dollars on the table, gripped her overnight case, and went outside to the taxi rank. The row of cabs all had their engines running, and exhaust plumes drifted skyward. The cab controller waved his arm, and a checkered cab shot up in front of her. As she settled onto the cold plastic seat covers, Morris hoped she was not coming home to another series of constant phone calls from Phillip. She had had her unlisted Georgetown number changed twice, but the requirement that she leave the number with her office had allowed him to uncover it both times.

Morris found it difficult to imagine just how she had ever become involved with him. He was handsome, Ivy League, and all, and she had once liked the way he knew people. Then she'd discovered that he was simply convincing in the way he passed their names around. She'd come to find that Phillip was content being an expert on Columbia and Peru for the State Department. He did not try to expand his knowledge. He socialized on the strength of acquaintance rather than friendship. Three years had gone by before she realized that he was simply an impediment to her career.

After the divorce, one Phillip had also sought, he had devoted several years to unending and boastful sexual conquests, until the women he was dating discovered that he was not a stepping-stone to a higher plateau. In the past fourteen months, he had refocused on her and set his narrow sights on reattaining what he called "their wonderful commonality of purpose."

Well, he was common, all right, but she was unique, and she was not having any of it. There was nothing Phillip had to offer that could not be obtained in a one night stand, and with more sophistication.

Five

Yuri Yurievich Malenkov belied the traditional description of a Soviet citizen. He was six feet in height and quite lean, appearing frail, and his pinched face, thin pale hair, and eyebrows accented the frailty. Fortunately, he was very intelligent.

Anatoli Malenkov, his father, who'd only reached the rank of captain before his death in a tank accident during exercises in the Ukraine, had planned Yuri's professional life for him. Anatoli had believed firmly in the tenets of the Communist Party, though he'd recognized class system within it, accepted it, and used it to gain for Yuri the education necessary to penetrate it. There were no obvious anti-revolutionary skeletons in the Malenkov closet which would have sealed doors, and Yuri had an innate ability and a grasping intellect which took him through many years of satisfying education. He had been schooled in mathematics and the physical sciences at Lomonosov University in the Southwestern District before specializing in meteorology at the Institute of Science.

All of which had led to his present uncomfortable position. He was sitting in a wooden shack in the frigid northern region of the Kamchatka Peninsula, waiting for the weasel Petrovsky to return with their distinguished and unwanted visitor from Moscow. Yakov's airplane was late. It was a long wait, and

Malenkov fidgeted and remembered.

The outer office was barren with grayed wooden flooring and pale gray walls which accentuated his personal claustrophobia. Dust particles floated in a shaft of the morning sun jutting through the single window. Below the window, there was a mild mutter of traffic on Dzherzhinsky Square. A few blocks away, if he were brave enough to get up and look, was a spectacular view of the spires and obelisks of the Kremlin. He remained seated. Except for two hard chairs and the small oak desk and chair of the male secretary, there were no other adornments in the office.

Colonel Yuri Malenkov had been waiting, watching the dust motes, for forty-three dragging minutes. The delay was an intrusion on his acute sense of efficiency. Time was so precious, too valuable to squander on bureaucratic processes. But he waited, for the process was absolutely necessary.

Finally, there came the muted ring of the telephone, and the secretary picked it up, listened, then said, "You may now enter, Comrade Colonel."

Malenkov disguised a deep breath as he stood and straightened his tunic, then marched through the doorway. Before the Chairman of the Committee for State Security, Malenkov felt positively sickly. The Chairman was shorter, but barrel-chested, exuding a physical power while his distinguished, blunt face, with very black eyebrows over deep opaque eyes, and silvery hair evidenced high degrees of self-confidence.

Chairman Felix Nemoronko rose to greet the colonel, displaying an impressively tailored gray suit. It was from London, thought Malenkov, who knew English and who had often considered the advertising in the rare Western magazines.

"Good morning, Comrade Chairman."

"Good morning, Yuri Yurievich. Do sit down."

Malenkov rotated to find a single rigid chair. It was an executioner's chair. He sat within penetration range of the cold gray eyes of the Chairman, who settled comfortably into cushioned black leather. Behind the Chairman hung a large portrait of the General Secretary, the sole decoration in the office. Judging by his office and its accoutrements, the Chairman was a man of simple taste. Or perhaps it was simply the facade he presented to subordinates.

"I am to tell you that the Politburo has read your proposal with great interest, Comrade Colonel. It has been discussed in detail."

"I could not have hoped for greater attention, Comrade Chairman." Malenkov chose his responses carefully. He wanted to present an image of respect and also an impression of his own worth. He tightened his sphincter muscle and repressed an involuntary shudder. Like many times in his childhood, when his father had returned from some engagement with a duffel bag containing gifts, Malenkov was anticipating the Chairman's gift with both dread and eagerness. There was the possibility of a negative response, and there was the potential for exalted status in the hierarchy. The latter was a dream he would like to have shared with his father or with his mother, who had passed away while he was at the University. He often missed the overstuffed, gray softness of his mother.

"We have concluded that there may be merit in what you have described. I have been delegated authority to proceed with a limited development of your proposition. But before we go any further, I want to discuss several salient points."

"Anything at all, Comrade Chairman!" Be calm. Let us not appear to be too eager.

The Chairman's gray eyes suddenly drove deep into

Malenkov's soul. "It is a very expensive operation that you have proposed," the Chairman said.

Malenkov had not even considered a budget for the project. "Comrade Chairman, I am not an accountant. The use of part of an air base, several airplanes, a hangar or two, a—"

"I am not concerned about material cost, Comrade Colonel. If the concept is a viable one, then the appropriate support will be brought to bear. I am speaking of the cost in terms of human life."

Malenkov sat straighter in his chair, if that were possible. "There are . . . some population impacts to be anticipated, as there have been in any great endeavor. It is a war we are fighting, and the West would . . . suffer some losses."

"These would be civilian deaths, my Colonel, not generally condoned by the Geneva accords."

"Yes, Chairman, I am aware of the accords. And certainly, I did indicate in my comprehensive report the necessity for the utmost secrecy throughout the term of the project. The objective is to accomplish victory without the appearance of having conducted a war."

"Yes. And provided that security is successful, the Politburo has little concern for a decrease in Western populations. Rather, their concern is for citizens of the Soviet Union."

Malenkov was lost. "But Comrade Chairman, there will *be* no retaliatory strike by the West."

"No. Perhaps not. Instead, Russian citizens will go hungry. If your project succeeds, there will be no American and Canadian grains for us to import."

"Comrade Chairman, the plan means that the entire economic structure of the United States will suffer, including agricultural output. If the Soviet Union might possibly have a poor harvest . . ."

"It can be expected," said Nemoronko harshly. "We have been required to purchase Western wheat for the past several years."

Malenkov had not read that in *Pravda* or *Izvestia*. He said, "I was not aware of that, Comrade Chairman."

"Nor are most of our citizens aware of what we must do for them," he snorted. "They concern themselves with demands for blue jeans and rock music."

"But Australia will be unaffected," Malenkov countered. "Do they not always have a surplus of grains?"

"True. However, if America and Canada are in need, where do you suppose the Australians will ship their wheat?" The Chairman did not expect an answer. "You see, my Colonel, your so-called comprehensive report did not consider the aspect of starvation.

"Starvation of Soviet citizens is one aspect that cannot be tolerated. It is not strictly the loss of life to which the Politburo objects, for as in any undertaking with proper political aims, casualties are an expected consequence. And I quite understand that you, as a scientist, are thinking entirely in scientific terms.

"However, it is necessary for the leadership of the Motherland to also deliberate in human terms. Once a segment of the population begins to hunger, it also becomes vocal. Starvation is not without its repercussions, possibly in loss of civil control. We cannot have that."

"I quite agree, Comrade Chairman."

"And then, there is the General Secretary's new openness with the West. That program cannot be damaged or compromised in any way."

"Of course not," Malenkov agreed.

"The General Secretary, despite appearances, has not abandoned the ideology of the Communist Party," the KGB leader said. "Rather, he believes that friendlier relations with the West cannot do any harm. A relaxation of tensions allows part of the military budget to be diverted to domestic needs. The eventual embracing of the Party by all members of the global community is but delayed."

"Perhaps, Comrade Chairman, this experiment is too . . ." He wound down, with nowhere to go.

Nemoronko offered a grim smile. "Too what, Yuri Yurievich? Too outrageous for our new political climate? That is not for you to worry about. Let it suffice, as far as you are concerned, that while domestic policies may be changing slightly, the Union of Soviet Socialist Republics has not altered her foreign policy in any way."

"Yes, Comrade Chairman."

"In the meantime, we must pursue our objectives by more subtle means."

"I fully understand, Comrade Chairman. And I admit to my blindness toward the overall view. Perhaps, rather than an immediate implementation of the project, there should occur a period of further testing, allowing for the stockpiling of grain?"

"Indeed. It is the considered opinion of the Politburo that it would be possible to increase our importation of foreign grain in the coming harvest, along with reducing what we utilize of our own harvest, so that an emergency store is available. It would mean that our people would have two, perhaps three, slim years, but that the possibility for civil insurrection would be nonexistent."

Malenkov saw his reward growing more distant.

"Then the following year would be the operational period for my project, Comrade Chairman?" He made reference for the first time to the ownership of the procedure.

It was not wasted on the KGB chieftain. "The USSR's process could possibly be initiated in the following year, Colonel Malenkov. It has been suggested that a limited test should be first conducted to determine that it actually works and to test your ability to contain knowledge of the project. Does that not seem feasible?"

A rivulet of perspiration made its way down Malenkov's back, uncomfortably penetrating the cleft between his buttocks. "Of course, Comrade Chairman."

"And I must ask if there is anything about the apparatus that has not been revealed in your report, Colonel. Anything in its usage that would hint to the Americans that something was amiss?"

There was just a little radiation side effect, so minute that he had not reported it, but that would soon be suppressed. "Nothing at all, Comrade Chairman."

"By making a commitment to this proposal, the Politburo is committing itself to the expenditure of billions of rubles, which are in short supply, my Colonel."

"I appreciate the cost, Comrade Chairman."

The Chairman's eyes narrowed, and his mouth hardened. "I take upon my shoulders the responsibility for that decision. Your shoulders must also bear the weight."

Malenkov swallowed involuntarily, certain that the movement of his Adam's apple was exaggerated. "Of course, Comrade Chairman."

"I, and the Politburo, will not be disappointed?"

"Assuredly not."

"The risk is the highest we have ever undertaken. Should the West become aware of what is truly the initiation of warfare, the counterstrike retaliation could come in nuclear form, Yuri Yurievich, and the Motherland would be the eventual loser."

Malenkov mustered his remaining resolve. "Secrecy will prevail, Comrade Chairman. The United States will be brought to her arrogant knees, without knowing why or how, and without a shot being fired."

"It must not fail. Not because of the loss of life, or

the shortage of grain. Within the next ten years, we will no longer have the surplus amounts of gold with which to purchase energy and wheat. Failure is embarrassment and subjugation, Yuri Yurievich."

"I will not fail you, Comrade Chairman."

"There will be two parts to the operation, Colonel Malenkov. Stage I will be the testing series. Stage II will follow, should the plan hold together. I am reassigning you from the KGB Science Division to what we will call Special Department XX in the First Directorate. The project is provided the code name of Rain Cloud. It is, after all, to appear as an experimental project devoted to the effort of increasing our harvests. You are assigned as commander of the project, reporting directly to this office, and not through the First Directorate. A special communication code will be utilized. Is that understood?"

Malenkov nodded gravely.

"I have assigned Major Boris Petrovsky as your adjutant, to handle non-scientific operations and security. He is to be trusted completely, and is also to be utilized in the recruitment of your supportive science and technical staff."

"But, Comrade Chairman, I have. . . ."

"You have identified some thirty scientists necessary for the project. However, we cannot have men of distinction at universities and institutes simply disappear for two years. Adequate cover stories must be devised. Major Petrovsky will make the arrangements."

"Yes, Comrade Chairman."

Malenkov knew that Petrovsky would also be there to watch him, and to provide yet more reports to the Chairman.

The Chairman stood abruptly. "Every success," he said.

Malenkov hurried to his feet, but his legs were weak. "There will be."

However he might resent these visits by bureaucratic busybodies, Malenkov also knew that he had to build a political base of his own if his future beyond the project was to be secure. In the past two years, he had had contact with the most influential individuals in the Party and the government, and he had to continue developing those contacts. His activities in the Far East required financial and political support from many areas, especially because his project did not appear on any budget document.

Whenever there was a visitor on the grounds, he devoted his entire being to providing them with the limited comforts available at the base. He also provided them with the information that he deemed they might be capable of understanding. He did not enlighten his visitors with the details of the key ingredients in the catalyst. At some point in his future, having sole possession of that knowledge might well insure the status he expected to achieve.

Malenkov peered through the frosted window to see his Volga ease to a stop at the outer gate, to be examined by the GRU guards. Those men belonged to the military counterpart of the KGB and were utilized by Petrovsky as the security force for the compound. Credentials, including the driver's and the guest's, were examined thoroughly before the automobile was allowed to proceed.

The process was repeated at the next gate. The compound was entirely encircled by two fences, each three meters high, topped by four strands of barbed wire and two strands of electrically charged wire. All movement to and from the compound, except for the project aircraft, went through these gates.

Malenkov donned his greatcoat and stepped out of the office to greet Politburo member Viktor Yakov.

"Amazing security, Colonel Malenkov," said the

visitor. "I am impressed."

"Entirely the province of Major Petrovsky, Comrade. A wonderful job."

Major Boris Petrovsky admitted the compliment by curling his lips.

Malenkov continued, "If you would like, Comrade, we might pursue a tour of the grounds, then come back to my residence for refreshment."

"By all means, Colonel. I am quite open to your direction."

They re-entered the car and drove down a wide street, its asphalt hidden by packed snow, though its disrepair was revealed by frequent lurches into potholes. Malenkov pointed out the small building that was command headquarters, his own small quarters, the small house for field grade-officers—occupied by Petrovsky and his aide, the guest house, the old officers' barracks for aircraft crews, the officers' mess. These were followed by the soldiers' mess, the civilians' mess, the civilians' barracks, then two barracks buildings for the GRU soldiers.

Requisition of the buildings by the project had had an impact on the rest of the base, where already crowded facilities had had to accept those evicted from the Rain Cloud site. The base commander, General Belushkin, complained bitterly, regularly, and ineffectively to higher authorities about the drastic drop in morale among his troops. Barracks housing fifty men in an eight-by-sixteen-meter floor now had seventy men forced into the same area. Indeed, it was difficult for a man to turn around in his space without risking injury or retaliation.

The visitors never observed that part of the base. Instead, they were released from the Volga to examine cursorily the living quarters of the company of GRU guards, which were immaculate and spacious, with twelve men housed in the same space as seventy on the main base. Malenkov knew how to maintain morale among his troops. His contingent received plenty of food, vodka on one night a week, and imported prostitutes under heavy security twice a month.

The barracks for the civilian scientists had been subdivided in order to provide each man with a private space. The effort promoted harmony and swift accomplishment of the project in the desolation of Kamchatka. Motion pictures, books, games, and female companionship on a commercial basis were provided for the civilians.

On the northern side, set well back from the street, were three gigantic hangars. Except for small windows in doors to avoid collisions by persons approaching from both sides, all windows had been painted black. The first hangar, nearest the main gate, was utilized as a supply and storage warehouse. It was crammed full of the stores, the scientific supplies, and the spare parts for the aircraft.

The second hangar had been converted to laboratory utilization. It was subdivided into a major laboratory, a small, private laboratory where Malenkov alone assembled the catalytic component, a fabrication plant, and a test center with a pressurization chamber. Malenkov's scientists worked in shifts around the clock, and the building hummed with electrical motors and electrical discharge. There was a continual odor of sour chemicals and of ozone in the air.

The second hangar was connected to the third by means of a fifteen-meter-long wooden tunnel. In the third structure were the six MiG-25 aircraft, their very expensive presence a sign of the commitment by the Politburo and an impressive semi-finale to the tour.

The group entered the hangar after touring the laboratory, and Malenkov explained the geography. "This hangar adjoins the inner fence and the doors open up on the space between fences. The aircraft proceed directly through an outer gate onto a taxiway. They return in the same way."

Pointing across the hangar, above the huge doors, he continued. "Up there you can see the observation platform. It is occupied by a guard who overlooks the interior of the hangar and the space between fences."

A spiral open-grid stairway was suspended from the lowered ceiling at the front half of the hangar, and Malenkov led the ascent to the upper floor hallway.

"On the far end of the floor is the communications and computer facility. On this end, to the right, we have storage, and on the left, the project command center."

Malenkov liked to show this room to his distinguished and powerful visitors, hoping to impress them not only with his efficiency, but with the control he exercised over the operation. One wall contained a plotting board with the outlined masses of the northern Pacific area, including the western coastline of the United States. On the wall to its right was a large map of the United States, covered with Plexiglas, and currently demonstrating a set of swirls and waves and arrows made from blue grease pencil.

Before the plotting board was a large table containing telephones and microphone headsets with long cords. A computer terminal stood against the door wall.

"It is a very impressive operation, Colonel," Yakov assured him.

"We like to think it helps us accomplish the task, Comrade."

Yakov led the way back to the ground floor and looked up at the nearest MiG. Painted a matte black, the droop-winged creature looked menacing even in repose.

"Tell me about your aircraft," the Politburo member ordered.

Malenkov enjoyed the subtle reference to "his" aircraft. "We have stripped them of all armament and electronics not necessary to their mission. A combat aircraft requires twelve thousand seven hundred kilograms of fuel for a flight of seventy minutes. With our first try, in what we designated the Type I aircraft, we were able to extend the flight time to eighty-five minutes, which was not sufficient. We then—"

"Why not use aerial refueling to accomplish the end sought?" Yakov asked.

"We must fly our missions on days of appropriate atmospheric conditions, a trying struggle for the pilots, let me assure you, and under conditions not suitable to refueling at altitude. Aerial refueling is accomplished shortly after takeoff and again before landing, if required."

"I see. Go on."

"In Type II aircraft, some components were rebuilt to allow for additional fuel storage, and external fuel tanks were also employed. The flight time was further extended, but not sufficiently.

"With the Type III craft, we have also fabricated new titanium panels to replace many of the original panels which were made of steel."

Malenkov carefully went no further in explaining that the MiG-25's were unfortunately all-steel aircraft, the Mikoyan factories denied access to lightweight titanium alloy. He also did not mention that the electronics were vacuum-tube-based, adding tremendous weight in themselves and in the required extra size of the airframe needed to house them. Their best two aircraft had electronics obtained from Japanese sources, just like some of the combat aircraft in other commands.

"With the Type III, we can now keep an airplane in the air slightly more than two hours. It is a significant achievement," he boasted, "but naturally suitable only for our purposes. Combat craft still must have the necessary armament and radar."

"And the reason for the extended flights?"

"As you saw on the maps upstairs, we must get the airplanes to the necessary altitudes and coordinates for proper deployment of the modules in the jet stream. At times, the aircraft must hold in the target area for some time before the modules are launched."

"I see. But won't the American reconnaissance satellites and perhaps their naval radar be suspicious of these flights over the Pacific?"

"We took the precaution of initiating flights sometime ago, always in poor weather, to create new patterns. By the time we entered the testing phase, the flights should have become a normal expectation. In addition, Comrade, extended flights of MiG-25s, with aerial refueling, have been accomplished in the North Sea and the Mediterranean. The objective is to ease the potential fears of foreign intelligence concerns."

Yakov nodded his acceptance of the explanation, and they re-entered the Volga for the return trip to Malenkov's residence. Inside the sparse quarters, heavy greatcoats were removed, and Malenkov offered his guest a drink. The eager affirmative brought out the vodka and three glasses. A toast to the General Secretary emptied them, and they were refilled.

Yakov hoisted his glass. "To the day when the United States becomes a republic of Soviet Russia, and lays her yield at our feet."

They all downed the warm liquid, heated by it and the sentiment of the toast. Boris Petrovsky generously refilled the glasses from Malenkov's bottle.

"There is one thought that has crossed my mind, Colonel. Was much credence given to developing control of our own weather?"

Malenkov thought immediately of the radiation by-product he had so far been unable to eliminate, and he crushed the thought just as swiftly.

He provided his standard answer. "Part of our research here is centered on domestic uses of the apparatus, after the primary objective is accomplished. To be frank, it is my impression that the Motherland's resources are rapidly being depleted. To preserve our store of gold and other strategic metals, and to simultaneously achieve the downfall of capitalistic control over other resources of the world, the present course of action appeared most hopeful. In a matter of two or three years, Russia will achieve economic and productive superiority in the world, and thus be able to demonstrate the naturally appropriate place of communism.

"Then too, Comrade Yakov, the *rodina*'s economy will be achieving new heights just as the American economy achieves new lows."

"Affecting other nations, of course."

"Of course. Japan and West Germany will have to find another place to send their little cars and their cameras when the United States can no longer afford them."

Malenkov always promoted the Party line. He was himself a rather newer member, though not necessarily commited fully to its dogmatic tenets, except in public.

"Excellent! You have my fullest support."

"Thank you, Comrade Yakov."

And Yakov proposed another toast to the success of the project.

71

Six

Garrett went down to the second floor of C-ring and entered a large room with no windows. The sign in the corridor indicated that the room was AFI's secretarial pool. A dozen women sat at desks, in various modes of production. Typewriters clicked and computer terminals cast green letters. There was a little congestion at the three copy machines.

In the far corner, an older woman sat before an electronic IBM, her fingers blurred over the keys. She looked to be in her late fifties, with neatly tended blue-gray hair, a number of wrinkles turned upward rather than down, and a slightly plump figure clad in a bright yellow dress. A mist-blue scarf was tucked around her throat.

Garrett guessed that she had been in the pool for a long time, since the younger women tended to be requisitioned for front office work with the honchos. He did not have those hang-ups.

He acknowledged several hopeful smiles with a noncommittal one of his own as he threaded his way through the maze of desks to the corner of the room. The black plastic standard on the desk identified her as Agatha Nelson.

She put her fingers on hold, looked up, and smiled when he reached her desk.

"Mrs. Nelson?"

"Yes, Colonel Garrett?"

His reputation had preceded him. It was either that or the news that Jessica had retired. Garrett wondered why AFI had a communications center in the basement when they had such a hot grapevine right here.

"Have you been here long, Mrs. Nelson?"

"I started with the section eight years ago," was the direct answer, her blue eyes unwavering. "Since my husband passed away."

"Do you have a security classification?"

"Yes, sir. Secret."

The clearance was not very high, but then, anything higher he generally kept to himself anyway. "Can you take dictation?"

"Not very well, sir. But I work off the dictaphone quickly."

"Good. Because I don't dictate very well. And I don't even write legibly enough to read my own notes. Would you like to be my secretary?"

She smiled, her eyes wide. "Yes, sir. I would."

Garrett picked up her name plaque. "That's done then. You notify Personnel of the change, and I'll sign whatever is required. Shall we go?"

"Well, sir." She indicated the page in the typewriter with a clear-polished fingernail. "I should complete this. I don't like to leave things unfinished."

He liked that. "Whenever you're ready then."

He walked back to his office, put Mrs. Nelson's identification on the desk in the outer office, then went back to his phone.

Garrett called the general number at Langley and asked for Howard Carson, only to find that the operative was now assigned to Hong Kong.

"How about Carl Brent? He around?"

"I'll connect you."

"Two-two-five-four."

Langley people always thought that the last four

digits of the phone number was the neat way to answer their telephones.

"Carl. Brandon Garrett here."

"Garrett? I'll be damned. Long time."

"You hungry? Good, I'll buy you lunch."

They met in a small pub out on 16th, near Howard University, which was British in decor but American graduate school in clientele. Brent was waiting for him in a back corner booth, and they both ordered British ale and Reuben sandwiches.

When they had plates in front of them, Brent chewed on a French fry and asked, "Why me?"

"You still in ops?"

"Nah. Moved to Intelligence four years ago. Regular hours. Regular pay. Dull as shit."

"Makes the family happy, though."

"This is the truth. Again, why me?"

"You've got good intuitions, Carl."

And he did have. Garrett had first met Brent in Saigon, where he had been working for Howard Carson, running counterespionage units composed of American Navy SEALs and Vietnamese indigenous personnel. Brent's success ratio had been much higher than the average because he was able to put himself into Charlie's mind, interpret the intentions, and then prepare countermeasures for them.

"What do I get out of it?" Brent asked. He had to cover his own ass.

"Anything I get hold of that affects you."

Brent bit into his sandwich, his eyes firm on Garrett's. "Shitty weather we're having, huh?"

"C'mon, Carl. I ever stiff you?"

"No, I guess not. Okay, I'm working Eastern Bloc analysis. You get anything in that line, let me know."

"I will."

"I've got eleven networks feeding me."

74

"Don't tell me about the networks."

"So what do you want to know about the Eastern Bloc-heads?"

"Nothing in particular," Garrett said. "I want to know about Suitland."

Brent's eyebrows went up. "Navy, huh?"

"Maybe. Just maybe. The way it happened, we've got a source in Red Banner Fleet headquarters. The source produced an item that was supposedly only available from two people at Defense Intelligence, one at AFI, and one section at Navy Intelligence."

"You excused yourselves right away, of course."

"Of course." Garrett grinned.

"Hell, I don't have any contact—not many, anyway—at Suitland."

"Yeah, but those you have are reliable. All I'm asking is for you to make a couple of telephone calls, see what you can hear."

"Why not? I'll ask around and give you a call in a couple days."

Garrett worked on his sandwich for awhile. It was well put together. The pickle was fresh.

"I get the impression you're not enjoying the paper end of your job?" he asked.

"It's all right, I guess. The crap we're getting is pretty old hat. Some schemes to interfere in German elections, military unit shifts along the Polish border, like that. New units moved south, toward Turkey. They're having hard times in Afghanistan again."

"But there's been something strange that you don't like?" Garrett suspected the man had something he had been sitting on for awhile.

"Not that I don't like it, Brandy. It's more like I don't understand it. This past fall, we had a couple black mountains suddenly show up in the satellite photos. At Polotsk and Nikolayev. Later, there was another one a few miles out of Dubovka."

"Black mountains?"

"Black plastic stretched over piles of wheat. Millions of tons. A hell of a lot more than they have permanent storage for. We sent some people in to check it out. Big damned deal. We thought it was wheat. They reported it was wheat. There's some corn and oats too."

"This isn't all Eastern Bloc," Garrett noted. "You're roving a little?"

"I get bored."

"So you think they're storing this grain for later in the winter?"

"I don't know. Maybe. They've never stored it like this before. Sometimes, they've had smaller accumulations in the open. Mostly, it's moved directly to the mills and processed. The other thing, *Pravda*'s been reporting that the harvest was way under projections and exhorting the people to conservation."

"And what do you read out of it."

"Semi-hidden stockpiles of wheat are scary. Like someone's planning for a time when they will need it."

"Maybe it's part of the General Secretary's economic plan. Maybe he's changed policy."

"You're very likely right, Brandy. It still interrupts my sleep."

"I'll put out some feelers, Carl, and get back to you."

Garrett drove his Corvette back to the Pentagon, and found that someone had parked a black Chrysler in his slot. Garrett's name and license plate number were on a small sign staked in the two-foot grass median at the head of the parking place. Prior ownership of the slot had not bothered the driver of the black car. Garrett nudged the Corvette's front bumper up against the Chrysler's rear bumper, got out, locked the roadster, and left it sticking out into the aisle.

On the concourse level, he ran into Marty Acker-

76

man, the *Washington Post*'s reporter for defense and intelligence. Ackerman was young, always slightly unkempt, and bright. Garrett liked him.

"Hey, Colonel!"

"Hey, Marty!"

Ackerman fell in alongside him as he headed for the elevator bank. "Any hot shit?"

"No news is good news, the way I hear it, Marty."

"You uncovered the network in Germany last month. That's the word making the rounds."

"Two assholes do not a network make," Garrett told him, without acknowledging his own participation.

"How about Petrie then? You heard about his new job, I guess?"

"Nat Petrie is a credit to his generation."

"He is, huh?"

"Most of his generation is retired. Or should be."

Garrett got in the elevator, and Ackerman turned away, grinning, and jotting in his notebook.

Leaving the elevator on his floor, Garrett wandered down the hall to his office. He found Mrs. Nelson moved into the outer office, watering a plant with a small pitcher.

"Getting settled, Mrs. Nelson?"

She looked up, "Oh, yes, sir. And please call me Aggie. It's easier."

"I'm all for easy."

She pointed to the several plants perched on her desk and the corner table. "I hope you don't mind?"

"Not at all. Bring in whatever you like."

She gave him a stack of telephone messages, and said, "General Danton would like to have you attend a meeting in the Conference Room at three."

"All right."

He leafed through the messages. Most of them were in-house. There was one from Tom Eaglefeather and one from General Bellows, who was now Chief of Air Force Personnel, but who had once been his commanding officer.

He spent as little time as possible returning the in-house calls.

Eaglefeather wanted to have dinner, and Garrett set a time with him.

He called Bellows.

"I heard about Harvey Landers," the general said.

"It's a damned shame. It shouldn't have happened to him. Or to Connie."

"I remember him as a hell of a pilot. About as much of a hot dog as you were. You were pretty close when you were both in my squadron, weren't you?"

"We were close. Stayed that way."

"That why I've got a morning report on my desk with you listed AWOL?"

"That's why," Garrett acknowledged.

"Okay, Brandon. I'll take care of it."

At a couple minutes past three o'clock, Garrett headed up to the meeting in the Conference Room. He thought he would be fashionably late.

He detested meetings, and this one was typically boring, but also refreshingly short. Afterwards, he went back to his office for his topcoat, then out to the parking lot.

An Air Force AP was leaning against his Corvette, watching a civilian rant and rave as he surveyed the predicament his Chrysler was in.

The civilian said, "Get a goddamned tow truck and haul that piece of shit out of here, Sergeant."

The AP said, "Actually, sir, it appears as if you're in his parking place. According to the tags, sir."

"Well, goddamn it, do something! The son of a bitch is parked clear out in the driving lane."

Garrett sauntered over and tried to appear interested as he surveyed the Chrysler pinned by the Corvette. He walked around the vehicles. The parking slot on the other side of the median, directly ahead of the Chrysler, was open now. It was a pretty high median, curbed and grassed, and currently covered with six inches of snow and ice. The "Reserved" signs poked out of the snow on thin wooden stakes.

The civilian looked at him.

Garrett stood to one side and looked back at him. The sergeant watched them both.

Garrett said, "Got a predicament?"

The civilian said, "The military's got a lot of fuckhead smartasses. Can't fucking drive!"

"You must be with Congress?"

"I head Representative Bymer's staff."

Which was about what Garrett had suspected. "I guess if it were me, I'd go out the other way."

"Over the median? Knock down the signs?" The staffer walked to the front fender and looked it over.

"Depends on the hurry you're in," Garrett told him.

"Fuckheads!" The staffer got in his Chrysler, started it, and made a couple tries. The front-wheel drive made a valiant effort in the two feet of space it had before reaching the curb, but slipped back. It nearly slid into the Corvette.

Garrett and the sergeant positioned themselves at each rear fender and pushed.

The car leaped forward, climbed the curb and the ice, lurched across the three-foot median, and knocked down the small signs. The front wheels dropped off the other side of the median.

And did not reach the pavement.

It was high-centered, resting on its chassis. The front wheels spun uselessly.

The staffer got out, swearing.

Garrett unlocked his Corvette, got into it, and started it. As he backed away, the staffer was swearing with a great deal more heat.

Well, damn, Barbara Morris thought, she had brought with her to Petrie's office the letter requesting transfer to another section, but after her interview, she'd elected to keep it in her purse.

During the general meeting of some twenty people, her new title kept echoing in her head.

Executive Assistant to the Director for Consular Operations.

Maybe she had been impatient, trying to move too fast. Petrie had recognized something in her file, and he was giving her a chance to roam a little, to quit specializing on the Soviet Bloc desk, and really, a pretty good title.

He had shaken up the section heads a little, transferring some to new duties, shifting others back to the field, or over to new desks. Some people were missing from the general meeting, and she had seen desks cleaned out. There was an aroma of fear in some of the corridors.

She said nothing as the others raised questions, primarily about their new areas of responsibility.

She turned her attention back to Petrie as the questioning died away.

"Hey, you old reprobate!" Eaglefeather had arrived.

Thomas Eaglefeather was one-eighth Lakota Sioux, and he had a long, tanned face, dark black, militarily short hair, and a lean and hard body. His jaw was always blue-black from his heavy beard. He had been a sophomore at UCLA when Garrett and Landers were seniors, and Garrett's friendship with Eaglefeather through ROTC and Air Force Intelligence assignments together had historical solidity.

Garrett grinned. "Hiya, Chief."

Eaglefeather coiled his length into the chair opposite Garrett.

"Goddamn. I heard about Harv Landers. I also heard you were there?"

"Close by." Garrett briefly related the story.

The Sans Souci waitress brought two Scotch-and-waters, and Eaglefeather said, "Brandy, you know how I feel? Sometimes I think the goddamned Fates have got their wires crossed. Like the engine-failure indicator lights on Boeing airplanes. Get an emergency light, and they shut down the wrong damned lives."

"I know. Thanks. I got a wire from Kij too."

"Amazing, isn't it, where his ears are placed? I don't know how he stays ahead of all the data he's got coming in. Or why he bothers. He's got to be close to seventy now."

"He's never failed to drop a line on my birthday," Garrett said.

"Nor mine."

They caught up on personal lives while waiting for their table, then ordered Veal Oscars when it opened up. After dinner, Eaglefeather ordered some ancient Napoleon brandy and two large cigars.

"I see you're still on the job," Eaglefeather said.

"I just wander around in a daze."

"It was you who tapped the shoulders of the two assholes at Tempelhof."

"I was in the vicinity."

"That should have been me. DIA's supposed to have its eyes open."

"Not necessarily, Tom. It was Air Force Intelligence that picked up on it first. We've got a stooge in East Germany's *Volkspolizei*. I just followed up."

"Still, I feel responsible for not catching it."

"Don't. It happens."

Eaglefeather took a long drag on his cigar. "Okay. I don't feel responsible."

"Good."

"One of my people saw you with Brent."

"Goddamned spies are everywhere. And most of them are our own." Garrett laughed.

He didn't think about it being the first laugh in two weeks. And he thought nothing of being recognized by either friendly or hostile operatives. He had been in the field for too long.

"You looking for anything special?"

"No."

Eaglefeather did not have the right contacts in Navy Intelligence. He also did not believe him. He raised one eyebrow.

"Just keeping my contacts up to date, Tom. But you know, Brent has a strange item."

Garrett looked around to be sure they were unobserved and unheard, then told Eaglefeather about the abnormal wheat storage.

"More than usual?" Eaglefeather asked.

"I'm not certain what's usual, Tom. I don't know whether it's worth following up or not, but I'd like to see the pictures. You know anybody who owes you a favor at NPIC?"

Eaglefeather pursed his lips, then said, "Swallow. Clare Swallow. He's an Army major I worked with for awhile. Good man. In fact, now that I think about it, he's seen some new stuff too. Long-range Foxbats."

"How long-range?" Garrett asked.

"Three thousand miles. Not confirmed, by the way. There's a possibility of aerial refueling."

"Damn. I hope so."

"Me too. The Foxbat's a capable interceptor if it can accomplish its mission in about an hour. If the Soviets can make it an assault craft or a fighter-bomber by extending its range, it could be very threatening."

"Maybe the two of us should see what else we can find out about it? I like to know when I'm being threatened by new technology."

"Or old technology, like this damned snow?" Eaglefeather asked him. "I came in on the Arlington bridge, and I mean to tell you, the wind, over and under the bridge, has turned that baby into a skating rink. That's threatening."

Storm Cloud

Seven

Boris Ivanovich Petrovsky looked at his watch. There was still plenty of time before the tankers arrived. He sipped from the warm vodka and ignored the woman above him.

On the bed beside him, two hirsute women fondled each other's huge breasts, sucking and licking, just as he had told them to do. He watched for awhile, then focused on the younger woman, though her age seemed indeterminate. She was astride his erect penis, pumping, as she had been doing for twenty-five minutes, while Petrovsky otherwise languished, his head resting on three pillows. He always enjoyed demonstrating his prolonged virility, tormenting whatever companion he happened to have chosen.

She was panting loudly. "I . . . I've come again. You come too?"

Lying bitch! He slapped her hard across the face. "Keep going, bitch!"

The two next to him on the small bed also increased their tempo, afraid of additions to the red weals on their buttocks and thighs.

Ugly broads, he thought. Peasants. Not at all like the well-rehearsed and beautiful women of Paris, where the Chairman had sent him on his last assignment. He had to instruct these pigs in everything.

Repulsed, he let himself relax, shuddered once, and spent himself. Abruptly it was over, not satisfying, but then it never had been. Simply a release.

Petrovsky shoved the woman off his thighs, and stood up to dress quickly in the KGB officer's uniform that so many feared. He descended the stairs to the lobby. The old man who ran the town's only brothel was nowhere to be seen. He was afraid of Petrovsky.

Boris Petrovsky knew that he was disliked by a great many people, and he suspected that their dislike arose out of envy for his efficiency and dedication. Some, of course, knew of his secret relationship to the man who now headed the KGB, and their dislike grew out of fear.

It was the power of knowing the right people, and Petrovsky liked that, for he knew that his appearance would not intimidate. He was only fifty millimeters taller now than when the former Chairman had picked him from the gutters of Leningrad and had him tutored for very special assignments. He had a thin face and droopy mustache, black like his hair, and thick like the luxuriant growth that covered most of his body—a peasant's fertility. It was perhaps his peasant's heritage that made him despise the lower class so much. His dark eyes never revealed what was in his mind.

He never considered his appearance except whether it was appropriate for the locale or for the task. The only thing Petrovsky had really studied about himself was his eyes. Their opaque, unreadable quality, with a hint of malice, established him almost as well as did his KGB credentials.

Outside was Malenkov's black Volga. It was an automobile the man just had to have, to establish his status, and which had been air-freighted from Vladivostok. Petrovsky got into it and directed the driver to take him back to the base. The light was already failing in Ust-Kamchatsk, a large village of some 10,000 people supported chiefly by the sea.

The people also supported themselves by services to the air base, like the service he had just left. Income was also derived from the sale of trinkets and food and drink from the dozen shops along the narrow street paralleling the harbor. In the lower coastal region, farmer and logger and fisherman scratched a meager existence. In keeping with the new policies, the people here were allowed some freedom at pursuing their subsistence on a minor free trade basis. To do otherwise would have entailed not only a massive infusion of Soviet supervisors, but also the very possible threat of an uprising. These peasants were highly independent.

In the village of Ust-Kamchatsk, no one was likely to become rich or even well off, however, since the level of pay entrusted to the conscripted soldiers at the air base was poor.

And anyway, none of it was of concern or of interest to Petrovsky.

As the car labored up the steep snowbound hill leading out of the town, Petrovsky stared out the window. They were 1,800 kilometers north of the islands of Japan, situated on the eastern coast of the peninsula. In some places, the broadleaf and coniferous forests were almost impenetrable. The car climbed quickly, following the narrow gravel road, passing through a rolling strip of countryside, then rising through shallow canyons and more dark green forest to the plateau on which the air base had been situated.

Petrovsky's concern was the Chairman's word. It was the only law.

Currently, that meant overseeing the fueling of the aircraft in preparation for the morning's flight. And watching Malenkov, of course. He was the only one requiring strict surveillance since, other than himself, Malenkov was the only one allowed to leave the project area.

Each time Malenkov had departed the compound, Petrovsky had followed the man closely and unobtrusively, but the results had been disappointing. The colonel normally went to the base officers' club for a meal and vodka. Once, he had visited the brothel in Ust Kamchatsk — but unsuccessfully, the girl had told Petrovsky.

He wondered if Malenkov might be more of an introvert than Petrovsky already suspected. Perhaps he was satisfied with, and by, himself, lying there alone in his residence.

And then Petrovsky wondered if the Chairman would send him back to Paris after this was all over.

Grigori Illiyich Zanov was also a major in the KGB. His right leg was twenty-two millimeters shorter than his left and afflicted with a searing bone pain. The stainless steel pins that tied the tibia together had been improperly planted by inexperienced interns.

In addition, the scar tissue from the bullet which had passed through his cheek remained jaggedly purple and rough. He never would return to the field, to the crisp edge of danger and intrigue. He would not again work in another foreign country or enjoy the international travel denied so many of his fellow countrymen.

Forever more, he would be consigned to this tiny gray office without even a window to overlook Dzherzhinsky Street. His horizons had been shortened to a five-block limping walk and four-story climb to the drafty apartment which he shared with his wife of sixteen years. She was now fat and dumpy and whining. Forever more, he would shuffle papers and summarize coded cable traffic as a shift supervisor in the communications section of Moscow Center.

Because the man he now assisted in intelligence summaries had betrayed him.

It had been a terribly dark night, in a border hamlet north of Quetta in Pakistan, and Zanov had been disoriented. He had just arrived from Rome on an emergency command from Moscow. He had met Petrovsky, and the two of them had begun a sweep of the area, to determine the extent to which Western arms were crossing the border into Afghanistan and to disrupt the stream wherever possible.

They reached the outskirts of Chaman at two o'clock in the morning and parked the rented Land Rover in a grove of trees. Though they were of equal rank, Petrovsky had assumed a belligerent command.

He gave the expected order. "We will walk from here, Zanov, toward that large structure, probably a storehouse for grain."

There were less than two dozen buildings in the village, all dark, except for the dim crack of light around the doorway of the warehouse, an old barn. Side by side, the two KGB agents followed the shadows of trees, working along the edge of a shallow ravine to a point some thirty meters away from the building. Zanov carried his silenced SIG Parabellum in his right hand and five pounds of C-4 plastic explosive in his left. If they found what they expected to find in the barn, they intended to destroy it.

Zanov did not hear the footsteps approaching.

Petrovsky heard them. Without the decency of a whispered warning, Petrovsky lowered himself into a hiding spot in the ravine.

Zanov stood alone at the edge of the open, weed-covered field.

Petrovsky was a survivor and a schemer, and he knew that the approaching Afghanistan sympathizers, having heard something, would expect to find something. It might as well be Zanov.

Petrovsky fired two shots at the approaching

guards and then slipped away into the darkness.

The two members of the patrol — Afghan or Pakistani — reacted by diving for the ground and opening up with their automatic weapons. Bullets whined in the dark, and two of them hit Zanov.

The pain of the shattered leg was unbelievable, knocking him to the ground, but he was able to pull himself over the edge of the gully into a clotted stand of scrub pine.

Blood poured from his face. Pressing his face into his shoulder to stem the flow, he heard Petrovsky's running footsteps and the shouts of the patrol. His clumsy running through the crackling ground cover diverted the patrol in Petrovsky's direction. They scrambled to their feet and ran past Zanov's hiding place.

There was the grinding of the Land Rover's starter. Zanov heard the rocks pinging from its spinning wheels.

He heard six shots, apparently ineffective in stopping Petrovsky, though he prayed otherwise.

Petrovsky's escape had one beneficial aspect; it drew the patrol after it.

Morning brought cold and damp and a peasant flogging a water buffalo hitched to a high, two-wheeled cart. The man was naturally surprised to find an automatic pistol protruding from a bush, but was encouraged to help Zanov into the cart and to provide transportation to where he was able to telegraph the *rezidentia* in Quetta. Petrovsky had already left the country.

With his future absolutely constrained, Zanov was infuriated with the past four months' assignment to provide a digest of intelligence to the man codenamed "First Base," in Kamchatka. His office in Moscow Center was currently "Home Plate," someone's ironic usage of the American game of baseball. Through surreptitious detection, he had discovered that First Base was Petrovsky.

At first, he had thought it might be punishment for the man's defection in Pakistan, after Zanov had submitted his complete report on the incident. Later, he'd heard rumors that Petrovsky was in charge of a highly classified mission, one of the Chairman's pet projects.

That had enflamed Zanov.

Petrovsky was being rewarded for shooting and abandoning a colleague in the field. The only answer must be that Petrovsky had some hold over the Chairman of the Committee for State Security.

Petrovsky, of course, was unaware of him. Zanov had seriously considered providing the traitorous bastard with erroneous information if he could do it without connection to himself, and if it would lead to Petrovsky's downfall. To date he had uncovered nothing that would help him in that regard, for the information flow was one way, from Moscow Center to Kamchatka.

But he kept looking.

At nine o'clock, Colonel Yuri Malenkov stood in the small and overheated outer office of his headquarters building and watched Petrovsky's men searching the tanker crew. Major Petrovsky himself stood alongside the colonel, much more agreeable since his short journey into Ust-Kamchatsk. Malenkov assumed he had visited the whorehouse.

The driver of the 20,000-liter tanker truck was finally cleared, and the truck engaged its gears and went clanking toward Hangar Number One. The man at the wheel drove slowly on the pockmarked surface of the street. As it pulled away, the second tanker entered the no-man's-land between fences. A swarm of GRU guards crowded around it, looking into every crevice. They opened toolboxes and swept under the chassis with the beams from four-celled flashlights.

"I believe I'll retire early," Malenkov said. "Morning will be here too soon."

"A good idea, Colonel. One I will follow after my next tour of the perimeter."

Malenkov was up at four-thirty, shivering as he dressed in the cold bedroom. His valet was in the small living room, stoking coal into the potbellied stove, but it was not yet warm. Malenkov emerged from his small house into a crisply silent night. There had been no recent snow, but a white rime covered everything around him.

Across the street, a glimmer of light shone from the door window of Hangar Two, where the night shift of scientists and technicians were at work, or more likely, taking one of their interminable breaks for tea and cigarettes. Similar shards of light emitted from the aircraft hangar where ground crewmen were preparing the aircraft.

Petrovsky and his aide, Captain Konarov, came out of the command office. The captain headed for the guardhouse, and Petrovsky started walking up the street toward the hangars. Malenkov waited beside the officers' mess for Petrovsky to join him. Through the windows of the mess, he could see the two pilots finishing their breakfasts.

"A clear morning for the flight, Comrade Colonel," Petrovsky said. Despite the respect in his address, Petrovsky always gave the impression he was being condescending.

"Yes, but hopefully, it will be overcast to the east. I don't wish to abort this mission, as we did the one three days ago."

They entered the aircraft hangar as a small tractor was being attached to the nose wheel of one of the MiGs scheduled for the day.

Climbing to the control room, Malenkov shed his greatcoat and dropped into one of the chairs scattered about, throwing his cap on another. He surveyed the maps. The United States map showed a good concentration of the jet streams inland. There was a low-pressure area over Nevada, which should nicely draw precipitation out of the Northwest.

The Pacific Ocean map was also up to date.

Both maps were tended by two technicians with grease pencils and earphones whose cords trailed over the floor. The lieutenant who supervised all of the technical personnel also had a headset in place.

Another technician came in from the computer center at the end of the hall and sat down in front of the computer console. He flipped a switch to power it. He punched in an access code, and the screen reacted with green letters asking for another command, which he entered.

The screen displayed, "SYSTEM PREPARED."

The primary communications operator at the table looked to Malenkov who, reassured by the weather patterns on the maps, nodded. The operator spoke into his headset, and they soon heard the whine of the twin Tumansky engines in each of the planes.

Half an hour later, the MiGs were 700 miles away, being refueled by airborne tankers, to top off their tanks before they climbed into the maelstrom at high altitude.

Malenkov, who did not normally smoke, accepted an American Marlboro from Petrovsky and watched the plotting board. Long green dashes indicated the preplanned route of the two aircraft, with green numbers showing the planned time sequence. As the aircraft pursued their mission, the green dotted line would be replaced by a solid red line.

"We are one and a half minutes behind schedule," he told Petrovsky. "That is not bad at all."

At the bottom of the plotting board, a technician drew in the start of a purple line, rising obliquely across the map. The Molniya I satellite was moving

95

into position. Malenkov was happy to have satellites and computers available to him, although he did not fully understand their operations. Without them, the potential placement and release combinations would be impossible to control.

An orderly brought them breakfast while they waited for another half hour. Malenkov hurried through his biscuits and eggs, then stood and studied the yellow swoops and swirls that were the indicated winds aloft. They looked like a child's fingerpainting. At the bottom right corner of the board, a technician wrote out the conditions: The altitude was 21,000 meters; the wind speed was approximately 192 kilometers per hour; there was high turbulence and heavy cumulus formations.

Another technician, guided by relayed reports from the satellite, altered the yellow fingerpainting, straightening one line toward the southern boundary of Alaska, to flow across the northern U.S. A southern swirl was moved further south, touching the Hawaiian Islands group, threatening the southern California coast.

Malenkov studied the patterns and ordered a course change for the aircraft.

"It is a good formation, Boris. Usually, these fronts approach the continent depositing precipitation haphazardly, dependent upon atmospheric conditions prevalent at the time. What we will do today is to cause all of the precipitate material to be unleashed at once. If one or two of the modules can pick up a southern drift, I should like to add to the current discomfort in California."

Forty minutes later, Malenkov ordered the deployment of the spheres. The aircraft responded and then turned back toward the peninsula.

In the next hours, the red and purple lines disappeared from the plotting board, leaving the yellow swirls and a series of orange dots that indicated the self-reported positions of twelve modules. A lavender line grew from the bottom of the map, the second Molniya coming into play. Data from the first satellite was dumped to the computer of the second.

After six hours, the spheres were spread about 950 kilometers apart. They were approximately 1,200 kilometers from the Washington-Oregon coastline. Malenkov's wish for a southern drift had not occurred.

The spheres had tumbled to about 15,000 meters of altitude.

"I can't allow them to get much lower," Malenkov complained to Petrovsky.

He stood up, his back stiff and sore from so much sitting. Withdrawing a packet of twelve computer cards from his breast pocket, Malenkov leafed through them. Moving across the room to the computer terminal, he motioned the operator aside and sat in the man's chair.

Malenkov inserted the cards, one by one, into a slot on the terminal face. He slipped them into the slot in the order in which he wanted them to detonate.

The computer read each card, compared the data against the information it had already received via the satellite, and stored the information. After the twelfth card had been read, the computer flashed, "MORE?"

Malenkov typed, "NO."

The screen scrolled up, "CODE?"

Malenkov typed in his own sequence of three secret codes, not even known to Petrovsky, which did not appear on the screen.

The screen printed, "READY FOR IGNITION. PRESS Y WHEN READY."

Malenkov pressed.

"IGNITION SUCCESSFUL."

Eight

The telephone light blinked, and she punched the intercom button.

"Mr. Morris is on line four, Miss Morris."

Damn. If she did not take it, he would keep calling. "All right."

"Hi, dollface."

"What do you want, Phil?"

"I'm taking you to lunch. Something expensive, to celebrate your promotion."

"I'm busy."

"Not too busy for lunch. I'll be up at noon."

Phil Morris was accustomed to command; the interrogative was not part of his makeup. "I said no, Phil. I have another—"

"I've got a proposition for you you'll like."

He always had propositions, from re-marriage to living together and sharing girl- and boyfriends. Phillip Morris thought that he was imaginative.

"Not today."

But he had hung up.

Damn it, why couldn't he leave her alone? She was depressed enough, as it was. With the damned report on Soviet education that Petrie had assigned to her, and now Phil, she was having a bad day.

On the desk in front of her were the uncompiled summaries that were to be edited into "An Estimate of Soviet Educational Standards." Someone at the State Department had raised the question of U.S.-USSR comparative standards two weeks before and Petrie had come to her with the assignment.

"Barbara. Somebody, which probably means the issue arose in the White House first, read some newspaper account about the national standing of our high school and college students. It was a disappointing report, to say the best, with a steady decrease in levels for the last decade. State wants to know how Soviet students compare. Look into it, will you?"

She had assigned four people to the collection of data. It came from the directorate's current files, from embassies in the Soviet Bloc, and from information stored in the CIA's computer files.

And what she had in front of her was just what it sounded like: a regurgitation of dry numbers. She felt as if something was missing, or as if she was missing something. For her first major assignment in her new job, she wanted to produce something worthwhile. Not a report that would get filed before it was read.

One of the reports from CIA's Intelligence Directorate, which was a discussion of Soviet institutes of education, was based on information collected by Air Force Intelligence. Since she had not tried them, she hit the intercom button and asked her secretary to get the Director of AFI on the line.

The bay was placid, flat and blue, and the air was calm. The warm air foreshadowed a midday temperature that would be uncomfortable, but at the moment, it was quite pleasant on the fantail. To the southwest, about twenty miles away, Yakama could see the distant peak on Corregidor towering over Manila Bay.

He sat back in the canvas deck chair patiently

while the cabin boy, newly acquired in Macao, served his normal breakfast of one egg, two slices of bacon, and one piece of rye toast, lightly buttered. His breakfast was a ritual learned during the American occupation of the Islands.

Yakama's palate was an international one, relishing the native menus of twenty nations, if only the more delicate of those dishes. His mornings acknowledged American taste, and his luncheons and evening meals examined the other lands where responsibility had taken him. The chef aboard the yacht was widely acclaimed by visitors. Of French heritage and minus a leg from the Moroccan campaigns, the galley master also commanded an impressive *pensione* for that hopefully distant prospect of his retirement. Yakama compensated his crew well financially, and he expected subservience in return. It was an equitable arrangement.

He was a solitary figure in his yellow chair on the broad stern deck. The glass-topped table at which he sat held hundred-year-old Rose Medalion china and gold-plated utensils, acquired in Bangkok. He leafed through the small stack of cables as he ate.

There were six cables this morning, all responses to communications he had originated, prompted by the computer suspense file. As in his travels, when he paused to greet an occasional old friend, like Morilund in Manila, Yakama wrote a quick note by post or telex at least once a year to all his old friends. Ostensibly, the practice was just to keep in touch, but the responders knew that someday it would be time for debts to be incurred or discharged.

Of special interest this morning was the cable from Garrett. Garrett's note was quick and brief, acknowledging Yakama's condolences for the death of Harvey Landers, inquiring after his health, and reporting nothing new in the American intelligence community. Behind the words, he could feel Garrett's deep sorrow.

Below it all, of course, was the nicety that Garrett still held his high position of trust in Air Force Intelligence. It might prove beneficial one day, although Garrett was one of the few to whom Yakama was indentured. He turned the telex over and jotted a note to update the computer file.

Roger Hornby was an old acquaintance from Southeast Asia days. Though the information was not bandied about, he was a longtime operative with British MI-6, and he was waiting for Garrett in his sumptuous office at the British Embassy on Massachusetts Avenue.

Garrett rarely wore a uniform in his job. That day, he was dressed in a good dark gray wool suit that had paid for his tailor's daughter's orthodontist. Roger Hornby had outspent him by a thousand U.S. dollars on his Saville Row pinstripe.

"You've just missed tea, old man," Hornby said, a toothy grin dominating his elongated face.

"Roger, you know I love your tea. It was you who set the time for the meeting."

"And so it was. My error, chappie, and I'll correct it next time." He held out his hand. "It is good to see you again, Brandon."

"And you, my friend. You have a title here?"

"Press Secretary. Grand, is it not?"

They moved across the large office to sit in two maroon velour chairs. "How is Pamela?"

"She's simply ecstatic over this posting, Brandon. We were last in Burma, you know. Dreadfully humid, Rangoon. Washington, while overly warm in the summer, offers cultural delights that intrigue her."

"Somewhere along the line, there have to be a few rewards," Garrett said.

"Undoubtedly. How can I be of service to military

intelligence?"

The distinction was not lost on Garrett. Hornby, in his position, was concerned with more global matters than the issues related to simple military intelligence needs. He would approach discussions with the CIA and with AFI on two different levels.

"Roger, you're aware of the renewed interest in encouraging U.S. Navy and Royal Navy cooperation?"

"Oh, rather. Condoned by the Prime Minister, naturally." His voice dropped half an octave. "Grenada didn't help, you know?"

Garrett knew. While the results of the intervention in Grenada were satisfactory, Queen, Country, and PM had been miffed by the diplomatic breakdowns. The island was in Britain's area of influence, after all.

"We're seeking ways to improve the communication," Garrett told him. "But we also don't want to feed the Royal Navy bad intelligence."

Hornby raised an eyebrow. "How is it that you are involved in Naval concerns?"

"A related matter that will be, hopefully, short term."

"I don't have a problem with that, Brandon, especially as I know you're involved. However, I don't know of anything out of the ordinary at present."

Negotiation was an absolute necessity, even with old friends. Give a little, and prod for a response. And never denigrate the other man's service.

"We've a couple of puzzlers, Roger. Not for publication just yet. First, there are Foxbats on new courses, way beyond their normal ranges."

Hornby smacked his substantial lips, worrying the square-cut teeth with the tip of his tongue. "Any particular areas?"

"Pacific, the Med, North Sea."

"North Sea? That is strange, old man. You know that we get our satellite photos as a handoff from the

NPIC, but we've either not received those, or our people have missed the significance."

Garrett dug into his inside breast pocket for his notebook, then flipped pages until he found the entry. "It's in one file. Ask for 9-81-0853-17. That'll give you an idea, and maybe some of your analysts can add something to it. We certainly can't."

Hornby wrote the number down on a memo pad, then said, "And the other?"

"This is between me, you, and whoever you think can be discreet."

"Of course, chappie."

"We may have a hole in Suitland's ship."

"Hmmm." Hornby's broad brow wrinkled. "That explains your role then."

"If true, it's not good for either you or us."

"I'll ask about and then ring up up."

"I'd appreciate it, Roger. That's all I /have."

Garrett started to stand.

"Well, let's hold on for a minute, Brandon. While I think of it, there is something about Polish universities. Let me check."

He got up, crossed the office, and rummaged through papers on his desk.

"Yes, here it is. Lady in London could not reach her brother, name of Polodka, who teaches in a Warsaw university. She asked for Embassy help, but did not get a great deal. Apparently, the brother had taken a long leave of absence. No way to reach him."

"Those long leaves of absence tend to be permanent."

"Rather. However, one of my newer mates, a frightfully impetuous fellow actually, took it upon himself to investigate the case further. He came up against a typically Eastern brick wall, but he did determine that another teacher at the same institution is also missing."

"Hmmm. What were the fields?" It was easy for

Garrett to assume the past tense in these situations.

"Meteorology and nuclear physics. Both men quite competent, I understand."

The door opened, and Hornby looked to it. "Yes, Miss Southby?"

"There's a note for Colonel Garrett, sir."

She brought it in, and Garrett found that Mrs. Nelson had made a luncheon appointment for him with a Barbara Morris from State. He would have ignored it, but the note also indicated that Merle Danton had set it up.

He looked at his watch and said, "Roger, I had better run. My calendar's being filled for me."

"I'm glad you stopped by. If I hear more on either of these matters, I'll be in touch."

"Thanks. Give my love to Pamela."

The cab took longer than usual making its way to Langley on the snowpacked roads. There had been no snowfall in two days, but overburdened removal equipment was not making much headway against what was already on the ground.

After showing his credentials twice, Garrett found himself in Swallow's office, heralded by a sweet young thing named Susan, whom he had met two weeks before when he had asked Swallow to investigate the new pattern of Foxbat flights on a worldwide basis.

"Good morning, Colonel," Swallow said.

"Good morning. Brandon will do."

"And Clare."

"You have any luck?"

"If luck's the right word, I had a little. Sit down, Brandon. Coffee?"

Swallow poured them each a cup of coffee, and unwrapped a cigar after Garrett declined. He clipped it while he continued. "Okay, what do you know about Foxbat?"

Garrett knew the aircraft. "MiG-25. Born in '64,

and production probably started in '69. Goes like a bat out of hell on twin Tumansky engines, and it has about eighty-thousand feet of service ceiling, close to the eighty-six thousand of our Blackbirds. In '77, one version set an altitude record of over one-hundred and twenty-thousand feet. Most of what we know about it comes from dismantling the one with which Lieutenant Belenko deserted to Japan. It weighs twenty-two tons empty, compared to one of our F-15 Eagles at twenty tons fully fueled and missiled. It takes fourteen tons of fuel. The Foxbat has a ferry range of fourteen hundred miles compared to the Eagle's thirty-seven hundred miles."

"Why the big difference?"

"The Mikoyan aircraft design team was in a hurry and didn't take the time to develop new engines for it. They used a design that they had on hand which will out-accelerate damned near anything but a Titan missile. It really is a rocket disguised as an airplane. And it has outdated electronics and is built with steel instead of lighter alloys. Titanium is used only in high-heat structural areas. Still, for all its clumsiness, it does what it's designed to do very well—interception and high-altitude reconnaissance. Later versions have been set up with side-looking radar, or cameras, or whatever the mission calls for."

"You got it." Swallow smiled. "Okay, the flights are getting longer."

"It's not Flogger, the MiG-27?"

"No. Flogger has three times the range of the 25, but it lacks thirty thousand feet in ceiling. This is Foxbat."

Swallow swiveled around to his terminal, keyed it, and brought up photos to demonstrate. "My people went back over the last five years. About two years ago, extended flights started showing up in the Mediterranean and the North Sea. It was nothing to get excited about—clear days and obvious aerial refueling. There was a weekly pattern in addition to the regular patrols of the old prop-driven Bears. It looked like they just wanted some high-level snapshots.

"Okay. We go over to the Pacific, and there's a difference. We come up with photos of some eight flights in the same time span. The difference is that every flight we caught was on a day of extremely poor weather, and in no case did we see airborne refueling over the ocean. All of the flights take place at altitudes the tankers can't reach."

"Where are they going?" Garrett asked.

"That's a damned good question." Swallow rotated back. "In the North Sea and the Med, there's obvious reconnaissance targets. In the Pacific, at the coordinates where we find them, they must be shooting whales."

Garrett ruminated. "Can I assume something?"

"It won't go out of the room."

"Two assumptions. One, the Pacific MiGs can actually go the distance on their own. Two, the Med and North Sea flights are covers in case the opposition happens to spot something unusual in the Pacific."

"I can buy the cover story, I think; the Russkis would do something like that. I'm not sure I can live with two-hour Foxbats."

"What would they have to do to the 25 to up it to that range capability, Clare?"

I'm no engineer, Brandon, but I think they'd have to strip armament and unnecessary electronics. There'd have to be two or three external drop tanks. They might have to rebuild with lighter alloy panels in place of some of the steel skin. Or maybe the planes are special-built at the factory in the first place.

"All of which means that these particular Foxbats are not an obvious military threat. No armament.

106

They're built for a specific mission. Maybe scientific experimentation of some kind."

"At a time when the Soviets don't have extra rubles to spare on non-defense projects. Plus there's the high cost of the cover flights. I don't know what it means, Clare, but I think we'd better keep an eye on the Pacific flights. I wouldn't worry too much about the others."

"Okay. We had a Pacific flight just three days ago. We're going to start tracking them on infrared now, so we can peek through the cloud cover."

Garrett thanked him and headed for the elevators. There was a taxi available on the front drive, but again, the trip into the District and 23rd Street was prolonged.

His name had been left at the checkpoint protecting Consular Operations, and he was passed right through.

Twenty minutes late for his appointment with Barbara Morris, Garrett found her in the hallway outside her office. He assumed it was she. She was a good-looking woman, tall, with green eyes and dark auburn hair.

She was also pinned to the wall by a tall, handsome man in gray slacks and a blue blazer. He had a tight grip on her elbow, pinching her flesh, and was leaning forward against her. He was very intent.

Garrett almost turned away, not wanting to interrupt some personal argument, when he saw the look of distaste on her face.

He overheard the man. ". . . I transfer over here, just think of the team we'll make. Now . . ."

Garrett stopped a few feet away, causing the man to look up. "We're busy, joker."

"One of you seems to be. Miss Morris, I believe we have a date?"

"That's right, Colonel. I'm ready."

The man dropped his grip on Morris's elbow and

107

backed away, perhaps intimidated by Garrett's title or heft. "Now, hang on, joker."

Garrett narrowed his eyes, which were going to gray. He smiled. "You know, the last guy that called me joker took six weeks to recover."

The man lost some of his tan. "Look . . ."

Barbara ignored him and reached out to take Garrett's arm. "Shall we go?"

They turned toward the elevators and left her suitor standing in the corridor.

"I guess I wasn't intruding?"

"The cavalry to the rescue in the nick of time."

They did not speak until they were seated in the top-floor executive dining room by a window overlooking Virginia Avenue. It was a cold view of icy asphalt. It was also cold in the dining room.

The waitress took their orders, then Morris told him, "Sorry I didn't introduce you upstairs."

"We haven't even introduced ourselves."

"I'm Barbara Morris. I'm the executive assistant to Mr. Petrie."

She smiled nicely, and Garrett wondered how long that would last, working for Petrie.

"Brandon Garrett. I hang around the Pentagon."

"The jerk in the hall was my ex-husband, Phil."

"He's not in agreement with your divorce?"

"He was at the time. He's changed his mind. How do the spooks on your side of the river get rid of someone you don't want around?"

Garrett grinned at her. "Want me to put out a sanction notice?"

"I'll look for a milder way."

Her salad and his club sandwich arrived, and she told him of the assignment given her by Petrie.

"I was to compare Soviet and American levels of academic preparation, like with our SATs, but I'm at a dead end. The Soviets have several series of test instruments to evaluate whether or not a student goes on for more advanced education. Since 1984, students attend a ten-year school and are then tested. Some go on to vocational schools and some to universities and specialized institutes. However, passing scores, national norms, and the like are not available."

"Who'd you use as a sources?"

"Embassy and diplomatic offices. Intelligence files. One of the reports came out of AFI, and when I checked over there, they said that you had acquired the data."

Garrett had to think about that. Two minutes went by before he recalled the circumstances.

"Somebody's misled you, I'm afraid. It was a by-product of another operation."

"What does that mean?"

"I was . . . in an unfriendly nation's education ministry offices, looking for something else entirely. Since I try to make my trips worthwhile, I grabbed some snapshots of a few extra files. Hell, I didn't know what I had until I gave it to the analysts."

"Oh." She looked disappointed.

"I've never looked for that kind of thing, Barbara, but let me put out some feelers and see what we can come up with. Would you want anything else?"

"Maybe. I don't know. When we couldn't get the test results, I tried to look at it from several different slants. One is the reputation of the institution, but what we found there was overabundant propaganda about faculties and programs, with no real explanations of the definition of high quality.

"Another way of looking at quality is by examining the faculties. That's a drudge job, so we skipped humanities and literature—they're downplayed by the Soviets anyway—and looked at the hard sciences. In a number of fields, there are names that mean something to American academics, and are revered for their expertise. Then, comparing the listings of faculty members in the catalogs against reality, we found that a substantial number—twenty-four I think it was—aren't really there. They're on leaves of absence."

Garrett recalled his conversation with Roger Hornby. "You remember what fields?"

"It varied. I remember some physics, chemistry, and nuclear specialties."

He told her what he had learned from Hornby, though he did not reveal his source.

"I didn't look at Poland, but I can check further. What were the names?"

"Polodka was one. I'll have to get the other name for you. They haven't shown up elsewhere, have they? It could simply be a transfer between institutions."

"I suppose that's right. I'll double-check."

They resumed eating, and Garrett wondered what her goals were. She had an aura of strict professionalism, and though the wine-red wool dress clung provocatively to her, the high collar and the light green of her eyes suggested that she was never in a mood for dalliance. On the street, she would be unapproachable to any man with common sense.

Based on his experience, of course, he would be the last to say that any woman was predictable.

Tom Eaglefeather was, however. He arrived in Garrett's office a few minutes before their three o'clock appointment while Garrett was staring out at the snow which had just begun again. The paper had reported flooding in Louisiana, and the water experts were already issuing dire warnings about spring floods.

Garrett heard Eaglefeather chatting with Aggie in the anteroom. The man always ingratiated himself with other people's secretaries. "You're looking lovely today, my dear. Can that be a new plant?"

The outer office was being slowly transformed from a greenhouse to an Asian jungle, and Aggie had successfully infiltrated two plants into Garrett's own office.

She told Eaglefeather, "Thank you, Colonel. And there is a new plant, but I'll bet you don't know which one."

"This one right here. Because it's on your desk, and closest to your heart."

Aggie said, "A susceptible woman could fall for you, Colonel."

"If only she would, love."

Eaglefeather appeared in the doorway, his voice a bass boom. "You awake in here?"

"I am now.

"I thought as much. You lazy fu . . . fellows over here want the Army, Navy, and Marines to do your work, while you hit the embassy receptions."

Eaglefeather picked a cup up from the sideboard and poured coffee. Garrett refilled his own cup, and the two or them took castered chairs at the conference table.

There was a trust and cross-reliance between the two men that went a long way. Once, when Eaglefeather had become entangled with a group of Laotian bandits, Garrett had flown a beat-up old twin Otter in to retrieve him. Eaglefeather would do the same for him.

Garrett asked, "You ever shave?"

Eaglefeather ran his hand over his blue-black cheek. "On Sundays. If they happen to fall on the seventeenth of the month."

Garrett grinned. "Why are they paying you at DIA? Or is it 'ears only'?"

"You know the Soviets keep the ruble off the international exchanges? We're devising a plan to draw the ruble involuntarily into a black market exchange on this side of the border. We'd like to have the Kremlin laying out domestic currency for stereos, radios, jeans, food from foreign markets. Start draining the Soviet economy of currency. We're not operational."

"That's a Defense concern?"

"It's a little sideshow, Brandon. More drains on the economy mean fewer tanks and artillery."

"That would strain them, wouldn't it? Cut some more slices out of their economic pie."

"The idea is to put pressure on domestic needs, so they have to reallocate out of defense. Stop the big buildup, and give more incentive to discussing disarmament."

"With resources as stretched as they are, I wonder whey they continue pouring money into risky projects."

"We do it too," Eaglefeather observed. "Hey, we got a report that Afghan rebels downed a big bird bound for Kabul with advisors aboard. There were some top Soviet brass, maybe a couple of generals. That's even more costly."

"Got a good source for that?"

"East Indian, via CIA."

"They opening up with you at the Company?"

"They were, until I hired Brighton away from them. I may have made a tactical error."

"They'll get over it, but I'm surprised Brighton left the Agency."

"He didn't like the recent shake-up in operations."

"He's not alone, from what I hear. Have you had time to look into this Foxbat thing?"

"A little. There were a few in Defense who were concerned about it for awhile, until a pattern emerged. The official line is that it's just high-level recon."

Garrett related his conversation with Swallow, including their vague theory.

"Son of a bitch! Special mission, huh? I'll kind of sneak in a suggestion like that with our strategists.

We can see what they come up with."

"Anything else happening in your shop?"

"Watch the papers in the morning. I'll bet we have another leak about radiation."

"How's DIA involved?" Garrett asked.

"The Joint Chiefs were puzzled by the last news leak because the traces found were so far away from reactors. Personally, I think they were scared shitless that Air Force or Army weapons plants or storage sites might be involved. So we've been monitoring NRC reporting, and damned if they're not picking up even more radiation traces. Some of it's not within a hundred miles of a reactor. I'm betting whoever's in charge of leaks over there will have something to the *Post* by tonight."

"No doubt. Have you heard anything about missing professors?"

"Whose?"

Garrett explained the circumstances from his two different sources.

"No, I sure as hell haven't. Optimistically, I'd hope that a bunch of those guys decided they couldn't take it and have gone on strike. Maybe they'll all want to defect."

"And realistically?"

"Realistically, I'd put my money on a series of new graves out back of the Lubyanka."

"I gave up betting," Garrett told him.

Nine

COMMITTEE FOR STATE SECURITY
MOSCOW
12-21 DIGEST

TO: Authorized Personnel
FROM: Moscow Center

1. General V.M. Sagrev died during the night as a result of injuries sustained in Afghanistan crash.
2. Four Sherman Class destroyers, one destroyer tender, and one Austin Class Assault Transport joined the U.S. fleet off Lebanon.
3. Peter Bowles, British citizen, detained by KGB Surveillance Directorate in Leningrad. Possible smuggling of Radio Free Europe receivers.
4. U.S. newspapers and television continue outcry over widespread radiation detection.
5. French government seeking W. German aid in stabilization of franc.
6. Soviet operative in Ghana dispatched, per directive, Chairman, KGB.

7. U.S. President again to declassify satellite photos purporting to show Soviet installation in the Caribbean. Source, U.S. State Dept.
8. Col. B. Garrett, AFI, pursuing inquiry into missing Soviet academic personnel. Source, U.S. AFI.
9. Lt. Cmder. J. Reynolds, U.S. Navy, to be court-martialed regarding charges of mistreating prisoners aboard ship.
10. Capt. M. Sutherland testified in hearing that a small explosion was heard prior to the breakup and sinking of the crude-oil tanker *Ghatsu* near Capetown.
11. T.S. Potter arrested in Rhode Island following nuclear protest.
12. Argentinian Minister of Commerce died in automobile explosion outside his home.

Major Grigori Zanov reviewed the list. It had been a quiet night and it was a short list. "Item Eleven, here. This man Potter in Rhode Island, Corporal? Is he one of ours?"

"I do not know, Comrade Major."

"Well, the First Directorate brought it to our attention, so I suspect that is the case. The Chairman will be concerned about how much the man knows, so see what more we can learn of the circumstances."

"Yes, Comrade Major."

"And send Items Two, Three, Five, Six, Seven, Ten, Eleven, and Twelve to First Base."

Zanov thought that Item 6 would be of interest to that bastard Petrovsky. Soviet agents who erred did not often err again.

And none of the rest of it would have any bearing at all on whatever the hell Petrovsky was up to.

Let the bastard find out his own information.

The General Secretary's morning office ritual included a quiet time in which he could read the briefs prepared during the night. They kept him abreast of the activities in which the Soviet Union had an active or passive interest. In some circumstances, the General Secretary then requested the original report, saving the more detailed account for the last of his morning reading.

After reading the full reports on two topics, he was concerned.

The history of the U.S. radiation could be puzzling, if the General Secretary did not know better. He had been unaware of the first radiation scare bandied about in the newspapers, but would have approved the decision of General Zhukov in Disinformation to leak the news at the time. This time, though, given the scattered nature of the radiation, Zhukov should have waited until he knew more about it.

The General Secretary was not an expert on nuclear energy, but understood enough to know that the U.S. Nuclear Regulatory Commission's discovery of radiation traces far away from nuclear reactors was disturbing.

The report contained a map of the United States and Canada with the areas of contamination hashmarked across the top western half of the continent and down the western coast. Black circles indicated the known locations of nuclear reactors or military weapons sites. The two separate patterns demonstrated no logical connection.

What seemed logical to the General Secretary, given all of the available current impacts on the North American environment, was that Malenkov's weather apparatus was poisoning the atmosphere.

Realistically, he had to admit that because of the secrecy of the project Zhukov could not have made the connection. But that idiot head of the KGB should have seen the relationship and cancelled the news leak. And certainly, Major Boris Petrovsky at Kamchatka Air Base, who was receiving all of these reports, should have sounded an alert.

He was absolutely certain that the Rain Cloud project was behind the radiation. He was just as certain that Malenkov was aware of the radiation, but had not revealed it because of his damned ambition. Well, the bloody fool would gain recognition as the man who destroyed his country.

With enough time, the relationship between radiation and weather would be revealed, and would suggest to the American President a devastating method for eliminating the country's problems with radiation, adverse weather, and the Soviet Union in one swift action.

The General Secretary's first priority was to contain the damage already done and to ascertain that any logical connections made by American persons of influence not be permitted to rise to the Chief Executive. Despite pockets of resistance within the Soviet Union, his new programs were developing well, as was the public image of the USSR outside its borders. All of his work should not be imperiled.

The second report focused his attention on a possible suspect. The report included a biography of Colonel Brandon Garrett, indicating the man's complicity in the eradication of several Soviet intelligence networks in the past ten years, most recently one in Southeast Asia and one in the German Democratic Republic. He had risen through the military ranks steadily, displaying perception and intelligence in a number of field assignments. The *Komitet Gosudarstvennoy*

Bezopasnasti's crammed file on Garrett suggested he was a great thorn in its side.

And now the Western spy had stumbled upon the fact that a number of prominent scientists were not where they were supposed to be. He was asking too many questions concerning their whereabouts.

He would never find them.

Of course not. They were all located at that damnable project of Malenkov's.

If this Garrett was as astute as his history suggested, he would soon assemble the radiation, the missing scientists, and the horrible weather into one possibly cohesive whole. Located in the Air Force Intelligence Agency, he would have access to the right ears.

The source in AFI had not mentioned how many others were aware of the missing professors. The source only said that Garrett was asking questions.

The wrinkles on the General Secretary's brow furrowed and deepened. He could not wait. He could not seek the advice of individuals, many of whom were members of important committees and of the Politburo. Delay could bring annihilation.

He pressed the call button under the lip of the desk, and his secretary appeared in the doorway. "Yes, Comrade General Secretary?"

"Get the KGB Chairman over here."

"Immediately, Comrade Secretary."

"Then get Colonel Malenkov on the phone."

Yuri Yurievich Malenkov was in Hangar Two when the call was transferred from the compound headquarters.

Malenkov was irritated by the interuption of his discussion with Leon Polodka, the chief of his staff of six nuclear specialists. The man was brilliant, but in theory rather than application. Malenkov was having a difficult time urging the staff to make progress in diminishing the radioactive by-product.

He picked up the telephone and was astounded to hear the General Secretary. Why would the man make a personal call to him? Why not follow the normal communication routes? The contents of Malenkov's stomach turned to acid.

"Yes, Comrade General Secretary."

Polodka and one of his associates heard the form of address and moved away to the other side of the room. Telephone calls from such personages tended to herald ominous news. Too often, it rubbed off on those in proximity.

"Comrade Yuri Yurievich, I call to inquire about your progress."

"Our progress, Comrade Secretary? I have sent many reports concerning the weather damage in the United States."

"I am well aware of those, my Colonel. Instead, I am interested in an effect of which I was unaware. What about the radiation?"

Malenkov thought he might have a heart attack, the way his chest suddenly hurt.

Petrovsky. The bastard!

"Radiation, General Secretary?"

"Certainly. The American media are reporting it substantially. There is no known connection with the American nuclear power plants. I must assume that it comes as a result of your apparatus."

Malenkov finally had complete ownership of the process, he noted.

"Comrade Secretary, certainly there has always been an insubstantial production of radiation in the fission process, occurring when we supercharge the crystals, though never anything to be alarmed about. We—"

"Alarmed, Colonel? You have the whole Ameri-

119

can continent alarmed, and ready to understand that you have been poisoning their environment."

"But it cannot have been that much. We are making great inroads on completely eliminating any radioactive by-product at all."

"Colonel, you will cease operations immediately and prepare a complete report to be personally delivered to me. Is that understood?"

"Yes, General Secretary. Completely." Hold on to something. Keep an advantage. Malenkov gulped audibly and asked, "May we continue experimentation? Within the laboratory?"

There was a disturbing, unending pause.

"For the time being, yes. Laboratory experimentation only. But there are to be no more flights." He hung up, with a jarring crash that made Malenkov jump.

Malenkov turned to the knot of scientists. They fidgeted under his glare.

"If you had not overheard, that was the General Secretary. He is concerned that we are not making sufficient progress with the containment of the radiation."

Malenkov stomped away from the nervous group and went to check on the production of fiberglass modules in the fabrication room. He did not want to think about the telephone call, or its potential consequences.

Each sphere was fifty-five centimeters in diameter, composed of two fiberglass halves joined together by epoxy, and each pocked with several small access doors. The bottom half of the sphere held the silver iodide compound crystals. The upper hemisphere contained the paravane, the key component, the battery compartment; and the electronics.

Malenkov was proud of his design, the perfect shape enveloping such a powerful tool of peace and of war.

The General Secretary . . .

He forced himself to ignore the perfect tool just then, and went down the hall toward the rear of the hangar to unlock and enter his private laboratory. He would not halt production of the spheres.

He must find a way out of this. He had never given up before, and he was not about to start now. He would not succumb to lesser minds.

His thin hands were shaking, and he clasped them together tightly. He was becoming increasingly insecure. Partly, it was the changing aspect of the project. It had been conceived in the warm laboratories of the Institute as an aid for Soviet agriculture. The more he had worked with it, sensing its potential, the more he had come to see the benefits for Mother Russia, not only in agricultural output, but in world domination. Inwardly, he had begun to visualize the concept as a halo effect around his own head, tasting the things that success would bring.

He had never been in a Zil automobile, but its handmade black sleekness beckoned to him, its image an obvious mark of personal achievement. He had never been to the theater or the ballet, but others went and carried an aura of sophistication that Malenkov knew he should have. They also carried tasteless comments about particular actresses whom Malenkov could vaguely associate with pictures he had seen in magazines. Still, the comments suggested fantasies with which to people his dreams.

This particular setback was more an affront to him as a person than it was to his sense of serving the Soviet Union. He did not think that the radiation discovery could trigger ballistic missiles aimed at Russia. He did know that he must curb the radioactivity side effect, and quickly, if he was to achieve his goals.

There was no possibility of changing the key component, seven packages of which rested on a steel-shelved rack on the wall opposite him. The key component, for which only he had the formula, was the lockstone at the apex of the arch. When it was activated by the TNT trigger mechanism, it ignited a controlled chain reaction in the thirty-five kilograms of passive crystals. He had developed the component in a laboratory-controlled atmosphere of miniscule dimension, and the radiation measurements had been infinitesimal. He had discounted the measurements as insignificant.

Only in the full-scale testing had the measurements risen to a proportion that was disconcerting, and again he had discounted them. Malenkov was fearful of sabotaging his future. He had assigned Polodka and his sub-group of nuclear physicists to full-time concentration on the problem. Professor Polodka, however, insisted upon access to the key component. He seemed adamantly convinced that the one and only solution lay in altering the catalyst.

That was impossible. Malenkov had tried to alter the catalyst himself and found that the most minute of changes resulted in no atomic fission. There would be no changing the key component.

Malenkov was not conditioned for such pressures, and he ached to find a way to relieve them.

While Malenkov grieved, Petrovsky fumed. He had had his own conversation with Chairman Felix Nemoronko, who had heard from the General Secretary. It was a one-sided conversation in which Petrovsky learned of his ineptitude in matters of security and his laxity in things observable.

He had been unaware of some of the details the

122

Chairman mentioned, but the tone told him what he must do in order to resurrect his future. The KGB major had discovered from the Chairman's harangue two topics around which he must weave some fabric of knowledge.

One was radiation and one was missing scientists.

That both topics had been the subject of intelligence reports he had no doubt. That he had not received the reports, he knew.

The first place for him to determine reasons for the omissions was the communications complex at Moscow Center.

Snowfall

Ten

Christmas Eve was not a godsend for many on the North American Continent.

St. Petersburg, Florida, received two inches of rain during the day, and the forecasters were guardedly warning of another two inches during the night. Nashville was having a white Christmas, and the four city dump trucks with their new snowplows were not coping well. The Dallas-Fort Worth airport was closed with snow on the runways.

A Panamanian Airways DC-8, already delayed for three days and in a hurry, took off from Kennedy International with the entire contingent of Panama's United Nations delegation and went down two minutes after takeoff, coated with tons of ice. There were four survivors among the 163 passengers and crew.

The Eastern Corridor trains were still operating, but Amtrak passenger trains out of Chicago had been cancelled while crews tried to free an FP-45 diesel and three dual-level passenger cars from snowdrifts forty-five miles east of Cincinnati. Similarly, the old Rio Grande Zephyr, now operated by Amtrak, was three hours overdue in Salt Lake City, and some officials had begun to worry. The "Scenic Route through the Rockies," through snow-choked canyons, was not conducive to rescue operations.

The mayor of San Francisco placed a moratorium on the use of private cars at night. San Franciscans, most of whom had never seen a studded snow tire, were novices on the ice-slickened hills. Most of Highway 101 south along the coast was closed to traffic, mud slides and a few houses having blocked access.

In Hawaii, which was experiencing unseasonably cool temperatures, an insurance salesman from Waukesha was delayed eight days beyond the free five days he had won topping a million dollars in sales. He and his wife fought with thousands of other couples each day at the airport, waiting for transportation home. Angela had not been able to reach the elderly woman staying with Angelica and Parker Junior, and she was becoming increasingly frightened. Parker tried to remember how many times he had used his VISA, Diner's Club, and American Express cards. He was pretty close to the limits, he thought. Parker also worried about his new Sedan de Ville which was parked at the Milwaukee airport.

Further north, and over the plains of Minnesota and North Dakota, the winds were incredibly strong, the wind-chill index occasionally reaching forty degrees below zero. The frigid wind had taken down most of the off-ground and exposed electric and telephone lines, leaving rural residents isolated from each other and from the rest of America.

In Cherry County, Nebraska, in the heart of the sandhills, with some residents who still recalled the Blizzard of '49, drifts as high as thirty feet had buried houses in Valentine. Stockmen tried in vain to airlift hay to herds of whitefaced Herefords stranded against barbed-wire fences. Cherry County might have to give up its claim as the county with the highest beef production in the U.S.

Bernie Zacharias, in Buffalo, New York, missed his dinner at home and thought longingly about a steaming T-bone steak. His hands were full, though, with thirty-six snow-bladed trucks, nineteen road-graders, seventeen four-wheel-drive tractors, and four new rotary snow throwers out on the streets. Nine drivers had radioed in to the office for assistance, and he was trying to get towing help out to them. The Buffalo snow-removal operation was one of best in the nation, but they were sorely taxed by this latest storm.

The temperature in Washington, D.C., was two degrees above zero, and large fluffy snowflakes continued to fall, coating the freshly plowed parking lots around the Department of Defense. A few cars remained in several of the lots. At the back of Lot 23, a snow-covered sedan gurgled white exhaust and occasionally flipped its windshield wipers. The face peering through the wiped arc was swarthy, with strained, dark eyes, and unkempt black hair. He was known to three people in the world as Alexandre.

The building was cold and deserted when Garrett decided to give it up after six-thirty. He could not concentrate on his current project anyway. After some test runs with fake data passed through Naval Intelligence, he had narrowed his potential spy to a signals section. That still left him with sixty-three possible suspects. Neither Brent nor Hornby had come up with anything that helped narrow it further.

Garrett had turned down dinner invitations from

the Bellows, the Eaglefeathers, and the Jerry Greens—a friend over at State and his wife, not wanting to intrude upon their holidays with family. He was not much on Christmas anyway.

Garrett locked his office door and took the elevator to the main floor. He wished the air policeman on duty at the checkpoint a Merry Christmas and made his way along the mostly deserted concourse. He waved to the guard on the desk at the main doors, but the man was conversing with a furry coat.

He called out, "Hey, John, Merry Christmas!"

John looked up. "Sure thing, Colonel. Merry Christmas to you."

The furry bundle turned, and he saw Barbara Morris's face peeking out of the high collar.

She said, "Merry Christmas, Brandon."

Garrett stopped and walked back toward her. "Hello, Barbara. What are you doing here?"

"Waiting for a cab now. I was playing messenger earlier."

"You may wait a long time tonight. Come on, I've got a car."

"You sure? I'm over in Georgetown."

"So am I."

Garrett led her out to the Corvette and opened the doors. He started the engine and let it warm while the windows fogged with their breath.

"I thought you might have gone home for the holidays. Indianapolis, isn't it?"

"You remember everything in my file?"

"File? What file?"

"I assume you checked me out."

"I did take a quick glance," Garrett admitted.

"I looked at yours," she told him, "but there wasn't much there. Most of your activities seem to

130

be classified at levels only directors can look at."

"I'm a classy guy. But you're not headed for home and hearth?"

"I couldn't face the flight home. I'm not a good air traveler."

The stereo he had installed issued Ray Price and Willie Nelson, recreating Bob Wills's old song "Faded Love." He turned the volume down slightly.

"Not a flyer, huh?"

"Don't put this in my folder. I'm terrified of flying."

The admission was strained. Garrett suspected she did not often confess weakness.

"I'd say it's pretty much a sane desire to keep your feet on the ground in this kind of weather."

"But you're a pilot. Aren't you born to pursue the wild blue yonder?"

"In my case, it's only on sunny days."

He got out to scrape ice from the windshield, then got back in and backed out of his slot.

Garrett raced the engine to plow the Corvette through a ridge of snow at the lot entrance, and slewed his way onto the deserted street. He was a block away when a flash of lights struck his rearview mirror and he saw that another late departer had pulled out behind him.

He took the Arlington Bridge over the Potomac, then headed north on 23rd Street.

When they reached the Georgetown area, Barbara guided him through deserted streets toward her apartment building. She said, "I hope I didn't take you out of your way."

"Not at all. I'm just ten or twelve blocks from here."

He eased over a hillock of plowed snow and stopped at the curb.

131

She slid halfway out, then turned back and asked, "Do you have plans?"

He grinned, not sure why he did not lie. "I try to never plan anything."

"You want to come up for a drink?"

He wanted a drink, but he also would just as soon be by himself. He guessed that Morris, however, was not looking forward to a Christmas Eve by herself. "Well, sure, maybe one."

She closed the door, and he drove up to the corner and another quarter-block before he found a parking place. They walked back together. Everyone seemed to be staying by the fire tonight. There were bright windows in the buildings, but no one on the street in her residential neighborhood. One car passed them, moving slowly on the ice.

Garrett turned to look after it, noting that it was a dark blue Audi with D.C. plates and a single driver. Somehow, it made him uneasy. Old instincts died hard.

It continued down the street, finally turning several blocks away, and he smiled at Barbara's quizzical look, then followed her inside. They climbed the stairs to her second-floor apartment, and she unlocked the door.

Barbara hung their coats in the foyer closet, and Garrett surveyed the apartment. It was homey. There were nice decorative touches: an afghan across the back of the sofa, a picture grouping on one wall—parents, relatives, classmates, boyfriends?

"I like your place."

"Thank you. Sit down, and I'll fix something. Hot toddy, Scotch, vodka?"

"Scotch is easier."

"Toddy is warmer, if you're willing."

"Fine."

The kitchenette was divided from the living room by a Formica-topped counter with three upholstered stools, and Garrett picked one of them to sit on. Barbara kicked off her high heels and padded about, selecting bottles and mugs.

There was a forced cheerfulness in her next question. "Do you have a commitment for dinner?"

"Well, I . . ."

"All I've got around is spaghetti."

All he had around was a frozen salisbury steak. There were of a couple real ones in his freezer, but he did not feel like scooping snow off the patio to fire up the grill. Oven-broiled steaks had never interested him.

"If it wouldn't be any trouble . . ."

"It wouldn't be any trouble at all." She smiled. It was the first smile he remembered seeing from her. "I'm going to do it anyway."

She extracted a plastic pan from the freezer and shoved it into the microwave. "It's homemade, at least. Every fall, I cook up huge batches of sauce and chili, so I can come home to something besides cube steaks."

"I know what you mean."

She poured their toddies and came around the counter to sit beside him. She was wearing the same wool dress in dark red that he had seen before, and he was aware of how it clung to her. He could see the faint protuberance of her right nipple through the cloth.

They talked guardedly about their jobs while they waited for the sauce and then the spaghetti. They were both professionals in operations sections, but there were agency secrets to be maintained.

133

Barbara put half a loaf of garlic-buttered French bread in the microwave. He sensed from the way she talked that her life was centered on her work, but not on the work for what it accomplished. Like too many bureaucrats he knew, she was interested in the job for what it brought her—salary, recognition, whatever.

Garrett and some like him—Eaglefeather, Hornby, and God forbid, even Nat Petrie—performed their government service for the good of their country. The Jack Kennedy syndrome. It was an outmoded ideology, judging by the majority of federal people with whom he dealt, but still one that he never questioned for himself.

Garrett pulled the cork on a bottle of imported French Bordeaux while Barbara set two places at the small table next to the counter. He noted that she searched a cabinet for her best china and a drawer for what looked like family-heirloom silver. When they sat down to the two plates Barbara had overloaded, steamingly aromatic, he said, "I really do appreciate this, Barbara."

Her face softened, and her green eyes were dark under the tiny crystal chandelier above the table. She smiled again. "It's not like I worked all day on it."

He rolled spaghetti on his fork and said, "If it ever turns summertime, so I can dig my grill out of the snow, I'll reciprocate."

She was a good cook, pouring some expertise into those sauces frozen for a later thaw, and he enjoyed the dinner more than he thought he would. When they finished the meal, he told her that, and helped pick up the table and load the dishwasher.

When the counters were wiped clean, he waited for her to get his coat for him.

Instead, she asked, "Would you like a brandy?"

She was nervous, her hands betraying her in slightly unsteady fashion, but she obviously wanted some kind of companionship on this family kind of evening. Garrett decided he was not in that big a hurry.

"Sure."

They sat at opposite ends of the couch, holding snifters, and Barbara said, "I've got a list of names for you. Of the missing scientific people."

"Oh, good. And damn it, I forgot, but I've got a couple of tests for you."

"Tests?"

"I couldn't get any compiled results on standardized tests in Soviet-controlled countries, but a guy I know over at Treasury did have the specific test instruments for general knowledge, for social sciences, and for physical sciences. I didn't ask how he'd gotten them, and they're a year out of date."

"Hmmm," she said. "I don't quite know what we'd do with them."

"My thought would be to have somebody at one of the testing centers—SAT, maybe—look them over and compare them to the American equivalents. It seems to me that the quality of the test instrument itself might be revealing."

"Ah. You mean the level of national scores doesn't mean diddly-damn if the Soviets are asking easier questions of their kids than we are?"

"Or possibly vice versa. Anyway, I thought it'd be interesting."

"That's a good idea. I'll follow it up. What about the scientists?"

"I haven't heard back from all of my sources yet. To be truthful, I haven't put a lot of time in on it."

Barbara swung her snifter, watching the liquid

roam. "According to the list I have, they're all nuclear physicists, meteorologists, and physical scientists."

"That is strange. But there's lots of strange things lately."

Her eyebrows arched. "Like what?"

There was nothing classified about what he had, and anyway, her security clearance was near the top cryptographic levels. "Like Foxbats."

She did not know very much about the MiG-25, and he devoted five minutes to telling her about the performance aspects that were puzzling him.

"What else?"

"*Pravda* is crying wolf at the door about food shortages, and yet our satellites are showing millions of tons of grain stored all over the country."

"Maybe their almanac told them to expect a long winter too? Lord knows, we may need some of our own surplus if this weather stays bad into the planting season."

"I suppose you're right," Garrett said. "Maybe they were expecting a bad year."

A bad year of what? No imports?

"While we're talking about odd things, there's something else too," Barbara said. "Nat mentioned it to me yesterday. The President's really been coming down on the NRC people about the news leaks on radiation. And then the Environmental Protection Agency screwed up in some way. They had the data in their files, but no one had flagged it."

"The EPA is catching it lately."

"Well, it's no damned wonder, with this kind of performance. I gather that the character responsible, some guy named Shafer, had his mind on his girlfriend and completely missed the significance of the reports. They fired him, but now he's suing the

136

EPA for being discriminatory, arbitrary, and capricious."

"Figures," Garrett said. "He'd be one of my favorite bureaucrats."

"I didn't know you had favorites. That was kind of a nasty crack you made about my boss to Marty Ackerman. Nat was fuming for three days."

"We'd better not talk about your boss," Garrett said.

From the protective fire in her eyes, he thought it was the best course. She did not respond.

"What the papers said is true?" Garrett asked. "That the radiation is not confined to reactor sites?"

"That's what Nat told me."

"The whole world is going to hell." Garrett sipped from his snifter.

Barbara sat upright suddenly, her lips parted, and her eyes introspective. "You know. . . ."

Her voice drifted into silence as she pondered.

Garrett said, "What do I know?"

"Just a sec."

She went to the kitchen and came back with a yellow legal pad, sat down, and began jotting words down in clearly defined block print.

Garrett leaned over the coffee table and read:

Strange Things:

Missing Nuclear People	— Radiation
Missing Physics People	— ??
Missing Meteorologists	— Weather
Stored Grain	— Expected Bad Harvest
Foxbats	— ??
Radiation	— Non-Reactor Source Military Weapons

When she was done, she turned the pad around for him to read right side up.

Garrett looked at her list and remembered his meeting at NPIC, recalled what he had thought, and what Clare Swallow had voiced.

"Barbara, opposite Foxbats, you can write, 'Special Mission.' "

She did, but asked, "Why?"

"It's something that came up with someone else. These particular aircraft are refined to where they must be reserved for only one task."

"All right." She looked over her notes. "I'm not sure what I've got here. It just seemed like it would help if I put it all down."

"Sure, you're sure," Garrett told her, though he himself was having difficulty with the concept.

So was Barbara. "It's really rather preposterous, don't you think?"

"That the Soviets are screwing around with our weather? It sounds pretty damned farfetched, but I'd bet whatever's in my wallet that it's possible."

"In the next century maybe."

"Well, just let me summarize it," Garrett told her. "A bunch of top Soviet scientists disappear from their home bases. They congregate in some out-of-the way spot and develop some kind of . . . thing that can alter weather. It's based on a nuclear reaction that produces radiation. Specially built aircraft deliver the packages into the Pacific jet stream—that much is founded on altitudes and coordinates we know about. They do whatever it is they're supposed to do, spreading a little radioactivity in the doing. We know about that too."

Barbara interrupted. "Maybe they're just slowly poisoning the atmosphere with radiation. The bad weather is an unexpected development."

138

"That's possible," Garrett said, starting to give in. "No, it can't be. They know that with all of the monitoring equipment of the EPA and the NRC we'd spot something like that. It would lead right back to them, and present a chance of repercussion by missiles. No, I have to think that weather alteration is the product, and the radiation a by-product. They might not even know themselves about the side effects.

"To top it off, in their planning, they've laid by a year or two's worth of wheat, knowing that the U.S. would not have exports available."

"Just what I said. It's still preposterous, isn't it?"

"Goddamn. Yeah, it probably is." Having said it out loud, Garrett could see the logic, but felt less certain of it. No one in power was going to believe it.

"It's completely contrary to their recent posture," Barbara said.

"They've changed domestic policy, but not foreign policy," Garrett reminded her. "Still, yeah, it's a bit fantastic."

"And maybe not. But why?" Barbara asked.

Babe in the woods, Garrett thought. It comes from climbing the operations career ladder without having field experience.

"It's nothing some of the Cold Warriors in this town wouldn't have done, if they'd thought of it first, Barbara. Look around us: communications broken down, energy being consumed at high rates. The freight and passenger transportation systems are a shambles. You said yourself. If this goes on much longer, it'll kill the planting season. Think what a shortage of food and high prices will do to the economy. Hell, I read this morning that the beef production is already endangered, and prices are expected to skyrocket."

"It could be devastating," she agreed. "Is it possible, though?"

"I'd guess the technology is available. We already seed clouds in a rudimentary fashion. This is just one step up in the process."

"So what do we do with this now?" She pointed to her notes.

"I'll have to think about it, talk to a couple people. It's all circumstantial except for the photos of grain and Foxbats. Even then, I couldn't prove the exact mission of those MiGs. And if we raised a stink about the scientists, you can be damned sure they'd suddenly reappear."

Garrett's mind raced with the possibilities, and he looked at his watch. "Damn, nearly midnight. I'd better get out of your hair, Barbara."

She got to her feet, leading him to the front closet for his topcoat. He shrugged his way into it.

"Thanks for the drinks and dinner, Barbara. Especially the dinner. I enjoyed it." Garrett unlocked the dead bolt and rested his hand on the door-knob.

"Thanks for the company," said Barbara. "It's hard being alone on Christmas Eve."

"I'll thrash this out with Danton after Christmas and get back to you."

"And I'll talk to Petrie."

That did not thrill him, but it was what she was supposed to do.

Morris was in stockinged feet, six inches shorter than he, and her face tilted up toward his, her eyes warm and deep. She signaled by raising slightly on her toes, and Garrett did not know what else to do but kiss her. It was a light brushing of his lips against hers.

140

Friends.

"Thanks again, Barbara."

He let himself out into the hallway, tugging his leather gloves on.

Garrett tried to concentrate on the disturbing theory that the two of them had stumbled over as he walked the snow-covered sidewalk to his car. Jesus! If it was true, the consequences were beyond fantasy.

The first thing, he thought, he had to get hold of Brent and Eaglefeather and get their reactions.

His investigative logic on the first run-through had been quick and jumpy, and he went over it again in his mind, reorganizing what was fact and what was conjecture. The concept was outlandish enough that it was difficult to hold onto.

He completely ignored the old senses tugging at a buried warrior mentality.

When he reached the Corvette, he stepped out into the street and went around the back end. He stomped snow off of his shoes. With his glove on, it was awkward getting the key ring out of his pocket. He unlocked the door, pulled the key out, and dropped the key ring.

Garrett bent down for it as the bullet slammed into the fiberglass top of the Corvette. Glass tinkled around him.

Morris leaned against the door for two minutes before moving, her mind trying to cover a dozen shifting, melting concepts.

She had been lonely, not wanting this evening, and that was the only reason she had invited Brandon up. And then he had not been what she had expected him to be. Over time and after a number

141

of passes by overconfident senior officers, she had learned to detest military men. They were too aggressive and too sure of themselves. With Garrett, though, she never would have known he had the uniform tucked away somewhere.

There had been no pawing, no innuendos, none of the things she had come to expect from the men she dated.

And maybe no interest at all.

He'd spoken with intelligence and shown an interest in her work. He'd seemed sincere in thanking her for what she had provided, information and dinner.

And he was, maybe, a little handsome. Rugged, kind of weather-beaten, wide shoulders, barrel chest. Nice blue eyes.

And there was this weather thing to think about. It was unbelievable really, and she found little solace in the fact that she had pulled all of the puzzling aspects into a package and that Brandon had recognized the significance at about the same time she did. It could not happen, of course. Brandon would find that it was impossible when he checked with the others he had mentioned.

She wanted to call Petrie right then and spring it on him.

Morris finally pushed herself away from the door and poured another inch of brandy in her snifter. As she settled onto the sofa, she heard the report. It was sharp, though not exceptionally loud.

Twisting around and rising onto her knees on the couch, she shoved the drapes aside and pressed her nose and forehead to the cold window. The white landscape of the street looked vacant. She turned her head until she could see up the street. There was the Corvette, but she could not see him. He was probably warming it up.

No.

There was no exhaust plume.

Puzzled, she watched for another minute, becoming more alarmed. When there was no change after two minutes, she ran to the closet for a parka and loafers, and then raced down the stairs to the street.

A hundred feet away from the Corvette, she stepped out between two parked cars, then looked up the street. That was when she saw his body sprawled on the ground.

"Oh, my God!"

Eleven

Yuri Malenkov was very tired, and his eyelids felt like sandpaper. The flight had taken nine hours of his time and large chunks of his self-composure. It left him with a feeling of nakedness in this broad, gray room. In front of him, in a semicircle, was a row of tables behind which sat the General Secretary, the Chairman of the KGB, and Politburo members Yakov, Parensyev, and Gurenko—the Rain Cloud Project oversight committee. His own slight physique was wraithlike before the bulky and richly fed leaders.

He had brought with him visual aids as well as reports. The map on the easel beside him was well decorated with the hieroglyphics of the meteorologist's trade, but he was not allowed the use of it.

The General Secretary deferred to Viktor Yakov, who fluttered the three-page report and said, "Colonel Malenkov, we have read your report, and I believe we can dispense with your harping on the successes of the project. Too often, we live in the past, holding to our bosoms the better memories and burying the bad. Yes, all of us here know about California and Maine and Wisconsin.

"We are here to discover why we did not know of this radioactivity effect, and to learn what you intend to do about it."

Malenkov's composure eroded further as his presentation disintegrated before it even began. He had counted on a recapitulation of his successes to temper the aura of malevolence in the room.

Be strong. Be brave. Think about nude ballerinas dancing around the bed.

No, not that.

Concentrate instead on your health, which is not good.

His stomach danced.

"Comrade Yakov," Malenkov began. "in the early experimentation, with small amounts of catalyst and passive crystals, no radiation was noted." Or considered noteworthy.

"So I see here," Yakov said.

"It is Comrade Polodka's learned opinion that the combination of large amounts of material in each module and ten to twelve modules per mission resulted in the radiation becoming measurable. Barely measurable. In no way could the atmosphere be jeopardized."

"You spread the blame to Polodka?" the General Secretary asked.

"He is the nuclear specialist, Comrade General Secretary. I am but a meteorologist."

"My concern," said the General Secretary, "is not with the atmosphere. Rather I fear that the Soviet Union could be jeopardized. This telltale trace of radiation could provide the trail followed back to its source."

"General Secretary, the most distinguished of our scientists have devoted their full time to the problem since it was discovered."

Malenkov did not consider it important to relate that the time elapsed was well over a year.

"And?" prodded Yakov.

"And substantial progress has been made, Comrade Yakov. A change in the composition of the passive crystals has reduced the radiation measurements significantly." The reduction was four per cent.

Parensyev asked, "But it is still measurable?"

"It is still measurable *if* each mission is carried out in the same manner as in the past, with twelve spheres deployed four times a month."

"You have a suggested change in the timetable for the future then?" Gurenko asked, getting his name into the discussion.

Malenkov took his mental deep breath. "Comrades, my suggestion: We have made a tremendous impact on American weather patterns. If we were to cease operations, that impact would be slowly erased, and two years of devotion and expenditure would be for naught.

"Instead, we must maintain a pressure on what we have initiated in order to extend the pattern into the planting season. We must shorten the growing season and assure springtime flooding along all major rivers. We must force the overconsumption of energy."

"That was your original plan," the General Secretary noted.

"It was, Comrade Secretary, but we may now alter the method. With the blanket of precipitation already created on the continent, we need not add to it, but maintain it. We can do this by reducing the number of modules released from twelve to eight, and by reducing the number of flights to three times a month from the previous four.

"The combination of fewer flights, fewer modules, and the new passive crystals will make any radiation by-product undetectable. And the Politburo objectives will still be reached."

He waited.

They all waited.

The General Secretary went on. "That may be, Comrade Colonel. I understand your devotion to the project, and I am certain that your zealousness toward that end would not influence your report to this panel.

"There are additional considerations. For instance, an intelligence officer in the United States Air Force has raised questions regarding the absence of renowned scientists from our prestigious institutions. That was not to have happened."

The statement took Malenkov by surprise, and he was immediately happy that he had not participated in the recruitment of personnel. "Comrade Secretary, I was not apprised of that situation. The recruitment was arranged by Major Petrovsky."

There, he had said it. That should get the little, ferret-eyed bastard.

"And handled, perhaps, with less finesse than might have been expected," the General Secretary admitted. "Still, the disappearances have come to the attention of an American intelligence officer."

Malenkov felt pale.

"The decision was made to contain any dissemination of the information by eliminating the repository of the knowledge."

Malenkov suppressed a shudder.

That meant murder.

It was one thing to change the weather, knowing that some deaths would occur—that was more natural and infinitely more remote. But to deliberately order someone to cold-bloodedly murder a particular man . . .

"We continue to research the topic, and will take whatever steps are necessary to prevent the linking of apparently unrelated facts with the reality at Kamchatka.

"But, Comrades, whatever we decide here, keep in mind that we may have to eradicate any evidence of the project's existence. Should the Americans develop enough evidence to interest a court of world opinion, we would certainly have to invite a neutral team of examiners inside our borders. We would have to prove their fears groundless. Am I understood on this point?"

Utterly.

Malenkov had a new vision of an entirely different future. Even if the operation was entirely successful, Malenkov now harbored doubts that the Politburo would risk returning the involved personnel to their old posts to chat with academic colleagues.

The masters of the Kremlin would leave them to rot in Kamchatka or possibly . . .

Malenkov said, "Comrades, it would also be possible to disguise our operation as a scientific experiment, with limited testing on domestic weather. A history, logs, records could be fabricated to show this. It is, after all, the long-range projection."

It was at best a reserve position, an attempt to show these influential men an alternative that did not mean the destruction of some of the finest minds in the USSR. It could also mean a lifetime of exile in the frozen wasteland of Kamchatka. Still, with that reprieve would come the time with which to develop other proposals.

"I like that," Gurenko said. "Whatever is decided here, I believe that the colonel should be directed to develop an alternate set of experiment records, whether they will ever be used or not."

The General Secretary looked closely at each of his colleagues, and appeared to note either affirmation or at least no objection.

He said, "It is so ordered, Colonel Malenkov.

You are to return at once to Kamchatka and begin to fabricate new documents. You will await further orders in regard to the current activities."

In confusion and relief, Malenkov left the room.

After the door closed behind Malenkov, the General Secretary pointed to the three telephones in the corner, one of them red. "I do not want to have to take a call on that telephone, Comrades, and have the American President tell me one of his homey little stories and then accuse me of poisoning the United States.

"Conversely, the time has also come to assume greater risk. Mother Russia's ability to mine her resources at the same rate she expends them is at an end. Changes beyond our control in the price of exported petroleum will decrease our revenues by several billions in hard foreign currencies. There will be a substantial deficit in our balance of payments at this year's end.

"We can risk the world's condemnation, and possibly a nuclear strike, or we can eliminate the project and starve to death. Those are the courses available to us, and the decision is upon the hearts of the men in this room. What shall that decision be?"

At Kamchatka, Boris Petrovsky decided to take care of another piece of unfinished business, though he would relish it more if it could have been accomplished in person.

He had learned through his sources in the Second Directorate—the KGB division that handled internal security—that Major Grigori Zanov was responsible for compiling the intelligence digest forwarded to him from Moscow Center. That alone was a surprise. He had thought Zanov dead in a ditch in Pakistan.

Now he wondered why nothing had been said to him by Chairman Nemoronko as a result of the report that Zanov must have filed. Perhaps Zanov felt lucky to have escaped at all. Still, Zanov would know that Petrovsky had regained the Land Rover and left his partner to face whatever music the Afghans had composed. With the events in Pakistan on Zanov's mind, however, it would explain the selection of the information reaching Petrovsky.

He ordered Corporal Marienkov to place the call directly to Zanov's apartment in Moscow.

"Hello. Who's this?"

"Why, it's Boris, Comrade Grigori. You certainly remember me."

"Petrovsky? You don't mean it. Where are you? I haven't seen you in—"

"Zanov, you know exactly where I am. And I will tell you exactly why I am calling, and then you will do exactly as I say."

"Listen, Major, you can't—"

"Yes, I can. It has come to my attention—from the General Secretary, in fact—that you have omitted certain crucial items of information in the intelligence digests forwarded to me." Mention of the General Secretary would establish an informal authority.

"Petrovsky—"

"Shut up! The omissions have resulted in the lapse of certain security concerns, and naturally I had to lay the fault at your feet."

"Comrade Major Petrovsky, I . . ."

In the response was the expected new subservience. Good.

"Perhaps your age has made you careless. I understand you carry wounds. Perhaps a medical retirement would be in order, Major?"

"No! Certainly not, Comrade Major."

"Then you will see to it that I receive all of the intelligence information that is considered necessary to my command?"

"Certainly, Comrade Major."

Petrovsky hung up without saying good-bye. There was much to be said for power. He liked the tone of fear in the voices of those whom he addressed.

Twelve

"Absolutely goddamned not!" Nathan Petrie was adamant.

He looked at Morris sitting in the chair on the other side of his big, new teak desk. Her face was red in either embarrassment or fury. Her shoulders were hunched forward and shook a trifle. He decided it was fury.

She spoke in evenly paced syllables in an apparent attempt to control her anger. "But Nat, you have to admit it's possible."

"It's possible. Damned unlikely, however."

"If it's remotely possible, why not take it to the Secretary? Let him decide whether or not to carry it further."

"No one is going to take any chances fucking up the General Secretary's new program of openness," Petrie said. "Especially the Secretary. And least of all with this bit of horse shit."

"You believe in *glasnost* then?"

"What I believe doesn't have a goddamned thing to do with it. Sure, the Soviets are trying a new tactic. My personal opinion is that economics and social pressures have forced it. And I think the whole Soviet mentality and ethos cannot change overnight. I wouldn't trust the bastards now anymore than I did thirty years ago."

"Then let's present this to someone. To anyone," she said.

"No. You've got a lot to learn about politics, Barbara. You haven't got shit for data. I'm not going to have the Secretary embarrassed by this. Let AFI do it. Let Garrett and Danton take the heat. It's about time Garrett got stuck with some bad PR."

"And if they do, and they're right?"

Petrie grinned. "If by any chance, they come up with hard evidence, CIA will take it over anyway. That'll put Garrett on the sidelines."

The day after Christmas, Garrett went to his office in the afternoon and settled into the padded brown leather of his chair. While he waited, he tried to read a number of reports stacked on his desk, and finally gave up in frustration. Damned paper.

He heard several voices in the outer office. "I'll give you forty bucks in cash for the raggedy-looking elephant-eared thing, Aggie."

"No!"

Clare Swallow's voice followed. "Tom, you're pretty cheap, you know that? It's worth at least forty-two, and I'd go forty-five, Mrs. Nelson."

"That much, Clare? Well, hell. I'll do forty-seven-fifty, but that's tops," Eaglefeather said.

"Neither of you would know how to care for it. Not for sale!" Aggie told them.

Eaglefeather sighed loudly, "Well, what's next best? Your boss in?"

"Yes. But General Danton said he was supposed to take a couple of days off, Colonel."

Eaglefeather appeared in the doorway.

"You bothering my lady friend again?" Garrett

asked.

"Protecting her from Clare."

Swallow followed him into the office. "Hello, Brandon. You're looking alive."

"Thanks. What's this?"

Brent came in toting a briefcase and said, "I hear you've taken up targeting, Brandy. You mind if we sit on the other side of the room?"

"There's a bench on the sidewalk in front of the building, if you're really worried," Garrett told him.

Brent and Swallow sat at the conference table, and Eaglefeather searched the cabinet on the side wall. He came up with glasses and a bottle of Black Label.

Garrett moved to the conference table. "Make yourself at home, Chief."

"Thanks. I will. Holidays, after all."

Eaglefeather poured straight Scotch into four glasses, then closed the door to the outer office.

"I have the feeling you guys have been up to something," Garrett said.

Brent said, "You notice how cold and miserable it's been lately? Makes you wonder if somebody's fucking around with the weather."

So Eaglefeather had passed it on after Garrett had tried the theory on him. "Crazy, isn't it?" Garrett observed.

"Maybe not," Swallow said. "One of the indicators is the attack on you."

Garrett said, "If that was ordered by somebody out of Moscow Center or the Kremlin, it was on the basis of something I didn't know I had."

Eaglefeather said, "Like I told you earlier, it was a professional hit. At least, there are three of us treating it that way."

Garrett had thought it professional too. Since he

had been unarmed, he had lain in the snowy street after the slug whined through the top of the car, shattering the driver's window, and tried to consider a course of action. The good ones did not miss. It had to be a combination of distance and bad weather.

He'd been sorry he did not have a weapon with him. He'd lain there, listening for movement, ready to slide under the Corvette or leap to his feet and run. Or see how far he got before a second shot brought him down.

Then Morris had come running, and Garrett was not sure whether that was good or bad. It might have scared off his attacker, or it might have put her in danger. He'd hustled her into the Corvette, whipped a U-turn out of his parking place, and driven a mile to a phone booth. He'd called Danton first, then Eaglefeather.

Danton had told him to keep his head down.

They'd met Eaglefeather in a bar in Virginia, introduced Barbara to him, and related the story.

Eaglefeather had said, "You're a lucky son of a bitch, always have been. I remember the time you were shot in Laos, though you caught that one in the butt."

Morris had been confused. "What was that?"

Eaglefeather had told her. "I got jumped by bandits. But I'm pretty damned good, of course, and I held them off for a couple hours until Brandy stole an old airplane and came in after me. To tell you the truth, I was less afraid of the bandits than I was of that rackety Otter and his flying. And the damned thing didn't have armor under the seats. He took a ricochet in the ass."

Morris had nodded, but she'd still looked stunned by the night's episode. It was, Garrett thought, the problem with operations people who had come up the analysis ladder rather than the field ladder.

Garrett had asked, "What do you think, Tom? You've got that old, no-coincidence look."

"Ah, well, I don't know, Brandy. Seems strange. The old gut instincts say it was professional, and therefore an intense reaction to something you've done or said. What else are you working on?"

While Garrett had given him the short story of Suitland, Eaglefeather had examined Morris as if wondering at her status with Garrett.

"It's nothing that I thought was important enough to draw this kind of response, Tom."

"Well, something had to be important," Eaglefeather had said. "The KGB doesn't lightly order a termination on someone of your rank or with your position in AFI. Hell, I can't remember the last time we suspected the KGB of wet operations within CONUS."

"It's the weather thing," Morris had said.

"We didn't even put that together until tonight," Garrett had said.

"That would excite the KGB if it's right," Eaglefeather had said.

"If it's right."

"I'd go with it as if you've got it down pat," Eaglefeather had said. "What's your next step?"

"Call Petrie and get a couple intimate friends for Barbara."

"Now, just a damned minute."

"You don't have a choice, Barbara. I've been talking to you, so you need some protection. I'd better make some calls to other people I've been seen talking to also. You're on that list too, Tom."

"I'll watch my back."

He had called Brent, who could pretty well take care of himself. Through Consular Operations' deputy for security, he had arranged a temporary security for Morris without going through Nathan Petrie. He'd called Hornby, without divulging the entire story, and the Brit had said he would take precautions. Eaglefeather had gotten on the phone and arranged for Army coverage of Swallow.

The security would only last seventy-two hours, unless they came up with some hard evidence.

Now Eaglefeather sipped Scotch and said, "There's two things to think about, Brandy. One, if it is KGB, as soon as they know they missed, they'll try again. The other thing is, we've got a leak somewhere."

They were all quiet. No one liked to think that his particular agency had a deep Soviet plant. Chasing a phantom at Navy was one thing. Having a mole close to him made Garrett mad.

"Your office clean?" Brent asked.

"Swept this morning."

"Good. I don't relish standing in the middle of a park to exchange confidences on a day like today."

"Well, who have we talked to about radiation, wheat, MiGs, or scientists?" Garrett asked.

Swallow got a piece of paper and wrote down the names as each of them recalled the people to whom they might have mentioned something. It was a short list.

Eaglefeather said, "Army Intelligence has a minor contact in Moscow Center. We need to drop a little story, with different data for each of these people, and see what turns up in Moscow."

At the affirmative nods from around the table, Eaglefeather said, "Give me a day to come up with something logical, and the variations on it."

Garrett passed the bottle around. "So you guys buy this proposition?"

"Until something better comes along," Swallow

157

said. "We thought we'd try to put together a package. Carl, you want to kick it off?"

Brent took several manila envelopes from his briefcase. "Sure. I talked to Morris this morning. She was pissed at the world in general and at ConsOp in particular. Petrie laughed her out of his office."

"Merle Danton may laugh louder," Garrett said.

Brent went on. "Anyway, I started with the radiation bit and had the Company computer talking to every other computer in town."

He displayed a long computer printout. "This is what we got out of it, but I'll summarize. The NRC and EPA monitors picked up trace radiation a year ago, in January, in a pattern that covered the West Coast and the North, up into Canada. Then it disappeared.

"It reappeared in mid-October of this year and has been getting a little stronger since then. Yet it's nowhere near lethal and barely shakes a Geiger counter."

"The timing of which suggests," Garrett said, "that the radiation accompanies bad weather."

"Hey!" Eaglefeather said. "Your head's all right."

Brent continued. "Then we followed up on our earlier conversation about the wheat, Brandy. I asked Clare to do some backtracking, and he burned the butts off of some of his people."

"Yes," Swallow said, extracting photographs and papers. "Shipments began in mid-July, most of them out of Galveston and New Orleans. We've traced every Soviet bloc freighter and some that were leased from the Japanese. There's an appendix here that lists each ship's name, country of registration, and the tonnage loaded. The next appendix lists the dates of arrival for each ship at Murmansk, Vladivostok, Leningrad, Riga, Odessa,

158

Rostov, and Astrakhan.

"In all cases, we traced each freighter by satellite or SR-71 photograph to its port. From the ports, the grain was transshipped by truck and rail, and due to the photo frequency, we lost track of some of it. Still, I'd guess that we tracked at least ninety per cent of the original shipments. Part of the problem is that domestically produced grain was merged into the transportation stream, along with Canadian and Australian grain entering the ports at the same time. It was difficult to keep it separate.

"However, we can still define a trend. Of the American grain, we can say with relative certainty that not one ton was shipped to a mill. At Petrozavodsk, Polotsk, Nikolayev, Dubovka, and Kiev, the grain was dumped on the ground and covered with plastic. Canadian, Aussie, and domestic wheat is included. In photos ninety six through one hundred and twelve you can see both uncovered and covered grain.

"You'll notice also, in photos eighty four, eighty five, and eighty six, that the storage sites were prepared in May and June. They were planning ahead on this."

Eaglefeather was pleased by the detective work. "On hard data, Brandy, 1981 was the USSR's largest previous purchase of wheat from the U.S. It amounted to two hundred and twenty five million tons. This year, they bought one hundred and seventy two million tons, and some of that was negotiated through satellite countries—Hungary, Romania, Poland, Czechoslovakia—though none of it was shipped to those countries. It's as if they were wary of our knowing just how much was purchased.

"However, I checked with some of my Canadian and Australian sources and found that they picked up another one hundred and six million tons from them. Total two hundred and seventy eight million tons, up fifty three million from their largest-ever purchase."

Garrett said, "Those are nice statistics. Can we prove anything with them?"

"Maybe that they have poor farmers," Brent said. "By itself, it doesn't mean much."

"Now then, on the Foxbats," Eaglefeather said. "I've checked around quietly at Army Intel, DIA, and at the National Security Agency."

"And I checked the Company," Brent added.

"It's difficult to tell if anyone knew or cared about the extended flights at all, since no one was going to admit that they had not known. They put it down to aerial refueling. And of course, we don't have any evidence to the contrary."

"The missing profs?" Garrett asked.

"They're missing."

Garrett waved his hand at the stack of paper and photos and said, "Look, what in hell am I going to do with it?"

Swallow said, "I think you could say we. Everything we've got is sketchy, but there are four of us who go along with the idea, Brandon."

"Make that five. Let's not forget Miss Morris," Eaglefeather said.

Garrett said, "Let me run the errand and the risks then. Tom, you're too far up on the full-bird list to upset anyone at the Pentagon."

"You can depend on that. What's an Eaglefeather without an eagle?"

"What I'll do is take the package to Merle, and see if he won't push it to the Director. If we can reach him, then it might get to the National Security Council."

"This is wonderful, of course," said Brent. "You

know what will happen then?"

"Yeah, I know."

Though some of the old hands in different offices could often get along with each other, the heavyweights sometimes got wrapped up in politics and interservice rivalries. They hated to admit that one or the other was ahead in data-gathering or strategy.

"There's going to be a very real problem of ownership," Brent said. "Some people just can't buy an idea unless they thought of it first."

"This time, it may be a problem of disownership," Garrett countered.

Garrett got up and locked the files in the safe secreted in the credenza behind his desk. He said, "There's another thing we could be doing. Clare, with the location of the flights, Kamchatka Air Base seems the likely base. Can we get some close-ups?"

"Sure thing."

"When will you try Danton?" Eaglefeather asked.

"This afternoon, when he gets back from the Hill. You know Merle, though, Tom. He's going to be skittish about the lack of links between data. He'll carry it for me, but he won't be happy about it."

Every time he put his weight down on his leg with the slightest bit of imprecision, the pain shot downward from his thigh to his calf, and upward along his spine to crash into the base of his skull.

Grigori Zanov clenched his teeth and slowly worked his way into the chair at his desk.

Damn that bloody Petrovsky!

His telephone call suggested that he did have some connection with the Chairman or the General

161

Secretary. Petrovsky had risen through the ranks considerably faster than any of Zanov's colleagues. Rumor also had it that Petrovsky, if not secretly a colonel, was drawing a salary equivalent to that of a colonel.

The bastard had some hold over someone, and he had a future.

What future had Zanov to look toward? There would be no more foreign assignments. There was only the tiny apartment and Natasha constantly nagging for more clothes, a better apartment, and more food. She also wanted daily mounting, a feat that was becoming impossible. Whenever he neared the crest of his own completion, he would move wrong, and the pain of his leg would cancel his satisfaction.

Natasha did not understand.

Maybe Boris Petrovsky did. Soon after Zanov had received the frightening phone call, establishing which of them had the most authority, Petrovsky's demands had increased. He wanted all backdated digests to ascertain no other items had been withheld. He wanted dossiers on a General Belushkin and a Colonel Malenkov.

After he had seen the report regarding missing scientists, he had asked for the file on Colonel Brandon Garrett.

Zanov had had no choice but to comply with each of the man's wishes. When he'd pulled Garrett's file, however, he'd found interesting entries. In 1975, Garrett had been assigned to Bangkok. The record suggested he had participated in covert activities in a number of areas. He had probably been one of the couriers financing Air America, and he had also probably been instrumental in the political re-education of key provincial chieftains. The record identified Garrett as responsible for uncovering a Soviet intelligence network resulting in the imprisonment and execution of thirty agents of varying nationalities.

Not in the file, but clear in Zanov's mind, was the fact that Major Boris Petrovsky, then a captain, had been posted to Phnom Penh during the same period and was the source control for that network.

That suggested a reason for Petrovsky's interest in Brandon Garrett. But why did it arise now, after better than a dozen years?

More astounding was the next to last entry in the file of Brandon Garrett. "Termination ordered—highest authority."

Garrett, a full colonel in the Air Force Intelligence, should have been considered in a position beyond such an order. That high up in an intelligence organization, much less within the borders of the United States, an assassination created far too many ripples.

Zanov thought the last entry was also interesting: "Compliance delayed."

That was the current euphemism for failure. Somebody had blown the attempt on him, and now Garrett would be surrounded with security.

Zanov wondered at the connections between Petrovsky and Garrett. Had Petrovsky asked someone of "higher authority" to sanction Garrett? Because of 1975? Or because of the ultra-secret project? And who was this Malenkov?

"Comrade Major? The night traffic."

"Thank you, Corporal," Zanov said, and picked the first cable off the stack. It was from London, a source in the British MI-5 who kept harping on Lady Diana's exploits. He would send a cable ordering cessation in that particular area.

The second cable came from Boston, Massachu-

163

setts, routing a message from the informant in Air Force Intelligence. The gist of it was that the Nuclear Regulatory Commission had discovered extremely high radiation levels near St. Louis, in Missouri. The President had determined to suppress the information.

Zanov would have to send that information to Petrovsky in Kamchatka, to the General Secretary, and to General Zhukov in Disinformation.

The AFI plant also responded to a question posed by the General Secretary. The decoded answering message read: "FOR MANAGER: G IN CONTACT MORRIS STATE COMMA BRENT CIA COMMA EAGLEFEATHER DIA COMMA SWALLOW NPIC RE ISSUE."

Zanov thought that "G" was likely to be Garrett. He had been working with people in the State Department, the CIA, and Defense Intelligence in regard to whatever subject the General Secretary had asked about. He would send that message directly to the Secretary's office by hand messenger.

Zanov went through the rest of the cables, not concentrating well. His leg hurt, and he kept thinking about the things he would like to do to that bloody Petrovsky.

Thirteen

Naturally, it took several days to get the National Security Council together.

On the last day of December, Garrett sat in Danton's office and listened to the NSC's damning verdict from his favorite general.

"There were several influences, Brandy."

"What influences?"

"First and important, it's New Year's Eve, and an emergency session of the National Security Council was not first on everyone's list of priorities. Not all participants were particularly enthusiastic. I'll bet some of the bastards were only worried about getting through the storm to their parties."

"Did they bother considering that this is a reason for the storm?"

"It always snows this time of year. That's a given. General Wake pointed out another given: Colonel Brandon Garrett frequently goes off half-cocked."

"Shit."

"CIA thought it was pretty farfetched. So did Treasury and the Bureau."

"Jesus, Merle! Did they get around to talking about the data at all?"

"Well, yes. But I'm trying to give you a feeling

165

for what else went into it. On data, Energy was very supportive. They like having someone else to blame on the radiation bit. CIA said they had been following the grain stockpiling, period. On the Foxbats, CIA and the National Security Agency are all naturally aware of the extended flights. They are also unconcerned since your pictures happened to miss the aerial refuelings."

"That's because the data was there, and they're pissed because Air Force found it."

"Maybe. No one seemed to know about the missing scientists, but all promised to look into it after the first of the year."

"They going to set up a committee?" Garrett asked.

"Damn it, Brandy, that was the good side. On the counterargument, several agencies pointed out that the Kremlin is normally a sieve on projects of this size. That's true, and there hasn't been a peep from any of our sources about a weather-modification project. And the National Security Advisor asked the Director if he felt strongly enough, given that weather alteration was an attack on the nation, that he would recommend to the President a counterstrike. Naturally, the Director had to back away from that."

"Naturally," Garrett said, but admitted he himself could not make that recommendation.

"And we were informed by the National Security Advisor that the White House is especially concerned that none of this get out. There is some degree of fear that such an accusation against the Soviet Union, developed out of—as it were—thin air, would bring embarrassment upon the United States. Especially in these times of openness, no one wants to step on Kremlin toes. The Secretaries of State and Defense shared that opinion."

"Of course." All of this was raising some doubts in Garrett's mind.

"Brandy, how firmly are you committed to this?"

"Here's the latest, Merle." Garrett slipped a sheaf of photographs across the wide desk.

"These are from Satcom Eighty-Seven; the first photos capture most of the Kamchatka Peninsula. Midway down the peninsula, by that hook there, is a bay and the town of Ust-Kamchatsk. To the west, in the next photos, about eight miles inland, is the air base. It's a standard Soviet Far Eastern base. There are two three-mile runways, barracks for maybe three thousand enlisted troops. Next picture, we get an idea of the mission of the base."

"Isn't it a training base?" Danton asked him.

"There's some training going on, though it's not a major training command. Instead, its an eastern defense command. The older MiG-21's are used for training. There's also several squadrons of MiG-23's, 25's, and 27's. They're performing reconnaissance with the Foxbats and one squadron of old Bears. In addition to the fixed-wing complement, there are four reinforced helicopter squadrons.

"The next pictures have a lot of grainage in them because they're blown up so much. Down on the southern edge of the base—near the end of the runways—is another grouping of hangars and buildings. These are fenced off from the rest of the base. Now you tell me, Merle, who in hell fences off three hangars from the rest of an air base? And with two parallel fences."

Danton leaned over his desk and pulled his Tensor light closer to the photographs. "My eyes aren't what they once were. Is this gray area between the fences . . . what is that?"

"Our guess is that it's a trail left by a walking guard between the fences. I know the Soviets are paranoid, but what are they guarding so well from themselves?"

"It's a point," the general conceded.

"Next photo, Merle. Taken two years ago. There were no fences back then."

"Two years ago?"

"Uh, huh. At that time, the training command was housed in that area, along with a squadron of twenty-four-hour alert aircraft."

"And you think all this is to . . ."

"Protect some very special aircraft. And a very special project."

"It may be just a confidential scientific project. That came up in the NSC."

"Damned right. It's the same thing I've been talking about, General."

Danton sat back, sighed, and said, "You going to answer my question now?"

"How firmly am I committed? Damn it, I wouldn't push the nuclear button, Merle. But like Eaglefeather, I can't believe we have four or five coincidences here. There's something to it."

"What chance have we got of getting more evidence? Something hard to link all this together. We went into the NSC on the thin side. I sat against the wall behind the Director and didn't participate, but there were some very skeptical faces."

It was Garrett's turn to sigh. "So okay. We don't get any help from NSC on this."

"The other agencies are supposed to look into it. That's what came out of it."

"They won't buy my information, Merle. They want to have their own, so they'll start from scratch, and when it's snowing in Biloxi in May, they may come up with something. By then, it'll be all over, and the Soviet apparatus will have disappeared."

"We need a lot more evidence before we can go back to the Council."

"Okay if I buzz Kamchatka and take a few pictures?"

"Oh, shit, Garrett! Be serious."

"Maybe I am. I don't know what more we're going to get from here."

"There's no way the Director can authorize a close-in reconnaissance without going to the Joint Chiefs and the DCI, and you know how Wake will react. Is it okay if I turn you down without going through the motions?"

"More and more, the damned politicians and bureaucrats in this town reinforce their protective cocoons, don't they, General? Where's FDR and Jack Kennedy when we need quick action?"

"They had advisors too," Danton pointed out.

"Yeah, but they had better advisors."

"Go home, Brandy, have a good New Year's Eve, relax a little. Next week, let's get together and determine just what more we need."

Garrett went to his office, found the Johnny Walker bottle, poured a drink, then flopped in his chair and put his feet up on the desk.

More documentation. Keep after it, but sure as hell keep it out of the papers. He did not know what more he could do, other than to push Clare Swallow for pictures showing a complete Foxbat flight. And that was unlikely in those weather conditions.

He was damned close to abandoning the idea. It was close to being beyond anything he could put together to satisfy the big boys. If only . . .

Harv and Connie.

For the first time, Garrett consciously connected it.

The thought had been fluttering at his mind all week like a moth just out of reach. There was a connection, but he had suppressed it or stayed busy enough that he did not have to consider it.

If they died because some son of a bitch was playing games with the weather, then by God, he was going to find out about it. And take some kind of action.

Garrett had never thought himself capable of revenge, but when he let the concept boil its way up in his mind, it firmed up his purpose. Certainly, he had no other goals at the moment, and this one was as good as any other.

"Well, Je-sus Christ! Having a party and didn't invite us."

Eaglefeather and Morris came through the door, saw his face, and knew right away.

Garrett shoved the bottle across the desk while Eaglefeather found more glasses and pushed two chairs close.

"We got turned down, lady and gentleman!" Garrett said.

Morris's eyes lightened in anger.

Eaglefeather said, "We couldn't have expected more than what we got, Brandy. There's a bunch of goddamned dummies up in the god chairs."

"We all went to the same school, Tom. I was asked if I would push the button. I said no. What would you have said?"

"Same thing. You tell Clare or Carl yet?"

"No. I suppose I should."

Garrett punched the private line on his phone and dialed NPIC. He found that Swallow had gone home and got him there, receiving a cautious greeting. "Hello?"

"Clare. This is Garrett."

"Okay. Damn, I'm glad you called. I tried to get you, but the switchboard said your office was empty."

"It might as well be. We got shut—"

"Brent's dead."

Garrett sat up in his chair, his hand tightening on the handset. "What!"

"It was an auto wreck, apparently. His car went into the Potomac."

"When?"

"Probably around five-thirty this afternoon. I passed it on my way home and recognized the car as the cops were towing it out of the river. I stopped to check, and I wish to God I hadn't."

"Clare, stay home."

"I intend to."

"I'll see if I can get some more security for you."

"Ah, hell."

"Let's not take chances."

Garrett hung up, dialed the Air Force Security number, and gave his request. Air Force did not know that the Army Intelligence coverage for Swallow had been pulled. They agreed to provide a stakeout for seventy-two hours, based solely on Garrett's assurance that the national security was at stake. After that, they would want documentation.

When he hung up, Eaglefeather asked, "Brent?"

"Yeah. Car wreck."

"Shit! What are we going to do, Brandon?"

Garrett swirled the Scotch in his glass. "Take some close-up pictures."

Morris said, "What?"

"I go to Kamchatka."

171

"Like hell you do," Eaglefeather said.

"I'm the logical choice."

"Bullshit! I'll go."

"You've got Sandy and the kids, and you don't speak Russian."

"You don't speak the language either," Eaglefeather countered. "At least, not very well."

"I do," said Barbara Morris.

It was snowing heavily when Garrett pushed the Corvette through the snowdrift on the sidewalk and parked it in the garage. The snow had drifted four feet high against the side wall of his house. He got out and unlocked the door.

Garrett pushed the door open, standing to the side of the doorway, and reached around the casing to flip on the light. He peered through his foyer into his living room and was relieved to find it vacant.

He had never had to move with such caution in his own home before, but he let the habits of old govern his movements. He viewed himself as a man with his head twisted continually backward, but he had seen nothing behind him on the trip over from Virginia. Which did not necessarily mean that there was not someone there.

He made a quick tour of the house. It was just as he had left it.

"Come on in, Barbara."

She came around the doorjamb and closed the door behind her. Shrugging out of her coat, she dropped it over the back of one of the oak chairs at the round table.

"Nice place."

"Whenever I get a chance to use it."

He stepped into the kitchen, extracted Scotch, bourbon, vodka, and brandy bottles from the cabinet that served as his bar, and set them on the counter along with a tray of ice cubes. "You want to mix us a New Year's celebration while I do some searching?"

"Sure. What do you want?"

"Scotch is fine."

Garrett went into the living room, tossed some logs and kindling into the fireplace, and got a fire going. Opening the front closet, which was under the stairwell, he went to his knees and shoved a stored suitcase aside, exposing his built-in safe. He spun in the combination, opened the door, and fished among the documents for his passport. Finding it, he closed the door, re-located the components, and closed the cabinet.

In the drawer of the octagonal table next to the couch was one of Garrett's arsenals. He rifled through it and came up with two boxes of ammunition, his Walther PPK in its oiled leather holster, and the nickel-plated .22-caliber Beretta 950 he had bought for some reason. He hauled the hardware over to the oak table.

Barbara came out of the kitchenette and gave him his drink while he checked the weapons.

"You always have lethal things around?"

"You know anything about guns?"

"They kill people."

"Sometimes."

He fed six rounds into the Beretta's magazine, slapped it into the handle, and quickly showed her how to operate safety and slide. "Put this in your purse."

"Brandon, I don't know. . . ."

"You never know. And you probably don't have

173

much of a chance if you aren't aware you're a target."

He loaded six nine-millimeter rounds in the other clip and locked it into the Walther, slid the automatic into the holster, and set it aside.

"Like you didn't know you were a target?" she asked.

He picked up his drink and sat back on the sofa. "Neither of us knew what we had."

She put her brandy—in a kitchen glass she had found—on the table.

"You looked at the condition of your refrigerator and cabinets lately? Booze and TV dinners and bread and bologna. The bread's stale."

"You snoop in everyone's kitchen?"

"I have this thing about nutrition."

"I have a housekeeper, but she hasn't been able to get in for awhile," he said in defense.

"Weak excuse."

"Anyway, you know you're a target, Barbara. I don't know what I said to whomever, but it triggered a reaction in Dzherzhinsky Square, and now Brent's dead. He talked to me, and so I have to believe that anyone I've spoken to could be on the same list. Keep the gun handy."

"What about Colonel Eaglefeather?"

"He's an old hand. He knows the routine. You and Clare don't, and I worry about you."

She smiled grimly, "Do you?"

"Sure. You're in operations, but you haven't faced the tiger."

She bristled at that, but did not respond.

Other than Christmas dinner and this weather theory, they had not explored deeply any subject of common interest. Without the weather, he was not sure he and Barbara Morris would have a common topic.

He was aware of the thrust of her breasts against her soft blue blouse, the flare of her hips in the navy skirt, the deft smoothness of her hand as it gripped the odd brandy glass. The tip of her tongue tested the corner of her mouth. In the flickering light from the building fire, her eyes provided a deep green, gold-flecked gaze. Her auburn hair was loose around her neck and long.

It was time to change the internal meanderings, he thought. She was a colleague and wanted to be thought of as a professional.

"Sorry about the quality of dinner."

"I like pizza," she said.

They had stopped at a small Italian restaurant since Garrett had been aware of the condition of his refrigerator. He would have avoided coming to the house if he had not wanted to dig out his passport and the automatic for her.

Barbara said, "You keep changing subjects."

"Do I?" Garrett got up to make himself another drink and to add brandy to her glass.

"Uh, huh. You're not really thinking of crossing Soviet borders?"

"I'll talk to Merle first," he lied.

"It's ludicrous, Brandon. You could get killed."

"I could get killed in D.C. But I've been inside Moscow's fences before."

"Oh." Her eyes drifted off, thinking. "I meant what I said, that I'd go with you."

"Now, *that's* ludicrous. You have no field experience, Barbara, no inkling of what it's like and what could happen."

"This is one way to get the experience, isn't it? Think what that would do for my resume."

Garrett wondered just what she would not do in

175

her pursuit of career enhancement. It was the one aspect he did not like about her.

"This is not a training mission. And by the way, these excursions never appear on the record. Are you prepared to kill someone?"

He saw the lie in her eyes, even as she said, "If I had to. Besides, I'm going to lose my protection tomorrow. I'd be better off out of the country."

That was bothersome. After what had happened in the National Security Council, he would not be able to persuade either the CIA or the DIA, not to mention her own ConsOps, to continue the security for her. With a little machination, maybe Eaglefeather could do something with the Army, he thought.

He would call Eaglefeather first thing in the morning, he promised himself. She needed security coverage, and he sure as hell was not taking her with him.

"I know this is a hell of a New Year's Eve, but I'd better take you home."

"Midnight's still an hour away."

"You wouldn't want your bodyguards to freeze to death for nothing, would you?"

They were out on the street in front of her apartment building in a government sedan.

"I suppose not, Barbara said.

"I'm going to pack a bag, and then we'll go."

"All right. I'll pack when I get home."

For the time being, Garrett let her think what she wanted to think.

Blizzard

Fourteen

On the first of January, a major winter storm crossed the Pacific Northwest, adding an additional eight inches of snow to a base of some fifteen inches. The storm was accompanied by record low temperatures and winds gusting to forty miles per hour, bringing the wind-chill index down to minus fifty degrees.

Seattle shut down. The city crews could not cope with the fallen electric lines, the failed traffic-signaling systems and the flow of white powder over briny ice on the streets. There were over five hundred automobile accidents in one day. The mayor of Seattle spoke with the governor and the governor called the President requesting federal assistance.

By the fourth of January, the storm had carried itself across the nation and the gubernatorial pleas were repeated. Idaho, Montana, North and South Dakota, Minnesota, Wisconsin, Illinois, Michigan, Ohio, Pennsylvania, New York and all of New England sought designation by the President as federal disaster areas. The Air National Guards in each of those states, already in partial use delivering pharmaceutical supplies and food to small towns, were activated to full strength, but were impotent in the face of the weather. Old C-130's and battered Huey helicopters remained lashed to the ground.

The ground forces of military reserve units and National Guard contingents were nearly as ineffective. They served well in urban areas, as emergency transportation for medical and food supplies, as backup police, and as rescue for stranded motorists, but were unable to reach small communities in force.

In tiny mountain towns in Colorado, Utah, and the Sierra Nevadas, beset with twice the snowfall of a normal year, the residents fared well. They were hardy pioneers or neophyte survivalists who had accepted the premise that contrary nature or nuclear war were possible contingencies. If the storms lasted well into the spring, they could, with rationing, last with them. The cellars were full of canned vegetables and fruits, the outbuildings hung with dried venison and beef, the backsides of cabins stacked high with split wood. And there were neighbors who would share.

Some neighbors in New Orleans, Louisiana, parts of which were again under a foot of water, took advantage of the opportunity to stock up on TVs, stereos, guns, refrigerators, three-piece suits, and video tape recorders at the expense of their fellows.

The President had reluctantly asked Congress to cut back the request for defense funds for the next year and approve a shift of funds from defense, education, and environmental protection to federal emergency assistance and necessary social programs.

Congress could not convene. Three-fourths of the House of Representatives were still attempting to return to Washington, D.C., from their home-district holidays. Only four Senators from west of the Mississippi were available in the capital.

Travel was restricted to absolute need, and tended to follow a southerly flow. By bus, by car, or by train, priority travelers worked their way south into Arizona, Texas, and Alabama, where air traffic was hampered primarily by rain. Then they made their respective ways eastward to congregate on the airport concourses in Tampa and Miami and Atlanta. Whenever there was a break in the weather, or a promise of plowed runways at Dulles and National, 737's, 727's, DC-8's, and Tri-Stars made a rush northward.

The Chairman of the Committee for State Security rested his elbows on his desktop and pressed his fingertips together. Felix Nemoronko was impressed with their strength and cleanliness. He was vaguely aware that most visitors to his office became mesmerized by the gesture, focusing on the power in his hands. It was the power to inflict happiness or pain, life or death. The Chairman himself felt comfortable with that aspect of his office.

"Your report, Pyotr Davidovich?" he asked the First Chief Directorate leader, General Pyotr Korontoyev.

"Alexandre did miss on his first attempt, Comrade Chairman. The weather—"

"Is only an excuse. Meanwhile, this Garrett is still able to discuss . . . thoughts he may be having. Alexandre has become overconfident of his

181

abilities, Pyotr Grigory. He should have insured his action."

"Of course, you are quite correct, Comrade Chairman. I will recall him and a have a serious discussion with him."

"Not just yet. A moment." The Chairman broke the spell of his hands and lifted the flimsy paper of the cable from the polished surface of his desk. He rescanned it quickly and thoroughly.

"The ripples expand, and we may become powerless to stop them. If your Alexandre had been successful, we might not now be in this position. According to this, the American National Security Council has been made aware of some . . . suspicion generated by Garrett."

"And they have turned him away, Comrade Chairman. The source said there is no action taken."

"Perhaps."

"And we do not know what information was presented," the First Chief Directorate Chairman pointed out.

He was fishing for information himself, Nemoronko thought, aware of the difficulties the man faced in not knowing all of the facts. "Yet as I said, Comrade General, the ripples expand. There are now more intriguers."

"But Comrade Chairman, Alexandre was quite successful with the CIA agent named Brent. And he will soon make another attempt on Garrett."

"And the Morris man?"

"A woman. Executive Assistant to State Department's operations director. She too—"

The KGB chairman nearly gasped his anger. "What! Why did I not know this earlier?"

"Comrade Chairman . . ."

"I do not like this. We are becoming entangled at echelons that draw far too much attention. And how certain are we of the information we are obtaining from Air Force Intelligence?"

"Quite certain, Comrade Chairman. The source has always been reliable."

The Chairman pondered the General Secretary's earlier remarks about risk-taking. He said, "The General Secretary has not rescinded his directive. We must go forward."

The chairman of the FCD nodded his big head slowly. "You understand, Comrade Chairman, that I am still left in the dark? I do not know why this man Garrett or his contacts are important enough to require executive action. I have been left out of the chain of communications for whatever operation it is that is taking place."

"Believe me, Pyotr Davidovich, I understand your concern. However, it is for the best."

"What would be best for me, and for all concerned, is if I knew the rationale for—"

"It is also at the General Secretary's instruction, Comrade General Korontoyev," the KGB chief told his subordinate.

"Yes. Very well Comrade Chairman. I will urge Alexandre to greater achievement."

"Provide him some support."

"He prefers to work alone, Comrade Chairman."

"His preferences are not your concern, nor mine."

In Washington, Lieutenant General Merle Danton regretted doing it, but he put Garrett on leave.

Garrett was so hung up in this weather thing that he was unable to concentrate on more demanding projects, like the Suitland information leakage.

Everyone liked to blame the weather for a number of misfortunes, and Danton understood that. He had also found Garrett's proposal almost plausible, and so he had carried it to the Director and urged its consideration by the members of the NSC.

The reception the proposal had received at the NSC, however, was embarrassing, and none of the other agencies appeared to be in a hurry to follow up on any of the hypotheses. Danton was aware of the suspicion that arose between agencies. So what else was new?

"I'm sorry, Brandy, I just can't try it again."

"They haven't seen the Kamchatka Air Base pictures."

"Get me something solid."

"Okay, Merle. I'll draw some expense money and go get what you need."

"Damn it, Garrett, I already told you that any operation of that nature needs approval right at the top. You won't get it. Also, Security told me that Morris and Swallow are losing their protection tonight."

"Damn it," Garrett said. "We're going to have a few more casualties."

"My hands are tied."

"Merle, maybe I should take a few days off?"

"How about thirty days of leave?"

"I'll see you in February, if I can get through

the drifts."

"You won't do anything stupid?" the general asked.

"You mean like get caught?"

"That's what I mean. And I don't want to hear more."

Garrett walked out of his office, and Danton damned the system and its obstacles for awhile. He did not like circumventing it like this.

Garrett went directly back to his office and called Barbara Morris.

"I'm leaving."

"With authority?" she asked.

"With enough. My own."

"I'm going along."

Well, hell, he thought. He could not leave her unprotected when her own agency would not cover her. He could not take her to Kamchatka either. But he could dump her somewhere safer than Washington.

"They're pulling your watchdogs off anyway," he said. "So I guess you're going along."

He called Eaglefeather, but the man was out of his office, and Garrett did not want to leave a message.

Swallow was in.

"I'm going to be gone for awhile, Clare."

"Take care, Brandon."

"You're losing your security. Keep an eye on your back. Dig up a gun."

"I'll do that."

Garrett cleared his calendar and the rest of his desk swiftly by simply stacking all of the paper in one pile on the credenza.

He went into the outer office. "Aggie, I'm going to be gone for awhile, a couple weeks. You hold the fort down, will you?"

"Is everything all right, Colonel?"

"It'll be fine. I'm taking some leave time."

"How long will you be gone, if anyone asks?"

Garrett snorted. "I doubt anyone will ask. Don't let the plants dry up, huh?"

Agatha smiled at him. "Oh, I won't, Colonel. You take care."

He went down to the duty office and signed out on leave after arguing with a major who insisted on orders. The major finally got them orally from Danton.

Garrett got his bag out of the Corvette, but left the roadster in the lot and took a cab into the District and then to the State Department. He went to the first-floor stairwell, where he had agreed to wait for Barbara.

This was completely stupid, she told herself, this running off on some spy mission. She was old enough to know better, and Brandon had told her as much, resisting very strongly.

He had finally relented, though. At least she thought he had relented. Maybe he was not going to wait downstairs for her!

Morris doubled her efforts, hastening the explanations to her secretary on the dispositions of correspondence and the compilation of two reports. Then she grabbed her coat and purse and stepped out into the hall.

She walked directly into Phillip.

"Hi, lovebug. I was just coming to see you."

"Phillip, I don't have time for this," She pictured Brandon looking at his watch, making a final decision to leave without her.

"Ah, honey, you've got to stop resisting the inevitable. Look, it's only an hour until lunchtime. Let's take off early, and—"

"I have a meeting, Phil, an important one."

He grabbed her wrist. "Barb, we've got to settle this, once and for all."

"You and I were settled quite a few years ago, Phil. Now let go of me."

He did not, but her secretary appeared in the open doorway, concern on her face. Barbara said, "Sylvia, would you call security and ask someone to come up here?"

"Certainly, Miss Morris."

"Now hold on! No need to get carried away. We've just got to devote some conversation to each other, hon. Tonight, at dinner."

Phillip spun around and left.

"What in the world do I do, Sylvia?"

"I don't know, Miss Morris, but I certainly feel for you."

"Thank you. Well, I'll take off."

"Have a good vacation. I hope you find some sun."

Half an hour after Colonel Garrett left, Agatha Nelson took her lunch hour. It was a half-block walk to the nearest pay phone. While she walked along the snow-covered sidewalk, she thought of her errant and idealistic son, who had defected from the Army in Vietnam, and was now resident in the Soviet Union. He was now thirty-eight-years old. However much she hated the circumstances, there was no way she could deny her love or the tasks she must perform to protect his life.

The booth was vacant, and she pulled the door shut against the stinging snow. Her purse always held a large quantity of dimes and quarters for these contingencies, and she stacked a few of them on the small shelf. She lifted the receiver and dropped a quarter in the slot.

Then she dialed the number in Boston.

Almost an hour elapsed before Karl Baronikov received the information. He was registered as American Medical Association lobbyist Charley Wales at a small hotel on Constitution. Under the name of Baronikov, he was officially Assistant to the Trade Attaché at the Soviet Mission to the United Nations in New York. He was fluent in German, Dutch, English, and weapons of a wide variety, though he was not extremely well versed in commerce.

Baronikov was dark, with a small scar on the side of his neck—the result of an incomplete attempt to slash his throat one summer day in Vienna. He was but five feet, five inches in height. Every inch, however, exuded competence and terror when he was performing under the code name Alexandre.

He knew his own competence thoroughly, and protested the two baboons someone had pushed onto him. Now they had fumbled, as he had known that they would. He should not have put them on the entrances of the Pentagon and the

State Department, looking for Garrett or Morris. He should have sent them to the Grand Canyon, out of harm's way.

According to the message that had traversed through Boston to Moscow, to New York, then to his hotel in Washington, with all of the attendant stops for perusal along the way, Garrett had left his building over an hour and a half before. The stooge at the Pentagon had not reported in on the high-frequency portable radio.

Baronikov gathered his radio and his competition quality Tokarev automatic pistol and made his way to the door. Garrett had not made his plans known to the Air Force Intelligence source. Baronikov would send the stooges to cover his house in Georgetown while he tried to reach Barbara Morris himself. Failing that, perhaps he could reach one of the people he knew had contact with her.

Perhaps her secretary. He knew the name, Sylvia Willox, and he knew the face.

He had almost reached his car when the stooge babysitting at the State Department called on the radio.

"The broad ain't here no more."

The goddamned bitch!

Phil Morris fumed at his desk for most of the afternoon, and finally went to his supervisor and complained of a migraine—which he had never had, but for which he had developed a reputation.

Some way, someday, he would get back at her for all of the substantial humiliation she had brought him over the years. Shortly after the divorce, everyone of consequence he had known had severed their social ties with him, though not with her. He knew she had initiated a campaign of poisoning people's minds against him. And all of the women he had elected to take out had quickly dropped him after she had reached them with her innuendos.

After he had figured all of this out, he had determined the best way to stop her was to begin courting her again. He had also calculated that her smear campaign was designed to drive him back to her. But he had held off for too long. Just as he was giving in, she had been promoted to that goddamned new title and suddenly was too good for anyone.

And she had been snared by the goddamned Air Force man, falling for a damned uniform. Some fucking hero who got his name in the papers. Morris would not easily forget the day in the hall when she had opted to walk off with Garrett, leaving him twiddling his thumbs.

Goddamn her!

Phillip Morris tried to slam the door as he left the building for his Peugeot, but the hydraulic damper slapped it back at him, bruising his knuckles through the glove.

He slushed his way through ridges of snow to the back of the lot, pulling off the glove and sucking at his stung knuckles. He stepped between two cars and looked up at some dark figure, just as the heavy boot was swinging upward. The steel-tipped toe caught him in the groin, driving his testicles upward, smashing them.

Morris doubled over in the worst pain he had

ever experienced. Agony crashed into his mind, interfering with his breathing.

He hit the ground on his side.

The foot lashed out again, catching him in the ribs, and he rolled onto his back.

A knee dropped into the middle of his chest.

He could not breathe. The pain in his crotch was unbearable.

Morris thought he would pass out, hoped he would. He sucked for air, gasping, feeling squishy, wondering if he would die.

He groped for his balls.

Seconds passed before he realized he could not pull his knees any tighter against his chest because someone was kneeling on him.

He was suddenly very afraid.

And he opened his eyes.

What he saw made him feel faint. The slenderest of stainless-steel blades, drops of moisture beading on the flat surface, was held directly in front of his eyes. He could not look away from it.

A dreadful voice intoned, "I am going to cut your balls off."

"Oh, my God! No, no, no!"

"You may keep what is left of them if you answer quietly my questions. And quickly."

"Yes, yes!"

"Where is Barbara Morris?"

"I don't know."

The blade flicked downward, just a tick against his cheek, but he was instantly aware of warm blood flowing over his face, dripping on his neck.

"My God, my God! I don't . . . I don't! She went . . . on vacation. That's . . . what they told

191

me . . . after I followed her to the lobby. I saw her meet . . . another guy."

"Who?"

"Garrett. Brandon Garrett. He's . . . he's a colonel, he's . . . intelligence."

"Where did they go?"

"The tunnel! The tunnel! I . . . don't know from there. I was . . . mad."

"Tunnel?"

"Under the city! Damn it! That's all I know!"

And then he was alone in the snow.

His assailant vanished, and in his agony he was very happy to be by himself. He closed his eyes and pulled his knees tightly against his chest.

It was nearly eight o'clock when Garrett made his call from a public telephone outside a pancake house in Durham, North Carolina. The phone rang twice, and Tom Eaglefeather answered.

Garrett uttered ten digits and hung up.

It was an old code, but Eaglefeather would know to slip two digits and reverse the last five.

While he waited for Eaglefeather to find a public phone, Garrett belabored himself: Was he doing the right thing? Were his logic and his sanity really together on this, or was he suffering the kind of delusion the brass and the secretaries on the NSC believed he was? And what kind of a jackass was he to bring Morris along?

He had almost given up on her when she finally appeared on the stairs, breathless, and they had gone below ground and taken the subterranean tunnel over to Treasury. From there, they were able to catch a cab. They went first to the bank, where Garrett withdrew ten thousand in cash from one of his savings accounts.

At an independent automobile rental agency, Garrett was able to rent a four-wheel-drive American Motors Eagle on a solemn promise to keep it in the city. The agency did not want its cars spread all over the Eastern Seaboard in this kind of weather.

As he might have known, Barbara was not prepared to leave the country immediately. They drove to her apartment so she could get her passport. When she reappeared six minutes later, she was carrying a small overnight case. She got in, and he squirted streams of snow from under all four of the Eagle's tires in his hurry to get out of the area.

"Damn it, I told you just the passport!"

"All I got was some makeup and toothpaste."

"We can buy that anywhere along the way."

"Sorry."

He let his voice carry his anger. "Maybe you should stay here, Barbara."

"And get shot in the night?"

He just grunted.

"I'm sorry. I promise to follow orders exactly from now on."

They were uncommunicative on the trip south, trapped in private thoughts. Garrett was concerned about his ignorance of the people involved in the Kamchatka project. A good field agent knew as much as possible about the opposition's leadership, and he had nothing more than the weather to go on.

The roads were hellacious, and there was no noticeable improvement in conditions until just

193

south of Richmond. Then the improvement would not have been notable except in relation to the roads they had just passed over. They averaged less than thirty miles per hour, and it took almost seven hours to reach Durham.

Garrett was fatigued, eye-strained, and butt-weary as he waited in the telephone booth.

When the phone rang, Garrett grabbed it and said, "Safe?"

Eaglefeather's bass came back, "Safe. Where'n hell are you?"

"South, going south."

"You're going through with this then?"

"There's no other way. The boss turned down other alternatives."

"You have unfriendly company?"

"I don't think so. We did a little foot-shuffling before leaving town."

"We?"

"Of the other gender."

"Is that wise?"

"No. But unavoidable at the time. It'll be solo on the last leg."

"You have resources?"

"Some green. Enough to get where I'm going."

"I've news on the decoy story."

The fake information leak they had devised had turned up in Moscow, and Eaglefeather's plant had fed it back to Washington.

"Who?"

"High radiation levels in St. Louis," Eaglefeather told him softly.

St. Louis. Oh, damn. They had given the St. Louis form of the message to Aggie.

"Son of a bitch! I'm getting too old. Are you

picking up on it?"

"Not just yet, I think. We may want to send another message."

Garrett would not try to shift blame. "I ran background on her. What did I miss?"

"I'm guessing. There's a son who's listed as an Army MIA in Nam. The odds are the bad guys have him stashed away somewhere."

"You'll let my boss know?"

"Not yet."

"You have a reason for that?" Garrett asked.

"With you . . . on leave, she's insulated. Let's just leave her in place until you're back."

Garrett hesitated, but said, "All right."

"Need anything else?"

Garrett considered. His plan was fast assuming a shape that might be successful.

"Maybe. Most of what I need should be available along the way. There are a couple of things."

"Shoot."

"I need a cable sent out tonight." He read off the lines he had prepared mentally.

"Got it. What else?"

"My . . . partner will serve as backup. If my trip is fruitful, but incomplete, she'll need an address for any evidence there might be."

Eaglefeather mulled that over, then offered a code. "Analog."

"Fine. We'll be in touch."

"Be very cool, my friend."

"In this weather, is there another choice?"

"I hope that it will be warm soon," Eaglefeather said.

"Watch your back," Garrett warned.

It was warm enough, quite balmy, but the over-cast skies dampened normal enthusiasms, and made old age more imminent. Looking out into the bay, Yakama felt a strange foreboding. It made him wonder if all the preparations he had made toward those years over which he had no control were entirely complete. He would have to spend some time reviewing them.

But to the moment.

He picked up the flimsy paper and read it again:

TO: EORCH

FROM: JAGUAR

APPRECIATE INVITATION STOP MEET HK SOONEST STOP

JUST REWARDS STOP

"Jaguar" was the code name the Soviets had given to Brandon Garrett.

"Just rewards," could mean anything, but certainly, he could not allow Garrett to pay him for anything the man might need. That was out of the question.

Also questionable was Garrett's mission. Yakama was unaware of anything of an important covert nature taking place out of Air Force Intelligence.

This could be interesting.

The invitation, of course, had been extended

two decades before and was always open.

Yakama chewed tentatively at his lower lip, then picked up the telephone that rested on the glass table by his side. He dialed the bridge. "Captain Timura, let us get underway for our home port."

Fifteen

The traffic regarding Garrett was getting hectic. After the message from the Air Force Intelligence plant, which Zanov had dutifully reported to the office of the KGB Chairman, to the chairman of the First Chief Directorate—who was now interested, and to Kamchatka, there had been many telephone calls.

Because a man went on leave?

Grigori Illiyich Zanov went back over the message copies accumulating in Garrett's file. He knew something about missing scientists apparently, and therefore had been marked for execution. It was very strange, though he had to admit that men had been killed for less.

It was strange enough that Petrovsky had called once again and demanded prompt notification of any change in Garrett's status. It was strange enough that General Korontoyev in the First Chief Directorate had come down to the sub-basement to use a scrambler telephone to make a call to the Soviet Mission in New York.

Zanov, because he no longer had other pursuits to capture his attention, had learned to pass the long hours of his shifts attempting to unravel intrigues within his own service.

He would especially like to unravel any that

might possibly affect Major Boris Ivanovich Petrovsky in a negative manner.

So he attempted to monitor Korontoyev's conversation with New York. He was aided by the overheated basement, which forced Korontoyev to leave the door to the soundproof cubicle ajar. Though he placed himself in a similar cubicle, on an apparent similar communication, Zanov was unable to overhear more than "Washington, D.C.," "Alexandre," and "Garrett." The words told him little.

He knew by hearsay that Alexandre was one of the Motherland's top assassins, and now he knew the agent was controlled through New York. A bit of deduction with the roster of the Mission might help him pin down the identity. At the very least, it gave him an investigative game to play while wasting away his time in the basement.

When Korontoyev left, he told Zanov to give top priority to any messages arriving from Alexandre.

"Alexandre, Comrade Chairman Korontoyev?"

"Yes, Major. He is to be given priority on all requests, and my office notified promptly. And I want you to stay through the next shift to handle it."

That had been gratifying, knowing that he still had a talent that was wanted, and Zanov happily remained at his desk, forgetting to call Natasha and mention his added work assignment.

Nothing at all happened for several hours.

Finally, there was the cable saying that Garrett had apparently left the city with Morris by way of a rented car. It asked that agents in all American and European cities with international airports be alerted to the couple's possible arrival or departure.

Zanov immediately sent the alert to all of the affected embassies, consulates, and residencies, then informed Korontoyev and received a compliment.

As an afterthought, he had an informative cable sent to First Base in Kamchatka.

Hours later, he was going off duty to painfully return to the drab apartment when the next key message came in: Garrett and Morris had been observed in Madrid, and the agent-in-place wanted to know what he should do about it.

There had been an Alitalia flight out of Dulles, headed for Paris, but Alexandre had been unable to find a place on it. His instructions had mentioned only that Garrett was too interested in a secret project taking place in the Motherland, and his best assumption told him that the intelligence man would head for West Germany. Under that assumption, Garrett would take the rented car south to where it was easier to obtain transatlantic transport.

He was able buy an exiled Cuban's seat on a DC-9 to Florida for $500, and was in Miami when he placed an overseas call to Moscow Center through Lisbon, then received the disturbing news that Garrett was already in Madrid.

In accordance with his normal bad luck where Garrett was concerned, there were no flights scheduled to Spain for seven hours. Twenty U.S. one-hundred-dollar bills were required to obtain the airline ticket to Rome from a seventy-year-old blue-haired lady who was a competent negotiator and a patient traveler.

From Rome to Madrid would be easy.

Garrett had not slept well on the flight, nor had Barbara. They were both fatigued as they waited in the baggage area for the luggage he had bought in Durham.

After they had eaten a sparse meal at the pancake house, Garrett had found a discount store and bought them two large suitcases, toiletries, a couple of changes of clothing, a large can like Grandma used to keep candy in, and a heat-sealing food-preservation kit.

They'd spent ten hours driving to Atlanta, with Barbara handling part of the route after the snow turned to slush, then to wet asphalt. While she drove, Garrett packed the Berreta automatic and the PPK in paper, then in the decorative candy can. He slipped the can into a plastic bag, which he sealed with the heat device in a men's room at a gas station in Charlotte.

It was a little risky, and the weapons would not be immediately available to him, but it was quicker than trying to find similar hardware in Europe. With the can packed in a suitcase sent directly through baggage handling, the possibility of detection was slight. Going through customs at their destination would be the test.

At Atlanta International Airport at three A.M., Garrett risked using his and Barbara's AFI and State Department credentials and got them on the first flight to Europe. He would have preferred using a phony name and papers, but he had not wanted to take the time to let Eaglefeather take care of the task for him.

Two hours later, after a rough takeoff that had Morris gripping her armrests with white knuckles, the 747 found smooth air. Garrett thought it was warm and relaxing in their first-class seats. Barbara was pale, and the tremble in her hands betrayed her nervousness. He squeezed her forearm once in reassurance.

"I hate this."

"Best way I know to get around the world. It's done all the time by the best of people."

"I still hate it."

Once the warning lights went off, a number of passengers promptly made for the upper-deck lounge, but there were still too many English speakers around for candid discussion between them. Garrett found out more about Indianapolis and Harvard and Barbara's aspirations than he wanted to know, and he let escape a couple of old memories.

"But how did you get into intelligence?"

He grinned. "Would you believe it was your boss, Petrie?"

"Really?"

"It was his Saigon group. At first, they just needed a pilot. Stupid me, I liked to fly."

"Lots of bad stuff?"

"Some." He did not talk about it.

"Takes a dedication to the job, doesn't it?"

"Not to the job, Barbara. To the country."

She had been watching him closely, and when he made the statement, her eyes darkened, and she settled back against the cushion of her seat, newly introspective.

It was ten P.M., Spanish time, before they successfully completed the customs examination in

Madrid. The plastic-covered candy can was only cursorily probed. Leaving the customs area, Garrett did not see anyone extraordinary watching for them. He had an itchy feeling, however, and so he went to the men's room and recovered the PPK. He shoved it in his belt at the small of his back.

After completing that preparation, he checked with several airlines and purchased two tickets on an Air France flight to New Delhi. The plane made one stop in Ankara. It did not leave until mid-morning on the following day.

A quick telephone call got him reservations, and a taxi got them downtown to the Villa Magna on the Paseo de la Castellena by eleven-thirty.

The walk from the terminal to the cab had been a shocker. It was warm, and there was no snow on the ground. The airport was crowded, but the mobs seemed less harried and more courteous than those to which he had become accustomed in Washington, people beset by cabin fever.

The hotel was an elegant, faded remnant of grander days and Barbara told him that it was lovely.

Standing on the sidewalk while the doorman sought a late-night bellman, Barbara asked him, "You've stayed here before?"

"A few times. I have a thing about decent hotels."

She pointed south on the tree-lined boulevard. "What's down there?"

"The Cultural Center. Then the Prado Museum. Over to the southeast, there, you can see the lights at the top of the Royal Palace."

"It's all so magnificent. I wish there was time to see it."

"You have to get out of the office every once in awhile and get on an airplane," Garrett said.

She may have had a retort, but the bellman showed up and took their luggage.

Garrett paid for two adjoining rooms, exchanged some currency, then tipped the bellman to take their luggage and overcoats up to the rooms. He led Barbara toward a dining room half full of patrons.

"I'm starved," he said.

"You should have eaten on the plane."

"On Atlantic flights westward, when the cuisine is German or French or Italian, it's worth eating. Eastward, it tastes like plasticized aluminum."

The maître d' seated them at a tiny table with candlelight that gleamed on white linen, crystal goblets, and heavy, ornate silverware. The flickering light played a warm sonata on the planes of Barbara's face.

"This is quite romantic."

"Is it?" Garrett did not want it to be romantic.

She frowned at his response, then said, "Except for once to Puerto Rico, and once to the Bahamas, I've never been out of the country before. I like it."

"There's a lot of this world worth seeing."

"And protecting?"

"And protecting."

He let their waiter recommend a traditional Spanish dinner, but selected his own 1978 cru bourgeois red Bordeaux to go with it, and the combination was satisfying. They did not hurry it. When he found a restaurant he liked, Garrett tried to not rush the pleasure.

After dinner, he ordered Napoleon brandy and

coffee. The coffee was heavy and aromatic.

"Sure you don't want a cigar?"

Morris wrinkled her nose at him.

Garrett stopped and bought a bottle of Johnny Walker in the lobby's liquor store, and they took the elevator to the seventh floor.

"Nightcap?" he asked.

"I'd like that."

His room was large and furnished with heavy Mediterranean pieces. The walls, drapes, and bedspread were brocaded in burgundy. A wrought-ironed balcony was visible through the windows. Barbara settled into one of the two wing-backed chairs that flanked a small table.

"This is the first time I've felt safe in weeks. And warm."

Garrett shrugged out of his suitcoat and pulled his tie loose. He poured Scotch into two real glasses.

"I wouldn't get too comfortable. We may have shaken them for awhile, but they're too good to stay shaken."

He could not rid himself of the uneasy feeling he had had at the airport. If the KGB was involved, there would be alerts on the Soviet international net by now.

Morris stood up abruptly. "It has been many, many hours since I have known the luxury of water. Hold my drink, will you, while I go wash off the dirt?"

Garrett saw her to her room, which was similar to his own, told her to engage every lock she could find, then went back to his drink. He turned on the radio, but found only hard rock in several languages, and gave up on it. The TV had given up the ghost.

He could then hear the drumming of the shower next door, and pushed away an image of her under the water by mixing himself another drink.

Garrett took his own quick shower, finishing with a jet of cold water, and redressed in slacks and a shirt. When she knocked on the connecting door, he opened it to find her in a terry-cloth bathrobe—and not much else, he suspected. Her hair was wrapped high in a fluffy white towel, and her face looked scrubbed and clean. A slight halo of steam rose from her. The green of her eyes was darker than usual.

"Better?" he asked.

"Much. I feel like I'm fit to be seen in public again."

He noted the twin protuberances of her nipples against the soft azure material. "Dressed like that? You'd draw quite a crowd."

She blushed minutely and slid past him, a heady aroma trailing after her. She picked up her drink and sipped at it as she turned to look at him, her eyes large over the rim of the glass.

"You don't mind, do you?"

"Of course not."

They talked for twenty minutes, Barbara rising once to replenish their glasses, and the action provided him with a momentary glimpse of her pale thigh. Her perfume was as intoxicating as the liquor.

Finally he said, "Long road behind us, and a long road ahead, Barbara. We'd better get some sleep."

Her eyes were on his. "I suppose so."

He followed her around the bed to the connecting door, conscious of the sway of her buttocks.

She stopped and turned around to face him. She leaned against him, raised her arms, and wrapped them around his neck. "How about together?"

He placed his hands on her hips and drew her tightly to him, feeling the pressure of her breasts against his chest, the heat of her, then the very soft, very hot touch of her lips against his own.

Morris lay beside him, a single sheet covering them.

She had never been a prude, though she had always been selective. Somehow, Brandon had brought out an undiscovered freedom in her. All through the long night of driving and the interminable frightening hours on the airplane, she had grown more conscious of him. She had let the awareness supplant the other things she should have been thinking about, like just what in hell she thought she was doing, trying to be some kind of spy.

The dinner had intensified her thoughts. Not the dinner, but the setting: old Madrid, warm night, wine, and candlelight. Candlelight making the planes of his face less hard, his blue-gray eyes moodier. Up in the room, she had nearly made the proposal in a cruder way, feeling weak-kneed and squishy in the stomach, and had put it off by leaving for a cold shower. Soaping herself in the shower, she had decided, damn it, why not. If he would not make a pass at her, then she would make one at him.

Brandon was quiet beside her, his breathing even, though not at the frequency indicating sleep.

He had not said a word during the frenzy of their lovemaking, though his ardor and intensity had said enough. She rolled onto her right side, placing the palm of her left hand on his flat hard belly and shifting her left leg to lie across his thigh, feeling new stirrings in him. "Brandon?"

"Yes?"

"I'm too pushy, aren't I? No patience."

He chuckled lightly. "Why don't we just say you're forthright."

Morris leaned forward to kiss his shoulder. Her lips found the hard tissue of a scar. There were lots of scars on him.

He rolled toward her, laying his arm over her waist, and kissed her lightly on the lips. "If you'd left, I'd have been in the shower all night."

Morris moved her hand down his stomach and gripped the hardness of him. "I've got a better idea than a shower."

They made love two times before finally falling asleep, entwined in each other's arms. And they awakened in the new time of seven o'clock to once more explore each other, drawing out new pleasures.

By eight o'clock in the morning, Morris was ready to forget the mission.

Garrett slapped her on the bottom and hustled them both into the shower. By eight-thirty, the bags were packed and stored next to the bellman's desk.

They went into the coffee shop and had toast and coffee for breakfast.

"What time does the plane leave?" she asked him.

"Ten-thirty-five. We need to leave here about

208

nine-thirty."

"Can we take a walk along the street? I'd like to look in some of the shops."

She could tell by his expression that he did not think of this as a shopping trip, but gave in and said, "All right."

They walked out into the bright sunshine. My god, how different from Washington! How lovely to feel the warmth on her bare arms. Garrett took the outside of the sidewalk, and they walked casually north on the boulevard. The trees were not leafed out, but she could imagine what spring in Madrid would be like.

They stopped occasionally so she could peer through windows into shops that were not yet open.

She sensed a tenseness in him.

"Relax. At least we're exhibiting our tourist cover," she said.

"I'm not so sure." His voice sounded taut.

She was startled, and started to look around.

"Don't look back!"

"What is it?"

"Let's just keep walking. Just keep it easy. There's a guy in a car back in front of the hotel. He's been watching us. Turn here."

They rounded a corner onto a side street. It was too early for more than a few people to be on the street. Several tall buildings made the sun's splash on the street harsh next to deeper shadows.

Behind them, she heard a car turn the corner, and she felt Brandon's grip on her upper arm tighten. The car, a small black one she did not recognize, went on by, pulling into a parking place further down the street. They kept walking, peeking into windows.

Morris's scalp tingled the closer they came to the car, but she kept her attention on the dolls and jewelry, making offhand comments to Brandon. He released her arm as they came abreast of the car.

She would never know exactly what happened. One minute, there was just tension, and the next minute, the loudest explosion she had ever heard.

She fell down on her right side.

No. She did not fall. Brandon had thrown her to the ground. She looked up and to her left, terrified. What she remembered was the jagged glass shards left in the car door window, and behind it, the surprised and fascinated eyes of a dark little man. His arm draped over the back of the seat, holding a blue pistol. There was a bloody red hole in the middle of his forehead.

The windshield was splattered with a ghastly gray and red gore.

"Quick! This way!"

Garrett grabbed her arm roughly, pulled her to her feet, and they ran to the next intersection and around the corner. They were almost alone on the block.

With effort, she willed her panic to subside and concentrated on running on the soles of her feet so as not to break a high heel.

In half a block, Garrett pulled them to a walk, and it took forever to reach the corner, where they turned right. They entered the side door of the hotel, retrieved the luggage from the storage room off the lobby, and had the doorman call a cab waiting at the taxi rank.

She found she could breathe again as she settled

against the cushion of the seat. Her pulse was still racing. The street, the people, the buildings seemed much brighter and sharper, as if her eyes were seeing in a strange new dimension.

It was difficult for her to understand how Garrett could chat so casually with the driver as they sped toward the airport.

She was trembling, and Garrett took her hand. She pulled it from him quickly.

Morris felt an overwhelming sense of repulsion. He had just killed a man.

Sixteen

When Felix Nemoronko learned of the events in Madrid, he railed for fully five minutes against the incompetent bloody bastards who made up the First Chief Directorate.

Then he considered the advantages.

The Chairman of the Committee for State Security was detective enough to deduce several important pieces of information from the fact that Garrett was now on an airplane for New Delhi, according to the *rezidentia* in Madrid.

It required putting oneself in, say, the place of Garrett's supervisor, Danton, in Air Force Intelligence. If Garrett came to him with some story of missing scientists and radiation and suggested some thesis concerning weather patterns, it would be difficult to believe, to say the least. Even if Garrett had added to that concoction some other clue, the whole idea was still fantastic. There were no linkages.

The story would be just as fantastic to the National Security Council.

Of course, there was nothing to suggest that Garrett had made the connection to weather. He might be singularly concerned with the missing professors, as had been reported by the asset within Air Force Intelligence. It did seem likely to the Chairman that Garrett felt there was a relationship between the disciplines of the scientists and the radiation reports in the United States. That might have led him to the northern Pacific MiG-25 flights. Again, it was all very tenuous.

And when ideas were tenuous, and when one had a man as stubborn as Garrett's file suggested, then one expected the man to firm up the ideas.

So.

Garrett was on his way to find more evidence to convince his nervous superiors. There were some niceties in that. The United States Government had not yet acquired the true story, and Garrett and Morris were outside the country, and therefore more accessible.

Nemoronko had to admit that Garrett probably had some idea of where he was going. If he had selected Kamchatka, then one of his other clues must be the hybrid MiG-25s.

Still, his journey meant that whatever had been presented to the National Security Council was not substantial enough to convince the dunderheads who comprised the hierarchy of the United States.

The Chairman called in his secretary and dictated three memos. The first was an informative one for the General Secretary outlining Nemoronko's rationales. The second memorandum was an imperative one for General Korontoyev in the First Chief Directorate instructing him as to further actions relative to Colonel Brandon Garrett. The third was a suggestive memo for First Base.

Then he sat back, placed his elbows on his desk, pressed his fingertips together, and studied the strength inherent in his hands. All it took was a snap of the fingers.

* * *

When Boris Ivanovich Petrovsky was a youngster in Leningrad, obtaining his warmth from stolen coats and his sustenance from the dustbins in alleys behind famous restaurants, often he had had to fight to stay alive.

His unknown paternity—that was the side he blamed—had left him with a stature considerably inferior to others of his age, so he had learned to make up for the difference in size with ferocity and determination. An iron pipe slammed across an Adam's apple or a judiciously placed knee or half an ear torn off with sharp teeth did much for his reputation and his ego.

Sometimes Petrovsky missed the simple human contact of those days. The existence he had already accepted had been interrupted when he had run from a restaurant with the wool and ermine-collared coat belonging to Yuri Andropov. He had not run far when he was apprehended by two previously unnoticed bodyguards. Andropov had studied him silently for ten minutes, asked five questions, then shipped him off for the beginning of his schooling. Progressively, as he had advanced in the KGB, performing the special services for Chairman, then General Secretary Andropov, and then for his successors in both posts, he had grown away from the eye-to-eye relationship with his adversary. Boris Petrovsky had had to rely on a remote manipulation of people and events in order to achieve his goals. Completing his victories from a distance was not as satisfying as hand-to-hand confrontation. There was very little adrenaline involved.

Petrovsky went back over the cables of the past

214

hours. It looked as if Garrett was coming gunning, like a character out of the American movie *High Noon*. Baronikov—Petrovsky was one of the few who knew the man was Alexandre—had missed him in the United States. And in Madrid, Garrett had been the quicker adversary, or it appeared that way. The resident had reported Alexandre shot to death in his car. Now, the First Chief Directorate would try to intercept him in Ankara.

Petrovsky fervently hoped that the assassins missed Garrett again.

Instinctively, he felt that Garrett knew more than Moscow Center was letting on. Moscow-based strategists tended to be overly optimistic in their assessments. Petrovsky felt that Garrett was coming to him in Kamchatka. And that was fine with Petrovsky. That was almost too good to be true.

Back when he had been less experienced, less reliant on an agent's instincts, Garrett and he had confronted each other, though not in the satisfying personal sense. Their combat had taken place by remote control, each countering the moves of the other, between Bangkok and Phnom Penh. Garrett had had a few more moves, and the network Petrovsky managed had collapsed in tattered ruins.

The thought of having the American present in Petrovsky's realm, face-to-face, was desirable.

Less desirable was the sentiment expressed in the specially coded message from the Chairman which Petrovsky had had to decode himself:

TO: First Base
FROM: Home Plate
Special Alert All Offices Primary Ankara For
Col B Garrett And B Morris STOP Knowl-

edge Spcl Prjct And Poss Location STOP Double Security Effort STOP Prepare Eventuality Termination Project With Prejudice STOP

Petrovsky committed the lines to memory and tossed the thin paper sheet into the wastebasket which contained paper destined for shredding. He was incensed over the Chairman's questioning of his security. The man had never seen it or tested it. The security of the project was more than adequate. Petrovsky had tested it himself many times.

The last line was defeatist in tone. It suggested that Garrett might be successful, and that the project might have to be eradicated.

That would be a massive undertaking. There were thirty-four scientists, twenty technicians, the flight crews and ground support. Even the custodial and kitchen personnel would be subject to the order. After them, was he to include the complement of GRU officers and guards? And the whores brought in for the soldiers and scientists? There would have to be clarification in the final order.

From the window of his quarters, Malenkov watched as Petrovsky and one of the corporals left the building on another of the man's incessant rounds of inspection. Malenkov pulled on his greatcoat and his gloves for the short walk to the office.

He had been avoiding contact with his adjutant, the decision stemming from an observation of the man walking through the general laboratory, testing the air with a Geiger counter. Obviously, someone in Moscow had provided instructions for Petrovsky to add empirical data to the reports he was already submitting. Seeing the radiation check had undermined Malenkov's confidence even more.

There was some consolation in the fact that Petrovsky was ignorant of the scientific section and had not, as far as the commander knew, tested the atmospheric pressurization chamber, where the radiation could be measured. So he suspected that the reports being submitted to Moscow Center were limited in their findings.

Whatever the cause, the result was to be found in the Chairman's reinstatement of flights on the restricted basis Malenkov had recommended. He was allowed eight modules per flight, three flights per month. If he followed the prescription, it would ease the pressure on fabrication and manufacture, allowing more time for experimentation. He worried, however, that the effects in U.S. weather patterns would be substantially reduced.

The trouble was, he did not know.

Malenkov stomped the snow from his boots as he entered the headquarters building. Corporal Marienkov was tending several red lights on the switchboard which controlled telephone traffic in the compound. The switchboard was limited to the compound. Only Malenkov and Petrovsky were allowed outside communication on two dedicated lines.

He went directly into Petrovsky's office and walked quickly around the barren room, checking the stack of papers on the desk and the scraps of paper in the wastebaskets. Malenkov found it detestable that he, the project commander, was reduced to searching his adjutant's office for information affecting his personal project. He had taken up the practice several weeks before.

There had been a large number of messages lately, messages to which he was not allowed access. The basket marked "For Shredding" held one crumpled piece of paper, and he bent over to retrieve it. The words almost did not register as he read them hurriedly. He tossed the paper back into the basket and started to leaf through the requisitions stacked on the major's desk when he heard Marienkov's boots crossing the floor in the outer office.

The corporal came inquisitively to the open doorway, peeking around the jamb to see what his commander was doing.

"Corporal Marienkov, have you seen the order for the silver iodide?"

"On my desk, I think, Comrade Colonel."

"Good. I want to increase it by twenty-five kilograms before you send it out."

He followed the large Marienkov into the overheated outer office and changed the amount on the requisition. Then he retreated shaken to his own office.

His worst fears surfaced. They were in black and white, and approved by Moscow.

The Chairman's assertion that the West was cognizant of the operation was apparently true. If this man named Garrett was not stopped, then the last sentence would take effect.

Colonel Yuri Malenkov had been a part of the Committee for State Security for long enough to know what the phrase "termination project with prejudice" meant.

Ongoing passengers did not deplane in Ankara,

Turkey. They waited in their seats while the cabin interior heated up and baggage and freight were exchanged in the airplane's belly.

Garrett picked out the two men immediately. They were two of nine new passengers who boarded in Ankara.

He had expected them after the play in Madrid. In that episode, his quick glimpse of the assassin, whom he had never seen before, had been enough to prompt the instincts, to tell him to draw and kill. He thought his reflexes had been a trifle slow. Maybe he was getting too old.

Reflex was important when dealing with the KGB, for only timing and accuracy created survival. He had survived before in such situations by not thinking too much before pulling the trigger.

Killing was obviously not one of Barbara's preconceptions about this mission, even after the death of Carl Brent. She had seen a Garrett that she had not expected after the sex play of the night before.

He was becoming more concerned about her lack of field experience. She was one of those bureaucrats he frequently complained about. Her heart was in her job, but not necessarily in the goals of her job.

Perhaps it was better that Barbara had undergone such a shock to her sensibilities this morning. Her new view of him would keep the proper gap between them for what was to come.

Garrett turned his head and found her green eyes, much lighter today, studying him.

"Problem?" he asked.

"You killed him."

"That's true."

"You've done it before." It was a statement.

"Yes." Another statement.

Garrett was no longer amused by her pouting. "Barbara, sometime soon, you're going to have to grasp the fact that this is no academic exercise entitled, 'Practical Seminar in Intelligence Gathering.' We live in a very real goddamned world where people get hurt and get killed. There's nothing here for your resume and your eventual promotion to Director. That wouldn't happen anyway."

Her eyes widened, the green going pale. "You're saying it's a man's world."

"I'm saying you're a civil servant, Barbara. The operative word is 'servant,' and you're just about as high as you're going to go in operations. The DCIs and directors will come out of a political world you're not in tune with. Their motivations are different. They believe in something besides the job; they believe in the country."

Tears started to well in her eyes.

"Don't get me wrong. You're just like me. I'm a military servant. I'm happy with what I decided to be. I don't want Merle Danton's job. I don't want to be a cabinet member. But by God, I share a motivation with Danton and with most of the cabinet members I know. And that makes whatever I do more than just a job."

His little speech was intense, though pitched low to avoid nearby ears that could understand English. He gave up on it as she turned her head away, the tears getting bigger in the corners of her eyes.

She stayed that way, avoiding him, until forty minutes out of New Delhi, where it was just after seven P.M.

"Barbara?"

She rolled her face to him. Her eyes were puffy and flat. "What?"

"Are you still with me?"

"Do I have a choice?"

"You might have. I can leave you on the plane."

"Yes, I'm with you."

"All right. In Row Nine on the aisle is a heavy-set blond man in his fifties."

She leaned over him to look. "Yes."

"Next to him is a younger guy, brown hair, about one hundred sixty pounds. The young one spoke French well enough with the stewardess to actually be French. I'd guess him as a contract player, picked up quickly as backup to the other guy, but not knowing much about what's going on. He won't have the same ideological commitment as the older man. That one's probably KGB. I think I've seen him, or his picture, somewhere before."

Barbara's knuckles went to her mouth. "My God, Brandon! When does it end?"

"Not for awhile. They won't be armed on the plane. Their hardware will be in their luggage, and I want to keep it that way. When we land, I want to take off fast enough to keep them from picking up baggage. They'll have to split up if we do, and that's better for me."

Garrett explained what she would have to do. "Can you handle that?"

"If I have to."

"You have to."

When the plane parked at the terminal, they pushed their way forward, past Row Nine, before the agents realized what had happened. The two agents were still jammed among the deplaning passengers by the time Garrett and Morris had descended the stairway and started across the hot tarmac.

Inside the terminal, it was hot and humid. Passengers and visitors shared Western dress and Indian garb about evenly. The air was thick with incense and with the aroma of spicy curries offered by concourse vendors.

Garrett headed directly toward an administrative area and saw Barbara enter the ladies' rest room. Behind her, the Frenchman came hesitantly to a stop, then took up a station outside the rest room, leaning against a pillar.

The Soviet sauntered along behind Garrett.

Garrett took a right down a long hallway which had Indian and English signs indicating airline administrative offices were located along its length. So was a small rest room, out of the normal traffic pattern for travelers, and he turned into it. It was vacant, and he waited behind the door for only two minutes before the agent decided that this was as good a place as any other.

The door opened tentatively, then wider, as the apparent vacancy alarmed his pursuer. As soon as his head was inside, Garrett stabbed swiftly with the heel of his right hand, catching the man in the throat. He felt the larynx crush and give under the blow.

The man gagged.

With his left hand, Garrett grabbed a handful of hair and jerked him into the room.

The agent choked on his own blood, which quickly appeared in the corner of his mouth. His eyes flared in terror, and he was more concerned about his imminent death than defending himself. He landed on his face on the white tile, leaving a smear of blood.

222

Garrett dropped knees first into the middle of his back, forcing the lungs to spew air at the blockage in the throat. The result was a Soviet panic in which he flailed his arms helplessly, banging them against the tile, trying to reach back for his antagonist.

Garrett found the nerve in the top of the man's shoulder with his thumb, pressed hard, and unconsciousness soon relieved the man of his fear.

He hoisted the heavy body onto its knees, pulled open the door to the rearmost of the three stalls available, and unfolded his burden onto the toilet. He eased him back into the juncture of two walls, positioning the feet to make the cubicle appear suitably occupied. Locking the door from the inside, Garrett listened for a moment, then pulled himself up and over the partition.

He did not know whether or not the agent would die before he regained consciousness and could yell for help, and he did not care.

Garrett quickly wiped the blood from the tile floor with a paper towel.

If he was any good, the second man would not give up his post when he became concerned because Barbara did not reappear. If he left his station, Barbara was to proceed on the next stage of her errand. Garrett had told her that he would allow fifteen minutes for impatience to set in.

Garrett stood over the sink and washed his face and hands. He was forced to wash them again when a dapper little Indian in an airline uniform entered, used the urinal, washed his hands, and combed his hair. The Frenchman pushed the door ajar and poked his head inside.

Garrett ripped paper off the paper towel roll and slowly dried his face and hands as the con-

223

tract agent entered, went to a urinal, and unzipped his pants. In the mirror, Garrett saw the puzzled look on his face as he tried to survey the room, looking for his partner. He spotted shoe tips under the door of the last cubicle.

The Indian exited, and Garrett did not waste time.

As the door whooshed shut, he simply turned and lashed out with his right foot, kicking the Frenchman in the middle of the back.

A man with his penis in his hand tends to feel vulnerable anyway, and he was too slow to counter the kick. His face smashed into the tiled wall. His chest crashed into the flushing handle, and Garrett heard ribs crack.

Dazed, he tried to turn toward Garrett, but Garrett reached out, twisted his hand into the long brown hair, and slammed his face into the tile four times. There was a lot of blood from his nose speckling the tile by the time Garrett was through.

The Frenchman was ensconced in the stall next to his Soviet comrade when Garrett caught up with Barbara leaving the TWA counter.

"Where?" he asked.

She had been told to buy two tickets on the first plane to anywhere. "Rangoon."

"It's the right direction. When?"

"Twenty minutes."

"Great. I'll get the suitcases."

"Brandon!" Her eyes were frightened.

"What?"

She changed her mind. She did not want to know. "Nothing."

Nathan Petrie called Eaglefeather and said,

224

"Tom, I'm looking for Brandon Garrett."

Eaglefeather said, "You don't say. I didn't know you two were on speaking terms."

"We shouldn't be after the snide remark Garrett made to Ackerman, but it's important."

"We'd better have lunch, Nat."

They met at a tavern in Virginia whose plastic appointments were unsuccessful in achieving the Old World ambiance they sought. Normally, it was a fifteen minute drive, but Petrie's chauffeur got the limousine bogged down twice in traffic jams created by heavy snow piled along the streets. It took half an hour, and Eaglefeather was waiting for him.

Petrie did not know the Air Force light colonel well. They had only crossed paths a few times in twenty years.

"You know where he is, Tom?"

Petrie got an affirmative nod from him, but Eaglefeather was not forthcoming. He was quite moody really—and maybe a little ticked off at Petrie?

"Where?"

"Why do you want to know?"

"I assume he's with my assistant. You know her?"

"I know her," the lieutenant colonel said.

"She took off without my permission."

Eaglefeather shrugged.

"I mean, she left a note that she was taking personal leave, but she didn't actually ask me."

"What do you need her for?"

"We've got a lot of projects going."

"That's bullshit, Nat. You ready to take the weather theory to NSC?"

Petrie hesitated. "It's very farfetched."

"But I believe it, Nat. All the way."

"Damn it. If you all could just come up with a little bit more."

"We will."

He watched Eaglefeather sip his beer, then said, "No. I can't take it anywhere yet. Look what happened to Danton and the AFI. They were damned near laughed out of the clubhouse."

"Your people didn't help in that meeting," Eaglefeather accused. "You were doing most of the laughing."

"Goddamn it, I need to know where they are."

Eaglefeather studied the ceiling intently. "Not from me."

"So I go to General Neilson. It takes a bit longer, but I still find out."

Neilson was Eaglefeather's boss at Defense Intelligence.

"You're an asshole, you know that, Nat?"

"I'm doing my job."

"What's your job?"

"To make sure there's no fuck-ups taking place."

"You're awfully concerned with image," Eaglefeather told him.

That was when Petrie began to be afraid. "The order came through channels from the White House. It's the same order I'll use with General Neilson."

Eaglefeather frowned. "He's probably in Hong Kong by now."

"Shit! He's going in."

"Yes."

"Goddamn it! Doesn't he know what repercussions that will have? Fuck! If he gets caught, the Soviets'll have a field day with a public trial."

"There won't be any public trial, Nat."

226

Eaglefeather's statement was entirely sincere and his demeanor morose.

Petrie, who was quick to pick up nuances, asked, "What in hell do you mean by that?"

"I don't believe he's worried about getting out, Nat. He will if he can, but he's simply not planning on it. There won't be any trial."

Seventeen

The island's peak cast a long shadow over the harbor as Yakama waited by the boarding ramp for the return of Captain Timura and the launch. The edge of a typhoon passing in Pacific waters had encouraged many ships to take refuge in the harbor. Several passenger liners and over two hundred freighters mixed with the pleasure boats and junks. One of Yakama's favorite scenes was that of a beautifully crafted Chinese junk placed in the forefront of Hong Kong's glass and steel skyline. The old and the new, his view of history.

The last time Garrett had been aboard the *Eastern Orchid,* he had been a captain. It suddenly seemed very long ago. The occasion had been a dinner party, a sumptuous one of roast pig, garnished with a pineapple and brandy sauce, for a few diplomatic friends in the American, British, and French consulates. The yacht had been anchored off the coast of Thailand by four miles to create a gulf between it and the whores and beggars in small boats who thrived in the canals and outreaches of Bangkok like frenzied ants encircling a half-eaten chicken leg.

During the cocktail hour in the main salon, with most of the treasures secreted elsewhere, Garrett had approached him with the knowledge and location of a group of 227 Japanese nationals brutalized and enslaved by the Pol Pot regime in Cambodia.

Yakama had been able to arrange the extrication of 221 of his countrymen from Cambodia. The feat had brought him contentment, though it also had increased his debt to Garrett. The American agent only appeared when he had information to further leverage the balance of payments between them. It was an art of which Yakama was master, and he had always been amused that Garrett so often bested him.

This time it would be different, and Yakama thought that he would more happily join his ancestors if his debts were settled. He watched with that anticipation as the launch finally appeared, skirting a junk under full sail, and coasted toward the boarding ramp. Two white-uniformed seamen stood ready to secure it and assist the guests.

From his vantage point at the teak rail, Yakama could see relatively little change in Garrett's appearance. There was a touch of gray at his blond temples and a few more wrinkles around the eyes, but his eyes appeared very tired. Or worried. Not defeated.

He was dressed in the distinctively far Western cut of an American suit, nicely tailored in light gray, though rumpled from the journey. For an American, Garrett had always displayed better than average taste.

Yakama was mildly surprised at the appearance of his companion. Until Garrett had called from Kai Tak Airport, he had not known there would be another, much less a woman. Where women were concerned, Yakama's memory did not require a computer's prodding, and he quickly added her to his listing of beautiful women.

There was a tension between the two of them, like magnets with opposing poles, pushing them apart. She declined Garrett's offered arm and struggled up the steep companionway on her own, an independent and forceful woman.

Beautiful, yes, but he suspected that her demeanor was not to his taste.

"Welcome, Miss Morris, and my good friend Brandon, to the *Eastern Orchid*. She and I place our humble services at your disposal."

Yakama smiled broadly, indeed very happy to again see his friend.

Garrett thought Barbara looked ill-at-ease—she had complained about the disarray of her traveling dress—when she said, "I'm pleased to meet you, Mr. Yakama." She used a diplomatic tone of voice.

"Please, Miss Morris. With my friends, I have become Kij, and would be most happy to have you join Brandon as my friend."

"Thank you . . . Kij. And I am Barbara."

"Enchanted."

The fragile Japanese turned to Garrett, beaming. "Brandon, you're looking marvelous."

"And you lie as well as ever, Kij. It's damned good to see you."

They bowed toward each other, then hugged each other with affection, not a Western gesture.

"Come. Let us repair to the salon."

Yakama led the way along the narrow side deck to where a young cabin boy in a white uniform opened a pair of wide doors to the salon.

The main salon of the yacht was twenty feet by twenty feet, with a teak deck protected by a hand-woven Persian carpet of lustrous fiber, intricate design, and hidden value. On the carpet were placed various conversational groupings of furniture, all low and cushioned in red silk laced with threads of very real gold. Several black-lacquered and glass-topped tables accompanied the settees and chairs.

Each of the four bulkheads was centered with a glass case containing one of the four collections— jade, ivory, sapphire, and diamond. It had been a long time since Garrett had viewed them, but the pieces seemed slightly different. He had always suspected that there were other, hidden collections— and probably some in gold and silver also—from which Yakama rotated pieces. These, though, would be the artifacts Yakama took the most pride in, in addition to the dozen priceless paintings adorning the silk-clad bulkheads.

Garrett was glad to see that the jade elephant, which he had acquired from a frightened and grateful Laotian chieftain, was the center of attention in the jade collection. Or had Kij rearranged it for his visit?

The cabin boy efficiently extracted Barbara's preference in liquor, not bothering to ask Garrett since that information would have been spilled from the computer's memory banks prior to their arrival.

When the drinks were delivered on a gold tray, Garrett sipped at his Johnny Walker Black Label, generously poured over a single ice cube.

"Your memory never falters, Kij."

"Ah, but age imposes its will implacably, Brandon. Electronic prods become the substitute for deteriorating brain cells."

Yakama tasted of his own strange, amber liquid. His quick eyes were evaluating Barbara.

"We will have this drink of greeting, my friends, then allow you to retire to your cabins, to freshen up. Henri has reverted to his national preference and prepared a *Chateaubriand* for us this evening. A culinary achievement I am certain you will find beyond parallel in the Orient or the Occident."

"Not the roast pig?"

"Brandon. *Your* memory does not fail. I too remembered the main course of our last meeting, too many years ago. Had I known you enjoyed it, I should have not let Henri have his head."

"There is nothing at all to fear from your table, Kij." Garrett told him. He noticed Barbara's head was cocked slightly as she listened to them, and she nibbled at her lower lip. He liked the look.

Yakama's face told him that his host was pleased with the comment.

Barbara's eyes moved slowly, perusing the room, and she said, "Mr. Ya . . . Kij, would you mind if I looked closer?"

"Not at all, my dear. I will be happy to serve as your escort."

They started on the port side, with the diamond case, and Barbara said, "These are unbelievably beautiful."

"I am fortunate to be able to enjoy some of the finer beauties of this world, for that space of time which I am allotted, Barbara. It is beauty which becomes more rare as time progresses, and as people find newer considerations to relish and to debate."

"I am not an expert, Kij, but I would guess that these might be considered museum quality."

Yakama smiled his pleasure, "I think that the majority of the pieces are, yes. Eventually, the collections will repose in a sanctuary available to the rest of the world."

The comment seemed somewhat fatalistic, and Garrett wondered if there was something the matter with his health. Or perhaps it was just part of Kij's penchant for planning every operation thoroughly.

Though he had been on a similar tour before, Garrett followed politely, listening to the occasional anecdotes regarding the acquisition of the art objects. Some of the tales sounded as if they had been fabricated from thin air, though they were probably factual. The tour ended at the jade case, where some seventy pieces of miniature sculpture were anchored on white velvet. The elephant was in the front center.

Barbara exclaimed over it. "I've never seen such carving!"

The sculpture was an exquisite representation of an Indian elephant, some six inches in height, counting the ornate royal carriage strapped to the back of the elephant. It contained a handsome chiseled Indian *rajah* and his favorite *ranee*. The carving had been estimated by Yakama to be several hundred years old. It was made more rare by the fact that it was accented with finely cut diamonds which were probably smuggled into India from South Africa.

Yakama smiled, looking up at Barbara. "I have always been most fascinated by the mineral, and the ability of the fine craftsmen who chose it as their medium. This particular specimen is done in jadeite, characterized by its emerald color. It is several centuries old, and was most likely carved in India. I suspect it was transported by bandits to the Malay Peninsula.

"It is my favorite, not only because of the intricate detailing and character, but also because it is the gift of my friend, Brandon Garrett."

Garrett shrugged his shoulders and said, "Your collection improves with age, Kij, and may eventually match your immaculate taste."

It was the host's turn to shrug in modesty. "I am

233

but a servant of destiny, Brandon. A most fortunate servant. Before I allow you to escape to your cabins, perhaps we could quickly put aside the business that I know you carry."

Kijuro Yakama's oblique glance at Barbara suggested that he was not entirely approving of feminine participation in such business.

They moved to a grouping of chairs and sat down. Garrett outlined his theory, taking his time, and explaining the sources in detail.

"I'm afraid, Kij, that I did not bring along any documentation."

"It is unnecessary, Brandon."

Garrett was uncertain whether the minute change in Yakama's expression denoted disbelief or dismay that he, as a master spy, was unaware of such a Soviet endeavor.

"I have," Yakama said, "based my knowledge of the processes of nature always in a traditional manner, always fallibly human, perhaps affected by the whims of one of your, or my, gods. The technological progress of this century defeats me quickly and encourages me to save what little is left of craftsmanship and beauty and nationality. That such a procedure as you describe could be available, I do not doubt. That the Soviet hierarchy would utilize such a process in aggression, I also do not doubt. If I have a suspicion at all, it is in the ability of the Soviet intelligence structure to maintain secrecy for so long. It would be a security measure almost unheard of in the beleaguered existence of the KGB."

"In the broad reaches of the organization, perhaps," said Garrett, "but not if the new Chairman really put his mind to it. And possibly circumvented the basic structure of the KGB."

Yakama bowed his head in agreement. "This is

true. And the new General Secretary has determination, ability, and a heightened intellect, when forced."

Yakama paused, then looked directly into Garrett's eyes. "Your mission is unsanctioned, Brandon."

"It is that. I've not had sufficient evidence to convince all of the players on my team."

"There are often too many players involved, especially in American intelligence agencies. Be that as it may, I am your servant."

"I will need some equipment, and a way into the Kamchatka Peninsula."

"And out?"

"I can play that by ear. I've done it before."

Garrett saw the startled expression on Barbara's face, as if she had not fully considered the slim chances. But then, this was only one more elective course in her particular school catalog.

She said, "That will be equipment for two, Kij. I'll be going along."

"That is incorrect," Garrett said. "You will be standing by the radio."

"I came into this, Brandon, planning to go as far as necessary."

"Your plans are not part of my plans, however. You've come as far as you're going."

Yakama sat back, bemused.

"Not yet, I haven't." Her face was flushing.

"Are you prepared to stick a gun in a man's face, and blow it to hell?"

"I . . . uh, I . . ."

"For God's sake, Barbara, answer me."

She dropped her head and did not answer.

Yakama was embarrassed and hurried along. "Speaking of untimely death, Brandon, there has been news from friends in Madrid. The friendly services do not know quite what to make of it, and sources in Moscow confirm nothing but that Alexandre is no longer with us."

"Alexandre? I'll be damned. I knew I hadn't seen him before, but I had no idea."

"It was your confrontation?"

"The first of two."

Barbara's head came up, "Who's Alexandre?"

Yakama answered, "He *was* one of the Soviet Union's top assassins. Twenty-nine or thirty executions have been attributed to him, though never confirmed."

Barbara had new information to confuse her.

"How about you, Kij? Do you have reservations?"

Yakama smiled. "Only that you did not choose to do this in July when northern cruising is more temperate."

Garrett laughed.

"Ah, Brandon, let me see. We have seventy, or perhaps seventy-five, hours of cruising to the Japanese northern islands, and then another sixty to achieve a position off Kamchatka. We will have ample opportunity to discuss the details. I believe, while the two of you refresh yourselves, I should have Captain Timura plot a course and get us under way."

They all stood, and Garrett and Barbara followed the cabin boy to their separate cabins. Garrett stood in the corridor while Barbara opened her door into a spacious cabin. It contained a queen-sized bed, huge closets, a private bath, and two original Gauguin oils.

"My God!" she said.

"And you thought the spy business was all bad."

She turned to look at him. "He's a fascinating man, Brandon. How long have you known him?"

"A long time."

"Do you mind my asking? Why did you give him the statuette?"

"Because I had no use for it, Barbara. And Kij appreciates it."

"But it must be worth a fortune."

She still did not understand friendships and loyalty.

"A Greek offered me a quarter million at the time, though I suspect it's priceless. But it's only money, Barbara. Friends in this profession are better."

She changed topics abruptly. "You won't let me go with you?"

"No."

Barbara closed the door on him. Garrett went to his cabin as a flurry of rubber-soled traffic could be heard on the upper deck.

That would be Kij's servants packing the artwork. Yakama always moved the collections to a safe haven whenever he was taking the *Eastern Orchid* into chancy waters.

Clare Swallow recognized the State Department operations man though he had never met him before. The description of Petrie he had heard—height, stature, and pinched face—gave him away.

He rose from his chair to his feet. "Mr. Petrie. Good afternoon."

"Good afternoon, Major Swallow. Please sit down. And may I?"

"Of course, sir."

Swallow flopped back into his chair and put out the cigar smoldering in the ashtray. What in hell was Nathan Petrie doing in his office?

"How can I help you, sir?"

237

"I understand you've been doing the photo interpretation for Colonel Garrett?"

"Yes, sir."

"Well, Garrett has taken a few days' leave, and he either has the one set of prints with him, or locked up somewhere. I would like to have another set."

Swallow had talked to Eaglefeather, and he knew that Garrett was going to attempt a penetration of the peninsula. He did not know how much Petrie might know about it, and decided to keep his trap shut.

Okay, follow the man's leads. He was too high up in the organization to do much else.

"That's easy enough, Mr. Petrie. Just a sec, and I'll get the file."

The computer codes were an indelible part of his memory now and came readily to his fingertips. He called up the file, then typed in the command which would queue it into the one of the laser printers in the print room.

"Okay, sir, on the way. Anything else?"

"Yes. As I understand it, there were some pictures of Kamchatka Air Base?"

"They're part of the same file now." Swallow touched his intercom button. "Susan, run down to the print room and pick up a pack of prints that should be coming in now, will you?"

Petrie asked, "There's nothing new in the last few days, is there?"

"No, sir. I wish there were."

Swallow unconsciously picked up a cigar from the box beside the phone, peeled the cellophane, and decided against lighting it just then.

"So do I, Major. So do I." Petrie stood.

Swallow stood up also.

"I'll get out of your hair. By the way, you don't

know if Brandon uncovered any more leaks out of either of our offices before he left, do you?"

"I don't think so, sir."

"Just the one, then, this, uh . . ."

"Aggie Nelson. That's all that I'm aware of. And I'm sure the colonel is quite unhappy about that."

"Yes. He is. Thank you, Major, and please let me know if there are any further developments."

"I'll do that, sir."

Swallow knew that Petrie and Eaglefeather and Garrett went back a long ways together, but for some reason, he felt quite uneasy about this meeting.

He finally lit his cigar.

Petrovsky stood in the doorway to Malenkov's office, and the commander waved him in. "Would you like some tea, Major? You look very cold."

"Please. I have just completed my rounds."

"And your security is as strict as it always is, I am certain."

"Stricter, Comrade Colonel. I have added three guards to the perimeter patrol."

Malenkov knew of the cable mentioning the Americans, but could not allow the man to know that he was aware of the tentative orders to terminate the project. The words of that cable had left him baggy-eyed.

"Is there a new concern, Major?" He handed the security chief a teacup.

"Thank you. Yes. A new concern. I have information that a spy, an American named Garrett, will make an attempt on the compound."

Malenkov acted surprised. "This is a fact?"

"According to sources of the KGB, Comrade Colonel, he and his colleague murdered one of our

239

agents in Spain and disabled two more operatives in India. He can be considered dangerous to the mission here."

"Colleague?" Malenkov did not know what else to ask. Murder was not a part of his experience, but if it had occurred, the situation was deteriorating quickly.

"A woman named Morris. She is a member of the American CIA."

"Is it not strange that a woman would be assigned to such an operation?"

Petrovsky grinned at him, the ferret eyes not reflecting an accompanying humor.

Malenkov fidgeted.

"Perhaps it would be strange to our operations, Colonel, though we often utilize women in an appropriate role—on their backs. But the American feminist movement has encroached on a number of areas."

"I see."

"To their downfall." The KGB agent raised his teacup in toast.

Malenkov echoed the gesture. "You are not worried then? That the knowledge of the Rain Cloud project is rampant in the West?"

"No, Colonel, I am not. I have it on excellent authority that suspicion is limited to a very small circle. It is the reason Garrett must come here, to gather evidence. His capture will end it."

"We should continue to fabricate the alternate set of records?"

"By all means. As a precaution."

"Very well. And the flight scheduled for the day after tomorrow? We are to proceed with that?"

"Certainly, Colonel." Petrovsky lit a cigarette, shaking out an extra for Malenkov. "You will be fueling aircraft tonight?"

240

"The tankers are scheduled for tomorrow night."

"We will be ready, Comrade Colonel."

In his new office suite at Langley, Nathan Petrie was also making his preparations. It had not required much scanning of his excellent memory to make the connection from Eaglefeather's statement that Garrett was in Hong Kong.

Petrie also knew Kijuro Yakama from his own Southeast Asia experiences.

They had never been friends, however.

His man on the Pacific desk, Beech, had been able to take it from there, and was now on the other end of the line. "Yeah, Nat, I got hold of Howard Carson in the Embassy, and he did some checking around. Yakama's boat has been and gone. It was last spotted off the main island of Japan."

"But is Garrett aboard?"

"Well, it's not confirmed, but one source saw a Caucasian couple taken out to the yacht in a launch. Best bet is that it's Garrett and Morris. We may know more when our people in Japan pick up on it."

"All right, thanks. Keep me posted, will you?"

"Sure will."

Petrie hung up and wondered how he could use his information.

Aggie Nelson might be a key. What an ass Garrett was, allowing an intelligence leak in his own office. Petrie had been certain that Moscow had an ear somewhere in AFI, proven by the assassination attempt on Garrett after he'd started screwing around. Major Swallow had pinpointed it for him.

Petrie knew where the leak was, and he had a fair idea of where Garrett was. By the next day,

Beech should have more for him.

He would have to act soon if this was not to escalate into a major international scandal. Petrie had reached one of those times when he truly did not like his job. He felt quite alone in this new job. The responsibilities weighed more heavily, and he was determined to make no errors that would reflect upon himself, the Secretary, or the President.

But then, Petrie had been alone before. He survived well.

Eighteen

"We have obtained a Maiden for you, Brandon," Yakama had said.

"What?" Morris asked, her voice unbecomingly shrill in the quiet of the salon. They had moved their small meetings from the fantail to the salon as the winds and seas turned cold and slate gray.

"A Maiden. That's the NATO designation for the Sukhoi Su-9U. It is an elderly aircraft, and almost totally replaced by Su-11s, Su-15s, or MiG-23s as an all-weather interceptor. Actually, the Su-9 was the fighter, introduced in the fifties. The 9 U is a trainer, seating two persons. The one we have, or rather that the Japanese government has, was used by a Red Air Force instructor and his student for defection almost a year ago."

"Where is it?" Garrett asked.

"Hakodate Air Base."

"Can I fly it?"

"You know that better than I, Brandon. It is a single turbojet aircraft. One gets in it and pushes the buttons in the correct order. You do still fly?"

"I still fly, Kij. Hell, I'm willing to try it."

Then in the black of night, off the island of Honshu, they were met by a small cruiser and took on equipment for Garrett. There were copies of the aircraft manuals which had been pirated by some enterprising associate of Yakama's. They were written in Russian.

The arrival of the manuals helped, for Morris found herself an essential part of the preparations. It was she who helped Brandon through the translations. They closeted themselves for hours, working page by page through the loose-leaf binders. Brandon was relatively proficient with short Russian phrases, but the complex technical terms escaped him. To top it off, his handwriting was nearly as indecipherable to her as the Russian Cyrillic alphabet was to him. She printed the English translations in clear block letters in the margins of pages containing illustrations of cockpit details.

The hours they spent side by side at the card table in his stateroom increased her awareness of him, and of his increasing remoteness.

After having learned that the man called Alexandre was a top assassin, she had revised her estimates of Brandon. When it had happened, she had been appalled that Brandon had not even given the man a chance, had not forced him to drop his gun, or whatever. There had just been the instantaneous judgment, the booming explosion, and the tiny hole in the man's forehead.

Now she understood that they were alive only because Brandon had made the quick decision. Having grasped that fact, Morris was able to reconsider the night before the killing. She had wanted him badly, and she had been much more brazen than she thought herself capable. She knew herself well enough to know it had not been love, just an overwhelming desire to be in his arms and to have him touch her.

It had been pleasurable, frenzied and tender, and yet, she had not really reached him. He had said nothing to her about that night.

He was entrapped in the preparations for this operation, and she had become aware of his dedication to an ideal. The job was all-important, but only as it led the protection of the United States.

What had really disturbed her was the Redeye rocket and launcher.

Her protests about that strategy had gone unheard by either Brandon or Kij.

Morris knocked on Garrett's door.

"Yes?"

"Can I come in, Brandon?"

"Sure."

She pushed open the door and found him arranging his equipment and packing it into a large backpack. Everything was white. He was dressed in white snowpants and white rubberized boots. A white anorak lay on one of the chairs. The backpack was white.

"Taking a trip?" she asked, trying to be light.

"Short one. I'm trying for my Eagle Scout badge." He grinned at her.

"You like this, don't you?"

"Truthfully, I hate camping out. I'm more the Ritz type."

"Brandon, we need to talk."

His face was instantly sober. "We'll talk when I get back, Barbara."

"If you get back."

"I always get back."

"Then why that rocket thing?"

As both Kij and Brandon had explained to her, the rocket was an outdated Redeye surface-to-air missile, complete with its own launcher. The whole thing was about four feet long, and had originally weighed twenty-nine pounds. It was lighter now because the explosive warhead had been removed, replaced by a screw-on aluminum canister that held some kind of electronic homing device and an inflatable sac to give it flotation. Kij's experts said that the rocket should now travel ten to eleven miles compared to the original two miles. The idea was for Garrett to drop his exposed rolls of film into the canister and launch them out to sea where a boat from the yacht could retrieve them.

"Purely insurance, Barbara."

Her resolve broke, cracked by feelings she could not define. "I don't want you to go."

His smile was kinder, compelling, but contrary to his words. "I have to go. It's the only way we'll convince the brass. Have you forgotten what it's like back there?"

The news reports of snow and rain in the U.S. had continued to be dismal. "I haven't forgotten."

Garrett leaned down and kissed her. Morris raised her arms to encircle his neck and pressed against him, but his ardor did not change.

It was still a good-bye kiss.

Garrett stood alongside Yakama, letting the deckhouse block the icy wind. The seas were rough, and the wind whipped the tops of whitecaps into frigid spray.

"Okay, Kij, I meet Kyboto ashore and he'll get me to the plane. You'll be off the Kamchatka coast the day after tomorrow."

"Yes. It must look as if we are on a continuous cruise for Anchorage, Brandon. We will be alert to radio transmissions along the way, but only in a span of three to four hours after dawn on the second day will we be in a position to recover your rocket pod."

"I know, Kij. I'll try to get the damned thing off the ground."

Garrett pulled his gloves on. "And Kij. Thanks."

"I have yet to do enough for you, Brandon. May the winds of fortune be at your back."

Garrett gripped his friend's shoulders in a hug, then turned to Barbara, whose eyes were red-puffed. From the wind, he told himself, and kissed her lightly.

The dinghy bobbed in the high waves, bouncing against the steel hull of the yacht. Garrett timed the crest of a wave, then dropped into the center of it. As it rose out of a trough, he lodged his feet against the stern motor mount and pulled the starting rope on the fifty-horsepower motor. It caught on the first try, echoing the preparation given it by the crew. Once it was idling, he turned back to receive the two packs lowered to him, then tied them down in the center of the dinghy with ribbon-like straps. A wave crashed over the bow, drenching the interior and sluicing off his slicker.

Immediately, the line that tethered him to the yacht was released, and the protective hull moved away. It was quickly gone in the foggy dawn. He twisted the grip, the motor roared a response, and he drifted the bow around toward the island of Hokkaido. Garrett's guide was the compass attached to his glove with a short chain.

The vista ahead evolved into whiteness that blended with the snow. The sea was an angry gray, and he could not trust his senses completely, but his familiarity with instrument flight allowed him faith in the brassbound compass.

Behind him was a swiftly departing Yakama and ahead lay a rocky beach. Also ahead was a possible patrol of the Japanese Defense Force that would not take kindly to his clandestine entry onto Japanese sovereign soil. He and Yakama had decided this way was best. It would not do to advertise his arrival in Japan by more conventional methods. Since he was a known intelligence officer, he would have picked up both friendly and unfriendly companions by entering through a harbor.

It took six minutes for Garrett to close in on the coast. He heard it first, the heavy crashing of waves on rock. The way the sound echoed back, he suspected he had found a shore with sheer cliffs.

The wave crests became higher, their faces more precipitous. The dinghy shot downward, crashed into the next wave, and shipped frigid water. Garrett retarded his throttle, trying to match the speed of the waves, and the bow slithered around.

He felt the rubber bottom scrape over rocks, ripping and tearing, before he saw the cliff wall. The propeller hit some obstruction, and the motor bucked forward. Throttling back, Garrett felt the vibration which indicated mortal damage to the prop.

Fine spray erupted around him, raining down.

Water splashed over the rubber sides and washed around in the bottom of the boat.

A line of foamy white told him where the water ended, twenty yards ahead. He tilted the motor for shallow running, then gunned it. The steering handle nearly vibrated out of his hand as the bent propeller rotated.

The bow followed a wave up onto a shallow ledge that had just become his destination. The ledge was ten feet wide and backed by a cliff that towered upward into the gloom of the fog. Coarse, heavy, salty spray cascaded from the shiny rock. It was not inviting, but it was all he had. The motor would not take him further.

Cutting the ignition as the bow bounced on the ledge, Garrett pulled at the slip knots holding his packs. The canvas straps were frozen by the cold spray, and they crackled as they broke loose. The surf pounded the shore in an ungodly din, and he fought his way forward though the water-filled dinghy. He heaved both packs shoreward just as a breaker slid underneath, raised the rubber boat high, and flung it against the cliff face. Garrett spilled out of it onto the granite ledge, taking a jolt against the back of his neck which starred his vision momentarily.

He shook his head, pulling himself upright as the dinghy was sucked back and thrown once again at the cliff. Scrambling, he caught both packs before they were washed away. On his knees, Garrett worked his way back to the cliff face. Footing was difficult on the salt-rimed ice covering the rock. His feet slipped out from under him, and he crashed to the ledge on his hip.

Holding the pack straps in his left hand, he looked to his right and left. Two routes were open to him. He could feel the sub-zero temperature biting at his face. There was an icy dampness inside his gloves. It was time to hurry, and he scrambled to his feet, then headed south.

It was rough hiking as he slipped on salt and ice, battered by the sea, but within a hundred yards he found a wide crevasse leading up. He followed it by lodging boots and hands against the side, levering upward, and eventually reaching the top of the thirty-foot cliff. A quarter mile inland, he found a copse of pine trees which sheltered him from the wind. He worked his way into the middle of the shrubbery and dropped to the pine-needled and snow-covered ground.

Garrett gave himself two minutes to rest, then unclipped the rain slicker and slid out of it. The loose foul-weather pants came off next. He exchanged the soaked gloves for a fresh, dry pair.

He buried the weather gear under a bush, shoving broken branches in on top of it.

Shedding the drag of the cumbersome storm clothing refreshed him, and he pulled up the hood of his anorak and started out in a southeasterly direction. The ground undulated under him, dangerous under a coating of three inches of snow. Two hours of steady hiking were required before he reached the road.

The going was much easier on the surface of the highway, and he reached the village just after eight in the morning. He found the man named Kyboto already waiting in a car idling next to the post office.

Ignoring introductions, Kyboto hustled him into his rusty 1957 Chevrolet sedan, and soon had them both squatting in front of an old, potbellied stove in a small hut outside the village. It was clean and warm, and Garrett appreciated that, although he detected the faint smell of urine in the air.

Garrett sipped at the hot spicy tea Kyboto prepared. It was good, and the warmth spread slowly into his cold limbs while he studied his host. The man was stocky and short with a smiling face and lank, black hair.

"How does it look, Mr. Kyboto?"

"Very good, Colonel, just as Mr. Yakama asked. I checked yesterday afternoon, and the aircraft has been examined and fueled. It was moved to a new place over near the operations building. A copy of your orders has already been posted in the operations log."

"Excellent."

"The weather report is not good, Colonel, but acceptable, according to my source at the base. And I have borrowed a taxi for tomorrow. From a friend."

Garrett was bothered by the weather, not in itself, for it might lend cover to his mission, but because he would be flying a strange jet aircraft in it. Any aircraft new to a pilot could be tricky as hell, and storm conditions were not the best to learn in.

"Very good. How about the equipment?"

Kyboto retrieved a cardboard box from the corner of the room.

The pressure suit looked large, but then Garrett was not planning on any maneuver that would create G-forces to be countered by the suit. The helmet was Air Force blue, with "Maj. R.S. Pillsman" stenciled across the front of it. An oxygen mask was clipped to it.

"How about the couplings, Mr. Kyboto? What do you know about them?"

"The couplings? Oh, yes. I have not seen for myself, but I understand that the oxygen and pressure suit couplings in the Russian airplane have been altered to fit those of American equipment. Also, the connections for the power cart have been adapted to start the engine."

"Mr. Kyboto, I am thankful for your help."

Garrett shoved his hand into his pocket, retrieved his roll of bills, picked through it, and held out a sheaf of fifties and hundreds.

Kyboto said, "It is taken care of."

"For your expenses then, and those of your friends."

"I cannot."

"Then a charity of your choice."

"That I can do." Kyboto accepted the money. "By the by, Colonel, they also said that there is a hydraulic leak in the landing gear extension mechanism. It is repaired, but may be inadequate."

"As long as they come up once, it will be

enough."

"I will see you at six o'clock in the morning."

The small man backed out of the hut, bowing once. Garrett returned the bow. Minutes later, he heard the old Chevrolet growl away.

After he left, Garrett checked the parachute harness, then unpacked the backpack, setting out the Air Force fatigues, bomber jacket, and peaked cap, all identified as belonging to Major Pillsman. He repacked his snow gear after setting aside cans of food, several packets of instant coffee and the copies of the Sukhoi flight manuals. He spent most of the day reading the manuals, interrupting his study by cooking a can of chili on the top of the stove and making instant coffee from time to time.

The manuals helped immensely to increase his confidence. Despite the Cyrillic lettering for gauges and warning devices, not much was different from aircraft he had flown before. The block letters of Barbara's printing made him think of her.

He was happy that she was in Kij's care and out of the line of fire.

Pictures of the cockpit interior aided him in identifying each instrument. He would constantly have to make calculations and translations for he found it difficult to think in metric equivalents.

Late in the evening, Garrett finally slipped the manuals into the stove and watched them burn.

He went over his papers. He had forged Pillsman identification in his wallet along with two pictures of a fictional family. The deceptive legend made him think of Harv and Connie Landers, Tad and Jay.

Garrett's throat constricted. He closed his eyes and went to sleep.

* * *

Nathan Petrie had been haunting the telephone of the man who had replaced Barbara Morris on the East Asian and Pacific desk. He did not know what else he could do.

Beech said, "We still have a Navy frigate in the area, and they have a radar contact on the *Eastern Orchid*'s position, Mr. Petrie, but there's nothing further to report."

"Where is it now?"

"It passed through the Tsugaru Strait early this morning and is now east of the Kuril Islands."

"On the way to . . ."

"Yes, sir. To Kamchatka. That's my best guess anyway."

"All right. Keep me posted."

Was that dumb son of a bitch going to try a water landing on the peninsula? Christ, he would be caught, sure as hell. And with Petrie's luck, that damned Morris woman would be captured along with him. And then there would be the trials, and the pointing fingers, and the resignations submitted.

Petrie would have to resign, of course. Morris was his employee, and an unwarranted invasion of Soviet territory by his executive assistant was unthinkable.

The Secretary would lose his job too. Guaranteed.

Christ! The careers Garrett would take with him. Danton. The Air Force Intelligence director. Maybe the Director of Central Intelligence. All good people who had a hell of a lot to contribute to the country.

Because Garrett thought he knew how to do it better. Bastard.

Petrie thought that what he ought to do was to get somebody from the Company to fly in there and sink that fucking yacht. That was what he ought to do.

Garrett sat in the back seat of an old yellow Toyota taxi as Kyboto drove them toward Hakodate Air Base. Beside him on the seat were his backpack, the elongated pack, the parachute, and his helmet. His pulse rate increased as they pulled up to the guardhouse at the gate.

A white-hatted military policeman saluted him sharply and he returned it with proper casualness while rolling down the window.

"Good morning, sir," said the Japanese policeman in excellent English.

"Good morning." His driver was completely ignored while Garrett produced his ID and a copy of the expertly forged orders, with the signature of some adjutant at Kimpo Air Base in Korea.

The soldier produced another salute. "Thank you, Major. You may proceed."

Garrett returned the salute, and the cab moved forward.

Ten minutes later, Kyboto wished him luck and abandoned him in front of the operations building. Garrett carried his gear into a large room with a long counter bisecting it. He presented his orders and a copy of the flight plan he had filled out to a small, crisp man.

The Japanese officer spoke a flat, unaccented English. "Oh, yes. Major Pillsman. We received your orders earlier, and the aircraft is prepared. What do they want with that old plane anyway, Major?"

"I'm damned if I know. Though I did hear something about testing the alloys in it, or something to that effect. Since I'd flown one before, they just

254

told me to get over here and pick it up. Has it been here long?"

Garrett was anxious to leave, but he did not want to appear as such to the conversationally minded Japanese operations officer.

"It was here when I transferred in, so that is at least nine months."

"Well, I hope it's in fairly decent shape."

"They put a good crew on it, Major. It should be fine." He slipped a paper across the counter.

Garrett pointed at a line at the bottom of the Japanese form. "Right here?"

"That is correct."

He signed Pillsman's name, then pushed the form back across the counter.

The officer ripped off a copy of the release he had just signed and gave it to him.

"Okay, Major. You're off at 0900 hours. The control tower will give you a green light. If they can find the green light. I don't believe they have worked with a non-radio-equipped aircraft in a long time."

The Sukhoi had radios, of course, but they were confined to frequencies utilized by Soviet Air Force authorities who did not want their pilots conversing with enemy aircraft and countries. The arrangement was fine with Garrett. He did not want to have any dialogue with air control once he was in the air.

"Thank you."

"And thank you, Major, for taking that piece of junk off our hands."

Finding a dressing room, Garrett shed his fatigues and pulled the pressure suit over his woolen underwear. He slipped into the blue bomber jacket and carried his belongings out onto the tarmac where the Maiden awaited him.

It was an ugly Maiden. The delta wing looked clumsy and the cone emerging from the gaping hole in the nose was halfway obscene. It was not armed but it had two drop tanks of fuel hanging from the fuselage below the wing. Several men scurried around it.

As he approached, the crew chief saluted him, and Garrett introduced himself.

Then the crew chief introduced him to the members of the crew, all of whom were justifiably proud of the work they had done. Garrett followed them around the airplane as they explained in inadequate translation just what hydraulic lines, mechanical components, and electrical faults had had to be fixed.

"As requested, Major Pillsman, we painted new identification numbers on the airplane. It will confuse the Soviets if they see the plane in flight."

Garrett had not known that Yakama had considered such details. It was the reason that Yakama was as good as he was.

"Very good, Sergeant. The engine runs well?"

"Exceptionally well, Major."

They completed the inspection, Garrett shed his jacket, and one of the crewmen helped him into his parachute. He climbed the ladder and reached back to take the paraphernalia handed to him. The cockpit would leave him little room for personal maneuvering once he was in the air, so he leaned the backpack and the rocket pack against the back of the front seat, but in the rear compartment. He secured them in place with one of several bungee straps he had brought with him. The flight jacket and his peaked cap he laid on the rear seat, and buckled in place with the seat harness.

Easing himself over the coaming, he settled into the seat. The crew chief climbed the ladder with his

256

helmet and helped strap him in, settled the helmet on his head, and connected the oxygen and pressure suit couplings.

"Are you ready, sir?"

"Let's light her up, Sergeant."

The chief signaled to his men on the ground, but stayed by Garrett's shoulder, watchful.

Garrett began to flip switches labeled neatly in Cyrillic characters.

A red glow behind the instruments told him he had aircraft electrical power. He found the altimeter where it was supposed to be and set the barometric pressure from the reading he had taken in operations. He nodded his head, and the crewmen latched their makeshift couplings from the portable starting unit into the jet's receptacle.

Garrett thumbed the toggle for fuel pump, then raised a red, metal protective flap, and closed the switch for the starter. He felt the turbine begin to turn, but nothing happened. Turning to look at the crew chief, he saw a puzzled look on the man's face.

Releasing the switch, he thought back over the checklist. He tried reversing two toggle switches and hit the starter again. Again there was no ignition. And again the sergeant's eyes narrowed.

Back to first base. He closed all toggles, flipping them back as he went mentally through the checklist. Maybe he should have kept the pirated manual. Ah, he had missed an ignition toggle.

He pushed it, raised the red flap, and turned the starter motor again. The reward was a whoosh, then the steady whine of the turbofan.

Testing each of his control surfaces quickly with rudder pedals and control stick, Garrett raised his right hand in an "okay" signal to the sergeant, who slipped down the ladder to the ground and removed the ladder.

He still eyed Garrett carefully.

The portable starting unit was disconnected and shoved back, and the chocks pulled from the wheels. Garrett was almost home.

He found the canopy control, and it whispered into place, cutting off the cold breeze and the flecks of snow. A rheostat knob was labeled "Heat," in Russian, and he turned it fully clockwise. He looked down to see if all the men had cleared away from the plane.

The sergeant had dug out his copy of Pillsman's orders and was carefully interpreting the English writing. Air Force abbreviations would slow him down, Garrett thought, but he began to worry that the sergeant had sensed that something was wrong.

Looking in his rearview mirror, Garrett saw that the crew chief had started toward the operations building.

Garrett released the brakes, and the Sukhoi wanted to roll without his applying throttle. He let it go, using a little jab of the right brake to line himself up with a yellow line on the wet, black asphalt.

In his mirror, he saw the crew chief now running toward the operations office.

Garrett remembered to turn on the wing deicers, which were electrically driven. He accomplished that as he followed the broken yellow line toward the taxiway, braking right to follow it for a quarter of a mile to the end of the runway. The left brake turned him toward the runway, where he stopped, looking directly at two F-4 Phantoms dressed in Japanese insignia perched side by side, awaiting takeoff instructions.

Hillocks of plowed snow rose on the other side of the runway, backgrounding the F-4's.

He appreciated the sleek look of the Phantoms, feeling clumsy in the delta-winged Su-9U. The F-4's had a full load of rockets, and the Japanese pilots looked over at him and waved. He waved back.

Then they were gone, trailing a dark wisp of kerosene vapor.

Garrett swung his helmet left and right, saw no incoming aircraft, and released the brakes. The plane eased to the center of the runway, and he aligned it with the center stripe. He held the brakes down and looked to the control tower. He found the flap control and gave himself twenty degrees.

A green flash.

Running the throttle forward, he released the brakes, and the plane began to roll. He had just converted his airspeed to forty-five miles per hour when he saw the quick flash of red at the tower window.

It was Morse code, flashing, "S-T-O-P."

There was either an emergency on the field, or the crew chief had convinced someone that his orders should be further examined. A quick scan of the skies revealed only the F-4's climbing and spiraling away to the east.

The plane was still gathering speed, so he ignored the signal to stop. At the far end of the runway, two miles ahead, there was a flurry of activity and blinking red lights. They were blocking the runway with emergency equipment and fire trucks.

"Oh, shit!"

He shoved the throttle full forward and engaged the afterburner.

Garrett was slapped back in his seat as the Lyulka turbojet, with the afterburner engaged, whipped out 19,000 pounds of thrust. Using the afterburner would be suspicious, but all he wanted now was to get airborne.

In seconds, he was abreast of the control tower. The signal light was still winking red at him in his peripheral vision. He ignored it and concentrated on using the rudder against a slight crosswind in order to keep the white line centered under the nose.

His side vision began to blur.

He would never know if there had been a real emergency, for the afterburner gave him the required airspeed in a half mile, far short of the blocking vehicles at the end of the runway. The plane felt light, the control stick delicate. The Sukhoi bounced slightly, yawing from side to side, and he was promptly uneasy with the strange airplane. Easing the stick back gently, he watched the airspeed which, in kilometers per hour, told him he was way over what he needed for lightweight take-off. The nose rotated upward, he centered the stick, and he had an amazing quarter mile of altitude as he passed over the red emergency trucks.

It was definitely not a Cessna.

He retracted the flaps.

Pulling back on the throttle, he killed the afterburner, and then worked the lever which retracted the landing gear. Metallic clunks, three green lights, and an immediate increase in airspeed told him the hydraulic system had lasted long enough to get the gear up.

It might not matter if the gear ever came down again.

Nineteen

Petrie looked around Garrett's office, then rummaged through the drawers of his desk, observed from the doorway by a disapproving Agatha Nelson.

"You haven't seen a stack of photographs anywhere, Mrs. Nelson?"

"No, sir."

She was not going to volunteer much, Petrie thought, but then his mission in Garrett's office was not to seek information from her. Rather, he was going to provide her with data.

"Is there anywhere else he might have kept something confidential?"

"There is a safe in the credenza behind you, Mr. Petrie, but I don't know the combination."

It's just as damned well, Petrie thought.

"Damn! You suppose General Danton knows how to get into it?"

"I don't know, sir. Is it important?"

"Quite."

Beech had called Petrie less than twenty minutes before, catching him in his limousine en route into the District. His message was that Garrett had probably stolen a Soviet jet from Hakodate Air Base. The Japanese Defense Force had two combat aircraft looking for it. No, they would not shoot it down without a direct request from the President.

Petrie was certainly not going to the President, or even the Secretary, for this.

Instead, he went to Aggie Nelson.

"I'm afraid Colonel Garrett has stolen himself a Soviet jet airplane and is going to attack Kamchatka Air Base."

"No!"

"I needed those photos to help pinpoint it. I'll just have to try the Photo Center."

Petrie gave her a grim look and strode out of the office, leaving the blue-gray-haired secretary in not much of a quandary—he hoped.

If he could not do it, and the Japanese could not do it, maybe the Soviets would shoot Garrett down before he had a chance to screw up every international pact they were working on.

Within ten minutes Grigori Zanov had the information from the source within Air Force Intelligence, routed through Boston.

The source confirmed several other messages Moscow Center had received from assets in Japan. They reported a great deal of consternation and confusion at Hakodate Air Base, but offered no rationale and no details as yet.

This Garrett was proving to be quite resilient and resourceful, Zanov thought. He had come up against the mysterious and deadly Alexandre and left the field victorious. He had gone wading through the airport in New Delhi, beaching yet two more of the KGB's whales.

Resourceful.

Garrett now commanded a Soviet interceptor which, as far as Zanov was aware, no one in the

Red Air Force wanted to admit was even missing, and he intended to enter the *rodina*'s air space and assault Kamchatka Air Base.

The target was Petrovsky's highly secret project, of course.

If he did not act quickly to alert the Coastal Defense Forces, Zanov knew that the tough American might actually penetrate Soviet borders and drop a bomb or some other lethal material on the secret project, perhaps killing Petrovsky and discrediting him.

Zanov shifted in his chair, a jolt of pain in his leg leaving him white-faced except for the purple slash across his cheek.

He leaned over to his right and fed the message into the paper-shredder.

Malenkov entered the main laboratory and shrugged out of his greatcoat. He tossed it on a chair beside the door and threw his fur cap on top of it.

Professor Polodka approached him. His eyes were red and his face drooped like that of a bloodhound.

"Come, Comrade Polodka, let us talk."

The two walked over to a desk at the side of the huge room and Polodka collapsed tiredly into a chair. Malenkov leaned back against the edge of the desk.

"Colonel, you have got to let these men have a rest. The pressures lately have been tremendous."

Malenkov was aware that he had been unrelenting in his pursuit of a formula that would eliminate the radiation by-product, just as he had been simultaneously forcing increased production of the spheres. Increasingly, he had come to realize that

263

his only salvation lay in proving to the General Secretary and the KGB Chairman that the apparatus could successfully paralyze the West. He considered it his duty to protect his staff, and his command, from consequences they knew nothing about. None of these civilians were aware of the precipice upon which they stood. Their, and his, proximity to death at the hands of an efficient Boris Petrovsky was very real to him, if not to them.

He ignored Polodka's concern and asked, "Have the spheres been prepared for tomorrow's flight?"

"Ten of them. The last two will be ready in time, Colonel Malenkov."

If he were following the orders of Moscow, utilizing eight modules on each flight, rather than the twelve in the original schedule, the pressure on the project personnel would not be as great. However, Malenkov was terrified by the prospect that a reduction in the number of modules, combined with the reduced number of flights, would allow North American weather to improve.

"We are moving much too slowly on this, Comrade Polodka. Already, there has been a twenty-five-percent reduction in the number of flights. A quarter of your workload has dissipated."

"But with each series, Colonel, we are trying to test new crystalline formations. The men are doing two jobs at once."

"And what of progress on the RR-324 crystals?"

"None. In fact, there has been an increase in radiation effect in the atmospheric pressure chamber testing. I still insist that we be allowed to work on the key component. The source of our problem must be there."

"And I have told you that it is not."

"Could we at least follow the spheres in another aircraft and sample the atmosphere after ignition? Perhaps that would be helpful."

"Impossible. Keep in mind, Professor, that we have only three and a half months to go. The rewards for our efforts now will then begin to flow. And most copiously."

"And we will get to go home?"

"I have been given that assurance," Malenkov told him.

He marched across the laboratory, feeling the hostile stares of the scientists following him like the wake of a large boat.

Once in the sanctuary of his private lab, Malenkov settled himself on the stool at his workbench. He could feel the fatigue threatening to envelop him. He knew exactly what the scientists were going through, though he himself did not complain.

Additionally, it was he who must carry the burden of worry about the potential end of the project.

Petrovsky seemed edgier and angrier with each passing hour. Where was the spy Garrett? Why was he not yet captured, or killed, so that Petrovsky would not explode? Just like the spheres in the jet stream. Malenkov was becoming as eager as his security officer to hear that Garrett was dead, his mouth silenced.

Malenkov rubbed his eyes and looked at the rack of completed key component packages at the side of the lab. Eight of them. He must assemble another four before flight time.

And Polodka thought he and his scientists were overworked? It was extremely selfish of them, Malenkov thought.

* * *

The temptation was to climb into the cover of the overcast sky, but Garrett resisted it. A passage through the clouds might make him feel invisible, but would be clearly visible to both ground radar and the airborne radar of the Phantoms. His minimum altitude over land was supposed to be 1,000 feet, but he dropped under that as soon as he cleared the air field.

For awhile, he did follow his filed flight plan to Kimpo Air Base, crossing a series of small farms whose inhabitants looked up from their snow-covered yards to stare at the strange-looking airplane. When Hakodate was well behind him, he drifted into a northwesterly heading and watched the washed blue of the sea coming up quickly. To his left he could see a small village that must be Esashi. The landscape looked like a miniature Japanese garden finished in white.

Then he was over water. The slate-colored angry seas were not the kind he would want to go down in. Life expectancy would be under five minutes. He held course for two minutes and then banked right to a heading of ten degrees.

The airspeed indicator showed 900 kilometers per hour, and he eased the throttle forward until it registered 1,100 kilometers per hour. He calculated that that was about 700 miles per hour, or Mach .9. At sea level, the Maiden was rated for 720 miles per hour, just under the speed of sound. According to the manuals, it would do Mach 1.8, 1,200 miles per hour, in thinner atmosphere, without armament or drop tanks. However, Garrett was not planning for that altitude, and he was not in the least excited about breaking the sonic barrier.

Fuel consumption at that altitude was breathtaking, but he had calculated that, with the full drop tanks, he should have more than enough for his purposes.

He was more interested in keeping it level and on the course he had plotted earlier. Hopefully, Hakodate Air Control had seen him going toward Korea and had passed the flight off as legitimate. He was pretty certain that was a vain hope. They had attempted to block his takeoff, and he must keep watch for any hunters.

After three minutes, he rolled into a new heading of eighty degrees to cut across the northern half of Hokkaido Island, into the Sea of Okhotsk, avoiding the Soviet island of Sakhalin to the north.

The Japanese island appeared ahead of him, the hills looming up quickly, and Garrett climbed to 700 feet as he crossed the beaches. That was within radar visibility, but he was certain the hills would create enough ground-clutter feedback in a radarscope that he would go undetected. The island was fifty miles wide here, and the jet passed over it in six minutes. As soon as he reached the sea, he turned to forty-five degrees and lost altitude to a hundred feet over the whitecaps.

Garrett found the flashing waves under him mesmerizing and kept his eyes focused on longer distances. He searched the sky overhead to avoid the self-hypnosis. There were breaks in the low cloud cover, but not many of them. He spotted the low silhouettes of the Kuril Islands off to the front starboard side.

From a pocket in the leg of his G-suit, he pulled an aeronautical chart and stuck it behind an electrical conduit that ran alongside the cockpit. He checked his watch. Twenty-five minutes out of Hakodate. Would they have given up on him or was the alarm spreading?

For the duration of his flight, Barbara would be monitoring Soviet and Japanese military transmissions on Kij's elaborate radios. Garrett turned on the Sukhoi's radios and spun the selector to the frequency on which she would try to contact him on if she discovered that the course of his flight had been detected.

He retrieved the chart and drew a rough line for his present course. When he looked up, he saw two thin shadows shimmering through the overcast high above.

The F-4's.

They were moving across his course, and he could not tell if they were looking for him. Against the sea in the overcast and light snow, he might well go undetected in the radar feedback caused by the high seas, but he turned obliquely to their rear. As soon as the Kurils looked to be too close, he returned to his original heading.

The Phantoms continued their northwestern course, and were soon out of his sight.

The heater, if it worked at all, was highly inefficient. He fiddled with the knob, turning it both ways, but made no noticeable change in the cockpit temperature. It was close to freezing, he estimated.

When he had not seen the Phantoms for awhile, he turned back to due north. He would hold that course for some time before turning east to cross over the peninsula from the western side. The air base and most of the Soviet radar installations were on the east coast of the peninsula, while the western coast was relatively deserted. There were mountain peaks in the 15,000-foot range to serve as his landmarks since he was not plotting windage. He did not know the effect of wind on this particular jet aircraft.

Garrett's experience in jets was limited to the T-38A Talon trainer and to a couple of varieties of corporate jet. He had access to, and kept up his rating on, Air Force Intelligence's modified Lears.

An hour into the flight, Garrett became more comfortable with the low altitude. The conditions had remained the same: low clouds above and gray sea below. There was minor precipitation. There was no icing.

He had seen a few fishing boats and a dozen freighters. None of them apparently saw him, or at least paid much attention to him.

He recalled his flight to Aspen. He thought about Harv and Connie.

Memories were not good at this point in his flight, so he eluded them by action.

He rigged his homemade automatic pilot. From the pocket on his left leg, he extracted his last two bungee straps and a rolled piece of coat-hanger wire.

Once the rudder was trimmed in, the plane maintained a straight course with his feet removed from the pedals. The control stick was another matter. It tended to flop about. He locked it between his knees and clicked the hook of a bungee strap over an electrical conduit on each side of the cockpit. The other ends of the straps fastened to the stick and kept it centered, preventing the aircraft from going into a bank. Uncoiling the wire, he fashioned a brace from the adjustment knob on the altimeter to the stick. That would prevent any changes in the nose-up or -down attitude.

When the Rube Goldberg apparatus satisfied him, he laid the wire on top of the instrument panel, and let the straps hang at the sides of the cockpit. He checked his chart and his watch and turned to ninety degrees. He had seen no sign of land in the past hour.

Seventeen minutes later, he saw the coast of the peninsula. It was a rugged, rocky shoreline, edged with scrawny green trees against gray rocks, and backed by white and brown hills. Beyond the coast, thick forests clogged the hillsides. Slightly to port, he could see the hazy outline of a high peak.

"That's got to be Klyuchevskaya Sopha," he said aloud, wrapping his tongue around the name.

The air base would be directly beyond the peak. He decided to skirt the mountain to the south.

He crossed the coast at a hundred feet of altitude, spying a small group of huts in the trees, but no inhabitants. The topography rose quickly, and he climbed to 500 feet, losing airspeed. Still, the elevation rose faster than he anticipated, and a rocky outcrop appeared just ahead. Garrett rolled the plane onto its side, still climbing, and pulled away from it. He could hear the intake and exhaust of his own breath in the confines of his helmet.

Garrett decided the speed was too great for his reaction time at this altitude in unfamiliar territory, and he reduced his throttle until he had the metric equivalent of 500 miles per hour.

For several minutes, he kept his eyes trained intently on the mountainous terrain. The Sukhoi continually rose above cliffs, swinging left and right, always climbing. When he took a quick glance at his panel, he was amazed at the reading of 9,000 feet.

Garrett felt minuscule in the middle of all that grand and deserted splendor.

He reached his high point of 12,000 feet in

eighteen minutes. To port, he could see the towering peak of Klyuchevskaya Sopha still another 3,500 feet above him. Over land, the cloud cover had thinned considerably. The overcast became a blue haze, and the sun reflected blindingly off the snowy peak. Below, he saw his shadow racing across gully and trench and sheer cliff face. Off to each horizon stretched rugged, massive cliffs, and below timberline were the thickest pine forests he could ever remember seeing. It was stunning in its primitive, unspoiled beauty.

Damn, he thought. The Soviets have something even they have not spoiled.

Another high peak rose in front of him, and he banked left, beginning to follow the lowering terrain downward and to parallel the eastern coast, traveling northward. He had not yet seen another aircraft.

Ten minutes passed, and he could see the eastern coastline with the Bering Sea beyond. A dark smoggish haze marred the concrete sky. He watched it coming up and determined that it must be Ust-Kamchatsk. The air base would be eight miles inland, at about 1,600 feet of elevation. His altitude was 2,000 feet, and Garrett estimated he was about two hundred feet above the forested terrain. It looked much rougher, and much more intimidating, than he had anticipated.

Then he saw a helicopter in the far distance. It was apparently landing, for it dropped out of sight as he made a quick turn toward the sea. The chopper may have been four or five miles north of him, but it was difficult to tell in the strange geography. His depth perception felt like it was out of whack.

He would not risk detection by getting too close to the base. Coasting down toward the

271

shoreline, examining the ground, and slowly bleeding off speed, Garrett discovered a narrow plateau of softly undulating ground just before he reached the coast. He passed out to sea by about two miles, then rolled the plane back inland. Slowing to 250 miles per hour, Garrett engaged his wire-and-bungee-strap automatic pilot.

Stretching his stiff back muscles, Garrett got a hand over the back of his seat, released the retaining strap, and hauled his two packs into the front of the cockpit with him. The space available was limited, and the rocket pack nearly did not make the transition. Placing both packs on his lap, so that the D-rings sewn into their harnesses were adjacent, he snapped the hook of the drop cord affixed to his parachute harness to both D-rings.

Digging into a leg pocket, he found his gloves and pulled them on.

He craned his head around the packs and checked the terrain and the instrument panel.

Air speed 250. Altitude 1,200, about 600 feet above the plateau. It was too damned low, but he was going to do it anyway.

He switched the fuel feed from the drop tanks to the wing tanks.

The foothills were coming up fast.

He dropped his hand on the orange handle next to the armrest.

Canopy jettison. Pull!

There was a crushing change in the pressure as the front of the canopy lifted with a mild explosion, then caught the wind stream, and was sucked away. The wind whipped at his face. He had not pulled the Plexiglas visor down. It was bitterly cold, and the wind screamed. He grabbed at the visor with his left hand and nearly lost the packs.

His oxygen mask was not secured. Fuck it.

Pull the red handle.

In the wind shriek, the explosion of the ejection charge was muffled. The seat bucked, tearing at his spine, and he locked his wrists around the packs. There was a tremendous downward pressure and dizziness as he tumbled over backward.

A flash of silver, and the airplane was gone.

One thousand one.

Wind horrendous in the bottom edges of the helmet. Mouth hurts—slapped by oxygen mask, now gone.

One thousand two.

Sky-mountain-green-blue-white.

One thousand three.

Seat is slowing, riding air, wind scream dying.

One thousand four.

At five, the seat did not separate, and Garrett panicked. He searched for the belt release, but then the seat was suddenly loose on its own. Kicking it away, he counted again and saw trees and snowy earth rushing at him. Too soon. Too fast.

He released his right hand from his left wrist, letting go of the packs, pulled the rip cord, then quickly rejoined his hands around the packs.

The parachute casing popped, and the drogue chute streamed the fabric out behind him. Air filled the canopy with a loud crack, and the sudden deceleration nearly tore the packs from his grasp.

Garrett swung slowly, like a flexible pendulum. The sensation had been nearly forgotten in the twelve years since his last jump. He looked down. The chute had opened none too soon.

Paying out the twenty feet of his drop cord, he

lowered the packs beneath him. They reached toward the peak of a tall pine tree, and he grabbed the shrouds, dumped air, and sideslipped the tree. The packs dropped into deep snow, and Garrett followed them, knees bent for a classic landing, but the canopy caught in the branches of the pine, slowing him, and he landed softly in two feet of powdered snow.

He stood knee-deep in the snow, surveying his perimeter, and took a deep breath.

The air was fresh and frigid and carried the unexpected aroma of pine. It was deathly quiet, with just a hum of wind in the high branches. He unbuckled the harness and stepped out of it. Quickly, he began to pull in the shrouds and fabric, and when he had it bundled in his arms, he hauled it thirty feet to a stand of tall pine trees.

He had the canopy and harness nearly buried under pine branches and snow when he heard the distant *whoomph!* of explosion. He hoped the wreckage would spread wide and that the full wing tanks had ignited. Heavy destruction would hamper rapid identification.

A helicopter search pattern seeking an ejected pilot would be his first clue that the wreckage had been discovered, and he planned to be miles away by then.

Under the protection of a grandfather pine, Garrett changed to snow pants, wool shirt, thermal boots, parka, web belt, woolen stocking cap, and mittens.

He checked the condition of his backpack. The bedroll and tent were in the bottom with extra socks and mittens, several Sterno cans, a cup, and packages of dehydrated food. The portable radio seemed to be working, though he picked up no transmissions, and would not test its transmit mode. He stripped the foam rubber from the Nikon camera and the telephoto lens. The lens went into his pocket with the rolls of 35-millimeter film. He hung the camera over his neck along with the 7 x 50 binoculars. There was a silencer for the PPK and a Starscope which he shoved into his right parka pocket.

He tied the single tubular pack containing the rocket to the side of the backpack.

Lastly, he assembled the M-16 assault rifle, slapped one thirty-round magazine into it, and hooked the other two magazines onto the web belt. When he stood up, his pockets bulged, but the pack was considerably lighter, and everything, including the rocket and launcher, weighed under forty pounds.

It was extremely rough country, and several times, he had to backtrack and attempt a different route. When he found a small creek whose frozen bed led him to the east, down to the lower side of the plateau, he followed it for awhile, then struck north again. There were frequent slips in deep snow, falls on hidden rocks, detours around cliff faces, hand-and-foot struggles up tree-stumped slopes, jarring runs down the other side.

Garrett did not stop often to rest because that invited thinking, and he did not want to think about how his mission was almost over.

Twenty

Major Stalintayev, in charge of Flight Operations, was nervous on the telephone. General Belushkin told him, "Repeat that, please, Comrade Major."

"It was perhaps twenty minutes ago. A report from a logging camp. He suspected an aircraft, since he saw one flying in the area."

"Do we have aircraft aloft?"

"Yes, Comrade General. A flight of MiG-23's, in training. There are five helicopters. Also, there is one tanker aircraft for the training flight. All of our aircraft are accounted for."

"And were we to expect a flight arriving from another base, Comrade Major?"

"No, General."

Belushkin thought for only a moment. "Dispatch two MiG-24's to search the area. Let me know immediately if they find anything."

"Yes, Comrade General." The operations officer hesitated, then asked, "Am I to notify Colonel Malenkov or Major Petrovsky?"

"All we have at the moment is an unconfirmed report. I see no reason to alarm those at the compound."

* * *

At Eaglefeather's request, Major Clarence Swallow was conducting real-time surveillance of the Kamchatka Peninsula. It was close to real time anyway. With the signal relays between the KH-11 satellite and two communications satellites, he had the pictures on his screen within seven minutes of the event.

They were infrared pictures. The haze and the cloud cover along the peninsula coastlines prevented the use of more normal visual representation. The screen was mostly blue, a deep blue in the cold reaches of the land mass. The coastline was almost indistinguishable because it merged with the frigid waters of the Sea of Okhotsk on the west and the Bering Sea and Pacific Ocean on the east. Tiny villages along the coast, depicted in light orange, helped to define the shoreline, as did coastal shipping. Darker red spots, the centers of more populated and warmer areas, helped him to identify the air base and Ust-Kamchatsk midway down the peninsula and Petropavlovsk-Kamchatski closer to the southern tip. Aircraft flying out of the air base left hot trails on his screen. They had been there all morning, and the patterns suggested typical training exercises.

When Eaglefeather called him with the news out of Japan about the stolen Soviet jet, Swallow had arranged coordination with the Jet Propulsion Laboratory in Pasadena, set up the communication links on Argus satellites, programmed the KH-11, and then focused his attention on the areas north of the Japanese Islands.

He was pretty certain when he saw on his screen the lone streak crossing the Sea of Okhotsk. As soon as it penetrated the western coast, he called Eaglefeather and kept him on the line, describing the flight across the peninsula.

"It's got to be Garrett," Swallow said.

"I'm sure it—"

"Son of a bitch! Flame-out. I lost it. He went down."

"Ah, shit!" Eaglefeather exclaimed.

Half an hour went by, the minutes dragging. Swallow studied the screen, looking for anything. Eaglefeather talked to him about nothing, just to be talking.

Then he had action again.

"Here we go, Tom."

"What is it?"

"It'll be a while before I've got definition, but I'd bet on an air search. I've got two aircraft departing Kamchatka Air Base. Hold on."

Swallow entered the comparison command into his keyboard, and the computer read the infrared signatures emanating from the two aircraft, then searched the memory banks for similar signatures. He had the answer in less than a minute.

"They're both Mi-24 Hind helicopters."

"You suppose that's good or bad?" Eaglefeather asked.

"That's the hell of it. I don't know. You'd better see if the National Security Agency is trapping any voice traffic out of the air base."

Lieutenant General Merlin Danton figured he had waited as long as he could wait.

He had the information from Swallow at NPIC that Eaglefeather had given him.

He had confirmation from the NSA listeners at Fort Meade that Kamchatka Air Base was conducting an intensive air search five to six miles south of the base.

Pressing the intercom button, he told Donna,

"See if you can find the Director for me, will you?"

Danton waited for the phone line to wink at him. He found he had been thinking about the two Hind helicopters. The phone buzzed, and he picked up the receiver.

"What you got, Merle?"

"You're not going to like it."

"Shit."

"From the data I've got coming in just now, we may have Garrett down on the Kamchatka Peninsula in a stolen Soviet aircraft."

There was a very long pause on the Director's end of the line. "You are shitting me, aren't you Merle?"

"No, General, I'm not."

"What did you know about it, and when?"

Danton told him.

"You let him take leave, knowing he might do this?"

"Yes."

"You really do buy into this weather-alteration crap then?"

"Yes, I do," Danton said.

There was another long pause. "This is going to be politically sensitive. The State Department is going to come unhinged."

"They'll talk it to death," Danton said. "They won't do anything about it."

"Until the Soviets raise hell," the Director said.

"If whatever is in that compound is what Garrett thinks it is, they may not say a word. They may scramble to get it buried."

"That's hopeful thinking. As long as we're hoping, Merle, can we hope that Garrett was killed in the crash?"

"I wouldn't count on it."

"Well then, we'll just have to back him all the way."

"That would be my recommendation," Danton said.

Two helicopters streaked southward, bypassing him by several miles. The direction they came from identified his objective, and Garrett made a quarter-mile shift to the west across a small canyon, climbed a slope, and then the base was before him, spread all over the plateau.

In the last mile, Garrett estimated he had climbed about five hundred feet. The perimeter of the air base began close to the edge of the plateau. He was in shallow foothills that rose above the base. The wind on the treeless plateau was stiffer, and the snow had been blown into drifts against outcroppings. There were a lot of bare spots, showing hard gray earth and stubblefields of weeds.

Conscious of his footprints leaving a path in the snow, Garrett found a trail along a ridge running parallel to the southern boundary of the base and traversed further to the west, stepping on fallen logs, weed patches, and rocks. Looking back, he could not pick out any mark of his passage.

When he was almost directly in line with the main runways, Garrett found a niche in a tumble of giant boulders backed by stately fifty-foot pine trees. He dropped his packs on the ground, flexed his shoulders in relief, and crawled up on a boulder with his binoculars.

He had a slight elevation over the base. The landscape to east and west, as well as behind him, was heavily forested, but thinned quickly, with low tree stumps where the timber had been felled. Nature was not allowed too close to the boundary of the air base. With the binoculars, he could see the single chain-link fence with a snow-packed road just inside it. The compound, with its two fences, was in line with his position. The picture in the darkening field of the binoculars was the fulfillment of his expectation from the satellite photos.

At the compound, there were two guard shacks, one by each of the gates, and he could see very little movement within the compound itself. The inhabitants were staying out of the cold.

He slid down from the rock.

His march had kept him warm, but inaction now was making him aware of the penetrating cold. He decided that his current location was hidden from eyes within the air base, as well as from above, and he quickly erected the one-man tent and shoved his packs and the bedroll inside it. The site was protected by rocks, trees, and overhanging boughs, but after he crawled inside the claustrophobic space of the tiny tent, he was bothered by his inability to see outside. The gathering darkness would help.

Garrett unrolled the sleeping bag and sat cross-legged on it. Inside the tent, out of the wind, he felt a degree or two warmer. He dug in the pack for two Sterno cans and two wire racks. Lighting the cans, he set them on the nylon floor of the tent, set the racks over them, then stuck his head and arm outside the tent to scoop up a cupful of snow. He put the cup of snow on one of the racks and waited for the crystals to melt.

The soft blue flames enhanced the feeling of warmth, and Garrett cupped his bare hands near the flame. Pinpricks of pain accompanied the heat.

After ten minutes, he added instant coffee to the cup, not waiting to see if it would boil, and drank it down. The lukewarm coffee was absolutely delicious, and the warmth spread through him.

He started another cup of water while opening a can of beans and franks and setting it on the other rack to cook. The result tasted so good, he had another can of beans and chased them with four biscuits.

He extinguished the flames after completing his dinner and crawled outside to resume his position on top of the rock, now shrouded in inky darkness.

The lights of the base provided ambient light for the Starscope. He used it to seek out a path to the perimeter fence, selecting finally a small copse of stunted pine trees as his last rest stop before attempting the fence. The dwarf trees were opposite a shallow gulley that passed under the fence, then through a steel culvert under the perimeter road.

Having selected his route, Garrett returned to the tent, slid into the sleeping bag, and worked it up around him. It was primarily for warmth for he knew he would be unable to sleep in the next few hours.

Boris Petrovsky had had a cold veal chop for his dinner, and it was riding uneasily in a sea of vodka as he sat in a straight chair pulled up to the glowing stove. His boots were off, and his feet rested on another chair. He had been watching all of the lights and activity near the operations building for several hours. When he heard yet another helicopter pass overhead, his patience snapped, and he went to the switchboard and plugged into an outside line. It took someone in operations a long time to find an authority figure.

"Major Stalintayev."

"Major Stalintayev, what is going on over there?"

The operations officer responded slowly enough, and with enough unease riding in his voice, to start the old tingle of suspicion rising from the base of Petrovsky's spine.

"We have an aircraft down, Comrade Major."

"I see. What kind of plane?"

"It is a training craft."

"Casualties?"

"We don't know yet. The pilot appears to have ejected. We're starting a search for him now."

Petrovsky thanked him and started to hang up, when another question came to mind. "This was one of your aircraft, Major? From here?"

"Oh, no, Major! It is not. We're trying to locate the home base now."

Petrovsky slammed the phone down, pulled his boots on, took his coat, and stomped out into the night. He took Malenkov's Volga and raced his way impatiently through the two checkpoints. He parked in front of the aircraft operations office seven minutes later.

When he entered the warm office, the base commander was speaking with the operations officer, and both appeared nervous.

"What have you got, Major?" Petrovsky ignored the commander.

Still, the general responded. "There has been a crash of a flight trainer. Do you suppose that is a concern of yours?"

"When did it happen?" He continued to address Stalintayev.

The operations officer looked to his commander, but was not brave enough to ignore the man whom he knew to carry much influence in the KGB. "We had a report at one-thirty. We suspect the crash occured around one o'clock, and we did not find the wreckage until after three o'clock."

"But no pilot?"

"Not yet, Comrade Major. We still have helicopters searching the area. We found no aircraft seat at the site, and must assume the pilot ejected, perhaps many minutes and many miles away from the crash."

"What about radio contact? There was no emergency radio message from the plane?"

"None."

"Tell me why Kamchatka Control did not know about this airplane."

"We do not know. We are trying to determine which bases in the region might be missing an aircraft."

"Major, do you remember receiving a specific order from me last September regarding notification of unusual circumstances?"

The officer came slowly to an erect position, followed by the general. "Uh, yes, Comrade Major."

"Is an aircraft crash a normal occurrence?"

"No, Major, it is not."

"Then I find that you have erred in not informing me of this incident some five hours ago. You may halt your query as to the origin of the aircraft. It came from the West—Korea, Japan. The source is no longer important. What is important, and hear me carefully, General Belushkin, is that you locate the pilot quickly. That he survived the crash is not to be doubted. That he will avoid rescue may also be considered beyond doubt."

He waited while the general's face turned a sickly green, then added, "I want every available aircraft airborne, and every available soldier placed on ground search. You may airlift ground personnel to a spot near the crash site, spread them out, and march them back toward the base."

The general interrupted him. "Colonel, that is very difficult terrain. . . ."

"Everything would have been less difficult had I been notified of this five hours ago. Those are the current orders, General. Need I have the General Secretary confirm them for you?"

The air base commander strangled on his own voice. "No, Major."

Petrovsky returned to the car. It had begun.

Malenkov had also been aware of the extraordinary activity across the field, and he had seen Petrovsky leave in the Volga. The insolent bastard always took it without permission.

He had stayed in his quarters, frequently rising from the worn armchair to replenish his glass and to look out the window for Petrovsky's return. Something alarming was taking place, and he wanted to know just what it was.

When the Volga finally returned to the compound, Malenkov slipped on his coat and hat and walked to the headquarters building. Petrovsky was picking up the phone, but replaced it when the commander entered.

"Something has happened?" Malenkov asked.

"Why, yes, Colonel. Our spy has arrived."

285

"Ah. He has been caught."

"No. But it will not be long now."

Petrovksy picked up the phone. "If you will excuse me, Comrade Colonel, I must make a call."

To find out if the project is to be terminated? Malenkov went into his own office and settled into his desk chair. There it was: the end. The spy, this Garrett, had made it, and the General Secretary would have no choice but to bury any evidence of the project.

He could feel the fear welling up in him, a black wave rising to tidal proportions. Only the appearance of the corporal with a cup of hot tea held his fear in check.

Options. A good scientist always has options available, a new method for examining theory and evidence. Alternatives. He must think it out fully, and be prepared for—

The telephone rang in the outer office, and he heard Marienkov speak to Petrovsky. "Comrade Major, the fuel tankers are now ready at the fuel depot. They would like to know when to proceed."

"As is normal, Corporal." Petrovsky's voice was reassuring. "We proceed as is normal."

Malenkov sighed deeply. It was a little reassurance for the project commander. With Garrett soon to be a prisoner, there might yet be a bright day ahead.

Snowblind

Twenty-One

The bridge of the *Eastern Orchid* was richly spartan. There were four padded leather chairs bolted to the deck behind the helm centered on the forward bulkhead. The bulkheads were inlaid with teak and the deck covered with a durable brown carpet. Large windows provided views to either side as well as forward, above the rows of instruments which displayed the operating conditions of the Mercedes diesels.

Morris had seen an occasional glimpse of faraway mountains to the north, rising out of the sea like monoliths, and soon obliterated by clouds. Since four-thirty, the windows had become opaque.

Their eyes and ears had necessarily become electronic.

Just behind the bridge was a full-width cabin containing almost all of the yacht's electronic gear—major computer, sonar, Loran, radar consoles, and the massive radios for voice, satellite navigation, code, and telex communications.

Since Garrett had slipped off the yacht, Morris had remained close to the bridge so she would be among the first to know of changes in his status. She had scanned the frequencies, and a yellow pad beside the desk microphone listed the frequencies with military importance — radar installations, the air base at Kamchatka, an airport at Petropavlovsk-Kamchatski on the southern tip of the peninsula. She had heard only guttural Russian, most of it short aviators' phrases, but nothing to suggest that Brandon's entry into Soviet airspace had been detected until just recently.

Yakama went quietly about his business, content to have his crew inform him of developments.

There had been two developments.

The first was a coded message from Hokkaido informing them that the search for the Sukhoi by Japanese authorities had been abandoned.

Then Soviet communications had become frenetic. Morris had difficulty translating so many voices at once. She had called the yacht's owner to the bridge, and Yakama had explained the patterns to her. He'd suggested that the airplane had crashed as planned, and that the Red Air Force had launched the expected search for it.

So far, so good, he had said.

She did not think it was good.

In the last few hours, though, the number of blips on the radarscope had increased tremendously. The Filipino radar operator observed that the whole of Kamchatka Air Base appeared involved in the search.

That was not reassuring.

Morris had never felt so . . . deserted. Yes. Garrett had deserted her, left her to face a bleak future.

Oh, Christ! she thought. Here I am, setting metes and bounds, and Brandon has never once made a commitment. Then she was upset with herself for being unfair.

She could not avoid the anxiety, however.

They were to receive three planned one-word radio transmissions from Garrett, and Morris was impatient to hear his voice. In an emergency, he was to broadcast an oral report of what he had seen, though, as evidence, that would not be very satisfactory. She did not want to make such a report to Analog in Washington.

Morris sipped at coffee gone cold and thought of Brandon freezing in the snow. Maybe he had broken a leg in the parachute jump? Maybe he needed help? Maybe he was already captured?

When Kij came to the bridge, she asked him again, "Do you think he's all right?"

"In my experience, Brandon has always been capable. I would not worry unduly, Barbara."

Morris tried to imagine a thin strand, a web, stretching across the miles to the Kamchatka Peninsula, binding Garrett to her, providing a way back. The memory of his good-bye kiss snapped it.

"Kij, he doesn't think he'll get away."

Yakama's eyes were sad. "No, Barbara, he doesn't."

"If they . . . capture him, there will be a trial. Like Gary Powers?"

Yakama sighed. "No. Brandon would not allow that."

"But . . . how. . . ?"

"You do not wish to know, Barbara."

She had to know what was in Garrett's mind. "Yes, Kij, I do. Maybe I'm not entitled, but I came this far with him. I'm part of it."

Yakama sipped from his cup. "He took with him a cyanide capsule."

"Oh, my God, no!" She spilled her coffee on her blouse.

* * *

Garrett was alarmed by the heavy troop traffic and advanced his starting time. He took long-range orientation shots with low-light film, then discarded the telephoto lens. From here on in, he intended to get lighter, as far as equipment was concerned.

He kept the radio, camera, rocket, extra gloves and socks, a multi-purpose tool, his pistol, and some food. He filled the big pockets of his parka and snow pants and buried everything else—tent, bedroll, M-16—under broken branches. The ground was too hard to dig in.

Garrett pulled the radio close, turned it on, and extended the long antenna. He adjusted the volume and squelch and keyed the transmit button, which also had a sliding flap so that it could be held down. He spoke quietly into the built-in microphone. "Blue." His voice sounded strange in the wind-whispering quiet of the pines.

It had begun to snow.

He was about to try one more transmission when he heard, "Yellow."

It was Barbara's voice. He recalled the night in Madrid, and he thought that she might really be worried about him. Instead of about her job, for a change.

He wanted to provide words of reassurance, but turned the radio off.

He used a zigzagging pattern in his descent from the foothills and took half an hour to reach the small copse of trees, where he stopped to recover his breath. His exertion, from stumbling walk and creaking trot, reactivated his circulation and brought warmth.

Garrett waited in the scrub pines while a four-wheel drive vehicle went by on the perimeter road, scrutinizing the fence line. When it had passed, he rose to a half crouch and crossed fifty yards of open space to the gully, leaping five feet to its bottom. It was filled with loose snow, drifted among a slag heap of rocks and gravel exposed by the wind. Using the stones as his path, Garrett moved toward the fence. He did not expect another patrol for ten minutes. Because of the weather, the patrols were not on an exact schedule. He had previously timed them in a range of eight to twelve minutes.

As expected, he found several strands of barbed wire implanted with steel stakes underneath the chain-link fence, where the depression of the ditch dropped below the fence. There were five strands, each about eight inches apart, protecting the three-foot gap under the fence. At four points across the eight-foot width, the wire was secured by vertical wires to give rigidity. Garrett withdrew his multi-purpose tool and utilized the cutting notch in the pliers on the joints of the four vertical wires. They snapped loudly in the crisp air. He pushed the rocket under the fence, shoved the radio and camera inside his parka, then lay on his back and pushed the lowest wire high enough to wriggle his way underneath.

Once on the inside, he rearranged the vertical wires in their original positions. From a distance, it would pass, and he did not think the guards would leave the warmth of their truck unless it was absolutely necessary. He scooped up snow and sprinkled it where his heels and elbows had gouged the surface.

The patrol vehicle growled.

The road offered no concealment, and he could not cross it in the oncoming headlights, so he aimed for the culvert pipe, racing on his hands and knees.

The pipe was eighteen inches in diameter, with a four-inch-deep frozen layer of ice in the bottom of it. Once inside, he would be unable to move his arms up or down. Shoving the rocket in ahead of him, Garrett dove head-first into the opening, sliding, banging against the sides, using his fingers and his toes to propel himself forward on the iced floor. It was utterly black, with no suggestion of an opening on the other end, and he was unable to see backward, toward his feet.

His heart echoed back to him in the confined passage and the mist of his breath rose into his eyes. He had the terrible feeling that his boots were hanging outside the opening, visible to the eyes of the patrol.

Garrett knew he had made a terrible mistake when he heard the truck grind to a halt, its engine pulsing in the silent night. If he had entered the culvert feet first, he would have been able to defend himself.

He heard the door opening.

Feet crunched in the brittle snow.

He heard the rustle of clothing.

Had they seen him, a shadow against the snow? Was the cut fence suspicious? Had he left tracks somewhere in the gully?

He prepared to scramble with toes and fingers for the other end of the culvert.

Then heard the crackling tinkle of a man urinating.

He let his breath escape slowly and waited.

The truck door slammed, the engine accelerated, and he felt the vibration in the steel walls surrounding him as it passed over. Garrett counted to one hundred, and then used his toes and fingers to walk himself out of the pipe, dragging the rocket behind him. There was a puddle of steam alongside the opening.

Piss on you too, he thought.

A quarter mile ahead of him was the road which paralleled the one he was hiding behind. It led directly to the gate of the compound. Beyond it were the approach lights to the runways. Garrett hoisted himself to his feet, traversed the perimeter road quickly, and dropped back into the ditch on the other side. Crouching, he raced along its shallow bed for two hundred yards, until he was close to the next road and found an eroded depression in the side of gully. He flattened himself into it.

From that position, he could see the guard shacks clearly, each of the huts containing two men. Through the large, lit windows, he identified the heavy uniform greatcoats and gray fur caps of the *Glavnoye Razvedyvatelnoye Upravleniye*. The GRU was providing security, and that encouraged him minutely. Garrett thought there was less idealism in the military intelligence organization than in the KGB.

The beat of rotors forced him against the side of his crevasse while a large MIL helicopter passed several hundred yards to the east. He caught the silhouette of a troop-transporting Mi-24.

They were still searching, and he suspected they were searching for him. There were too many helicopters and too many troops involved for it to be anything else. The ruse of a downed Soviet training flight had run its course.

He wondered how long it would be before the ground parties crossed his trail and followed him in. With as many men as they were putting out into the search area, it should not be too long.

He would have to hurry it along.

Three hours later, however, he was still in the same position, and had reached the conclusion that he would have to circle back and try from another angle. The timing of the patrols within the twin fences of the compound had not altered once, and the air base's perimeter patrol trucks behind him passed almost as regularly. No one had entered or left the compound. The damned place was beginning to look impenetrable. The frequency of helicopter flights from the base had slowed.

Damn. It would take hours to work around to the other side of the compound, but he did not see another option. He flexed cold muscles and started to his knees.

Lights flashed over him.

Garrett ducked back down. Looking back, he saw a truck rounding the curve, its light beams passing over his position, then once again centering on the road. He pushed further downward in the ditch and examined the truck as it lumbered toward him. It was a semi-tractor, pulling a tanker trailer, its silhouette clear against the runway lights as it passed over the culvert on the interior road. It ground slowly along, dousing its headlights as it neared the compound and stopped before the outer gate.

As it went by, Garrett noted the white diamond emblazoned on the rear and was able to interpret the bold lettering. "AVIATION FUEL—HIGHLY FLAMMABLE." He judged the tank size at about 5,000 gallons, or whatever that was in liters. It looked to be about half the size of one of the Air Force's 10,000-gallon jobs.

What did that tell him?

Five-thousand gallons. It had to be for the MiGs, but the damned statistics labeled aircraft fuel loads in terms of weight, not gallons. His own thinking as a pilot was automatically attuned to weight.

Let's see . . . the MiG-25's took nearly fourteen tons of fuel. How much did a gallon of aviation fuel weigh?

He did not know. But he recalled that water weighed something like eight and a third pounds per gallon . . . 8,333 pounds per thousand gallons . . . about 41,000 pounds for a 5,000-gallon tanker . . . about twenty tons.

And oil floated on water; it must be lighter.

What else? There were always two MiGs together on the flights Swallow had captured on film. But this truck had enough fuel for only one and a half Foxbats. There had to be another tanker!

Garrett scrambled over the rocks and weeds, slipping on the patches of ice and snow, to the embankment of the road crossing the ditch.

The tanker had passed through the outer fence and was now being examined by several flashlights at the inner gate. Beams of light poked at the truck, and in their glare, he could see that the tanker trailer was similar to those with which he was familiar—an oval body with a square storage section on the rear housing the hoses and pumps. There was no place to hide on the trailer.

The tractor was a typical military tractor—boxy, flat hood, vertical windshield, canvas top, squared front fenders, spare tire mounted vertically against the back of the cab, tandem dual rear wheels.

Before he could analyze further, he heard another diesel engine coming from the north, and he pressed himself against the earth and watched the swing of the headlights. He pulled the strap of the rocket pack over his shoulder and head, hugging it diagonally across his chest, instead of his back. He pulled the straps tight.

When the wash of the headlights passed over the top of him, he quickly raised his head over the embankment to look at the approaching vehicle.

Tanker.

No helper in the cab.

Then he was on his feet, scrambling up the embankment, gaining the road, and running on the snowpacked road alongside the truck. Certainly, no guard on the gate would see him behind the headlights.

For as long as they stayed on.

They died, as the driver avoided blinding the guards.

Garrett was already alongside the frame of the tractor, running, slipping in front of the monstrous dual rear tires, trying to reach the chassis. He kept watching the cab, but the driver would be looking ahead.

There were patches of snow on top of the frame rails. Touching them would leave a trace of his passage. He reached down with both hands, arms clumsy around the rocket, to grab the underside of the U-shaped rails, the open end of the U facing inwards.

He lost his footing.

His legs swung around and trailed behind him, skiing on his heels in the snow. The strain on his arms and hands was tremendous. His back was downward, and he could just let go. The truck would pass over him, and he could try to find another way in.

Maybe.

Looking forward and up, Garrett could see the space between the frame rails, the bottom of the cab resting on the top of them. To his left spun the driveshaft. There was a pocket nearly two feet in width, from the frame to the driveshaft, and six feet in length, from the transmission support bracket to the frame member supporting the back of the cab. The upside-down pocket was fifteen inches in depth and was hidden by the gas tanks hung to the rear of the running boards, by the running boards themselves, and by the mounted spare tire.

Garrett pulled forward, his muscles aching, and gained two inches, then slipped one gloved hand, then the other forward for another gain of six inches.

And the truck stopped, already at the gate.

He thought he had had more time.

The stalled truck, though, allowed him to crab-walk forward until he could pull himself upward into the cavity. He inched to his right, packing his buttock into the open U of the frame rail, giving his back minimal support. His feet were leveraged against the rear frame crossmember and his arms were lodged against the transmission. The rocket launcher pressed into his chest, flattened against the floor of the cab. Within seconds, he felt the strain begin to increase on his arm, calf, and thigh muscles.

There were voices raised near the cab, and his limited knowledge of Russian phrases allowed him to translate part of what they were saying.

"You . . . anything besides . . . trip, Pyotr. . . ?"

A laugh. From the driver. ". . . desire . . . young girl . . . Dmitri."

". . . more liquid?"

Another deep laugh. ". . . in bottle. You . . . refreshed?"

"Open your door!"

Garrett could hear the boots crunching in the snow, then the door was opened. Probably to shield the guard from eyes within the compound while he took a swig or two of whatever was in the bottle.

Garrett's muscles screamed.

The snow underneath reflected light against the chassis as the beam of a flashlight was passed around below the truck. The boots crunched toward the rear, around the back of the trailer, then came up the other side.

Finally, he heard, "You may proceed, Pyotr . . . and many thanks."

There was a clatter of chain link as the gate swung open, a clash of gears, and the rear wheels spun on ice.

The pain spread into his ligaments.

The truck lurched forward into the space between fences. The other gate opened, the truck moved through it, then came to another halt.

Garrett composed orders for his muscles, one muscle at a time.

This time, the crisp snow was punctured by many boots. They swarmed around the tanker like bees to a hive. Light reflections bounced around the crooks and cranies of the tractor and trailer. Garrett almost lost his grip when one beam struck him fully in the eyes, coming through a gap between the running board and the cab. Metal doors clanged as the interiors of the cab and hose compartment were examined.

Garrett's torturous hold against the frozen metal of the truck frame threatened to sag away. His neck ached from holding his head upright.

And the voices. Concentrate on the voices.

". . . last load, driver?"

Pyotr replied, "Yes, Comrade Colonel Malenkov. It was . . . only two aircraft. I am wrong?"

"No. No." The reply in a firm voice. "Only two . . . morning."

A long pause, then: "Well, Corporal?"

". . . as always, Colonel."

". . . underneath?"

"Yes . . . Comrade Major Petrovsky."

Garrett, barely breathing, caught his breath. Surely no guard would get down on his hands and knees in the snow and crawl beneath the truck.

Petrovsky.

The colonel's voice. "Then . . . let it go on! All right, Major?"

"Proceed." A lower voice.

Again, there was a grinding clash of gears, and the spinning of the wheels until they found a grip, then the truck lunged forward.

Seconds later, all of the wheels on the left side, set by set, dropped into a cavernous pothole. The jarring crashes almost loosened Garrett's hands, and his left leg did drop from its precarious heel-hold. It required every ounce of his strength and concentration to raise it back into place.

Petrovsky. He knew the name. It had to be Southeast Asia somewhere.

Petrovsky. There was a first name: Boris. Boris Ivanovich Petrovsky.

Garrett had never seen him, but he had been a network control in . . . Phnom Penh. A captain then, with the KGB. Part of the network Garrett had eliminated.

The truck lumbered along in compound low gear and followed the street passing in front of the hangars. The groan of the engine drowned out other sounds Garrett might have wanted to hear, such as the crunch of boots walking along-side. Hanging his head backwards and angling it, he could see no legs marching near the tractor.

The next pothole was too much for him.

When the front wheel slammed into it, both of his feet were dislodged and dropped to the ground. He grunted and let go, falling heavily on his back, then rolling onto his side so the rocket would not catch on the differentials. The dual axles went by.

The trailer axle passed, and an airbrake housing clutched at the sleeve of his anorak. Then he was exposed to the yard lights over the doors of the second and third hangars, though they were several hundred yards ahead.

He rolled again, easing over the rocket, to the side of the road, toward the unlit hangar. Garrett cringed at the thought of the damage he could be causing to the radio and camera. Gaining his feet, he struggled against overstrained muscles and walked calmly toward the first hangar, hoping to appear part of the normal routine, though his white dress was far from normal within the compound. In the front wall of the building, a large freight door confronted him, with a small passage door let into its face.

Garrett paused to look around. Except for dim bulbs over the entrance doors to buildings across the street and the two floodlights over the doors to the next two hangars, the compound was unlit. It was an indication of the security man's over-confidence. With his perimeter so well guarded, he would consider it unnecessary to patrol the facilities on the interior.

He opened the door, looked in to find it apparently vacant, stepped over a six-inch-high threshold, then closed the door behind him.

A dozen dim red bulbs, high above, provided illumination in the two-story-high hangar. It could house seven or eight aircraft, but was now stacked with rows of wooden crates, cardboard boxes, and steel barrels. The Cyrillic lettering on the crates and boxes was mostly indecipherable to him since most of the markings indicated chemicals or various kinds of compounds. Along the left side, metal storage shelving housed numerous bins, boxes, and odd shapes. Against the western wall, fiberglass half-globes were nested in tall stacks.

Surprisingly, it was warm, and Garrett decided the heat was a requirement of the stored chemicals.

This could be all he would need, he thought.

Pictures of the stuff stored in here, with their labels, could be interpreted with conclusions drawn by the experts. Garrett found a cache in the crates, unwrapped the Redeye rocket, and stored it out of sight.

He retrieved the radio, extended the antenna, and turned it on. The building was metal-clad, but he hoped the radio was powerful enough to overcome the barrier.

Keying the transmit button, he said, "Orange."

The response was immediate and was again Barbara's. "Yellow."

He shut down the radio, and put it behind the crate with the rocket.

Garrett spent half an hour taking pictures of boxes, barrels, crates, and funny-looking fiberglass pots.

Kijuro Yakama stood on the bridge and held a very hot cup of American-processed coffee alternately in his hands. The view in any direction was

303

dismal indeed.

The cloud base was low and scattered fog reflected the yacht's running lights. The Soviet coast was fifteen miles off the port bow according to radar, and they would be the subject of scrutiny for coastal radar installations. With that in mind, the *Eastern Orchid,* though she could be pressed for thirty, was making a leisurely twenty-one knots, a speed which gave them the look of a slow cruiser on its indifferent way to somewhere.

The decks were coated with ice as thick as a man's wrist in places, and Yakama thought often of Manila Bay. These were not seas he was fond of cruising, and his stomach was upset, his chest constricted.

He had omitted dinner because of his upset stomach and, like Barbara, had begun to haunt the communications cabin.

The "Orange" signal from Garrett carried both relief and concern with it. He was in the compound, an achievement in itself, and he had time in which to work. The color code of orange also indicated that Garrett was on the right track, that he was seeing evidence to support the theory of weather modification. The choice of another color would have suggested that the secret project was engaged in different activities.

He and Barbara had discussed the other possible missions of the Kamchatka compound, but always came back to the weather alteration. Barbara had become more vehement about the bureaucrats in Washington, railing against them for forcing Garrett into this act. Yakama thought that Barbara was dealing with the real covert world for perhaps the first time, and she was not happy with what she was finding in it. It showed in her reddened eyes.

The two contacts with Garrett, in two words, had revealed strain in his voice. Listening to Barbara at the microphone, Yakama had detected the stress in her own voice, but the emotions were for Garrett and not for herself. If she was not in love with him, she was awfully close.

His own state of mind was not entirely clear. Based solely on his previous experiences with Garrett, Yakama had had a ninety-percent belief in the weather theory, reserving his usual ten percent of skepticism. Now, with the orange code, he had total confidence, though he was reluctant to consider the chances of proving it to anyone else without sufficient evidence.

Garrett was there.

He could get the photographic proof, but whether or not he could get it out of the compound was going to be another story entirely.

Yakama was beginning to believe he had made a tactical error in his manipulation of the Redeye rocket. He had been concerned first about the man, but now, the evidence was more important than the man.

Petrie was beginning to believe the story was all over town. Secrets were not sacrosanct in Washington and probably not even possible. Still, he had thought that the knowledge of Garrett's foray was limited.

Then the Secretary had called him in. "I want to know all about it, Nat, and right now."

Petrie sat in a soft leather chair. "Yes, sir. What have you heard?"

"Conjecture, probably. But I know this: AFI took Garrett's proposition to the NSC, and they turned it down flat. I thought that would be the end of it, unless Garrett came up with something more.

"Then, this morning, I get hit up by the Director of Central Intelligence, asking me what Garrett's doing. Naturally, going by what you told me, I say taking a leave of absence.

" 'In Japan?' he asks me."

"It seems that our Mr. Beech has been asking very loud questions about Garrett all over the globe."

"Yes, sir. I had him asking the questions."

"And now the Director of Air Force Intelligence has requested a meeting with the DCI, with me, and with the National Security Advisor. I want to know what in the ever-loving hell's going on."

Petrie told him.

"Goddamn it! Morris too?"

"Yes, sir."

"Have you done anything to try and stop him?"

Again Petrie sighed, and with real regret. He told his superior of his attempt to have Agatha pass information to the Soviets, hoping they would be able to down Garrett while he was still in the plane.

"I'm afraid it didn't work," Petrie added.

"It didn't work." The Secretary's tone was defeatist.

"The plane went down, but it wasn't shot down. The peninsula is overcast, and the only thing we're getting from satellite coverage is the infrared. We've also been monitoring radio traffic. The airplane crashed six or seven miles south of Kamchatka Air Base, and the Soviets have an amazing number of aircraft in the air, probably looking for the pilot. We think it's Garrett."

"Who else is covering this?"

"NPIC is doing the tracking. NSA is active. I

assume DIA and AFI people are agitated too."

"Jesus. You'd better get all the photos together for me. I want to know what the base looks like, what that compound looks like. And get everything Garrett had before together."

"You're going to argue his case?"

"Do I have a choice at this point, Nat? If Garrett's on the peninsula? And what about your Barbara Morris? Of course I am. Quietly. Because the President should be aware of what's going on. He might well think it necessary to go to some level of DefCon status, just in case the Soviets react rather violently to this. And on the other hand, I am also preparing my letter of resignation. You might do the same."

The National Weather Service, in concert with the U. S. Army Corps of Engineers, issued a bulletin in the afternoon, warning of the possibility of the failure of forty-one dams in the United States sometime in the spring, should precipitation continue at levels above normal. Neither agency wanted to do it, for fear of creating panic in populations along the Missouri, Ohio, Mississippi, and Colorado Rivers, but there was no other moral or ethical choice.

The Department of Energy was assembling new directives for signature by the President, as an Executive Order. The order would divert natural gas and electrical supplies from industry to residential requirements. Not even defense industries were exempt, and they already knew of the impending order through lobbyist grapevines. They were busily preparing layoff notices for their employees.

Other industries were in a turmoil also. Automobile factories had already shut down. Except for divisions producing winter wear, the garment industry had suspended production. Entertainment was suffering along with everyone else. A few sitcoms filmed in studios were still in production. Any feature requiring location shots was being delayed until spring. News reporters and weathermen were prominently featured on television. Almost all other programming had reverted to reruns.

In an atmosphere of ultimate pessimism, the Super Bowl was cancelled.

Twenty-Two

The diesel engines of the tankers roared to life, and they pulled away, bumping and clanking over the street toward the security gates.

Shortly after the tankers departed, two civilian scientists appeared from the tunnel, ushering three rubber-tired carts, each holding four spheres. Malenkov stopped the carts just inside the hangar. With a small screwdriver, he twisted open four Dzus fasteners on the curved access panels for each of the modules. He inserted each of his twelve coded cards into slots in the electronic apparatus, priming each module for identification and communication, and then closed the curved door protecting the electronics.

One by one, the scientists connected the umbilical cord from each sphere to its receptacle in the cavernous nose hatches of the two MiGs and lifted the globe into place. A technician climbed the ladder to the cockpit and closed the ejection hatch doors hydraulically.

As he completed the familiar ritual, Malenkov wondered why he was still doing it. Petrovsky had yet to capture the spy, though the man had apparently been in the country for over ten hours. Maybe he had already taken his pictures and escaped. If so, the project had reached an end.

What could he do to protect himself? He could leave the compound in the Volga, on the pretext of seeking relief at the officers' mess, and then leave the base. But for where? The Kamchatka Peninsula was so desolate, so far removed from any link to other parts of the Soviet Union, that he could not hope to reach any place of importance or safety. As if there would be a place of safety for him in the Motherland.

Still, running away seemed the only option open to him as long as the spy Garrett was at large. But he must be prepared for anything. He would have his driver refuel the Volga, so it would be ready, and he would stay close to Petrovsky, so he could evaluate any sudden changes in the man.

And he would continue this mission, as if all his world were yet normal.

If the Rain Cloud project could remain alive for an additional three months, then his dominance of the Politburo and his insurance of an exalted place in Soviet history would not erode, as had Stalin's, Khrushchev's, and Brezhnev's. The General Secretary would own half the world, and the other half would succumb in time. The new economic picture of the globe would show the Motherland a radiant achiever when compared to the chaos of America.

It was slipping away, however.

The General Secretary had just talked to Petrovsky and learned of the probability that Garrett was near the compound. He believed Petrovsky, and so he had made the only decision available to him.

"Boris Ivanovich, here is what you must do. If you capture Garrett in the next twenty-four hours, you must interrogate him fully. And finally."

"Of course, Comrade General Secretary."

"If you learn from him that others are cognizant of the project, the project is to be terminated immediately. I leave the details to you, but, evidence that it ever existed must be hidden. Be certain that you manage to save the sham records. In any subsequent investigation, Rain Cloud will be a domestic experiment that didn't succeed."

"I understand, Comrade General Secretary."

"If you cannot locate Garrett in the next twenty-four hours, then you must also proceed with the destruction of the project. Is that clear?"

"Absolutely, Comrade General Secretary. But if Garrett has only one or two confidants . . ."

"Then there is a dim ray of hope. Call me, and we will decide together."

At a few minutes after midnight, Garrett decided he had better take some pictures in the other hangars, especially of the aircraft.

When he eased the door open, he found that the time he had spent inside the warehouse had erased his acclimation to the cold. There was no wind, but the air was still and bitter. The snow on the ground gave the compound the illumination of early morning. The frigid atmosphere gave it crystal clarity. Wherever he saw a light, he saw tiny shatters of frozen moisture in the air around the bulb.

He took a deep breath and stepped out onto the path worn in the snow that ran along the front of the hangar, then closed the door behind him.

The path ran across the front of the first

hangar, spanned the space between it and the next hangar, and ended at the small door in the second building. It was the only route open to him since each of the hangars abutted the fence on the other end.

A cone-shaped light hung over the door of the second hangar. There was also a light over the door of the third hangar, but strangely, there was no path in the snow between the second and third hangars. He assumed there must be another route between them.

Garrett rushed across the open space between the first two structures, continued to the doorway, and put his hand on the knob, ready to pull the door open.

He jerked his hand off the doorknob as if it were molten metal when he looked through the small safety window.

Garrett ran westward, where no path had been plowed, and ducked around the corner of the building, feeling the cold corrugated metal press against his back. Breathing came hard.

It was a laboratory!

Goddamn. He had nearly walked right into it. The damned place had been converted to a lab. He did not know what he had expected. Supersecret equipment behind those black-painted windows, maybe, but not a full-scale laboratory full of men in white smocks. But then, he had forgotten about the missing scientists.

Garrett closed his eyes, trying to retain the brief image of what he had seen through the small window in the door. There were lots of tables, white-topped. There was a lot of glass tubing and hundreds of bottles on racks. He had seen white-coated men and maybe a desk or two, over at the

312

side of the room.

How many men? Ten or twelve? Had anyone seen him?

No. They would have come to the door by now.

What else?

Something seemed funny.

Oh, yes. He had seen only half of the interior, or maybe less than that. The hangar had been partitioned off into smaller rooms, so there were probably other special-use areas inside.

He needed pictures.

First, he needed to take his next step.

He certainly could not stay where he was, and he could not get into the lab building from the front. He might as well try the next building and perhaps get photos of the MiGs. They had to be there. That was where the tankers had discharged their fuel.

Looking behind him, he saw the reason why there was no path between the two hangars. There was a wooden tunnel constructed from one to the other. It was an alternate, out-of-the-weather route. It ran from laboratory to aircraft. He saw no way into it from where he was.

Peeking around the corner, he saw no movement in the compound, except for shadows inside the guard shacks at the fences. He stepped out toward the last building, creating new footsteps in the snow, paced to look normal, not like a man running.

The third hangar was the largest, and it took time to reach the door in the center of it. The snow was well-mussed here, where the tankers had backed up, where hoses had been hauled around and fuel spilled. The odor of kerosene still hung in the air.

He felt blinded by the overhead light when he looked through the small window in the door.

The interior was dark.

The door handle turned easily, so he opened the door and stepped inside. He sideslipped to his right, to wait for his eyes to adjust to the darkness inside. After a few seconds, he realized that ten or twelve dim red lights were in use here, as they had been in the first hangar, and he realized he was looking directly at the snout of a very large airplane.

Foxbat. MiG-25.

Few Westerners had ever been this close to one. It was painted a dull, flat black, but it gleamed in the shaded red lights from above, and the airplane emitted a deadly aura of power.

Garrett took two more steps to his right, and there was a new light, previously blocked by the MiG, high on the end wall of the hangar. A shadow moved in a red-lighted box. It was a guard station, mounted on the wall over the big doors, looking out on the secured area between fences. Always looking out, never in, he hoped.

His night vision was gaining clarity, and soon he could count six aircraft parked in the hangar. The camera was loaded with 1000 ASA film, and he hoped the red lights above were sufficient. There was always computer enhancement available if necessary. He aimed the camera, took one shot, and then watched the guard platform, as the click of the shutter seemed to echo against metal and concrete.

There was no reaction from up in the guard box. He took five more shots, having to guess at his focus each time, and following each snap of the shutter with a covert glance toward the guard.

Now the tunnel to the other hangar.

It might yet be possible to get near the laboratory unobserved. His confidence was increasing the longer he was in the compound.

Careful of each step, he began to make his way to the side of the hangar. He headed toward the area where the tunnel should join with the building. Garrett was watching the observation platform and did not see the stairway until he ran into it. It was like having an unknown, skeletal hand reach out of the dark and tap him on the shoulder.

He froze in place, wondering what it was. It took a few seconds to realize that it was a metal, spiral stairway since it was so out of place, set away from a wall. Looking up, he followed the shadowy outline to where it entered an upper floor some fourteen feet above. A second floor in the hangar?

What the hell, why not?

His rubber-soled boots made no noise on the stairs as he climbed, then peeked over the edge of the floor, and saw a dimly lit and vacant hallway. It was thirty feet long, and had three doors opening onto it, one at either side, and one at the end. He finished his climb upward.

He opened the door on the right, to find only stacks of boxes, and he closed it and moved silently to the door at the end of the hall. He turned the handle, and pushed the metal door open a few inches.

There was a light on inside. Garrett held his breath and opened the door until he had a six-inch-wide view.

Computers. Radios.

And a man.

He was in a GRU uniform and a swivel chair, his feet propped up on a desk, and if he was not asleep, he was close to it. His head kept nodding forward slowly, then jerking suddenly upright.

Garrett closed the door softly.

For the first time, he felt like he was totally surrounded by the enemy. Before that moment, he had concentrated on an objective, considering fences and guards only obstacles in front of the goal.

Ever more careful, Garrett retreated down the corridor, stopping to try the last door. It opened on a dark room, and he slipped inside and closed the door behind him.

He released a sigh of relief until he realized that, for all his careful preparation in planning and equipment, he had not brought a flashlight.

He would try the lights briefly. The switch was where he expected to find it and he looked at the opposite wall, then flashed them on briefly, then off.

There were no windows in the room, no way for a telltale light to alert someone in the compound. He turned the lights back on.

One wall contained a large plotting board of the northern Pacific area. A dotted green line departed Kamchatka and crossed out into the Pacific. Above the line, in Russian hand-lettering, he was able to translate, "Projected—0500." Similar projected times were written in at intervals along the line. Was a flight planned for the morning?

The tankers had fueled aircraft tonight.

Garrett could not believe the fortune that had made him climb that staircase. Who would have believed the command post for the mission was hidden away on the second floor of an old hangar? And under such light security?

If Petrovsky was responsible, he was conducting himself with as little foresight as he had shown in Cambodia.

On the wall to his right was a map of the United States, liberally punctured with red-headed pins, and smeared with writing from a marker pen. Interpretation of the flowing cursive writing was difficult, but it seemed to indicate meteorological readings.

Adjacent to the door by which he had entered was a computer terminal. It was similar in appearance to those with which he was familiar, but the keyboard characters were Cyrillic. He wished he knew more about computers and hated them less. He might have tried to access the programs.

Feeling as if someone might come along at any time, Garrett quickly rotated around the room several times, and took thirty photographs, then changed to a new roll of film. The laboratories were lit, so he used a 400 ASA roll.

Reaching for the light switch, he entertained the thought of sabotage for the first time.

His frame of mind, from the beginning suspicions to the execution of his mission, had been totally devoted toward the collection of evidence. He needed data to convince the damned bureaucrats and the pseudo-gods in the important chairs so they could pursue confrontation with the Soviets on a diplomatic level.

Now he wondered if he might be able to disrupt the operation, if only temporarily.

It was too damned bad the Redeye missile did not have a warhead. A good-sized charge of high explosive up the snout of one of the MiGs would take the whole building with it.

But there was one temporary solution.

The computer terminal beckoned.

He stepped around to the side of the terminal, trying to see the back of it. If there was no way for him to get into the software and play around, then he would have to get to the hardware.

A thick cable dropped from the base of the gray metal cabinet to the floor, where it was connected by way of a multi-pinned plug to another thick cable which entered the wall. Presumably, it led to the computers in the next room. Garrett mentally crossed his fingers, grasped the multiple plug, pushed out a springloaded clasp, and pulled it apart. The female side of the plug had receptacles for twenty-four pins from the male side. He selected a pin near the middle of the male plug and used his combination pliers to bend it back and forth until it broke off. He did the same with one more pin, then reconnected the plug, minus two circuits.

Looking around the room once again, he shut off the light, waited a minute to let his eyes adjust to the dark, then checked the hallway. He let himself out to silently descend the stairway. He had evidence of control, of the planes, of the location, of the charting of destruction, and of the raw materials used.

All he needed was a shot or two of the labs and maybe also the apparatus.

There were two possibilities for finding the apparatus: on the aircraft and in the lab. The aircraft were at hand, but getting into them in the dark, with a guard nearby, did not seem feasible.

Quietly, he moved back toward the tunnel entrance in the side of the hangar where he found unlocked double doors and thanked the jackass—Petrovsky?—who was in charge of security. He must be extremely proud of his first line of defense, the double fences.

The tunnel was dark and short and had double doors at the other end. A slight push on one revealed a well-lit but vacant foyer. Pushcarts were set against the walls, the only pieces of equipment observable.

Garrett slipped through the doorway. A few feet down, on his right, was a windowed door into the laboratory. He sidled along the wall and peeked through the window. This time he counted the people. There were fourteen, all in white coats, and all intently engaged in a variety of unexplainable activities. They all looked rather sullen, shoulders slumped, faces downcast. He raised the camera, snapped once, advanced the film, snapped again.

He ducked under the window and went further down the hallway, to where it ended by turning to the left. There was another door located there, but it had no window. The corridor to the left was empty, so he turned the handle slowly and eased the door open a half-inch.

A voice spoke out.

Garrett was paralyzed until another voice replied to the first. It was unhurried and conversational.

He could not see the speakers through the gap, but he could see a shelf stacked with round spheres—the two halves or the bowls he had seen in the warehouse joined together. It was the container. He eased the door back and slowly released the handle. He already had a few pictures of the fiberglass spheres.

The hallway ahead of him now went clear to the rear of the hangar; he could see the original aircraft doors in the far wall.

He moved forward and tried the door on the right. It was locked.

It was the first locked door he had come across, and that intrigued him. A hasty examination, however, revealed a steel door in a steel frame, with a substantial dead-bolt lock. He would not be entering it.

Moving further down the hall, he tried the door on the left, found it open and the room dark, and stepped into it. With the brightly lit hallway behind him, he decided to chance the room lights.

The room was about twenty by twenty feet, finished in gray paint that matched the corridor. It contained in its center a six-foot-diameter metal housing, banded in heavy metal. On one side was a thick metal door eighteen inches in diameter which had a heavy glass window imbedded in it. A profusion of knobs, valves, and piping were attached to the housing. He was reminded of a miniature Navy diving bell, or decompression chamber.

Atmospheric pressure chamber. He took four quick shots of it.

It was time to get the hell out.

He checked the hallway, found it vacant, and hurried to the end of it, to the back of the building. He discovered another hallway and followed the new passage across the back of the hangar. At the far end was a door that should let him out between the first and second hangars.

It did. He found himself in a trash area. Large bins were full of discarded cardboard, cans, and bottles.

He decided not to rummage through the garbage and headed back to the first hangar.

When he checked his watch, back in the warehouse, it was nearly four-thirty in the morning.

Petrovsky had risen at three-thirty and shaved away the night's growth of black beard, taking care with the trim of his moustache. He dressed and then banged on the door to his aide's room, yelling for the man to get up.

He walked over to the headquarters building and ordered the clerk to make him tea. Then he called base operations and asked for Stalintayev. If the bloody bastard had gone to sleep, Petrovsky was going to make some corrections in the man's schedule and rank.

"Major Petrovsky, there is nothing yet to report. The air search continues, though it has been extremely difficult in the dark. Most of the ground troops are returning to the base. Because of the very rough terrain, the lines are scattered, and some are still a few kilometers out. I'm afraid some of the men are missing.

"I imagine that they probably deserted, Major."

The major did not respond to that. "They found nothing at all?"

"Nothing, Comrade Major. Not the aircraft seat, nor the canopy. The ground is so rough, a trail would be difficult to locate in daylight, not to mention at night."

"Then we will give them a chance to try it during the day. Give them a few hours' rest and prepare to take them back to the starting point."

Petrovsky slammed the phone into its cradle,

cursing the incompetence of the base commander, the operations officer, and the conscripted troops.

It had been over fourteen hours since the Sukhoi had crashed, and yet there was no sign of Garrett. Certainly, he had had sufficient time to reach the base if he had parachuted from the aircraft somewhere in its line of flight to the crash site. There was no doubt at all in Petrovsky's mind about that.

Perhaps he had taken only telephoto pictures and had already made his way in the opposite direction? Those clods in the army would probably have simply waved at him, had they seen him. Or there was the possibility that he was already in the compound.

No, it could not be. The perimeter was entirely too tight. There were the fences, the dogs, the detailed vehicle inspections.

The inspections.

As he thought about it, he remembered returning from the operations tower in the Volga, and the trunk had not been examined.

Had his security detail become lax, at a time when laxity could not be tolerated?

And how thorough had been the examination of the fuel trucks? As with any routine, when firmly established, procedures tended to become expected and hasty.

In his organization of the security for the compound, he had given no thought at all to interior patrols.

He put his cup on the clerk's desk and got his hat and coat from the hall tree. Stepping outside, he called to one of the guards in the hut.

The man opened the door and stuck his head reluctantly out into the cold. "Comrade Major?"

322

"Bring a flashlight, and come with me. Now!"

The two of them started down the road. When they reached the first hangar, Petrovsky turned in from the street and clomped through the snow to the doorway. Under the beam of the flashlight, he could see many footprints in the snow, and a beaten path along the front of the building, but nothing particularly out of place.

He pushed open the door and looked into the dim interior.

There was no movement, no sound. Everything there appeared quite normal.

Petrovsky pulled the door shut and continued to the second hangar and past it. Aiming his flashlight ahead of him, he noticed one set of footprints in the eight-inch-deep snow. They stopped at the corner, went around it, then came back and went on.

That was peculiar. Out of habit, compound personnel took the tunnel route or, arriving from barracks or mess, entered either building directly from the street. Petrovsky stepped off the impressions. They obviously belonged to a tall man.

Garrett was six feet tall, four inches taller than Petrovsky.

The guard floundered along behind him as they entered the third hangar. Petrovsky ordered the soldier to turn on the lights, and the sudden blaze caused the guard in the wall-mounted enclosure to bolt upright from his dozing position. Shaking his head, he clambered clumsily to his feet and then saluted Petrovsky.

Petrovsky frowned and chewed reflectively on his lower lip as he wandered slowly about the hangar, looking intently at the aircraft and at the floor. There were chips of snow and ice melting into small puddles on the cement. Could it be from the fuel crews?

Petrovsky did not think so. Too much time had elapsed since the fueling operation.

Some instinct told him that Garrett had been in here and had walked unchallenged around these secret airplanes. The knowledge produced an icy thrill that moved slowly up his spine and into the back of his brain, much as if there were a sniper-aimed rifle directed at the center of his back.

Garrett knew!

The tunnel.

Petrovsky moved through it, looking in on the main lab, through the door of the fabrication room, then checking the locked door of the private lab. The floor was not marked with wet footprints here, but then any snow on the intruder's feet would have been cleaned off by the time he reached the hallway. With each step Petrovsky took, the more assured he became of Garrett's previous presence.

And the more certain he became that his failure to locate Garrett would disgrace him and his patrons.

He hurried now, his pace quickening beyond the ability of the guard's stubby legs. The man trotted after him, panting like a dog. Petrovsky turned into the long corridor across the back of the building and quickened his stride even more. He felt Garrett's presence beyond any degree of uncertainty the farther he went.

When he opened the little-used exit on the rear of the building and saw the footprints in the snow, he cursed.

"Major Petrovsky?" the bewildered guard asked.

"Go back and call the barracks. I want a squad

of men at the storage hangar immediately. Move!"

The man went racing back down the corridor, his feet echoing a cadence of fear. Petrovsky waited ten minutes, then followed the trail of footprints across the open space and to the front of the building. Ten guards arrived a minute later, some of the them only partially dressed.

The icy streak in his spine broadened and forced the hairs on the back of his neck to rise.

Garrett dropped the film rolls into the rocket body. Then he pulled a small notepad and a pencil from his pantleg pocket and wrote:

Boris Ivanovich Petrovsky, Major, KGB—security?
Malenkov, Colonel—commander?
14 scientists observed in lab, middle hangar.
Apparatus in three-foot fiberglass sphere.
Special hatch in nose/bottom of Foxbat.
Command center, 2nd floor, west hangar.
Atmospheric Pressure Chamber, middle hangar.
Smell of ozone. Smell of iodine.
Chemicals stored in east hangar.
GRU security force.

He heard running footsteps outside.

Shoving the notepad and pencil in with the film, Garrett screwed the canister back in place, dropped the rocket into the launcher, and picked up the radio. He turned it on and extended the antenna.

Holding the radio to the side of his face and keying the transmit button, Garrett said, "Green."

He decided he could fire the rocket right through one of the black-painted windows in the sidewall at the thirty-degree angle he and Yakama had estimated was necessary for a twelve-mile-long trajectory.

"Yellow," crackled over the radio.

The footsteps stopped outside the door. He could hear the rustling of clothing. A rifle bolt clacked.

Garrett keyed the transmit button and used his forefinger to slip the flap over it, to keep it in the transmit mode. He flipped the radio upward on to the top of a crate eight feet off the floor. Barbara and Kij would be able to hear whatever transpired.

The door opened, clanging against the metal wall. It was about fifteen feet away from him, and Garrett aimed the missile launcher at it. They would not know that it was not particularly lethal. He released the safety and activated the optical aiming system. There was no longer an infrared lock-on buzz to signal an optimum launch time.

A hand reached around the door frame, found the light switch, and bright fluorescent lights flickered on.

A voice, in stilted English, asked, "Colonel Garrett? I know you are in here. It would be most pleasant if you came out to meet me."

It was not surprising that they knew who he was, but he wondered what trail he had left for them to follow.

The voice probably belonged to the KGB security man, so Garrett said, "Major Petrovsky, it's warmer in here. Why don't you come in?"

Petrovsky was a brave man, and he stepped

boldly into the doorway.

His face paled immediately when he saw the rocket aimed at him.

Garrett lifted the launcher until the sight lined up with his eye. The scrawny major looked very sickly.

"Come on in, Comrade. Slowly."

Petrovsky took two steps forward and stopped. Cold as it was, a line of perspiration still appeared on his forehead. Garrett centered his sight on it.

"Colonel Garrett . . ."

Garrett rotated to his left, raised the nose of the weapon, sighted through the center of the window, imagined the gray sea of his target, and pulled the trigger.

Nothing happened.

Twenty-Three

"Typical of American weaponry, wouldn't you say, Colonel?"

There was no response from Garrett.

Petrovsky's voice carried a minor tremor. "Would you mind if I took a closer look at that?"

"By all means, Major Petrovsky."

"Ah, you know me?"

"You're a graduate of Phnom Penh, '75."

"Yes. Well, I am happy to finally meet you, Colonel Garrett. We have much to discuss."

"It may be one-sided, Major. I'm not much inclined toward nostalgia, I'm afraid."

"Perhaps you will be persuaded." The major's voice was tinny and ugly on the radio. "There is tea available in my office. Shall we?"

How could they be so damned polite, so military? Over the radio, she heard a shuffling of boots on concrete and a spattering of commands in Russian.

Morris clamped her eyelids closed, held her hands against the earphones, and listened intently. She translated for Kij, "He told somebody to search the building."

Then: "They're taking Brandon away."

She waited six minutes, hearing desultory conversation and the scraping of wood on cement. She was aware of perspiration breaking out on her forehead. Her armpits were damp. Kij appeared sick.

There was new, excited chatter.

"They found the camera," she translated.

Then came more shuffling and scraping. It sounded like wood on concrete.

There was a loud exclamation followed by silence and the loss of the radio carrier wave.

"And the radio."

Her heart pounded. When she had first heard the "Green" signal, the code that meant Garrett was preparing to fire the rocket, Morris had nearly knocked the Filipino communications operator out of his chair.

Then had come the tense, terrible voice of this Major Petrovsky.

She dropped her head on her arms. She thought of the cyanide capsule and thought she might get sick.

Kij patted her shoulder as if he were unaccustomed to consoling grieving women.

"Brandon found what he was certain he would find, Barbara. We know that."

She raised her head and took a deep breath. "But my God, Kij, they've got him."

"Yes. He thought that might be the case."

"And the rocket didn't work!"

"I am afraid I made a major miscalculation there. I admit it."

Morris swung around abruptly to face him. "What do you mean?"

"My assumption was that if the rocket did not fire, Brandon would have been forced to bring the films, and himself, back out of the Soviet Union. In the attempt to circumvent the necessity for him to use the cyanide pill, I arranged for the missile launcher to be inoperative."

They did not bind his hands, but one guard walked closely on each side of him on the trek to the building located next to the gate and just inside the fences. Just before they reached it, Garrett heard the whine of jet engines, and looked to the north to see two Foxbats taxiing away from the third hangar.

"As a pilot, you must admire the aircraft, Colonel. Beautiful, are they not?" Petrovsky asked him.

"Very pretty."

He was taken through an outer office cluttered with desks, file cabinets, a switchboard, two corporals, and a lieutenant. Petrovsky motioned him into a small overheated office. He stopped in front of a scarred old wooden desk.

Petrovsky said, "I imagine that you have a weapon, Colonel?"

"Yes."

"May I have it?"

Garrett unzipped the parka and extracted the Walther. He handed it to the major.

Petrovsky gave it to one of the guards. "Put this in the outer office, then send Marienkov in. Anything else, Colonel? In your pockets?"

"Just food."

Marienkov entered, searched his pockets, and came up with the cans of food, the combination tool, the extra gloves and socks, and the silencer for the pistol. His parka and gloves were taken from him and hung on a hall tree in the corner of the office. He was told to sit in a straight chair centered in front of the desk.

The other corporal brought in mugs of tea. It was hot and aromatic, and the heat spread through him, loosening taut muscles.

Garrett thought of the cyanide capsule in the hood of his parka. It might be entirely out of reach by now. He had had a chance at it on the walk over, but the failure of the Redeye had shaken him. He found he had a sudden reluctance to give up too early. All of the photographs were now in the hands of Petrovsky, and he could think of no way to get the evidence out to Yakama.

Would Yakama and Barbara be able to convince anyone in Washington based on the confirmation of his report in the code signal "Green"?

Petrovsky sat behind the desk. "You had a pleasant flight, Colonel?"

"Nice enough. It was a little rough coming over the mountains," Garrett told him congenially.

"Yes. It often is. And the final leg of your journey was also rough? By kerosene tanker, of course?" The weasel eyes narrowed.

"Comrade Pyotr was most helpful."

Raising a dark eyebrow, Petrovsky picked up a pencil and wrote a note on the pad in front of him.

Marienkov was at the side of the room fiddling with the Redeye.

Garrett said, "That's high-explosive there."

"He doesn't understand English, Colonel. Shall we get on with it?"

"Certainly. Brandon Garrett. Colonel, United States Air Force, 0-223154. Status, on leave."

Petrovsky waved a black-bordered file folder at him. "Good. That corresponds with what I already know. Now, perhaps you would explain your interest in our work?"

"Tell me about it, Major, and I'll tell you whether or not I'm interested."

Petrovsky smiled, started to say something, but was interrupted by the slamming of the front door. A GRU lieutenant brought in the camera and radio and laid them on the desk.

"Thank you, Lieutenant. That is all?"

"That is all, Comrade Major."

"You are dismissed."

The lieutenant about-faced and left the building.

Petrovsky opened the camera back and found it empty.

"It's not even used, Major," Garrett said. "I just got here."

Marienkov had the rocket out of the launcher and was examining it.

"And the radio, Colonel? Your Barbara Morris must be close at hand."

The bastard would know about her.

"I left her in Rangoon."

Marienkov figured it out. He twisted and the nose cone slipped away from the propulsion part of the rocket. The film canisters and notepad tumbled to the floor. Petrovsky's eyes were almost merry as he watched the corporal kneel and scoop them up.

One by one, Petrovsky fondled each roll, then slowly pulled the strips of exposed film from the canisters. Garrett watched the man and silently screamed as his evidence evaporated.

Petrovsky read the note.

"You have been as busy as the American bumblebee, Colonel Garrett. It also appears as if your mission has ended in this humble office. To make things brief, why don't you tell me about our project?"

The Military Code of Conduct notwithstanding, Garrett had no qualms about discussing subjects about which Petrovsky was aware. On top of which, Garrett was not on a mission sanctioned by his government.

"Sure. You've been modifying the weather patterns over the United States and Canada."

Again the front door slammed in interruption, and the voice of the night before erupted, "Major Petrovsky! We have to abort the mission! The . . ."

The excited chatter died as a tall, lean man in the greatcoat of a KGB colonel stepped into the doorway.

Petrovsky smiled. "Colonel Yuri Malenkov, may I present Colonel Brandon Garrett of the United States."

"May I?" Garrett asked Petrovsky.

"Surely."

Garrett stood, turned, and saluted his equivalent in a foreign service. The action took Malenkov by surprise, but he recovered and returned the salute.

Garrett said, "I assume that you are the project commander here, Colonel?"

"Uh, yes," Malenkov said. He seemed extremely hesitant and self-conscious.

Garrett sat down again and sipped his tea.

Petrovsky asked, "What seems to be the problem, Comrade Colonel?"

The commander, his anger dissolving in Garrett's presence, said, "The computer is down."

"I don't doubt it a bit. Our American friend spent some time in that area of the compound, I should think. Did you not, Colonel Garrett?"

Petrovsky's voice had hardened with the news from Malenkov. Maybe someone in higher authority would be extremely distressed that Petrovsky's security lapse had allowed the project to be sabotaged. Garrett hoped the bigwigs in the KGB were more than distressed.

He was also happy he had taken time with the computer plug's interconnecting pins. "Which area is that, Major?"

Marienkov had moved out of his peripheral vision, and Garrett did not like that.

The weasel eyes went opaque. "Let us go back to something else. Where is Miss Morris?"

"Taking the sun in Rangoon, the last I knew. She was awfully pale after Washington."

Major Petrovsky nodded to the corporal behind Garrett, and a gunshot shattered the quiet room.

Instant pain jerked his left arm straight, ran screaming to his fingertips, and spilled along his nerves. He dropped the tea mug on the floor.

He almost passed out from the pain. He bent forward at the waist and squeezed his eyes shut. He grabbed his left arm with his right hand.

After two minutes, Garrett caught his breath and opened his eyes to see the stain of tea spreading over the wooden floor like thin brown blood.

"You missed the elbow," Petrovsky said in Russian.

Marienkov replied in Russian, "I am sorry, Comrade Major. Again?"

"Not just yet."

Garrett's arm was useless.

He sat up and parted his fingers to look at it. Blood saturated the gray wool sleeve two inches above his elbow. He clinched his teeth against the pain, but thought it was not the deep pain of broken bones. He hoped the slug had missed bone as it passed through his flesh.

334

Petrovsky said, "We have time, Colonel, for a very long discussion. And the corporal is better with kneecaps. Who else knows of your little excursion?"

Garrett's mouth felt dry. His voice had cracks in it. "Moscow Center, I suppose."

Petrovsky sighed.

The tendrils of a morning sun, diffused by an overcast sky, had lightened the scene through the window, and Garrett could see the beginning outlines of the forest and the mountains. They looked good to him.

He took a big gulp of air and said, "And all of the American intelligence community, Major. How else would we get the satellite photos of the long-range MiGs, the pictures of the compound here, the stored wheat? Then, there's all those missing scientists, thirty-four of them, and the radiation by-product of the spheres. We knew all of that before I came in."

Petrovsky's face paled, as it had when Garrett had pointed the missile at him. He stood up abruptly and left the office.

To make a phone call? Did he require advice from his superiors?

It was what Garrett had counted on.

Marienkov, however, remained behind him, just out of reach, and Garrett was afraid his left arm was not up to any kind of a tackle.

Yuri Malenkov stepped back as Petrovsky came through the door, his face hardened into some kind of resolve.

Major Petrovsky called to the corporal seated at the switchboard. "Place a scrambled call to Moscow. You know the number."

The corporal left his desk and sat down before the switchboard.

So. This was it, what he had feared. All of America knew about the Rain Cloud Project. Malenkov believed the man named Garrett when he said that others knew.

And the burly men on the oversight committee would make their decision to hide the fact. The rulers of his beloved Motherland would destroy him in their attempt to protect themselves. Destroy him piece by piece, like the spy. He looked at the slumped figure of Garrett and felt sick. Petrovsky suddenly terrified him.

Malenkov glanced out the window at the Volga. It was fueled and ready, but Petrovsky would never let him through the gates.

On Marienkov's desk rested a blue automatic pistol.

Malenkov looked around the outer office. Petrovsky and his lieutenant were unarmed. The Kalashnikovs of the two corporals were leaning against the outer wall.

He was forced to this, he told himself.

He stepped to the desk, picked up the pistol, looked it over, unsnapped the safety, and slid the jacket back to inject a round into the chamber. He backed up to the opposite side of the door, where he could see inside Petrovsky's office as well as the outer office.

There was no other alternative.

He aimed the gun at Petrovsky.

Malenkov said, "Cancel the call, Corporal."

The corporal looked up at him, and Petrovsky spun around, staring in disbelief. "Malenkov, what — ?"

"Be quiet, Major. Marienkov! Get in here! And Colonel Garrett, if you please."

336

Garrett turned to look behind him, puzzled.

Marienkov also turned, saw Malenkov with Garrett's automatic, and raised his own pistol.

Malenkov shot him in the face, a small hole opening in the man's left cheek. A large glob of shattered white bone and bloody cranial matter ejected from the back of his head and splattered against the wall. The corporal fell backward onto the floor, dead. His pistol clattered on the floor, coming to rest against the baseboard.

Garrett forced himself up out of the chair, his left arm hanging uselessly, stepped over the body, and walked into the next room. "Colonel Malenkov?"

Petrovsky shifted, and Malenkov's finger tightened on the trigger. A shot rang out, and a hole appeared in the wall over Petrovsky's head. The major froze.

The corporal at the switchboard vomited on the floor, gagging violently. The lieutenant stood frozen in a half-step pose, and his face looked haggard.

Without turning to look at him, Malenkov said, "I will go with you, Colonel Garrett."

Petrovsky's face reddened in hatred. "You bloody frigging traitor!"

"Call me traitor, Boris Ivanovich. Your orders are to kill me and everyone here. It is you who are a traitor."

Garrett was beginning to understand. "May I have the pistol, Colonel?"

"Yes."

Malenkov stepped sideways and transferred the Walther to him. Garrett felt as if he had control of his fate again. It felt good.

"I will dress your wound," the colonel said.

Malenkov opened a desk drawer, found a first-aid kit, and rolled up Garrett's sleeve. When the blood had been blotted, Garrett felt better. The entrance and exit holes were both small puckers. About .22-caliber, he estimated. There was more pain than damage, he thought.

"So. You have been targeted for dismissal, Colonel Malenkov?"

"It was some time ago. I read the cable sent to Petrovsky."

"And what do you have to offer me?"

"Offer you?"

"Why would I take you out of here?"

The scientist considered the question. "I invented the process of weather modification. I alone know the formula for the key component, which triggers the crystals. No one but I."

"I see," Garrett said. "And in your absence, the project cannot continue?"

"It cannot. I am all you need. I am your proof, Colonel Garrett. I have much to offer as the process can also be used for peaceful means."

Garrett looked through the window and saw soldiers gathering around the building. They had heard the shots. If Malenkov was indeed the inventor, he was correct in saying he could serve as living proof.

The faces of Harvey and Connie Landers flashed through his mind, and he nearly converted Malenkov to dead evidence.

Was he really the only one who knew the formula?

"You are wearing a KGB uniform, Colonel."

"Scientific Division, until this project."

"And Major Petrovsky?"

"Assigned to the operation by the Chairman of

338

the Committee for State Security."

Malenkov was free with his information, and Garrett could detect nothing in his manner to suggest he was lying. He *was* nervous, his hands shaking as he sprinkled disinfectant over the wounds and wrapped gauze around Garrett's arm. In his place, though, it might be expected.

In the end, it would not matter if Malenkov were lying about his sole possession of some secret formula, Garrett decided. If he took Malenkov with him, he would have all the evidence he needed. It would not matter if the Soviets still had the ability to alter the weather. In any event, he did not have time to make tantalizing decisions.

Garrett directed the commandant in wiring the hands of their prisoners with coat hangers, twisting the wire tightly about their wrists with Garrett's combination tool. The prisoners were then eased to the floor and their feet clamped tightly together with more coat hangers.

Garrett pocketed his PPK and picked up one of the Kalashnikovs leaning against the wall. "Are there any more magazines around?"

"In the desk there."

He found five more magazines for the weapon in the desk drawer. Using his right arm, Garrett recovered his parka, hat, and gloves. He worked his way into the parka and Malenkov fashioned a sling for his arm out of a roll of bandage. The film was no good, but he put the cans of food back in his pockets, then added the bulky, thirty-round magazines. He hung the strap of the radio over his neck.

Malenkov was still wearing his greatcoat and fur hat.

"Quickly, Colonel. I want you to tell me how

the apparatus works."

The colonel gulped, his scrawny throat working rapidly.

"Now!"

"In the spheres, a passive set of silver iodide crystals reacts to a catalyst, which I have called the key component, when triggered by radio."

"All right. Now, are there more of these key components in the lab?"

"No. They were all sent on the mission today. They are on board the aircraft."

"And where are the aircraft?"

"Still en route to the target area. We were hoping to repair the computer malfunction."

"The spheres can be launched without the computer, and without triggering them?"

"Yes."

"Can you reach the pilots and tell them to jettison the spheres?"

Malenkov's expression told Garrett that the man had not thought about the modules still safely aboard the airplanes. They contained the catalyst which could have been broken down and deciphered if they were brought back to the base intact.

"Yes. I can." He picked up the phone at the switchboard, made a connection, issued orders, then waited.

Four minutes later, he replaced the phone on the switchboard and said, "The spheres have been deployed, and the MiGs have been ordered to return."

"Good. Next step. Can you give orders to those guards out there?"

Malenkov was apologetic. "I am afraid they do not listen well to me."

He would have to take Petrovsky along.

Garrett used his pliers to cut the wire at the major's feet, then pulled him erect with his right hand. Feeling was returning to his left arm. It throbbed with an intensity that threatened his concentration. The lights seemed too bright and on the verge of strobic pulsing. He assumed he was in partial shock. Heading out into the cold was not going to help that.

He shoved Petrovsky toward the door, taking care to not be gentle, and pushed the muzzle of the Kalashnikov hard into the back of Petrovsky's neck.

Malenkov picked up the remaining Kalashnikov from the corner and opened the door.

There were at least fifty GRU soldiers surrounding them, partially hidden from sight by parked vehicles and the corners of buildings.

"Order them back, Petrovsky!"

Petrovsky spoke loudly in Russian. "Get back! For ten minutes!"

Garrett translated the short phrase well.

He moved the muzzle of the automatic rifle slightly to the side and pulled the trigger once. He shot off the lobe of Petrovsky's left ear.

The man flinched abruptly from either the pain or the report of the rifle right behind his ear, or both. Blood oozed from the torn flesh.

"You want to try that again, Major?"

"Get back! And stay back. Go to the barracks."

The soldiers began to retreat.

Garrett saw two GRU officers gesturing toward slow-moving soldiers.

"We'll take the four-wheel-drive out there. You drive, Malenkov."

They exited the building. Garrett kept his back to the wall and rotated his head continually from side to side, looking for the danger spots. The guards in the fence shacks were on their knees, peering through the windows. He nodded to Malenkov, and the three of them rushed the short distance to the vehicle.

Petrovsky was reluctant, and Garrett slapped the muzzle of his rifle into the major's kidney. The project's ex-commander got into the truck behind the wheel, and Garrett pushed Petrovsky toward the passenger side. The blood from his ear was dripping down his neck.

"You could let me have my coat," Petrovsky said.

"I think I'll bring Marienkov's pistol instead," Garrett said. "I can work on your kneecaps, keep your mind off the cold."

He pulled the passenger seat forward and shoved the bound man into the back seat of the utility vehicle, then followed him and closed the door.

Malenkov started the engine, slid back the window, and yelled at the single guard now on the gate. The man immediately opened the gate.

Between the fences, crouched on their knees against the snow, four guards held two dogs in check. Malenkov engaged low gear and pulled out into the no-man's-land, trailing the running guard who was intent on opening the outer gate.

As they emerged from the compound, the truck picking up speed, Garrett shoved the muzzle of the AK-47 into Petrovsky's stomach. Behind them, dozens of figures were running all over the compound like headless chickens in a farmyard, lost without their commanders. He hoped they remained confused for a long time.

He wiped sweat from his forehead. Reaction to the wound, he told himself. He felt like sleeping for a long time.

Malenkov crossed the open ground to the perimeter road and raced along it. In a short time, he turned onto an asphalt road and slowed before a barrier at the main gate. A Red Air Force enlisted man stepped from the hut, saluted, then stopped in shock as he saw the weapon trained on the officer in back. His face drooped.

Malenkov slid back the small window and yelled, "Raise the barrier!"

The guard nodded and pushed down on the weighted end of it. It rose, Malenkov gunned the truck, and they were outside the air base. The asphalt road was snowpacked in places and spotty with ice. Within two miles, the morning was yet lighter, and the pavement petered out into gravel road that was totally snowpacked.

And Garrett had a problem.

He was free of the base, and he had his evidence.

But he had nowhere to go.

Twenty-four

"This is an unmitigated disaster," the National Security Advisor said.

He glared with open hostility at those surrounding the table. Supposedly, they were the crisis team the President had demanded.

Merlin Danton was not too happy with any of them himself. Petrie and the Secretary of State sat next to him. The others in attendance were the DIA director, the DCI with the Central Intelligence Agency's DDO, and General Wake, the Chairman of the Joint Chiefs of Staff.

The bits and pieces from all of the agencies had finally been put together in a sloppy report. Danton had not known that Yakama was involved, though it did not surprise him. He got his birthday messages from the retired Japanese intelligence officer too.

When Petrie had admitted to his scheme to down Garrett with Soviet fighters, he had apologized for his failure. "I'm afraid the message I leaked through the KGB plant got cut off somewhere. Garrett got through."

Danton had leaned over and told him in a voice too soft for the others to overhear, "Nat, I don't give a shit about your new office and your new feeling of power. You went too far on your

344

own, and I'm going to have your ass. Someday. Somehow."

Nat Petrie, who never showed fear, did just then. His eyes widened and his nostrils twitched. He stuttered, "Goddamn it, Merle . . ."

"There's too many damned agencies," the security advisor said, "running around like headless chickens. We've got to put some direction on this, and we've got to do it now. I don't give a damn about what's happened in the past few days. I don't care who believes what about this weather crap. We've got two known intelligence officers missing and probably within the Soviet Union. The issue is, what are we going to do now?"

Wake turned to the Director of Central Intelligence. "Recap what we know, will you, Mr. Director?"

The DCI had a voice that was powerful and always in control. He spoke with enunciated clarity. "Garrett is inside the Kamchatka Peninsula. We do not know where in Kamchatka, for certain, but the air and ground searches out of the air base have been called off. He may have been captured. We don't know where Morris is. Two more of the questionable Foxbats departed the base early this morning. It appears that their flight has been aborted early, and they are currently on the return leg."

"If Garrett has been captured, we may be hearing from the Soviet Ambassador shortly," Wake said.

The Secretary of State said, "There hasn't been a peep out of them yet."

"What about Yakama's yacht?" Danton asked.

"Whose yacht?" the security advisor wanted to know. Petrie had to answer. "We have maintained surveillance on its track, of course. The skies are overcast, but we've got it pinpointed with infrared."

"What the fuck is this about?" the advisor demanded. His eyes were hot with his anger.

Petrie fussed with the handle of his briefcase. "It didn't seem important at first, sir. Yakama only helped Garrett steal the Sukhoi."

"Where's the goddamned boat?" Danton shouted.

"It's fifteen miles off the eastern coast of Kamchatka," Petrie said.

"Why?" asked the National Security Advisor.

"I don't know."

"I do," Danton said. "He's going to pick up Garrett."

"I sure as hell wouldn't count on it," Petrie slipped in.

He had to say something, or the others would think him superfluous. Danton already thought that.

"You think Garrett's going to get out of this, Merle?" Wake asked.

"I know he pisses off some people around this table from time to time, but go back and look at his record. Find a failure for me."

The President's security advisor said, "All right. Let's give him forty-eight hours."

"Then what?" the DCI asked.

"Hell, I don't know." He turned to the DCI. "Mr. Director, you get your people going on a very close scrutiny of all of the USSR's defenses. If they go to alert status, I want to know within two minutes."

"Yes, sir."

"And General Wake, you be ready to go to

346

DefCon Three if the President feels it's necessary."

"Yes, sir. You really think it'll be necessary?"

"For all I know, Garrett's going to blow the shit out of that compound. If he does, it'll be necessary."

For over five decades, Yakama had fought his wars with his wits; he was not a man of personal action. Usually, the decisions he had made had borne fruit.

This time, he had made an error in judgment. He could have lived with that had it not been Garrett who had fallen prey to his error, for he owed to Garrett, not only the jade sculpture, but the lives of many of his countrymen. In all the years of their association, Garrett had not once before asked for help, and the one time that he had asked, Yakama had been found wanting.

Barbara was obviously distraught, near tears, when she said, "Kij, can you put me ashore?"

"I can do that, Barbara. To what purpose?"

"To get what evidence I can. About the project."

"You are trained in these matters?"

"No. No, I'm not. But I can try. Photographs, whatever. Even from a distance."

"Not to make some foolhardy attempt to free Brandon?"

She closed her eyes, rubbing them with her forefingers. "No, Kij. I'm trying to be realistic, and I'm sure I wouldn't know where to start. But we need the photos. That's what Brandon would want."

"Is that what you want?"

"It's my country too, Kij. I don't like what's

347

happening to it."

Yakama thought that Barbara had completed some radical change in her philosophy. Somehow, he liked her better. He told her he would think about it, and went below to sit in the teak-paneled warmth of his office.

By all rights, Yakama could reasonably expect that he had another ten years of active existence left to him, though in some respects, as with the young ladies that Timura found for him, he had become much more passive. What would those next ten years be like?

America was not his country, though he had been well-tutored by her. He owed her less allegiance than he owed to Garrett. Yet were America to be subjugated by the Soviets, and the balance of power delivered to a single, oppressive entity, his own world of the Western Pacific would not be a place in which he would enjoy his last decade.

His only option was to complete Garrett's mission. There were various ways of doing so, including the importation of highly qualified mercenaries, but time and position were of the essence, if he was also to serve Brandon.

He had not yet given up hope.

Position came first.

He got up and took the companionway to the bridge. Barbara was sitting in one of the observation chairs, and her eyes were red-rimmed.

"Captain Timura, I believe we want to reduce speed to sixteen knots, so as to not leave the area of Ust-Kamchatsk too quickly. We will hold for half an hour at that speed, then reverse course for Japan."

"Very good, Mr. Yakama."

Yakama ignored the venomous look in Barbara's eyes as she heard his order.

General Belushkin blew his nose in his handkerchief and looked at the agitated GRU captain. "You say Colonel Malenkov and Major Petrovsky have been kidnapped? That is quite unbelievable, Captain."

"But it is true, Comrade General! Major Petrovsky had his ear shot off!"

This was too good to be true.

"We need to launch a search, General!"

"We have searched all night to no avail."

"But that was for the American!"

"American? What American? No one told me about an American."

The GRU captain said, "It is classified information, Comrade General Belushkin. Now we must hurry!"

He let the captain fume a bit before saying, "Very well. I will come to the compound and look around before making a decision. Major Stalintayev, we have normal patrols up?"

"Two helicopters, General Belushkin."

"You may alert them, but do not send more until I get to the bottom of this."

There was no hurry that General Belushkin could see.

Malenkov drove fast on the infrequent straight stretches. He was apparently accustomed to the road, and there was no traffic.

The road curved away toward the east and soon began to drop away from the plateau, winding among heavily forested landscape, twisting down shallow canyons toward the coast. Malenkov was slowed to fifteen and twenty miles per hour by some of the sharp turns.

Garrett remembered from his maps that this road would intersect the coastal highway which wound northward for a mile to Ust-Kamchatsk and southward to a general harbor overlooked by Petropavlovsk-Kamchatski.

"How far are we from the coastal road?" he asked Malenkov.

"About five kilometers."

The *Eastern Orchid* would still be within radio range. To try to reach her by way of Ust-Kamchatsk, which had been his tentative original plan, would endanger her, though, since it was so close. The military at the base would be arranging some kind of pursuit.

Garrett needed Malenkov, but he no longer needed Petrovsky as an observer of his plans. "Pull over."

The man slowed to the side of the road. Garrett unlatched the door and scrambled out of the truck.

"I'm afraid, Major Petrovsky, that we must part ways. It's been grand."

The KGB man's eyes showed no fear, just extreme hate, as he struggled to get out of the back seat with his hands wired behind him. His ear had stopped bleeding and the blood was crusted brown on his neck.

All he said was, "It is cold."

"So be it. If you survive, wonderful. It's more of a chance than you had in mind for us."

Malenkov said, "Colonel, it would be better if you shot him. He is dangerous."

"Let's not get absolutely bloodthirsty, Malenkov."

Garrett knew that Malenkov was probably correct, but Garrett had not yet taken a life unless his own was in a great deal more jeopardy than it was now.

Petrovsky grimaced, "You, you traitorous pig, will find justice at my hands, no matter where you attempt to hide."

Garrett kept his pistol on Petrovsky as he led him back into the trees, unwired his wrists, then wired them again around a thick trunk. Petrovsky somehow looked forlorn, but Garrett was able to withhold his pity.

Garrett got back in the truck, motioned to Malenkov, and they pulled away.

Malenkov said, "Pardon me, Colonel, but you should have shot him."

"What I want to do very much, Colonel Malenkov, is to shoot you. I have no sympathy for defectors from any country, much less the man who caused the death of two of my closest friends. Don't push me." Garrett meant every word.

Malenkov's eyes left the road momentarily. "I am sorry."

"Don't be sorry. If they get close, if it looks as if we may not make it, then I will kill you."

A sneaking suspicion that Malenkov was some kind of egomaniac not telling him the exact truth kept him in check. There was that suspicion, and also a vague wish in the back of his mind to justify to Danton the accuracy of his assumptions. The inventor could do that.

The Soviets would be frenzied by now. Not only would the truth come out, but they would have lost the key to their weather program. He could expect an intense concentration of efforts to recapture them.

The coastal highway was coming up fast, if that narrow, twisting gravel road could be called a highway. The Soviet Union, east and west, was short of superhighways. Paved roads were restricted to population centers.

"Stop here."

Malenkov braked.

Garrett got out of the truck with the radio, extended the antenna, turned it on, and pressed the transmit button. He did not have a code color for this, so he repeated his earlier code, "Green."

There was no response.

"Green."

"Yellow." Barbara's voice.

"I'm on the lam. Hot pursuit."

Her voice sounded good to him, tinny though it was. She asked, "The bay?"

Garrett calculated the time it would take him to get down, steal a boat, and meet Yakama's launch somewhere, against the probability that helicopters were now taking off from the base.

"There's not enough time."

Yakama would be checking his charts, computing, giving Barbara the alternatives.

She said, "Petropavlovsk-Kamchatski. After dark."

"Copy that. Green out."

Garrett got back into the truck. "Let's get on it, Colonel. South."

Malenkov did not question him, just engaged the transmission and began to drive.

There was traffic on the highway, some of it military, most of it consisting of unidentifiable

352

relics passing for cars and trucks. They were piloted by civilians heading toward markets or work in lumber camps.

The road rose and fell, twisted around monstrously huge trees, occasionally rose to the plateau to follow level ground for awhile, then descended once again to the coast. Garrett estimated they were averaging about forty miles per hour. With another 260 miles ahead of them, that meant another six and a half hours, assuming they could stay on the road in a known military vehicle for that long.

Somewhere along the way they were going to have to sit for awhile and lose a few hours in order to make the rendezvous with Yakama.

His arm ached. He could feel the pain pulsing with the beat of his heart. His mind felt alert, though, out on the edge of peril. It had happened before, in Laos and Cambodia and Vietnam. It was adrenaline pumping, and it was fear, and it was . . . an unwillingness to give up, to lay down and die, while the bad guys won. Sometimes he forgot what it was like.

He wanted vengeance also, and had to struggle for control over his finger on the trigger of the AK-47 every time he looked at the man who had killed Connie and Harv.

"You're sure they intended to waste you, Colonel?" Garrett asked.

"Waste? I do not know the meaning."

"To kill you."

"Oh, yes. I saw the cable to Petrovsky. From Moscow. Resulting from your intervention, Colonel Garrett." There was bitterness in Malenkov's voice.

"You planned on making a success of yourself,

and of the Soviet Union, with this process?"

"Of course. I could do no less for my country. Would you not . . . are you not now doing the same for yours?"

It was a point that Garrett could understand. "So your country turned on you. Do you expect that the U.S. will be different, as far as your aspirations are concerned?"

"I have much to offer. I do not expect, or desire, charity."

"What about your family?"

"I have none."

"You're offering your weather-modification process?"

"What else? It can be used to beneficial result also."

"Radiation all over the landscape is a benefit?"

Malenkov's eyebrows rose. "There is a small by-product, yes. It has nearly been eliminated, and can be, with appropriate further research."

Garrett said, "You may not receive the attention you may be expecting."

Malenkov's head turned toward him in question, and the truck slid sideways in a rut. He deftly swung the wheel and returned to the twin ruts.

"I do not understand."

"Your wonderful process has resulted in a few hundred deaths. In loss of property, in hunger and deprivation, in economic problems. You will not be perceived of as a savior, Comrade. There will be people who want to pull this trigger as badly as I do."

Malenkov's shoulders sagged as the man realized a new vision of his work. He did not speak, and Garrett picked up the map he had found in the glove box.

He also found a pen, and in the margins of the map double-checked his calculations. It was, he thought, time to start checking side roads, looking for alternate transportation.

They passed one road. It was snow-covered. Helicopter pilots searching for them could easily skip the side roads with no tracks. If they left the highway, they would have to take a road that appeared well-traveled.

Then, he heard the thrupp, thrupp of rotor blades.

Sliding down in the seat, Garrett peered out the rear window. It was a Hind, and it was coming up fast. They had been spotted easily this early in the morning with no traffic on the highway. And the highway must appear like a white scar on a green torso, for towering forests rose on each side of the highway.

"Put it in the ditch!"

The Russian locked the brakes, sliding toward the narrow drainage ditch at the side of the road. Garrett opened his door and fell into the snow before the truck came to a stop. Malenkov dove across the passenger seat and out of the truck as the gunship screamed overhead.

The 23-millimeter machine guns stuttered.

Fountains of snow and asphalt erupted along the road. A dozen metallic clunks told him the truck had been hit.

The chopper climbed out of its dive and began to turn for another pass.

Pulling his gloves on, Garrett drove into the woods, followed closely by Malenkov. He scrambled over fallen logs and forced his boots through the thick underbrush. Fifty feet away from the road, they were hidden in the dense foliage.

He could hear the helicopter as it chattered back over the road, its guns silent.

There was only one helicopter, but he might be calling for his friends.

He and Malenkov would not remain free for long if they had to abandon the truck and stay in the forest. He looked at the Russian and found him pasty-faced. He probably had not faced hostile fire very often.

The helicopter had to go.

It circled around overhead, trying to spot them through the trees.

Garrett checked the magazine in his Kalashnikov and snapped off the safety.

Did they know he had a weapon?

Probably not, for they came back around low. The trees were dense enough that he had to track the helicopter's progress by sound and the downbeat of air from the rotors. He saw bushes and branches waving a hundred yards away.

The Hind moved closer.

Through the branches overhead, he saw its ugly snout. Garrett let go with a long burst. The AK-47 bucked in his hands, and he felt a stab of pain in his wound.

His staccato burst was rewarded with an immediate whine of the chopper's turbine engines and the recession of the rotor beat. If it had been hit, it would be attempting a crash landing back on the highway.

Garrett ran back toward the road, tripping his way through the underbrush.

He reached the treeline, a few feet higher than the drainage ditch, as the helicopter burst into view. It was trailing a wisp of oily smoke. The beat of the twin turbines was erratic. As it came sliding toward the road, he held his rifle against the trunk of a pine and squeezed the trigger. The result was two shots, and the magazine was empty.

Swearing at his lack of foresight, Garrett dropped behind the tree, ejected the empty magazine, and locked in a fresh one.

The Mi-24 hit the ground hard, its rotors dying. Doors popped open on both sides, and four men ran for the ditches and the forest. Garrett fired a one-second burst along the ditch line on his side of the road, and two men reversed course, one of them grasping his wrist. A soldier on the other side of the road fired a burst at him, and snow and ice stitched its way across the highway and climbed toward his tree.

Garrett dove backwards and landed behind a felled log.

He dragged the AK-47 around and laid the muzzle over the log.

The Hind sat in the middle of the highway, its tail boom toward him. It would have fuel aboard.

Garrett pulled the stock of the rifle against his right shoulder and squeezed the trigger. The stuttering bite of the stock was a welcome counter for the pain in his left arm. He worked the muzzle upward and to the left, spraying the entire fuselage.

There was a burst of red-yellow flame, followed by dark smoke.

The fuel tanks and ammunition were suddenly in jeopardy and the four men in the ditch on the other side of the road knew it. They scrambled backwards, running awkwardly in the underbrush for the forest behind them.

Garrett fired off the last of his magazine in

their direction. One man went down.

"Let's get out of here!" Garrett yelled at Malenkov.

The Russian nearly beat him back to the truck. Garrett clambered into the passenger seat while locking another magazine into the assault rifle.

"Hurry up, goddamn it!"

Malenkov slid into his seat and cranked over the engine. As soon as it caught, he slipped the clutch, and the truck blundered out of the ditch.

They were two hundred yards down the road when the MI-24 exploded. The concussion rocked the truck. Flaming fuel and debris fell around them. A chain reaction in machine-gun ammunition kicked off a long series of explosions.

Garrett looked back to see cherry-red flames licking upward from the shattered hulk.

It was a damned beacon for any other searchers.

He searched the skies while Malenkov fought the descending road. The truck slipped into and out of ruts. The next hill was steeper, and the truck slowed to twenty miles an hour before they reached the top.

Fifteen minutes later, Garrett had still not seen any other pursuers. Something was wrong. They should have been a hell of a lot closer.

Something else was wrong too.

Malenkov said, "Colonel Garrett, I believe we must have a ruptured fuel tank. We are nearly out of gasoline."

"Shit." Garrett leaned left and read the petrol gauge. About a quarter tank. One of the 23-millimeter rounds must have punctured the tank.

He bent over and retrieved his map from the floor at his feet, turning it around to find their position. He estimated that they were almost thirty-five miles south of the air base road.

Coming up on the left was a road which led down to the coast, passing through a small village.

When they reached the road, Garrett ordered the colonel to a stop.

"Where now, Colonel Garrett?"

"How easily are people bribed around here?"

"Bribed? I do not know the word."

"Take money to keep their mouths shut."

"Ah. I do not know the people of this region well, but I would guess they would be . . . bribed easily. They are an independent sort, and suspicious of government officials."

"Let's go down to the village."

Malenkov spun the wheel and they left the highway, coasting down a steep and narrow road, which curved around huge boulders. The forest closed in on them.

Garrett said, "I hope they are easily bribed with American dollars."

"Unfortunately, your dollars would be more acceptable than my rubles."

They rounded a final curve and were in the midst of two dozen unpainted shacks, wood smoke rising from tin chimneys. A long finger pier jutted its way out into a shallow bay toward the concrete sea, but no boats were in evidence. There were two cars, an ancient and scarred Volga and a Honda customized in dents.

Garrett had hoped to find a boat. He dug under his snow pants to his cloth money belt and came up with two thousand in fifties. He told Malenkov what he wanted, and gave him the money.

Malenkov looked over the bills and said, "If I convert correctly, that is a lot of money."

"Use what you need. And hurry."

Malenkov got out and headed for the shack with the Honda parked in front of it.

Ten minutes passed before Malenkov emerged from the hut with a young man, lanky, with blond hair hanging from a woolen cap. Garrett gathered the AK-47's, the radio, and the first-aid kit and got out.

The young man slid in behind the steering wheel, started the truck, and drove onto a rutted trail on the beach, headed north.

Malenkov said, "The boy is the village administrator's son. He will take the truck several kilometers to the north and abandon it. He will return by an alternate route. I gave him three hundred of your dollars."

"You could have given him more."

"I paid the administrator five hundred of dollars for the automobile."

"Will they keep their mouths shut?"

"They received money from me, and rather than risk losing it, they will say nothing."

The old Honda started right away and hobbled shockless back up the road they had come in on. It had no heat, no insulation, very little padding left in the ragged blue upholstery, and very little blue paint on its dented and abused exterior. The engine sang a weary, rattling tune that might have been a dirge.

The bouncing and jostling were killing Garrett. Every jolt sent a stab of pain down his arm, and he thought that his wound might be bleeding again.

Traffic was heavier by then and the decrepit

Honda blended well with the other vehicles.

Malenkov asked, "Do we stay on the highway?"

"I don't know what else we can do, except hope that Petrovsky has been waylaid for awhile."

Petropavlovsk-Kamchatski was about four hours away.

It could have been eternity.

Twenty-five

"Thirty years have passed since I have been unable to sleep at night," the General Secretary told the KGB Chairman.

It was not I who initiated this monster, Felix Nemoronko thought, but he said, "It is a difficult time for us all, Comrade General Secretary."

He had called the General Secretary with the information from Kamchatka that Garrett had escaped, after a much too brief detention, and with a defecting Malenkov. Petrovsky waited on the other line.

The General Secretary made his decision. "Garrett is to be killed. Malenkov we must keep alive until we have extracted all of his useful information. Bury the project. There will be another year for us, Comrade Chairman. I just hope it is soon."

"As you wish, Comrade General Secretary." He pressed the button to bring Petrovsky back on the line. His strong hand clutched the telephone receiver as if there were no strength at all in it.

Boris Petrovsky's wrists had been raw from the bite of the wire and his face blue with the cold when they reached him. One truck had gone by without hearing him, but the Red Air Force lieutenant in the second transport had heard his yell and come to a halt.

Wrapping his bleeding wrists with rags, Petrovsky had ordered the truck back to the base and found the compound in chaos, the gates wide open, and General Belushkin ensconced in the outer office. Petrovsky's aide sat nervously in a straight chair.

Belushkin grinned at him. "So my men recovered you, Comrade Major."

The heat needled his face and hands, but the fury in his mind ignored it. He picked up the phone and dialed while telling his aide, "Captain, General Belushkin and any of his men who entered the compound are to be detained in Barracks A. And shut the gates."

The general lost his grin very quickly.

After the Chairman passed on to him the General Secretary's very welcome words, Petrovsky called Major Stalintayev at operations and ordered a helicopter. Then he hung up, went to his desk for his web belt and holster, and left the office.

An ambulance was parked to the side of the outer gate, its attendants collecting the body of Marienkov. One of the corpsmen had briefly attended to Petrovsky's ear and wrists as he waited on the telephone.

He had listened to the Chairman's instructions with a high degree of anticipation. Garrett would die slowly. And Malenkov, the traitor, would gush forth everything he ever knew, once Petrovsky had him spread-eagled on a table.

There was not a doubt in his racing mind that he would soon have the two of them in custody. Though they had over two hours of lead time, they would not escape.

When the helicopter settled to the ground outside the gates, Petrovsky, his GRU aide, and four GRU soldiers passed through the gates and climbed into the back of it. Donning a headset, Petrovsky ordered the pilot to take off.

"We will first examine Ust-Kamchatsk from the air."

"Yes, Comrade Major, the pilot responded as the Mi-24 rose, dipped its nose, and headed eastward for the coast.

They had yet to reach the coastal road when one of the soldiers spoke up, "Comrade Major, there is smoke over there, to the south."

Petrovsky followed the pointing finger and saw the tall column of black smoke.

"Pilot, we will go south."

In less than eight minutes, they were hovering over the wreckage of the helicopter. Several automobiles were backed up to the south and north of the smoldering hulk. Petrovsky issued an order, and his pilot landed to the south of the wreckage. It was a total loss. The damned Garrett was formidable.

As he emerged from the helicopter, three men came running out of the forest toward him. One held a bloody handkerchief to his wrist. Petrovsky spent five minutes listening to their story.

He climbed back into his helicopter.

The pilot of the downed helicopter called after him, "Major, how will we get back to the base?"

"Walk. You blundering dolts deserve it."

They took off toward the south, and Petrovsky and the GRU captain trained their binoculars ahead and to the sides whenever they passed over an intersecting road. If there were tracks on the road, they detoured and traced them to coastal villages, to farms, to lumber camps. They did not see the truck Garrett and Malenkov had taken.

It was after nine o'clock when they came upon

a wide and well-used trail leading to the east, twisting through the forest until it reached a fishing village set above a small bay. It was a typical collection of drab weather-streaked buildings. A deserted pier jutted out into the small bay. Two small boys emerged from a shack and stared in awe at the helicopter.

The dwellings were clustered on the slope above the pier, and several doors opened to investigate the sound of their passage, but no one came outside. One of the larger buildings had an old Volga parked outside.

Petrovsky told his pilot to land. The icy streak was present in his spine.

The pilot landed on the pier, and Petrovsky and the captain crawled out. A light dusting of snow rose in the air from the rotors.

He selected the big house with the sun-bleached Volga, and the two of them walked up to it. A gray-haired, rugged old man opened the door.

"Who are you?" he demanded.

Petrovsky did not bother with his credentials. His uniform said all that needed to be said. He shoved the door into the man's face.

"Give me your name!"

"Wolontov."

These Easterners lacked both civility and subservience. "Why are you not with your fleet?"

"Who are you?"

Petrovsky's rage, barely in check as it was, surfaced. He unsnapped the flap of his holster and withdrew his Tokarev pistol.

The GRU captain at his side stiffened.

"I asked you a question, pig!"

There was defiance in the old man's eyes, but he said, "I am the village administrator."

Petrovsky pushed his way into the tiny sitting room, saw an aproned woman standing in the

365

doorway to the kitchen and a long-haired youth rising from a flowered sofa.

"I want to know immediately if you have seen two men this morning. A Soviet KGB officer and a foreigner."

"Very few strangers pass through our humble hamlet, honored sir." Disdain was evident in his tone.

Petrovsky shot the young man in the thigh. The report was thunderous in the small room, and the teenager fell to the floor, clutching his leg, but not uttering a whimper.

His mother ran to his side.

He leveled his pistol at the woman. "I have no time for bargaining. She is next."

The disdain was replaced with hatred. "They were here."

"When?"

"I do not know. I do not have a watch."

"How did they travel?"

"A military truck."

"Which way did they go?"

"Who watches?"

Petrovsky raised his pistol again.

"Back to the highway, I think."

Petrovsky spun on his heel and left the house. He ran down the slope to the pier and climbed back into the helicopter.

Demanding a map from the corporal, he opened it to the correct region. Garrett would have expected immediate pursuit, and he would have avoided Ust-Kamchatsk. It was too close. The wilderness of the peninsula offered a million hiding places. There were dozens of small roads and trails departing from the highway, all along the coast. Some led to lumber camps, some to tiny fishing villages, some to military radar installations. Petrovsky would be slowed considerably if he had to examine each of the potential turnoffs. He would have to order up more helicopters.

Or perhaps not.

The highway south went all the way to Petropavlovsk-Kamchatski in rough but passable condition. It was a major city of 150,000 population and offered in its port a maze in which a fugitive might hide for a long time, waiting the chance to be taken out by some gullible fishing boat captain. Yes, the city was a likely objective for Garrett, even though the winding road to it was almost 475 kilometers in length. A helicopter could cover the distance several times in the same amount of time it might take to drive it.

Garrett would expect pursuit.

Petrovsky would not oblige him.

Garrett's escape route must be by sea. An aircraft was too easily spotted. It would be a submarine probably, meeting him offshore. He ignored the implications of a submarine, which would assume that the United States Navy was involved.

If he placed his forces correctly, blocking the bays and ports along the peninsula, forcing Garrett southward, he would have a far better chance of recapturing the infiltrator and the traitor than he would by straining his eyes through dense forest or heavy snow.

Why flit about like the fly, when he could calmly await the closing of the web, like the spider?

Since Garrett's transmission, Morris had been delirious with hope. Her mind raced with possibilities, wondering what had happened, where he was, how he was getting around.

"I'm on the lam," he had said. He was being chased.

By whom? How many?

She and Kij had conferred quickly, then she had told him to go several hundred miles south. Now she could not believe that they had added that many miles to his chances, but Brandon had not questioned it.

Yakama and Captain Timura had huddled over their charts and examined their radar screens, then had turned the *Eastern Orchid* outward from the coast and had fallen into a track of southbound shipping traffic some twenty-five miles off the coast. Timura was relieved to have his own radar blip part of a trail of blips belonging to freighters and tankers and one passenger liner.

She squeezed her eyes shut. When Brandon had been captured, she had closed off feeling about him and had tried to concentrate on the things she would need to report to Tom Eaglefeather.

With his renewed freedom, she was again washed in the memory of his touch, the way his brown eyes looked so sad, the slight lift at the left corner of his mouth when he was amused.

Her emotions were on a roller coaster, but she was afraid to get off, afraid she would not find out where it ended. Like Space Mountain at Disneyland, with warning signs and exit doors all along the way to the start of the ride, Garrett had given her ample chance to quit at various stops along the way. She had refused out of stubbornness, and now she must finish the ride.

Twenty-Six

The city teemed with a life that Garrett had not thought he would see again. Traffic near the harbor was congested, trucks, buses, and automobiles vying for barely defined rights of way. It was an industrious metropolis with a frontier flavor, yet the faces were not happy ones. A sour melancholy characterized Petropavlovsk-Kamchatski.

Parking on a side street next to a slaughterhouse with an metallic overpowering aroma of blood, Malenkov took more of Garrett's dollars and left him to scout among the privately operated warehouses and fishing concerns clustered around decrepit docks.

He returned in an hour with an ill-fitting, ragged brown overcoat.

"I have purchased a boat and a place to hide. It required eight hundred of your dollars."

Garrett did not care about the money. "What kind of boat is it?"

"A five-meter wooden boat with an Evinrude motor made in America. It is old, but it seems to run well. I listened to it."

A wooden boat would be difficult for radar, and Garrett was satisfied.

"Good. Let's go."

Garrett shrugged out of his bloodstained parka and donned the overcoat.

Malenkov carried a paper sack with the first-aid kit and the radio. Garrett carried the two rifles with their remaining three magazines bundled into a scrap of upholstery torn from the back seat.

They entered a storefront building, half erected on earth and half on the rotting timbers of a wharf, its grimy windows crusted with a decade of dead flies. The sole occupant grinned mirthlessly and nearly toothlessly, his eyes fearful and greedy. Sparse shelving held greasy marine engine parts.

The proprietor was anxious to get them out of sight. "This way, quickly."

They followed him into a briny storage room randomly stacked with more hardware and several complete engines. A door off the back led to the dock, and a door on the side opened over the water. A beam crossed the ceiling of the room and jutted outside through a notch in the side door. It supported a block and tackle used to raise and lower heavy equipment from and to water level.

There was no heat in the back room, but Garrett did not care. He sank onto the quilt provided by their reluctant host, and rested his head against the wooden siding. The walk had exhausted him — he had been unable to sleep on the jolting journey, and his arm ached intensely.

Malenkov sunk to his knees next to Garrett. "We will need to check your wound, Colonel."

Garrett did not protest, but slipped out of his coat and let the scientist clean his wounds with water from a pail, sprinkle the puckered and purple wounds with disinfectant, then powder them with an antibiotic. The Russian applied fresh gauze and adhesive tape.

Five minutes after he was back in his rotten coat, he fell asleep.

Malenkov rested against a splintered wooden crate

and studied the sleeping Garrett. He took time to consider what he had avoided during the long drive. It was a situation in which he had certainly never expected to find himself in: he, a patriot, running from the KGB in the company of a wounded Western spy.

It was not an ideal he had chosen for himself, though it was probably a consequence of changing his ideals. He had been relatively happy in his first goal, the one nurtured by his Captain of Armor father, of perfecting his mind. In exchange for his devotion to scientific pursuits, the State had provided him with adequate shelter and nourishment. He had even received rapid promotion. Some things, a woman and family, had had to be deleted, or delayed, but it had not been an uncomfortable existence.

No, it was when he became involved in the fringes of the political world and allowed the vision of material gain to subvert his real training that he had strayed from the safe course.

The decision he had made that morning was still unreal. It had been made out of the primal instinct of survival rather than any intellectual deduction.

Was that what he had been reduced to? To basic survival? To killing a lowly corporal? He who could offer mankind so much of his intellect?

Yuri Yurievich Malenkov had not yet given the world all that of which he was capable. He knew that.

It had been snowing heavily for several hours and the temperature at water level was two degrees above zero Fahrenheit. A man could live in the water for less than a minute.

The snow and the night reduced visibility to fifty yards or less. It was much safer to rely on sound, which carried clearly for long distances across the mouth of the bay.

The bay opened to the south, with the harbor

tucked up against the northern shoreline, and from western coast to eastern point was three miles wide, a wide-open throat to freedom, or a narrow funnel to entrapment.

Five slowly moving patrol boats of the GRU border unit patrolled the mouth of the bay. Each gunboat was eighteen meters long and mounted a 30-millimeter cannon on the foredeck, 23-millimeter machine guns to port and starboard, and a rack of depth charges on the fantail. The searchlights were useless in the snow-fall, eliciting a blinding reflection that would inconvenience the crew more than the quarry.

Radar would be chancy if Garrett was escaping in a wooden boat, though it might pick up the mass of a large motor, and it did pick up the radar reflectors installed by law aboard the trawlers of the fishing fleet.

The radar scopes of the patrol boats were littered with the signals reflected by the fleet as it began to return an hour after sunset. There were 197 boats in the fleet that day, and they would be chugging into the harbor for over two hours, the varying rackets of their worn engines providing several octaves of orchestration floating low across the choppy surface of the bay, reflecting off the hulls.

The time the fleet returned to harbor would be the best of times for anyone fleeing the country.

Major Boris Petrovsky had worried about it since he had boarded the boat in the late afternoon, staying in the wheelhouse to eat a cold sandwich and drink hot tea. He wanted to be near both radio and radar.

He organized his patrol to compensate for weather, setting up listening posts on the western shoreline and on the eastern point. He spaced the available craft, moving like a single clothesline on pulleys, across the harbor mouth and placed two crewmen on each bow, ordered to listen for the sound of an outgoing boat. Radar operators were instructed to ignore the blips

372

of incoming vessels and to look for that one signal that would be going against the tide.

The radio operators were directed to scan all frequencies, seeking any odd or coded message that might betray the mother ship or the submarine which was bound to be off the coast somewhere.

Petrovsky might be blinded for the moment, but his ears would compensate.

The gunboats were capable of a top speed of forty-eight kilometers per hour, and could cross the five-kilometer mouth of the bay in four minutes. At their current speed of fifteen kilometers per hour, spaced as they were, there were no stretches of water unobserved longer than a minute.

It would not be enough time for a slow boat, and Petrovsky was comfortable with his arrangements. The cold stripe along his spine told him he was right, just as it had so often in the past. The true hunter knows when his prey is near.

By seven-thirty, Garrett had decided he could wait no longer. He had been awake for an hour, since the fleet began to return, and he was refreshed. His mind felt clear, and the throb of his arm was becoming more irritant than obstacle. He had abandoned the make-shift sling, and he tended to hold his arm partially bent at the elbow against his side. A sharp extension of his elbow made it feel as if muscle and ligament were tearing, but logic told him otherwise.

The marine store's proprietor had departed earlier. He wanted to be safely seated in a tavern with many friends around him should there be a hitch in their plans. Garrett could not blame him.

He and Malenkov checked the rifles, then slid open the side door. Garrett had thought it cold in the warehouse, but exposed to the harbor wind, his face felt the sting of hard-driven sleet. It was surprisingly light out, and that was not reassuring. They stepped out onto a narrow, unrailed balcony. A stairway led down to a small landing stage securing the boat Malenkov had purchased. They descended slowly.

Malenkov held the painter while Garrett clambered in and made his way over wooden thwarts to the stern. The motor did not have a self-recoiling starter rope. He had to wind the provided cotton rope around the pulley head three times before it finally started. It was loud and rackety with loose bearings, and its roar carried loudly across the water.

Malenkov took a seat in the bow, holding a Kalashnikov across his lap.

Garrett searched until he found a cable which was the broken gear shift, gripped it, and pushed the interior wire. The motor lurched into reverse. He quickly pulled it the other way, and the boat surged against the dock, scraping itself forward. He twisted the throttle grip on the steering handle, and they were under way.

The boat was heavy and the motor not strong enough to move it fast, but it soon found headway into the oncoming waves. Garrett gauged his speed at four or five miles per hour, which was fast enough to maintain a heading and slow enough to manuever around incoming boats. He rummaged in the paper sack for the radio, turned it on, and lodged it between his feet with the volume raised so he could hear a carrier wave over the wind and the motor.

Malenkov sat stoically listening in the bow, his head bent forward. Occasionally, he signaled for Garrett to turn to the left or the right, to avoid an inbound trawler. From the time he had awakened, Garrett had sensed a change in the man. He had been introspective before, but was now almost entirely enclosed within himself.

After awhile, the short choppy waves transformed into long swells, white caps slapped the wooden hull, and icy salt spray misted over them.

The *Eastern Orchid* was twelve miles from the mouth of the harbor at Petropavlosk-Kamchatski, traipsing on the heels of a freighter inbound for the anchorage.

Through Captain Timura, Yakama had ordered the first mate and one crewman aboard the launch, and it was now three miles off their starboard bow. The distance between them would be necessary in order to triangulate a fix on Garrett should he make a radio transmission.

The radarscope, where Barbara had stationed herself, did not look optimistic. Hundreds of harbor-bound targets were identified by the operator as the fishing fleet, and five targets continued to crisscross the mouth of the harbor. They were obviously patrol boats in such number as to suggest a dragnet for Garrett.

Kijuro Yakama flinched when he saw a sudden change in the pattern on the screen. One of the gunboats had reversed its direction.

He picked up a headset, held the earphone to his ear, and spoke into the microphone. "Yellow."

The first mate aboard the launch had been anticipating the message. "Jade."

Yakama read off the coordinates of the patrol boat. "Proceed with haste," he said.

The outlook was not hopeful. The launch was unarmed and could do nothing against a gunboat, even if it could reach Garrett before the Soviets did.

It was the gunboat behind Petrovsky's command boat that had detected a change in the harmony of engines entering the bay. The radar operator had unsuccessfully tried to wipe away what appeared to be a speck of dust on his screen. It persisted as a tiny pinpoint. To avoid any possible future charge of malfeasance, the lieutenant in charge of the boat had radioed the information to the ugly little KGB major aboard the command boat.

They were told to maintain patrol.

The major himself would investigate.

When Garrett heard the words "Yellow" and "Jade," he suspected Yakama was trying for a radio fix on his position. He lifted the radio from between his feet and held down the transmit button, counting to thirty. That should be long enough.

The thunder of the gunboat reached them first. Its bow abruptly appeared out of the night and snow, then it roared by ten feet off their beam, its wake rocking the little boat violently. Garrett grabbed the gunwale to avoid being thrown overboard.

The thunder died away as it swung in a broad bank, and started back toward them. Garrett shoved his helm over, aiming off their bows, but the larger craft turned with him.

Garrett idled back and struggled to keep his bow headed into the oncoming swells.

The gunboat could crush them quickly, either with the cannon he could see on the foredeck, or by simply running over them. Malenkov said nothing, and they both sat quietly as the craft came alongside.

"We meet again, Colonel Garrett! As I was certain that we would." The voice of the KGB major was a familiar one to Garrett now.

Garrett looked up at Petrovsky, standing on the deck of the patrol craft five feet above him. He did not speak.

"And you, our traitor!" Petrovsky said, the scorn in his voice flung against the wind and snow. "We would like both of you aboard. Now!"

There was an air of excited anticipation in his voice.

The larger craft rocked in the surge of the swells, and the small boat nudged against the steel hull, held there by the motor idling in forward gear. The deck gun was unattended, and a pair of sailors left their machine guns to aid in the embarkation. An armed sailor and an army captain with a drawn Makarov pistol were the only ones with currently threatening weapons.

"I'll go first," Malenkov said in English.

He stood up in the bow, and he brought his Kalashnikov with him. He swung the muzzle up without aiming, the trigger pulled home, and the rifle barked a staccato rattle that echoed over the water.

The sailor shot Malenkov, four slugs stitching across his stomach and chest before the sailor's face erupted into a cherry-red mass.

The army captain was hit and spun off the deck, falling toward Garrett. He threw up his right arm and deflected the man, or his body, into the sea.

Malenkov crashed into the bottom of the boat.

Garrett snatched his AK-47 from the thwart beside him and, without taking time to aim, shot the two sailors darting toward their machine guns.

Petrovsky's face showed contrasting flickers of curiosity and outrage. He held both hands out at forty-five degree angles from his body, as if to say he was unarmed.

"Colonel . . ."

Garrett glanced at Malenkov in the bottom of the boat, then squeezed the AK-47's trigger. Petrovsky took a dozen bullets, from his left shoulder down through his groin, blood spurting hotly from the punctures. The force of the slugs slapped him back against the deckhouse, then he tumbled forward and tilted momentarily on the railing. Finally, he overbalanced, somersaulted from the deck, and crashed face-up in the bottom of the small boat. Garrett would remember the man's sagging face, the mouth dropping in gagging reflex as the mind had its first view of the next life and recoiled. Then the body was empty, crumpled against the bottom of the boat.

The patrol boat's transmission engaged and the engines roared as the helmsman attempted to pull away from the carnage. Garrett guessed that the fuel tanks must be below waterline, and he emptied the magazine of his assault rifle. Holes punctured the steel hull.

He was reaching for his last magazine when the boat caught fire.

Garrett advanced his throttle and headed slowly into the sleet, hunting for distance.

When the boat exploded, flaming debris spewed upward, arcing out, and one charred life preserver landed smoking in the boat. Garrett left his helm and crawled forward to throw it overboard. Petrovsky's body was laying across Malenkov's, and he levered the dead major's legs over the side, then rolled the body out.

There were a dozen holes in the bottom of the boat jetting miniature fountains of water.

Malenkov's lips were blue, and there was a film of salt-water-diluted blood across his chest. Garrett could see the man's eyes staring at him, and his lips moved. He leaned forward to put his ear to Malenkov's lips, and the man spoke, but Garrett could not understand what he said.

When he looked again, the scientist was dead.

Garrett returned to his motor.

Behind him in the sleet, he could see the lights of more patrol boats converging. He hoped they were seeking survivors of the gunboat.

And he hoped his own boat did not sink too soon.

Warming Trend

Twenty-seven

There were floods. They were widespread along the Missouri, Ohio, and Mississippi Rivers, though they did not quite achieve the stages and the damage that had been earlier predicted.

Four small irrigation dams in high country gave way, and all of them might have contained the high spring runoff if they had been inspected and maintained properly. Nine deaths were attributed to those failures.

Slightly over nine thousand deaths were linked to the weather conditions of that winter, along with the loss of some two hundred thousand cattle, sheep, and hogs. The price per pound for beef rose twenty-one cents at the supermarket.

In Maine, Illinois, and Michigan, the state legislatures passed bills requiring natural gas and electric companies to absorb much of the abnormal cost of energy, on a one-time basis, for hospitals, for the handicapped, and for the elderly. By March, nine other legislatures had similar bills in committee.

It could be expected that other consumers would bear the burden of the costs to the utilities, sometime in the future, according to a report by the Department of Energy.

Farmers were already in the field, complaining bitterly about the soggy ground, though there had not been a significant snowfall for seven weeks. They also complained about the Soviet announcement of dramatic increases in their expected wheat harvest, that they would not be purchasing American grain that year.

The Department of Agriculture began in-depth studies related to the plight of the American farmer.

Railroad tracks were repaired, coal and ore trains began moving, steel production resumed, and automobiles rolled off the assembly lines, though in diminished numbers, and not one with more than six cylinders. Congress rushed through its committees, conferences, and caucuses a bill providing for a three-year, decreasing tariff aimed at protecting American automobile and high technology industries and adjusting the monstrous deficit in the balance of payments.

The Japanese and the Germans screamed the loudest, and the State Department tried to be diplomatic.

The Defense Department screamed also, in an anguish shared by the President, as funds were diverted from missile, fighter, and shipbuilding programs to support state welfare, highway rebuilding, and damage-cleanup programs. National defense, and the defense of allies, especially in NATO, would take years to rebuild, to catch up with the Soviets.

In Moscow, the General Secretary was pleased with that development since it meant that he could reallocate some of the Soviet Union's military resources to domestic programs. And though the details were sparse, he was also pleased that Boris Petrovsky, in his final act, had suppressed all evidence of the Rain Cloud Project. With the consensus of the Politburo, Boris Ivanovich Petrovksy was posthumously named a Hero of the Soviet Union. In the same Tass announcement, one line was given to the unfortunate and very explosive accident in the far eastern Soviet Union which claimed the lives of several prominent scientists, a few technicians, and a few soldiers.

Lieutenant General Merlin Danton had reassigned

Agatha Nelson to the secretarial pool, where she would be insulated, yet available if needed. Petrie called him almost daily, asking if he knew where Petrie's executive assistant was. And nine weeks after he had last seen him, Danton was still trying to locate his own special assistant. Garrett had not completed his assignment at Suitland.

Other than a message directed to Analog, and passed on to him by Tom Eaglefeather, Danton had no evidence to indicate that Garrett was still alive. The Analog message read: "Have a nice spring."

The cherry trees along Pennsylvania Avenue were blooming nicely.

The entrance and exit wounds were still puckered, but were now a deep purple which almost disappeared into the nutmeg tone of his skin. Garrett did not pay much attention to his wounds anymore.

He heard the ringing of the little brass bell on the front veranda as he waded from the blue water, bent to pick up his towel, and climbed the slope of white sand toward the thatched-roof cottage he had rented on the outskirts of Papeete. His muscles felt toned and strong after the swim.

He toweled the sand from his feet on the narrow rear porch, then hung the towel over the railing and went inside, letting the screen door slam behind him.

Barbara turned from the front door, where she had just taken a package from a very small boy.

"It's for you."

Garrett sat down at the table and eyed her bikini-clad figure speculatively.

"Don't do that! You'll make me self-conscious, and I know I don't wear these suits well."

"Only your opinion. You can always take it off."

"In a minute," she promised. "Damn it! Aren't you at all interested in what's in the package?"

"Maybe it's money. We can always use that."

"Hurry up!"

Garrett used a table knife to cut the tape.

"Only Kij and Tom know where we're at, so it's difficult to get excited."

"For you, maybe. Nat Petrie is probably sending us a bomb."

"Worried about your job?" he asked.

"No. It'll either be there when we get back or it won't be."

Under the wrapper was a white envelope, and Garrett opened it. It was from Yakama: "The possessor will always find ill will to his back and good fortune in his way."

Garrett knew then, and he gave Barbara the note to read and the box to open. She was childlike in her eagerness, with a new happiness that went well with the tan, the bright smile, and the relish for life.

She levered open the cardboard flaps, parted the flimsy white paper, and extracted the jade elephant.